THE BARD'S BLADE

D0037152

THE
BARD'S
BLADE

―――

BRIAN D. ANDERSON

TOR

A TOM DOHERTY ASSOCIATES BOOK

NEW YORK

THE BARD'S BLADE

Copyright © 2019 by Brian D. Anderson

Map by Rhys Davies

A Tor Book
Published by Tom Doherty Associates
120 Broadway
New York, NY 10271

www.tor-forge.com

Tor® is a registered trademark of Macmillan Publishing Group, LLC.

Library of Congress Cataloging-in-Publication Data

Names: Anderson, Brian D. (Brian Don), 1971– author.
Title: The bard's blade / Brian D. Anderson.
Description: First edition. | New York : Tor, a Tom Doherty Associates
    Book, 2020. | Series: The sorcerer's song
Identifiers: LCCN 2019041246 (print) | LCCN 2019041247 (ebook) |
    ISBN 9781250214645 (trade paperback) | ISBN 9781250214638
    (ebook)
Subjects: GSAFD: Fantasy fiction.
Classification: LCC PS3601.N49 B37 2020 (print) | LCC PS3601.N49
    (ebook) | DDC 813/.6—dc23
LC record available at https://lccn.loc.gov/2019041246
LC ebook record available at https://lccn.loc.gov/2019041247

Our books may be purchased in bulk for promotional,
educational, or business use. Please contact your local bookseller
or the Macmillan Corporate and Premium Sales Department
at 1-800-221-7945, extension 5442, or by email at
MacmillanSpecialMarkets@macmillan.com.

First Edition: January 2020

Printed in the United States of America

0 9 8 7 6 5 4 3 2 1

How do I dedicate this to a single person, when so many have been essential to reaching this monumental achievement in both my life and career? My son, who gave me the initial inspiration? My wife, who convinced me I had the talent to make it happen? My dear brother and father, taken from my life far too soon, whom I am still trying to make proud? My agent, who despite all the rough edges could see the potential in my abilities? My fans, whose love of the genre and willingness to give an unknown like me a chance enabled me to keep creating new worlds and adventures? There is a list I could make that would easily add twenty pages of text—each one deserving of this dedication.

The truth is, they are all pieces to this wondrous mosaic that is my career. While I cannot mention everyone, I hope they know that, spoken or unspoken, they are not forgotten. Every house requires a solid foundation. And it is the people in my life that have ensured mine is made from granite.

So for all who know me, either personally or through my work: I dedicate this book to you.

THE BARD'S BLADE

1

HEART INTERRUPTED

All things that end, begin anew.
Book of Kylor, Chapter Six, Verse Two

Mariyah leaned back in her chair, rubbing her neck and twisting the stiffness from the muscles in her back. Staring at the three ledgers and two-inch-high stack of papers on the small dining table in front of her caused an involuntary groan to slip out. This was Father's fault. His organizational ineptitude was a continual source of frustration. He was a master at cultivating the grapes and perfecting the wine, but when it came to the administration of their family business, he procrastinated needlessly, waiting until the work was so backed up that it took days, sometimes weeks, to put the books in order.

She cast her eyes around the kitchen, cursing as she realized that, as usual, she'd been too wrapped up in work to remember to light the stove and heat the kettle. Looking at the various pantries and cabinets, she ran through a mental inventory of their contents. Wine, wine, and more wine.

A deep thud and the clatter of breaking glass snatched her attention to the window. *Not again*, she thought.

Another crash and more breaking glass had her running

to the front door. Flinging it open, she saw Tamion standing over a crate, eyes wide, hands covering his mouth. Wine was seeping onto the ground around his feet, filling the air with its sweet aroma.

"Again, Tamion?" she said, with undisguised irritation. "How many does that make this year? Five?"

Tamion was nearly as clumsy as he was strong, but at least he didn't sneak away to drink when left unwatched. Wine from Anadil Farms, named for her great-grandmother, was a mighty temptation. One that few could resist, apparently. Tamion was the third hand they'd hired in as many years.

After old Chano died, more than three dozen had come calling, hoping to get hired on as his replacement. Initially, Mariyah hadn't understood why so many had applied, considering it didn't pay much and the work only lasted through the fall. It was when she'd found Milo, Chano's first replacement, in a drunken stupor behind the house, the wagons only half loaded, that it had become clear. Her back and arms twitched at the memory of loading more than fifty crates of wine by herself.

Tamion had a deceptively thin build, though he was by no means frail, having spent his youth working the fields. His close-cropped red hair and fair complexion still gave him a boyish appearance, even though he was nearly forty years old.

"I'm sorry," he said, his voice muffled by his palms. "I'll pay for it. Please don't tell your father."

Mariyah planted her hands on her hips. "It's not my father you should worry about. You know how long it took me to fill those?" This was an exaggeration. She had indeed filled and corked the bottles, but that was four years ago. This year her father had hired someone else to bottle and store the wine, and it was still aging in the main cellar. But this batch was of particularly good quality, even by her family's exceedingly high standards. Each drop was precious.

Tamion opened the crate with fumbling hands. "I'm sorry. Look. Only one broke. I mean, two."

"I should send you home before it's three," she said, but then softened her tone and forced a smile at Tamion's anguished expression. "It's all right. I was planning on keeping one for the house anyway. Clean out the glass and put it by the porch."

"What about your father? You don't think he'll fire me, do you?"

Her father had sworn if Tamion broke another bottle, he would do just that. And he was sure to notice the crate was short by two.

"I'll tell him I did it," she replied with an exasperated sigh. "Now you had better get back to it. You don't want to miss the festival."

Tamion was visibly relieved. "Thank you. I promise to be more careful."

Mariyah turned to the door, pausing just inside. "Take one for yourself," she called back. "I'll tell Father I broke three."

Tamion's eyes lit up and he bowed repeatedly, nearly tripping over the crate in his excitement. Mariyah closed the door, fearful of another calamity should she stay a second longer. Three bottles would be hard enough to explain away, particularly from this batch. Each full crate was worth enough coin to pay the average farmhand's wages for a week. *Father is not going to be happy*, she thought. But keeping Tamion in their employ was better than the alternative.

Mariyah returned to the kitchen and plopped back down at the table.

"Still there I see," she said to the pile of waiting papers. She sorted through the small stack until she found the inventory list. Thirty-five crates had just become thirty-four, and it was up to her to decide who would be shorted on their order. A tiny smile formed as the unlucky soul's name popped into her head. The smile stretched as she imagined the sour expression on Mrs. Druvil's face—though in truth Mrs. Druvil's expression was always sour.

———

A soft rap at the door told Mariyah she'd spent too much time in thought and too little on work. Through the window she could see that the sun was nearing the horizon. *To blazes with it. This can wait until tomorrow.* Not like her father would notice anyway. So long as the bills were paid, he couldn't care less about the books. Twenty was young to be trusted with the well-being of the family, but though her father was by far one of the finest winemakers in Vylari, it was their combined efforts that had in recent years increased their wealth to the point that they could expand the farm. This season they'd employed twice the number of hands as the previous, and next season promised to be even better.

Selene, Mariyah's best friend since childhood, had given up knocking and let herself in. Entering the kitchen, she let out an exasperated groan.

"Why aren't you ready? I told my brother we'd meet him before the festival starts. Or did you forget?"

"I was just finishing up here," said Mariyah. "Don't worry. We'll be there on time."

Selene sniffed. "That would be a nice change." She then twirled around, arms extended. "What do you think?" She was wearing her finest dress, blue with green stitching and a white sash, and her straight waist-length raven hair was tied back and intertwined with a silver ribbon. "Mother bought it for me; sent it all the way from Lake Merion."

"My father orders fish from Lake Merion. It's quite good. Though now that you mention it . . ." Mariyah leaned her head in and sniffed several times. "Is that fish I smell?"

"Stop it! That's not funny."

Mariyah laughed. "I'm sorry. I was only teasing. It's very pretty. Really."

This seemed to satisfy Selene. "Thank you. Now would you please explain why you're not dressed? The festival starts in less than an hour."

Mariyah had never enjoyed large crowds. The jostling about and the way folks squeezed tightly together made her feel trapped. And unlike the Spring Wine Festival, where she could stay hidden behind her father's tasting booth, she would be expected to mingle and hold conversations with people at the Harvest Festival.

"Lem's playing tonight?" asked Selene, as she pulled a bottle from the cabinet and uncorked it with her teeth. "I will never get what you see in him."

Mariyah could feel her irritation building. "For one thing, he never takes without asking."

Selene grinned and took a seat on the opposite end of the table. "You want me to put it back?"

"No. But could you at least use a glass this time?"

Selene took a long gulp directly from the bottle and then offered it to Mariyah.

Mariyah growled and pushed back her chair. "I can see you're planning on having a *very* good time tonight."

Selene grinned. "One of us needs to. All you ever do is pine over Lem."

"Jealous?"

Selene coughed a laugh. "Jealous? Over Lem? I would

never . . . I mean, he's just so peculiar. Always going on and on about music. And those eyes of his . . ." She gave an exaggerated shudder. "Honestly. You could do better."

"I like his eyes." She did. Unusually gray and large, they had the power to capture her whenever she looked into them.

It was true that Lem lived an unconventional life. But someone with his talent was in high demand. Admittedly, she hated that he was forced to be away so much. But it was something she had learned to tolerate. Some considered him odd—easily distracted and often preoccupied. But she knew that his passion for music was beyond that of normal folk. And his talent was made manifest when he played.

Her mother had once remarked that people often cast scorn upon things they thought to be out of the ordinary. Unlike her father, who wanted Mariyah to wed someone with what he thought to be a more stable profession, she was in favor of the match.

"Why Lem?" her father had demanded once, during a heated discussion about her future.

The previous evening, Mariyah had told him of Lem's marriage proposal. One would have thought she was planning to marry a wolf.

"What's wrong with Lem?" she countered hotly.

"Nothing is wrong with Lem," he admitted. "It's . . ."

She knew what he wanted to say, though he was refusing to say it. "So, he's a musician. There's nothing wrong with that."

"I know. And I have nothing against him personally. He's a fine lad. But what sort of life is that? You need someone more stable. I don't want you working yourself to death just because he can't support you."

"I have no intention of Lem supporting me. Mother works. Why shouldn't I?"

The fact was, however, that Lem was not merely a musician; he was far and away the best in Vylari. One did not hold an important event without hiring Lem. The coin he made from students alone earned more than enough to be considered respectable by any standards.

Setting aside these thoughts, she entered her bedroom and crossed over to the wardrobe, pausing to stare for a long moment. If Lem weren't playing tonight, she could have feigned illness or found some other excuse not to attend.

Only the thought of seeing him urged her to open the wardrobe doors. She pulled out a blue-and-gold dress her mother had bought two years prior for her birthday. Lem had remarked at the time how well it suited her. Mariyah smiled. *Yes. This will do nicely.*

By the time she was ready, she could hear Selene talking with her mother in the living room. This meant Father would soon be home also. She gave herself a quick, final glance in the mirror and hurried to join them.

Selene was sitting across from her mother near to the hearth, her wine now in a glass. Mother was wearing the tan cotton skirt and blouse she often wore when spending the day in the field inspecting grapes, and her salt-and-pepper hair was wrapped neatly in a bun.

"Aren't you coming with us?" asked Mariyah.

She smiled back. "Not tonight. Your father and I are going to the Sunflow."

Realization struck. "Your anniversary! I completely forgot. Should I come with you?"

"Not unless you want to be embarrassed," she replied. "Your father promised me a romantic evening. Besides, someone has to represent the family. People from all over Vylari will be there."

"Like we need more business," Mariyah laughed. "We can barely handle what we have."

"A testament to your father's skill," Selene chipped in, then drained her glass.

"And a testament to my daughter's keen mind," her mother added. "Do tell Lem that I expect to see him before he leaves again. He promised to teach me 'Dove of the Snowfall.'"

Mariyah crossed over and kissed her mother's brow. "I will. I promise."

"Now off with the two of you," she said, shooing her daughter away. "Unless you want to be questioned by your father for an hour."

This was all the prompting Mariyah needed. Father would insist that she not only tell him every moment of her plans, but swear several times to come straight home once the festival ended, and remind her for the thousandth time that Lem was to remain outside the door upon walking her home. Mother was more understanding when it came to their time together. *Young hearts need to be free*, she would say.

As they exited the house, Mariyah spotted her father approaching from the barn. "Hurry," she whispered to Selene.

The girls broke into a run, laughing as they went, not stopping until they were well down the road and out of earshot of her father's call.

———

The sun was nearly past the horizon, and already the lavender sky was strewn with starlight. Several travelers shared the road, mostly on foot, though there were some ox-drawn carriages filled with supplies for the festival.

The excited voices and laughter of children sang in harmony with the chirping of the crickets. Mariyah recalled how much she had enjoyed these gatherings as a little girl. Selene's parents ran a small bakery in the nearby town of Olian Springs, and would let the girls ride in the wagon atop the boxes of cakes and bread they sold from their booth. In those days, the two spent countless hours tromping through the vineyard or, if the weather wouldn't allow, reading stories to each other. Selene's mother had quite the collection of tales in her library and had taught them both to read almost from the moment they could walk.

Soon they could hear the flutes playing, and the scent of honey rolls, candied apples, fig cobbler, and myriad pastries and other delectables filled the air as they neared Miller's Grove. Dozens of large pavilions had been erected, and various acrobats, musicians, and theater troupes were performing to the delight of what was already at least a thousand people. Booths were set up in a massive circle surrounding the festival, where merchants and artisans from every corner of Vylari were plying their wares. At the far end would be games and contests. Selene usually managed to talk Mariyah into a race or two. Mariyah was an exceptionally fast runner, easily beating most of her friends.

Selene pulled Mariyah toward a group standing just within the entrance. Mariyah recognized most of them, including Kiro, Selene's brother. He was a bit older and had recently taken a blacksmith apprenticeship in Jordine, a hamlet two days to the north. Selene had hoped for years that Mariyah and Kiro would marry, but Mariyah had never felt any attraction. Kiro was friendly and charming and had always treated her with the utmost respect, but Lem had captured her heart. There could be no other.

As they walked up, Kiro was telling the group of his time in Jordine.

"I like the work," he said. "But Master Dorin is about as nasty a fellow as you could meet."

Mariyah tried to look interested, but could not stop herself from fidgeting. Lem would be playing by now.

"She's not really listening," remarked Selene.

Kiro laughed. "That's right. I nearly forgot. Do you know where he's playing?"

Mariyah took a moment, as if trying to remember, but she knew the exact spot and time. "Somewhere on the east side, I think. We can wait a while. He'll be at it for a few hours."

Kiro offered his arm. "Nonsense. I love hearing Lem play. Best musician in Vylari, I'd wager."

"You go ahead," said Selene. "Yemil promised me a honey roll."

Mariyah watched Selene take the arm of a young dark-haired boy standing a few yards away and vanish into the crowd.

The others decided to wander the festival for a while and then meet up later. This was fine by Mariyah. Hopefully once Lem was finished, they could sneak away without anyone noticing.

The distinctive tones of Lem's balisari reached them as they approached the edge of the blue-and-red pavilion. Only a few dozen folk were there. The majority of the crowd would come later, after shopping the booths and playing a few games. Blankets were scattered about where the early arrivals had set up for a relaxing meal. Sitting atop a stool on a raised dais at the opposite end was Lem, his instrument gripped between his knees as he plucked out a jaunty tune.

Mariyah's heart raced. His auburn curls fell around his shoulders, the claret shirt he wore accentuating his olive complexion. He was built thicker than most, even more so than Kiro, yet was quite tall. Selene could say anything she wanted; Mariyah thought him the most beautiful boy she'd ever seen.

His balisari, an unusual instrument and considered one of the most difficult to master, had a teardrop-shaped body and two necks, one broad, one narrow, joined at the top by an elegantly carved headstock that fanned out like the tail feathers of a bird. The rich burgundy finish was beginning to dull from years of wear, but with the gold inlay around the outer body and swirling up both necks, it was still strikingly beautiful.

Seeing them approach, Lem abruptly ended the melody and signaled to the small crowd that he'd be taking a short break. He wrapped Mariyah in a tight hug and gave Kiro a fond slap on the shoulder.

"Good to see you, Kiro. How goes the apprenticeship?"

Several disgruntled remarks drew their attention. The small crowd was growing, and newcomers were wondering why there was no music.

"I'll tell you later," said Kiro.

Lem nodded, then gave Mariyah a light kiss on the tip of her nose. "Are you staying?"

"What do you think?"

Lem picked up his instrument, and the peevish voices quickly quieted as he remounted the dais and resumed playing. Mariyah and Kiro found a spot nearby to sit and listen.

The first song, "Stars in the Water," was a tribute to the Sunflow River. It was a happy little tune with a bouncing rhythm that urged several of the spectators to their feet, who danced about and sang along with the lyrics. The second, "The Tree of Vylari's Soul," was a more serious affair, and one of Mariyah's favorites. It told of dark times and wicked deeds, when war and death had plagued the land, and how, in the end, the wise founders had banished the evils of magic and conflict to create a new paradise: Vylari. It was an old song, said to have been written at the founding, though admittedly Mariyah was unsure how true that was. No one really knew when Vylari had been founded or when the barrier that kept it safe was created. Truth be told, no one much cared. Vylari existed and was protected, and that was enough.

Lem's talent was obvious, and it was little wonder he was sought by the wealthiest families to play at their gatherings. And it was clear that he enjoyed entertaining much more than he did teaching. Unfortunately, festivals and other functions were largely seasonal, so students were a must.

After an hour, Kiro excused himself. "Better see what kind of mischief the others are getting into, and if I can keep them from getting into any more."

By the time Lem took another break, the pavilion was completely filled. Shouts of "Keep playing" and "Don't stop" followed him as he made his way to join Mariyah.

"I can't believe you have to go away again," she said.

Lem sighed. "I know. Me either. But you know how it is. I have to make as much as I can this fall, or I'll end up with twice the number of students this winter."

Mariyah wrapped her arm around his and leaned her head on his chest. "I wish I could come with you."

Lem chuckled. "And let the winery crumble in your absence? You know your father's hopeless without you."

"I know," she sighed. "But it's a nice dream." There was a long silence. Mariyah could sense there was something on Lem's mind. Before she could ask, he gently moved her away and took her hands.

"I was thinking about giving it up."

Mariyah furrowed her brow. "Giving what up?"

"This. Your father's right about one thing: This is no life for you. I need to stay closer to home. What kind of husband would I be if I constantly left you alone?"

"What else would you do?"

"I was considering asking your father for work," he replied.

Mariyah laughed. "You? Work with Father?"

"Why not? I'm strong enough. And I already tend the garden at my house. How hard could growing grapes be?"

Mariyah touched his cheek. "I would never ask you to give up playing. And there's more to it than growing grapes. Making good wine takes years of practice."

"We *have* years. I'm sure your father would say yes."

"Lem, I love you. I truly do. But sometimes you're as thick as stone. You'd be miserable. And if you're worried over leaving me by myself, I intend to come along with you."

"That's just it. You wouldn't be able to."

"And why not?" she demanded.

"You know as well as I do your father could never run things without you. And as much as it irks you sometimes, I know you love working at the winery."

The thought of Lem giving up his life was never a thing she had considered. It seemed cruel. "I . . . I don't know. I'll need to think about it."

"Of course." Lem kissed her hand. "We have all the time in the world."

Lem played for a few more hours, taking short breaks to sit with Mariyah. Selene came by once, though she stayed only long enough to tell Mariyah that they were leaving the festival to meet on the east bank of the Sunflow. Mariyah promised to join them after Lem had finished for the night, though she knew it was a lie even as she said it. Lem was only home for another day before heading north to Gunderton, which of the five towns in Vylari hosted the largest of the Harvest Festivals. But as much as she wanted to go with him, there was simply too much work to be done at home.

Perhaps it wouldn't be the worst thing for Lem to work with Father, she thought, then quickly banished the idea. Lem would be wasted as a winemaker. She would not be the cause of his misery. And working with her father would most assuredly be miserable.

When the final melody was over, Lem strapped his balisari across his back and walked with Mariyah to the row of food and sweets vendors. Lem picked out a few pieces of hard candy, making sure that at least three were tart apple, Mariyah's favorite.

"Selene asked us to meet them at the Sunflow," she told him, pursing her lips as the deliciously sour taste filled her mouth.

"If you'd like, we'll go," he offered.

"I'd rather not, if you don't mind."

Lem pulled her in closer. "I have all the company I need right here."

"Me too."

The booths were starting to close down for the night, and the crowd was thinning as people began making their way home. It was nearly midnight now, and Mariyah knew they needed to start back too.

As they exited the festival grounds, a chill air blew in from the north, sending a shiver through Mariyah's entire body.

"Winter's coming early this year," she said, folding her arms to her chest.

"That's what Shemi said too." Lem was doing his best to keep her warm.

"Where *was* your uncle tonight?" she asked.

Lem shrugged. "Who knows? I didn't see him while I was playing. Probably wandering around here somewhere."

Mariyah adored Shemi. He had a quick wit and casual manner that never failed to put her at ease. He was Lem's uncle, but he felt like family to many of the children in Olian Springs. As a youth, Shemi had spent most of his time wandering around Vylari, never settling down to a 'respectable' profession, earning a living doing odd jobs and selling the furs and meat from his hunts. Though it vexed some of the elders of the community, it meant he had a sense of adventure and countless stories to entertain the youngsters. Even now that he was an elder himself, his wanderlust had not diminished, though he typically stayed to the forests and hills within a day or two of home.

Lem and Mariyah turned from the well-worn causeway onto the lesser-used trail that would lead them to the eastern end of Mariyah's land. They'd only walked a few yards down the path when they heard someone shouting Lem's name from the road.

They turned and spotted Kiro striding urgently toward them, searching the faces of the passersby. Lem called back, waving his arm. Kiro broke into a run, sliding to a halt a few feet away.

"What's wrong?" asked Lem.

"You have to get home right now," he said, slightly out of breath.

"Is it Shemi?" asked Mariyah, a sudden stab of fear piercing her chest.

"No. Well, yes. Shemi's fine. He's the one who sent me.

He came looking for you at the Sunflow, but he didn't say why. Only that it was important you hurry."

"Can you walk Mariyah home?"

"I'm coming with you," she insisted, firmly.

"Your parents will worry. I'm sure it's nothing." When it was clear Mariyah was not bending, he placed his hands on her shoulders. "Please. I promise if it's something bad, I'll tell you."

After a long moment, Mariyah let out a huff. "Fine. But I don't need to be walked home."

"I don't mind," said Kiro. "To be honest, I'm grateful for any excuse to get away from Selene and her friends. They're unbearable when they've had this much to drink."

Mariyah cupped Lem's face in her palms. "You had better come get me if something's wrong."

Lem leaned down and kissed her. "On the spirits of my ancestors, you have my word."

Mariyah rolled her eyes at the overstated promise. "Off with you."

After a sharp nod to Kiro, Lem took off running. Mariyah watched until he was back onto the main road and well out of sight before starting out.

Lem was probably right in saying it was nothing. Shemi often quarreled with his neighbors. It was never severe, but Lem's was the ear his uncle would bend each time. Yes. That had to be it.

Yet as they walked, Mariyah could not shake the feeling that this time there was more to it than a neighborly spat. But she dismissed this as irritation over her time with Lem being cut short. She would have to give Shemi a scolding when next she saw him. A *sound* scolding.

2

THE STRANGER

Do not fear the darkness. I am the light that guides you. Do not fear the unknown. Nothing can harm you so long as your faith in me holds true.

　　　　Book of Kylor, Chapter Eleven, Verse Twenty-Six

L em ran, the balisari strapped to his back bouncing with each stride, fueling his already nagging anxiety. If the instrument was damaged, it would be an unmitigated disaster—it had been a gift from his mother, passed down through generations of her family. She'd told him that it had been brought to Vylari just before the barrier was created. There was no way to know if the story was true, though Lem had never come across another instrument quite like it.

Soon he was forced to slow to a brisk walk, out of breath and holding the stitch in his side. Though he was one of the taller, broader boys in Olian Springs, he always seemed to tire more quickly. Even the young children he taught seemed to have greater stamina. Of course, most boys spent their days tromping around in the forests, while Lem stayed at home practicing his instrument.

Likely he was worrying over nothing, he told himself as his breathing returned to a normal cadence. But it would be uncharacteristic for Shemi to call Lem away like this over something trivial.

Lem's fears were confirmed as he drew near the house he and Shemi shared. It had been his mother's house, and Shemi had been a welcome guest whenever he was in the area throughout Lem's childhood. It was a modest dwelling, set fifty yards back from the road, with a sturdy front porch and red clay tiled roof. Though in need of a fresh coat of paint, it was in good repair, due in no small part to Shemi's considerable carpentry skills.

Shemi was standing just outside the front door, talking to a tall woman with shoulder-length silver hair, clad in a long green-and-white robe and carrying an ash walking stick: Ferah, an elder on the council and highly respected among the people.

Shemi was still in the old leathers he wore on his long walks, his weathered features contorted into a deep troubled frown. Ferah was not a frequent guest; in fact, Lem had only met her once, when she had paid her respects the week his mother died. This was more than some minor spat between neighbors.

"Finally," said Shemi, visibly relieved. "I was afraid Kiro wouldn't be able to find you."

"What's this about?" asked Lem.

Shemi glanced over to Ferah.

"I leave it to you to explain the situation," she said.

Shemi nodded and took a long breath. "There is a stranger in Vylari."

Lem raised an eyebrow. "A stranger? What do you mean?"

"Someone has crossed over into our land," he replied. "Someone from Lamoria."

"What? How can that be?" No one had ever passed

through the barrier. Everyone knew it was impossible to penetrate.

"We're not sure," said Shemi. "It's happened only once before. At least that we know of."

Lem didn't know what to say. As shocking as it was, he couldn't understand why this news had led to Shemi sending for him urgently in the middle of the night. "And this has something to do with us?"

Shemi nodded slowly. "Yes. I'm afraid it does."

This was absurd. Once you passed beyond the border of Vylari, you could never find your way home—that was what protected the people from the threat of Lamoria, and prevented any who might wish to leave from divulging Vylari's location. This lesson was passed on to every child by the elders; it was an absolute truth. Despite Shemi's current assertion that it had happened before, as far as Lem knew, no one had ever tested the validity of the belief. No one had ever gone there. In fact, some speculated as to whether or not Lamoria even continued to survive. There were no *strangers* in Vylari, only people he had yet to meet. And should there be any doubt the barrier was real, the stories about the terrors of the outside world were sufficient to douse the flames of the more curious souls. Not even Shemi would have the courage to step beyond the border. This had to be a mistake. But the expressions on the two elders' faces said that they thought otherwise.

"What do you know of your father?" asked Ferah.

This question stunned Lem nearly as much as the news of a stranger. "My father? Nothing. My mother never spoke of him."

"Illorial was never a forthcoming woman. I did not know her well, but that much was clear. Still, you never thought to ask?"

"Of course I did. But she refused to say anything about him, so I stopped trying after a while. If she planned to tell me, she died before she could." He turned to Shemi. "What's this about?"

His uncle gestured to the door. "We should talk inside."

Lem stood firm, waiting until Shemi and Ferah entered before following. They passed through the living room to the kitchen situated at the back of the house.

His father? Lem had always assumed that his father not being there was due to some scandal. It happened from time to time; though in his case, it was the mystery that set tongues wagging. No one knew who he was or what had prompted Illorial's sudden departure and then her abrupt reappearance, belly heavy with child. She had refused to speak of it, becoming sad or sometimes angry when pressed on the matter. Shemi claimed not to know anything about him, though Lem was never completely sure he was being honest. There was a time Lem would look at the faces of men he met, looking for himself in their features, wondering if this were perhaps the one. He paid special attention to those to whom his mother spoke, hoping she would give something away in her tone or expression. But she never did. After her death, Lem had thought less and less about it. What did he care for a father who hadn't cared for him? More importantly, why would anyone be interested in his parentage now?

They took a seat at the small table opposite an unlit stove. There was an actual dining room, but Lem and Shemi did little entertaining, and the east-facing windows in the kitchen gave a pleasant view of the sunrise, so this was where they ate most of their meals.

"Out with it," Lem demanded. "Who is the stranger? What does it have to do with me? And why the interest in my father?"

"There has always been a mystery surrounding you, Lem," said Ferah. "One which you are unaware of. One which until now has not been thought important enough to solve."

"A mystery?" said Lem, coughing a sardonic laugh. "What? Because my mother had an affair? I'm not the only one in Vylari who doesn't know who his father is."

"True," said Ferah. "But you are the only one whose mother crossed into Lamoria."

Lem blinked several times, eyes darting back to Shemi. "This is a joke, right? Mother would have told me something like that."

"This is not a joke," said Ferah. "Your mother left Vylari. That alone is troubling, as we do not know what compelled her to do so. But her return was what had us most concerned. It is deemed impossible, and yet she managed it somehow. And while pregnant."

"Well, if you think I know how she did it, you're wrong," Lem asserted.

"I do not," said Ferah. "That much is clear. And in truth, I have been willing to dismiss it, until the stranger arrived. But he has. And that means Vylari is no longer safe. The barrier exists to protect us from the horrors of the outside world; without it, we are defenseless."

Shemi gave Ferah a sideways scowl. "We don't know the barrier has failed. Only that two people found a way through."

Lem understood why Ferah was worried, which made Shemi's irritation confusing. "You still haven't explained what this has to do with me. I don't know how it was done. I swear if I did, I would tell you. But I've never heard of any of this before."

"I am not doubting your honesty," said Ferah. "But I needed to be sure. A situation has arisen. The stranger's

arrival has brought more danger than I could have anticipated."

"*More* danger?" repeated Lem, still unable to fully accept what he was being told.

Ferah and Shemi exchanged glances. Shemi was clearly
unhappy, while Ferah's expression was stoic.

"Before we continue, you should show him," said Ferah.

Shemi looked down at the table and then nodded. Rising, he gestured for Lem to follow.

Lem hesitated. Without being told, he knew that the
stranger was in the house. *Why would they bring him here?*
Shemi led him from the kitchen and walked at a conspicuously slow pace down the hall off which the bedrooms and
Shemi's study were located. At the end was a spare room
used for guests. But no one had slept there in years, not
since his mother's funeral. Shemi's wanderlust had culti-
vated a great number of fascinating stories, but not many
roots in the town. They rarely had visitors, and none who
would stay for the night.

Shemi closed his eyes, taking a few seconds to steady his
breathing, then reached for the knob. The door squealed
open on disused hinges, and the dim light from a lantern
spilled out onto the floor. Shemi stepped aside, allowing
Lem to enter first. A tingle of fear seeped in as Lem peeked
around the doorframe. He could see that the bed was occupied. *The stranger.*

With wary steps, Lem drew closer. At first, he could not
make out the stranger's features. Beneath the thick blanket, he could tell that he was quite large; his feet poked out
and hung from the end of the bed. Lem picked up the lantern and held it above the stranger's head. His black hair
was short, neatly trimmed, and looked as thick and dense
as wool. His skin was the color of pine bark, and he had
a square jaw, heavy brow, and high cheekbones. *Powerful*

was the first word that came to Lem's mind, though beads
of sweat covered the stranger's face and his breathing was
rapid and shallow.

"Frila's boy, Chaud, found him this morning a few
miles from the barrier," said Shemi in a half whisper, "dis-
oriented and barely able to walk. He said only one word
before collapsing. 'Illorial.'"

Lem nearly dropped the lantern. *Illorial*. His mother's
name. "Are you sure?"

"As sure as I can be," Shemi replied. "I didn't hear it
myself. But Chaud has no reason to lie. That was why they
brought him here."

Lem took another long look at the stranger. Could this
possibly be . . . his father? *No*, he decided. He was far too
young. The man lying before him could not be more than
thirty. "What's wrong with him?"

"Ferah believes something happened to him when he
crossed the barrier," replied Shemi. "But then as your
mother passed through unharmed, there's no way to know
for sure."

The implications were mind-boggling. His father was
not from Vylari; rather, he was from the impossible land of
Lamoria. "Can you help him?" Answers to so many questions were within his grasp. The stranger *had* to wake.

"If I knew what was wrong with him, perhaps. But he
seems to be getting weaker by the minute. I think he's
dying."

"Could we send for a healer?"

"Ferah is as skilled as any, and she has no idea what to
do."

"Surely someone can help him?"

"I'm afraid not."

A feeling of desperation threatened to overcome Lem as
he looked down at the stranger. There had to be something

they could do. His mother had crossed the barrier unharmed. Why had it hurt this stranger? Was his mother
somehow different? Special?

An image of her on the porch popped into his head, a
tiny smile on her face while she patiently taught him the
balisari. An ordinary Vylarian by most standards—hard-
working, dedicated to family, good-natured, and kind.
There was nothing about her that would suggest she could
do something as incredible as cross the barrier. How could
she have kept something this important from him? Lem
placed the lantern on the nightstand and turned to face
Shemi. "Why haven't you ever told me any of this?"

"I never knew why my sister left Vylari. When she returned pregnant with you, she made me swear to keep her
secret."

"I had a right to know." Through the tempest of confusion swirling in his head, a low boiling anger was building.

"I wanted to tell you. But she was convinced that if you
knew, you would leave Vylari to look for your father. More
than anything, she wanted you kept safe."

"How did lying to me keep me safe?"

"No one lied to you. I don't know who your father is."

"How could you not know?" he said, voice growing
louder with each word.

"For the same reason you don't," he replied, unmoved
by Lem's display. "What should I have done? I couldn't
force your mother to tell me, now, could I?"

"How does Ferah know about it?"

"She was the one who found your mother when she returned," Shemi explained. "She helped her hide the truth . . .
until now. When Illorial went missing, it was thought
she must have drowned in the Sunflow or run afoul of wild
animals. When she came back, seemingly from nowhere,
people assumed she had run away, fearing a scandal. It was

easy enough to encourage that idea. I mean, who would think she could have left Vylari?"

"That doesn't explain why *you* kept it from me."

Shemi locked eyes with Lem. "It's what your mother wanted. It's not for you to question her wishes. Or me either. You can be angry all you want, but it doesn't do a thing to change the situation."

Lem knew his uncle was right. His mother had loved him fiercely. There was nothing she wouldn't have done, no sacrifice too great, if it meant his happiness. She'd watched over him like a treasure. Even before Shemi came to stay with them permanently, he'd never felt the absence of a second parent. His mother would have only hidden the truth to protect him. And Shemi loved him like a son, taking on parental duties throughout his entire life. Though Lem could not agree that he should have been kept ignorant, he couldn't fault the old man for doing what he'd felt was best. "And what *is* the situation?"

Shemi reached into his pocket and retrieved a folded parchment. "That will be for you to decide. The stranger had this."

Lem held it in his hand, staring down wide-eyed as if it might burn his fingers. An object from Lamoria. One which contained . . . he was afraid to know.

Lem's head was spinning, and for a moment he felt as if his legs would give way. "None of this makes sense. Why would Mother leave Vylari? And even if she did, how could she have made it back? There has to be more to it."

"I'm sure there is," Shemi agreed. "But there's no way to know what that is. One thing you can say about my sister: If she didn't want to tell you something, there was no way to force her. And believe me, I tried."

Lem stumbled to a chair pushed against the wall next to the door. "What do I do now? What will people think?"

"They'll be afraid, at least at first. But that's to be expected. In time, they'll come to accept it."

Lem turned his attention to the parchment. The chill of fear coursed through his limbs as he held it with trembling hands. "Have you read it?"

Shemi nodded. "It's nonsense, if you ask me. But I won't keep it from you."

For several seconds, Lem was paralyzed. He squeezed his eyes shut, his heart pounding in his ears. Somehow he knew that whatever it said would change things even more than they had changed already. Taking a long breath, he opened his eyes, unfolded the parchment, and looked down at what was written. At first he could not understand it. The lettering was strange, like nothing he'd seen before.

Lem concentrated, running his finger along the symbols. He had never been the scholar Mariyah and Shemi were. He wasn't dim, but he'd never acquired a genuine love of reading.

"They're the same letters as ours," said Shemi, noticing his difficulty. "Keep looking. You'll get it."

Gradually he recognized the familiarities. Yes. They were the same letters he had been taught. Some exactly the same, others reversed or with extra loops and squiggles in odd places. After another few minutes he was able to make out what it said.

To whomever finds this letter,

My name is Hylar Olivan of the Order of the Thaumas. As I am unsure what will become of me once I pass through the barrier, I am writing this should things go awry. The magic protecting this land is unlike anything I have encountered, and I feel woefully outmatched by its power. Simply locating it was a challenge. Still, I must try to make it through.

Should I fail, it is vitally important that this find its way to the woman named Illorial.

Illorial,

You likely do not know me. I was but a boy when you lived with us at the enclave, though you knew my father, Pyvor, well. I have been sent to warn you. What we feared for so long has come to pass. He is coming. Soon doom will be upon us all. Our seer, Oryel, believes our only hope rests with one who dwells among you—a child enormous of talent, with special gifts that have the power to hold back the darkness. She says that this person will have a deep connection to you. But it is uncertain what that connection might be. Only that they are a bridge between your world and ours. They must leave Vylari at once. Their strength will draw him like a beacon. The barrier will be no obstacle. Your land will burn and your people will die. Please. You must help us before it's too late. I know you have no reason to trust me. So I have been given these words: The wind shall guide you home. Oryel told me it was the last thing she said to you before you returned to Vylari.

Again, I urge you to hurry. And should I not make it through, tell my father I love him . . . and that I am sorry.

Hylar

He folded the parchment and handed it back to Shemi. He had never felt more confused and afraid in his life. The implications of the letter were immense. "Is that why Ferah is here? You want me to leave?"

"Absolutely not. I would never allow it."

"But if this is true—"

"You aren't going anywhere. You hear me? There's no way to know if any of this is true or not."

"But he knew her name . . . and where she was from." Lem felt as if the entire world were crumbling before his eyes; his dreams of marrying Mariyah, of working at the vineyard alongside her, of starting a family of their own were vanishing like a fog in the heat of the late morning sun.

Shemi shoved the letter in his pocket. "I don't care what this says. You're staying here, and that's all there is to say about it."

"Has Ferah read it?"

"Yes."

The short answer and tense tone were revealing. Ferah wanted him to leave. And if what the stranger claimed were true, for good reason. Lem pressed his palms to his knees and stood on wobbly legs. Shemi took his arm, and the two exited the room and returned to the kitchen.

Ferah was waiting silently, hands folded and eyes fixed on the tabletop.

Lem's head was still swimming as he sat heavily in his chair.

"So now you know the truth," said Ferah.

"Just because outlandish claims were made doesn't mean they're true," Shemi asserted.

"No?" said Ferah, her mouth turned to a deep frown. "Then how would you explain it?" Before Shemi could respond, she added: "It is clear that he knew Lem's mother. And he was willing to risk his own life to come here. Why would he do that for a lie?"

Shemi fumed but had no response to give.

Lem could see where this was going. And Ferah was right. The stranger was not lying. He had crossed the barrier knowing he might never return.

Finally Shemi regained a modicum of composure, though the anger in his voice was undisguised. "I will not allow Lem to leave. He belongs here. I don't care what anyone says."

"I am not suggesting he leave." In contrast to Shemi, she maintained a poised calm as her eyes shifted to Lem. "Nor do I think, should he choose to stay, anyone would force him to. At this point, I only weigh the possibilities. But if what the letter says is true, everyone in Vylari could be in great danger."

"The letter said nothing," Shemi retorted. "Vague claims of a coming evil? Insisting we send away one of our own kin? That tells us nothing. Why not just say what this evil is? No. I'll not take the word of a stranger without more than a few words scratched on parchment as a reason."

"It could have been written in haste," offered Ferah. "And do not forget it was intended for Illorial."

"Or perhaps he was a madman," said Shemi.

The voices of Shemi and Ferah drifted far away, their words garbled as they continued the debate. All Lem could think about was Mariyah. He would have to tell her. But what would he say? That his mother had done the unthinkable and left Vylari? That his father was from Lamoria and possibly even a wielder of magic? And worst of all, that his staying might mean that everyone in Vylari could be in mortal danger? The thought of the conversation caused a lump to form in his throat. Would she feel differently about him? How could she not, when *he* felt differently about himself? The image of the dying stranger insisted its way to the fore of his thoughts. More than anything, he wanted this not to be happening. Yet it was. How could Mariyah not feel uncertain about him, about their future, when his past had been built on a lie?

"Lem."

The touch of Shemi's hand brought him back into the moment. "I'll leave."

"You will do no such thing," barked Shemi.

Ferah's expression softened. "That is very brave of you, Lem. But your uncle is right. We don't know how true this is. Or even for certain if it's you that he came to find. And I would not have you make a rash choice based on fear. Frila and Chaud have seen the stranger and read the letter, so word will spread. There is nothing I can do about that. But that should not force you into a decision. Especially not one with such irreversible consequences."

"Listen to her," said Shemi. "I know you're upset. But give it a few days."

"What good will that do?" asked Lem. "Nothing will change."

"Perhaps not," said Ferah. "But running away is rarely the right thing to do. My advice is to wait until you've had time to settle this in your mind. Perhaps there is an answer to this riddle. Neither I nor your uncle are schooled in Lamorian lore, at least not beyond what is commonly told. There are other elders I can consult. Give me time to investigate."

Lem looked from Shemi to Ferah. He had never felt so utterly lost. Nodding almost imperceptibly, he said, "I'll wait."

Ferah smiled. "Good. In the meantime, you should stay close to home. Unfortunately, books dealing with Lamoria are rare. It will take a while to gather them all." She pushed back her chair. "It's late, and this has been an eventful night."

"Please," said Shemi. "There's no need to go back tonight. Take my bed."

"Thank you," replied Ferah, leaning wearily on her walking stick. "But my children will be frantic if they wake and I'm not home. And I promised my grandson I would take him to market in the morning for sweets."

Olian Springs town proper was nearly three miles away—a long walk at her age. Though not older than Shemi, the years had caught her much earlier. A stray thought entered Lem's head. Was the elder leaving because there was a stranger in the house . . . or him? This foreshadowed what might come. People would fear him; reject him. Child of a magic wielder. Yes, he used the shadow walk while hunting. But that was a natural talent, one possessed by all Vylarians, and not true magic. The mere mention of the word was like spitting a curse. The people of Vylari had closed themselves off from Lamoria, where magic was used to wage war and to spread death and pestilence. From childhood they were taught about the evils that lay beyond the barrier. Now, Lem was irrevocably tied to the very thing his people loathed and feared the most.

He imagined the eager faces of the crowd who had enjoyed his music tonight. The smiles and laughter resounded in his memory. And that was all it would be from now on: a memory. The people of Vylari would not be able to prevent themselves from fearing him. The stories they had been told would see to that. Would his jobs dry up? Would he become an object of curiosity and ridicule? The thought formed a thick knot in his stomach. He might be forced to give up teaching and performing altogether. At least he and Shemi could feed themselves. Shemi had taught him to hunt and trap. Though he wasn't as adept as some, he was good enough to keep them from starving.

Shemi walked Ferah out. Lem could hear their muffled voices in the foyer, the words *trouble* and *danger* drifting into the kitchen. If only the stranger would wake up, tell them precisely what his letter meant. What was this evil? How had he known how to find Vylari?

"I know what you're thinking."

Lem hadn't noticed Shemi return.

The old man began tossing wood into the stove. "Some tea will settle you down, I think."

A sardonic laugh slipped out before Lem could control himself. "Tea?"

"Never underestimate the power of a good cup of tea," Shemi said, ignoring Lem's tone. "You just rest your mind. Nothing is going to happen. Nothing we can't handle, anyway."

Lem sat quietly until the kettle was ready and a cup of steaming hot tea was placed in front of him. He held it to his mouth, concentrating on the heat rising, covering his lips with a layer of moisture, its minty aroma mingling pleasantly with the sweet scent of Shemi's pipe. He had never taken up the habit himself, but had always enjoyed the smell. It reminded him of evenings before his mother had died, when the three of them would sit on the front porch and Lem would play the balisari. She would laugh with delight as Shemi danced about and blew smoke rings in time with the music.

Lem puffed a breath over the tea and took a small sip. Though it warmed his belly and relieved some of the fatigue in his muscles, it was not enough to ease his burden. "I don't know what to do. It's just so . . . big. I feel like I'm drowning."

"Then don't do anything yet."

"I need to tell Mariyah, before she hears about this from someone else."

Shemi nodded. "I suppose that would be best. But you shouldn't worry. She loves you. She'll understand."

"Will she?"

Shemi's tone hardened. "Listen to me, lad. The two of you were made for each other. Anyone with half a brain can see that. Don't you go underestimating her. If you think she'd stop loving you over this . . . well . . . you should be ashamed for thinking that."

Shemi's words struck home. Mariyah had been a true partner to him since the day they'd met. He could remember exactly the words she'd spoken to him. He could even see the blue cotton dress she'd worn, with tiny silver beads woven into the shoulders and sleeves, and the white ribbon that had held back her hair. Every detail was a painting he could look upon anytime he wished; a sublime moment forever frozen into his memory.

That had been the first time he'd mustered the nerve to play publicly. One of his friends was going to be celebrating a birthday with a gathering on the banks of the Sunflow. Initially the family had asked his mother to play, but she'd insisted that Lem would be better suited to perform for what would certainly be a younger audience. It had taken no small measure of encouragement to convince him he was good enough. At the time, he'd only ever played for Shemi and his mother, and felt extremely self-conscious about his abilities. Mariyah would still tease him about it sometimes, saying he'd looked like a frightened deer, ready to flee a hunter's bow, as he perched himself on the stool unable to so much as look up for the first three songs.

"Good thing I eventually did," he would reply. "Or we'd have never met." This was an exaggeration, of course. Lem had been far too shy to have had much to do with it. It had been Mariyah who'd approached him. Left to it, he would have never found the courage.

She had been sitting on a blanket among a small group of friends. Lem had seen her a few times before, but never considered for a moment speaking to her. After all, her family owned Anadil Farms. While his . . . But as the evening wore on, their eyes met repeatedly, and each time she would give him the faintest of smiles, never once looking away. However, being the awkward boy he was, Lem took this for nothing more than her being polite. Or perhaps she was simply enjoying the music. Surely a girl so lovely could not be interested in him.

His mother had once told him that music and love were two parts of the same spirit. At the time, he hadn't understood her meaning. But as the notes flowed from his balisari that night, at last he did. He'd poured out his soul, and of all those gathered together, laughing and dancing beneath the stars, only Mariyah had seen it. By the time he was nearing the end of the performance, he knew that each note was played for an audience of one.

Lem had been kneeling beside the stool, packing away his instrument, when he heard Mariyah's voice for the first time.

"Were you going to leave without saying anything?"

He had not seen her approach, and was utterly dumbstruck as he looked up at her smile.

"I'm Mariyah," she said, offering Lem her hand.

Lem nearly toppled over as he scrambled up. "I . . . I'm—"

"Lem," she said. "I know. Your uncle Shemi talks about you all the time."

"Shemi?" he blurted out, still unable to form a coherent sentence.

"Shemi *is* your uncle, right?"

"Yes." He could not believe she was talking to him. *Say something, you idiot. Don't just stand there.*

Mariyah laughed. "Not much of a conversationalist, are you?"

"No," he stammered. "I mean, yes. I mean . . ." His shoulders sagged, and he let out a defeated groan. "I mean, I think I'll go drown myself now."

Mariyah laughed again. "I hope you don't. We can work on your conversational skills on the way home. Assuming you're willing to walk with me."

Lem glanced over at her friends, who were looking on with great interest, giggling and whispering to one another. "What about them?"

"If you would rather not, I understand."

It was in that moment that Lem's courage finally showed itself. He picked up his balisari and slung it across his back. "I would be honored."

Mariyah took his arm, and without so much as a farewell to the others, they left the gathering together. People would talk and rumors would fly. The daughter of Freyn and Leyna of Anadil Farms keeping company with the likes of Lem? But Lem did not care. As they walked arm in arm, he knew only one thing: He was the luckiest boy in the whole of Vylari.

And from that night forward, Mariyah had never shied from her feelings for him. Even in the face of her father's disapproval, she'd stood firm. How could he question it now? Yet he did, regardless. It was one thing to *seem* different; quite another to *be* different. But under his uncle's scolding gaze, he relented.

"Of course. I know she'll accept me. But it doesn't make telling her any easier. And there's her father to think about."

Shemi chuckled out tiny puffs of smoke. "Mariyah can handle him well enough. He'll not risk losing her over this. Sure, he'll complain. I can almost hear him now. But he complains as it is, you know? You can bet that Mariyah will have her way."

Lem finished half the cup and then placed it on the table. "I think I need to turn in for the night." His head was pounding, and a deep fatigue had crept through his limbs.

"Good idea. You get some sleep. Let old Uncle Shemi do the worrying for now."

Lem rose, kissing the top of Shemi's head before retiring to his room. The next day would be every bit as stressful as this had been. Just thinking about the dawn filled him with dread. He had promised Mariyah he'd tell her if something bad had happened. Well, something bad most certainly had happened.

After removing his clothes, he unclasped the silver locket that hung around his neck. He never went anywhere without it.

Lem placed it on the nightstand and slipped into bed. But after an hour, sleep had not come. The anxiety and fear worming their way into his mind would not be denied or forgotten. How many people already knew? Would Mariyah find out before he could tell her himself? And her father . . . Shemi's reassurances notwithstanding, Mariyah's father would do his best to keep his daughter away from him. He might be incompetent when it came to business matters, but he still was a very influential man. The trouble he could create for Lem could not be ignored.

Lem wanted to weep; to scream; to do something, anything that would take away the feeling of helplessness that threatened to overcome him. He threw back the blanket and placed his feet on the cold wood floor and slumped at the edge of the bed. *Perhaps a spot of whiskey might help.* Shemi kept some in the kitchen pantry. He didn't enjoy it as much as his uncle, preferring wine. But it had its uses.

A garbled cry sounded from beyond the door. Lem snatched up a lantern and hurried into the hallway, turning toward Shemi's bedroom. But another agonized moan from the spare room had him sliding to a halt and running in the opposite direction. The stranger was still in bed, but was twisting and groaning as if in horrible pain.

Lem placed the lantern on the floor and leaned over the ailing man, unsure what to do. "It's all right. Calm down. You're safe."

Shemi. He should get Shemi. He turned to call for his uncle, but a hand shot up and gripped his wrist.

"He's coming!" the stranger shouted, thrashing his head from side to side. "He's coming!"

Lem tried to pull free, but the steely fingers held fast. The stranger's eyes popped open and fixed on Lem.

"Is it . . . is it you?"

Lem could not form a reply.

Sweat drenched the stranger's hair and face. "You must go," he rasped. "You must leave this place. He's coming. You must go before he finds you."

"I'll get help," Lem finally managed to say. Again he tried to break free.

"No!" With irresistible strength, the stranger pulled Lem forward and wrapped his other arm around his neck.

Lem panicked, frantically pushing against the stranger's chest, but to no effect. In a single motion, the stranger leaned up, crushing Lem to his body.

A flash of white light covered Lem's eyes, momentarily blinding him. As his vision slowly returned, his nostrils were assaulted by the rancid stench of burnt timbers and rotten flesh. The bedroom and the stranger were gone. In their place was an open field roughly two hundred yards in diameter, completely encircled by a massive inferno reaching as high as the treetops. Heat assaulted him with brutal ferocity, but there was nowhere to run. Strewn across the ground like broken twigs were hundreds upon hundreds of bodies, mangled and twisted, some hacked to pieces, their faces contorted and frozen into their final horrorstricken moments. Many he recognized at once—friends, acquaintances, students. He averted his eyes, fearing that one of them might be Shemi . . . or Mariyah.

"This can't be real," shouted Lem. "It's a trick. What have you done to me?"

He is coming. The voice of the stranger called out from all directions. No longer shrill with madness, the enormous volume of the deep baritone reverberated in his chest.

He will find you. He will destroy everything you love. You must go. Hurry. Before it's too late.

The flames began to creep toward him, consuming the bodies as they approached. Lem looked for a way out, but he was trapped. His flesh blistered as the heat increased, until all he could do was drop to his knees and curl into a protective ball.

In a rush, all went black, and there was dead silence. The flames were gone, along with the pain from the burns. He was back in the spare room, splayed on the floor beside the bed. Slowly he held out his arms, relieved to see no injuries. *An illusion*, he thought. *Some form of foul magic.*

"It wasn't real," he gasped, reassuring himself, his heart still racing.

As he struggled to his feet, he could see the stranger lying flat on the bed, the blanket wadded up at his feet. The vacant stare told him that the last remnants of his life were spent. Whatever magic he had used must have been too much for him.

Lem could still see the flames; still smell the charred bodies of his kin, bringing on a wave of nausea that filled his mouth with saliva. Pressing his hand to the wall he spat, taking deep, even breaths until his stomach settled. *Is this what's coming? Fire and death?* Desperately he wanted to dismiss it as the insane ravings of a dying man. But in his heart, he knew better. The stranger had sacrificed his own life to give him this warning. He could not ignore it. He could not allow what he had witnessed to come to pass. There was no choice to be made. He must leave Vylari.

Lem pulled the blanket over the stranger's head and returned to his bedroom. Taking a seat by the window, he gazed into the night, tears falling freely. Already the sky was turning purple, soon to be joined by the orange-and-red glow of dawn. He continued to weep, praying to his ancestors for the courage to do what must be done, all the while desperately wishing for time to cease its relentless march. But it was a foolish wish—one born from fear and misery. The sun would rise. And Lem would spend his final day under a Vylari sky.

3

FAREWELL TO VYLARI

Kylor placed his hand on the man and asked, "Why do you weep?" The man wiped his tears and replied to our Lord, "Because I am alone. My family has abandoned me, and my friends refuse me their aid." Kylor smiled at the man and said, "You are not alone. I am here. I will never abandon you."

Book of Kylor, Chapter Twenty-One, Verse Seven

It was gone!

Panic gripped Lem as his fingers began a frantic search around his neck for any trace of the missing chain. His precious locket! But all he felt was bare flesh.

He would never have left it behind. Never. Not even the fog of despair could have made him forget to bring something so important. He was certain he could remember taking it from the nightstand and placing it around his neck. Be that as it may, it was not there now. Doubt began creeping in. He had packed in such a hurry and with so little thought . . . could he have? No. He remembered distinctly. He had just written Mariyah a note, explaining why he had to leave, a message he dared not deliver himself. It was just after he'd shoved the letter into his pack that he put it on.

He rifled through his pockets, thinking he might have

put it there in his haste. The contents were quickly removed and tossed onto the grass. Still nothing. In desperation, he unslung the balisari and pack from his shoulders, intending to search in a vain hope that he might have stowed it with the rest of his belongings.

As he placed the pack down, he felt something slide around in his shirt. Tearing open the top buttons, he thrust his hand inside and let out a loud moan of relief as he felt first the chain and then the locket attached to the end.

He closed his hands around it and dropped to his knees, pressing it to his brow. It took more than a minute before he could slow his breathing, and even then his heart continued to race.

He could see that the clasp securing the chain had snapped off. He held it up, gazing at it for a moment, tears ready to fall. From outward appearances, it was nothing special. Though well-crafted, it was not particularly elegant. The face side bore an engraving of lilies and grapevines woven together, while on the reverse two words were inscribed:

For Lem

He ran his fingers over each of the letters, the tips barely brushing the surface. Then, easing open the lid, he saw Mariyah's countenance smiling up at him, and a lump formed in his throat. She had given him this locket on the night he had declared his love. The night they had promised to spend their lives together. A promise he was now breaking.

It was too painful to dwell on. After tucking the chain and locket safely away into his most secure pocket, he gathered up the rest of his belongings. With a deep breath, he swallowed hard and continued walking.

As he crested the gentle slope of a low hill, he paused and shut his eyes. The soft rustle of the evening breeze caressing the tall grass seemed to be calling out his name, begging him to remain, insisting that he was still needed, still wanted.

He opened his eyes, his resolve teetering on the precipice. But there was no turning back. The safety of his people was more important. Still, an inner debate beleaguered his mind, one to which there could be no clear resolution. The stranger could have been lying, though the sacrifice of his life made that unlikely. He could have been delusional, made so by the power of the barrier. But then he had known the danger and had braved it anyway. For every objection, the part of Lem who knew what must be done had a reply. It was maddening. Desperation became rage, then turned to despair, then to sorrow, then back to rage in an unpredictable cycle of emotion. Why was this happening? What had he done to deserve this? All he had ever wanted was to live a peaceful life; to marry the woman he loved and raise a family. Was that so much to ask?

But the life he desired and the life he would have were two vastly different things. When he had found Mariyah's mother casually inspecting the vines, he had feared she'd already heard the news. In Vylari, gossip practically traveled on the wind. But to his relief she did not appear to know. Or if she did, she'd hidden it well. But Lem knew Mariyah's mother. She would read the letter before delivering it. Though she'd never opposed the match, it was a safe bet that she would now. Shemi may very well have been right in saying that Mariyah could stand up to her father. But her mother . . . her will was like iron. And her devotion to Mariyah was equally strong. It was her mother Mariyah took after more than anyone. To think of the two in a battle of wills . . . But that would not be a concern. By the time the sun set, there would be nothing for them to fight about.

The words of Uncle Shemi invaded his mind. Lem thought him to be in complete denial about the situation. *I don't care what other people think,* Shemi had said before leaving the house that morning to speak again with Ferah. *You're family, and that's that. You belong here.* Lem had simply smiled and nodded his agreement. Shemi's love for him rivaled his mother's, but love would not change facts. And the vision the stranger had shown him . . . Even had he told Shemi about it, he would have just claimed it to be another lie or delusion.

They had buried the stranger in the meadow as the sun rose that morning. It had felt wrong, as they did not know Lamorian customs or traditions. But they made sure to give him as much dignity as possible by offering some words to the ancestors on his behalf.

Lem had once asked Shemi about the world outside Vylari, a question every child posed at some point. The stories of the horrors that lay beyond the border were passed on almost as soon as a child could talk. He could picture the old man clearly, feet propped up on the kitchen table and an unlit pipe gripped loosely between his teeth. *It's no place for us, lad. Nothing but war and death out there. Best you keep your head here. No need to wonder about dark places and evil deeds.*

There was no doubt he would miss Shemi tremendously—almost as much as he would miss Mariyah. Guilt twisted through his heart like cold steel, guilt and regret. She would hate him for leaving—hate him for not saying goodbye—hate him for what he was. But it was better this way. Hating him would make it easier for her to move on and find a new life with someone else. A better life. One that did not hold naught but the promise of ridicule and hardship. She was every bit as strong as Shemi said. And in truth, she would love him regardless. She would have probably come with him had he asked. And there was a selfish corner of his mind that had contemplated the idea, if only for the wisp of a moment. The point of leaving was to keep those he loved safe. He was alone now. The dangers he would face were for him and no other.

Lem allowed himself a final look back, imagining her standing atop the next rise. She was clutching his letter to her chest, flaxen hair whipping across her tear-soaked face, her eyes pleading with him not to leave. But the vision faded. There was no one there: only the land and trees to mark his departure. As it should be.

After saying a silent farewell, he turned toward the road ahead. It was time.

He had never been so close to the border. Very few bothered to venture this far out; it wasn't worth the risk. One wrong step and you faced the terrible consequence of being forever lost in Lamoria. Elders, when the subject came up, never tired of saying that the people of Vylari were not meant to live there. That they were different. Better. They had created a home where war and magic could never find them. That was why the barrier had been created in the first place. That's what they claimed, anyway; though in reality, no one really knew the true reason, nor even how the barrier worked. The fact that it was made from magic was dismissed as unimportant, the contradiction willfully ignored.

It still was inconceivable to think that his mother had crossed over, and even more so that she had found her way back. What had she discovered there? Had she really fallen in love with a Lamorian? If so, why had she left him? But the real mystery that now plagued him was why she had not said a single word about it to him. In fact, she'd rarely mentioned her past at all. Most of what he knew of his family was from conversations with Shemi. Not that there was anything of particular interest—millers, weavers, and other various professions. All told, Lem's mastery of music made him the most noteworthy member of his entire line for at least as far back as Shemi could recount. This only served to deepen the mystery.

After his mother's death, Lem had searched through her papers and books, hoping to know her better, to understand why she had been so distant—particularly just prior to her sudden illness. But no answers had been forthcoming. He'd found drawings of strange creatures and places, images he'd dismissed as pure imagination at the time, but now he wondered if they might be things she'd seen beyond the barrier. Otherwise, he'd found only a few letters, mostly casual correspondence from her sister and her cousin, and none containing anything useful. There was only one letter that had seemed out of place—a request for his mother to visit the home of someone called Yularius. As far as Lem knew, no one by that name lived in Vylari; though it was always possible that Lem simply hadn't heard of him. He had considered asking Shemi, since his uncle had walked the length and breadth of Vylari many times throughout the years and knew just about everyone. But bringing up his mother's name always put the old man in a somber mood, and after a time, he had decided not to pursue the matter. It wasn't as if there was anything he could do about it. His mother was gone, and that was that.

The balisari strapped across his back felt heavy and awkward. It was the only thing of real value he had brought with him . . . the only thing apart from the locket he could not bear to leave behind. *Will there be musicians in Lamoria?* he wondered. Surely there would be. He couldn't imagine a place so brutish as to lack the ability to enjoy the pleasures of music. For Lem, life without music was a life not worth living.

Time passed unnoticed as he wound his way through the thick of the forest. The birds' songs went unheard, the voice of the wind ignored, as the narrow, seldom-used trail led him irreversibly away from all he had ever loved. He almost didn't see the marker carved into the ancient oak. Lem halted abruptly, his eyes fixed on the ominous symbol. It was a warning; a plea to turn back.

He strained his eyes to look as far beyond the oak as possible. Nothing appeared to be any different. There were no foreign trees or strange shrubs. A squirrel, looking just like any other squirrel, was leaping from limb to limb in the high reaches of a pine. Could the elders have been wrong? Was the border there at all? Maybe it was nothing more than a story told to scare people into remaining at home. Or maybe the magic was gone, withered away by time. Perhaps he would be able to return one day after all. Yet there *was* the dead stranger to give the story credence. Passing through the barrier had killed him. Or had it? There was no way to know for sure. If the stranger had been a wielder of magic, perhaps it was a spell gone wrong, or . . .

He scolded himself for his foolishness. Magic or no magic, there would be no return for him. Not while the possibility of the vision coming true existed. Taking a deep breath, he clenched his fists and willed himself forward.

For a moment his feet felt like lead weights fastened to the end of his legs. The finality of his decision was paralyzing. A wave of nausea had him gripping his stomach, making it a struggle to remain upright.

Squeezing his eyes shut, he tried to regain his self-control. *You can do this*, he told himself. *Just pick up your feet.*

The first step beyond the oak was uneventful. He felt no different, and a quick glance back revealed nothing out of place. After three steps it was the same. He allowed himself a tiny smile. That he *could* return was a comfort. Perhaps one day he could solve the riddle of the vision. Surely Shemi would be forgiving, even if angered by Lem's unannounced departure.

He took another step. This time, a rush of wind filtered through the treetops, wrapping itself around his body and giving him a mild shiver. He had been sweating, and he wiped his brow on his sleeve. He always perspired when he was nervous, and at this moment, he was bordering on total panic.

Turning back toward the oak for a final look at his home, he was immediately horrorstruck. It was no longer there. He had done it. He had crossed into Lamoria.

"That's impossible," he whispered. He had barely left the tree's shadow. Even so, it was true. Where the oak had once stood, there was now nothing but a patch of thick grass surrounded by a cluster of sapling pines.

He began searching the area, frantically tearing his way through the heavy brush. His breaths were coming in short gasps, and his heart thudded madly in his chest. The trail had completely vanished. He set off in the direction of what he felt sure was home, but could find nothing familiar. There was not so much as a footprint or bent blade of grass to show that he had passed through. After more than an hour, he was forced to accept the truth: He had stepped beyond the border. This was what he had set out to do, but the reality of it was more crushing than he had expected. The magic *was* real, and he could never go home again. He was now and forever exiled.

Staggering over to a small clearing, the realization overcame him. He would never see Vylari again.

"What have I done?" Helplessness and fear reached into him with cruel fingers, digging their way into the pit of his stomach. He sat with his head in his hands, wishing he could take it back, that he had never stepped across the divide.

But his cries went unheard, his voice swallowed up by the trees and wind without so much as an echo. No one would come.

It wasn't until he heard the chirping of crickets that he looked up again. Overhead, the dimming sky heralded the coming of the night. Already tiny pinpricks of starlight were shining through. About this time back home, Shemi would be dragging him down to the banks of the Sunflow. A moonless night always made stargazing better. His friends would likely be there too, begging him to play a song while they danced and sang and laughed until their legs grew tired and they collapsed in a weary cluster of fraternal smiles.

But he would never wet his feet in her cool waters again. Nor would he lie on her banks and call out each time the spirits tossed down the sands of heaven, watching in wonder as they streaked across the sky only to disappear into nothingness just before they reached the ground.

As the night set in, a chill wrapped around him. He was alone, truly alone for the first time in his life. He tried to tell himself that he'd known it would be this way. But he hadn't. All he'd felt was the overwhelming need to leave Vylari. Sure, he had tried to imagine what the world beyond would be like, but that hadn't prepared him for this feeling of complete isolation.

Unable to penetrate the shadows of the forest, he cast his gaze east toward the unknown. Another gust of wind sent fresh shivers through him, and for a moment he imagined he could feel death pressing in to offer the comfort of eternal sleep. *No*, he told himself, a small measure of courage returning, *that's not the answer*. He rubbed his arms to stave off the cold. As lonely and afraid as he was, he knew that he must endure.

"Your mother didn't raise a weakling," he said aloud, as if the sound of his voice would be enough to chase away the fears closing in. "*She* made it in Lamoria. So can you. But not if you keep up with this sorry display. If you do, you'll die before you're barely a day away from home."

After unslinging his pack and balisari, he set about gathering firewood. Though not as adept as Shemi, he could damn sure survive in the forest. He had brought a bow for hunting, though he wasn't sure what the game would be like here. And he had no idea how far he would need to travel before reaching a town or village.

One thing at a time, he thought.

Once the fire was lit, Lem unwrapped his balisari and plucked out a familiar tune: one his mother had taught him when he was learning to play as a child. Though he now had the skill to embellish and improvise, it was still basically the same song. Playing it had always made him feel better when he was sad. Closing his eyes, he lost himself in the melody.

As the final note faded away into the night, Lem felt the strength in his heart renewing. He would not shame his mother by giving up. He would find a way to survive. Whatever was out there, he would face it head-on, with the courage of a true Vylarian.

Even if he wasn't one.

4

THE LETTER

Do not cling to those who seek to fly far. In time they will
return. For all journeys end at home.
Book of Kylor, Chapter Four, Verse Seventy-Eight

Clutching a folded piece of parchment tightly in her
hand, Mariyah stormed up onto the porch of the
cottage and flung the front door wide. Just inside,
Shemi was sitting at the table, puffing on his long, slender
pipe, a cup of wine and a bowl of cherries in front of him.

"Where is he?" she demanded, cheeks flushed and wet
from recent tears.

Shemi jumped at her abrupt entrance. "What has gotten into you? Lem's not here. But I'm sure he'll be along."

Her lips trembled as her eyes darted searchingly about
the room, as if the old man might be lying. "Lem!" she
cried out.

Shemi placed his pipe on the table. "I told you he's not
here." His long gray hair was tied up and tucked beneath
a wide-brimmed straw hat. This, together with the worn
trousers and shirt he had on, said that he'd only just arrived
himself. "Now calm yourself and tell me what's wrong."

Mariyah flung the parchment onto the table. It bounced
once, hitting Shemi in the chest before rolling onto his lap.

"He gave this to Mother," she told him. Her hands were still clenched, and fresh tears were starting to fall.

He picked up the parchment, carefully smoothing it out on the table. As he ran his eyes over the message, his face gradually darkened. "I see. Did your mother read it?"

"Yes," she said, wiping her eyes. "That's why she waited until now to give it to me."

Shemi nodded slowly. "I understand." After taking several deep breaths, he looked Mariyah directly in the eyes. "We need to move quickly."

"Is it true?" When Shemi didn't answer, she stepped in closer. "Is it?"

He hesitated another moment. Lem had confessed everything in the letter, explaining that he had to leave in order to keep her safe. "And if it is?"

"If it is, I don't care. But I need to know all the same."

The old man's shoulders drooped, and a long sigh slipped out. "It's true. We hid it from him and everyone else as best we could. Until now, we were successful."

"So Lem didn't know?"

"He found out last night. I had hoped he would never need to. If the stranger hadn't come, he likely never would have known."

"Where is the stranger now?"

"Dead. We think crossing the barrier killed him."

Mariyah staggered into a chair, face pale, expression afflicted. "And the rest . . . the danger. Is that true?"

"I don't know. I don't want to believe it. But the more I think about it . . . maybe it is."

"Maybe?" she snapped, a torrent of anger surfacing out of her pain. "You mean Lem abandoned me on the word of the stranger?"

Shemi looked back down at the letter. "Lem said that

he was sure. Something else must have convinced him. He wouldn't have left otherwise. That much I *am* sure of."

"I . . . can't believe it. He can't be gone."

Shemi stood and held out his hand. "Perhaps there's still time. Lem is a stubborn one. If he thought he had to leave to protect you or me or Vylari, there's nothing that would stop him. But the thought of venturing into Lamoria would frighten him as much as it would anyone."

"You think he might still be in Vylari?" she asked.

"Let's hope so."

She sprang up, ignoring the offered hand, and rushed toward the door. Shemi grabbed his walking stick from near the hearth, pausing to snatch up a small pack hanging on the wall he kept prepared for short journeys.

"He could have made it to the border by now," he said. "But if he hasn't crossed, we'll find him."

The sun was waning as they hurried across the meadow beyond Shemi's cottage. A line of pines to the north swayed and groaned under the force of a wind that touched only the treetops. At ground level, it remained still and calm. It was as if Vylari itself were trying to attract their attention. But north was not their destination. The border leading to Lamoria was to the south. Shemi blew into his hands and rubbed them on his upper arms in an attempt to combat the cold.

"We can make the border by dawn if we hurry," he told Mariyah. He could see the look of doubt and concern in her eyes. "I'm fine," he added. "These legs aren't so old yet that they can't carry me where I want to go."

They started out at an overly fast pace. He was determined to prove to Mariyah that he meant every word. Having reached his one hundred and tenth year, he was in fine physical condition for someone of his age. He often went on long treks lasting many days to visit friends and relatives. Occasionally, he would accompany Lem on a hunt. *Well-preserved;* that was what he called himself. *Stubborn and thickheaded* was what the other elders said—a fool unwilling to accept old age. Tramping about the hills and forests was a pastime for the young.

Though it was not uncommon to live past one hundred and fifty, the days of vigorous adventure were usually long gone by the time someone reached one hundred, replaced by a life of relaxation and simple pleasures. Shemi, however, refused to allow his age to slow him in the slightest. He would often joke that should he ever slow down, death might well catch up with him.

The road to the border was little more than a wagon trail, pocked and pitted by erosion and poor maintenance. The few residents living out this far kept pretty much to themselves. These were tradespeople, mostly, without the need for large tracts of land or well-kept roads to transport produce to market.

They stopped by the home of Hron and Dansya. Hron was a potter, though they relied mainly on his wife's income as a tailor to support their family. This was just as well, seeing as how his skills at the potter's wheel were not exactly what anyone would consider masterful. Shemi bought a few jars from him from time to time, to be neighborly, and Lem had taught their children how to play the balisari in exchange for the odd shirt or pair of trousers whenever Dansya had extra cloth to spare.

The house was the last one along the road, and the only place that Lem might have thought to stop by. He was fond of their children, remarking that the youngest, a dimple-cheeked boy named Valian, had a natural talent for music. Hron was only a few years older than Lem, and though the pair were not exactly close, they were on friendly enough terms to go hunting together every so often.

The door opened before Shemi could knock, and Hron

stepped out onto the porch, his dark complexion and eyes made even more pronounced by his light tan jerkin. His brown, shoulder-length hair, tied back into a loose pony-tail, was sprinkled with tiny flecks of sawdust. He folded his arms over his chest, a sour expression on his face.

"I've no time for a visit today," he declared, without a hint of courtesy. "Too much work to get done."

Given Hron's relationship with Lem, this greeting came as a surprise.

"And a good day to you as well," Shemi responded. "Don't worry. We aren't staying. But I was hoping you might have seen Lem pass by here today."

"Why would he come this way?" Hron asked, his frown deepening.

"Please," begged Mariyah. "We think he might have come through here. Could you ask Dansya? Maybe she saw him?"

"She didn't."

"Would you mind asking her?" Shemi pressed, struggling to maintain his polite smile.

"She would have told me."

"What do you mean by that?" Shemi demanded, his smile now fading.

"I think you should go talk to Byrn. I want no part of this."

Hron began to close his door, but Shemi rammed his walking stick into the frame. "I think you had better tell me what you know, boy, before you catch a beating. Lem is your friend. Or have you forgotten?"

"I haven't forgotten. But I'm not getting involved. Do you hear me?" He looked down at the walking stick still wedged in the door. "So if you don't mind . . ."

"Actually, I mind quite a bit," Shemi growled. "Now tell me what you know, or so help me, you'll live to regret it."

His tone and posture suggested that he had every intention of carrying out the threat.

After a long moment, Hron threw up his hands. "What do you want from me, Shemi? You want my family to be ostracized? We already struggle to earn a living."

"Why would anyone ostracize you?"

Hron sniffed. "You know good and well why. Byrn's been going all over the valley telling folks about Lem . . . about who his father *really* is. Don't bother denying it. He told me about the stranger crossing the border. And about the message he carried. You think I'd let a wielder of magic in my home, around my children?"

Byrn was a close friend of Chaud, and a few years back he had tried unsuccessfully to win Mariyah's affection. It was no surprise that he would be spreading the word, if for no other reason than to get back at Lem for capturing Mariyah's heart.

"Lem is not a wielder of magic," Shemi stated emphatically.

Hron snorted. "He's always been different from the rest of us. You know that as well as I do. And now we know why. So please, just leave. I have work to do."

Shemi leaned in until their noses were almost touching. "The only thing different about Lem I can see is that he isn't a narrow-minded dolt like you." His hands trembled in white-knuckled fists. When Hron retreated a pace, he yanked his stick away from the door and stormed back toward the road.

Hron looked to Mariyah. "When you see him, tell him not to come around again. Assuming he's not driven out of Vylari. Which would be the best thing for everyone, if you ask me."

It was an ill-advised comment. Before he could blink, Mariyah jumped forward and landed a blow squarely to his nose. Blood poured down over Hron's mouth and chin. Eyes wide with shock, he staggered back, hands covering the lower half of his face.

"Lem's twice the man you'll ever be," Mariyah shouted at him, her face crimson, poised to hit him again. Spinning around, she marched after Shemi, who had paused and was now giving her a look of clear approval. From behind, he could hear Hron cursing as he slammed his door.

"Well done, my dear," Shemi told her. "Remind me to call in his debts come next harvest."

"Do you think he was right?" she asked, rubbing her knuckles. "Would people really ostracize him because of Lem?"

Shemi shrugged. "What does it matter? If those fools can't see that Lem is one of us . . . I just wish . . ."

"What is it?"

He cast his gaze to the ground despondently. "Some of the things I used to say. About the people in Lamoria."

Mariyah took his hand. "Don't blame yourself. Everyone says that sort of thing."

"My sister didn't."

"Did she ever tell you anything about Lem's father?"

"Not very much. Only that she loved him, and that he was a kind and gentle person."

"That's hard to imagine," she mused. "The stories my mother told me said that the Lamorians were all driven mad by greed and magic."

"I know. But now I wonder if those stories were only told to frighten us into staying in Vylari."

"But surely *all* the stories can't be false. I mean, the barrier was put there for a reason."

"I never really thought on it much until now. It was easy to simply say that Lamoria was evil and to be avoided. Why question it? No one can find us here, and no one leaves.

War is unknown to us." He glanced over, his expression racked with sorrow and regret. "I should have known better. I should have somehow convinced Illorial to tell me more."

They continued in silence until arriving at the trail leading to the border. Here, they found signs of Lem's passing and hastened their steps, keeping their eyes fixed on the light impressions he had left behind. Shemi could tell that his nephew had been walking at an easy pace, clearly in no hurry to leave. A faint hope rose that they would find him still at the border, unwilling to take the final few steps. But he knew it was unlikely. When Lem set his mind on something, he followed through.

Shemi could picture the scene in his mind. He could see the fear-stricken expression on Lem's face. He *had* to find him. Only the shadow of the large oak and the track's sudden disappearance snapped his focus back.

His arms shot out. "Not another step!"

Caught off guard, Mariyah stumbled into him, pushing him sharply forward and off balance. He gasped loudly as he spun around and began desperately clutching at thin air for support. With eyes wide and his body leaning precariously back at an almost impossible angle, he managed to catch hold of Mariyah's sleeve. Had he been any heavier, he would have undoubtedly pulled her along with him. As it was, Mariyah yanked hard, leaning back until Shemi succeeded in righting himself. He wrapped his arms around her, panting and gulping deeply for each breath.

"What is it?" she asked, unsure as to why he had panicked.

He pointed to the symbol on the oak, while at the same time firmly ushering her back several steps. "If we had gone any further, we could never have returned home."

Mariyah looked past him to stare at the seemingly normal expanse of forest ahead. "Are you sure about that?"

His eyes shifted to where Lem's footprints were still visible. "You see those? The way they abruptly end just beyond the tree?"

"What does it mean?" she asked, a slight quiver in her voice.

Shemi's posture deflated. Suddenly he looked much older and frailer. "It means he's gone. And there's nothing we can do to help him."

Mariyah heard him clearly enough, but made no reply. It was as if the shock of his words had frozen her into position. She simply stood trancelike for more than a minute, her eyes fixed on a point somewhere beyond the border, her face completely devoid of emotion.

Then, abruptly, she snapped out of it. As she turned to face Shemi, all the fury and pain of her loss burst forth. She strode past him, straight for the border.

"Where are you going?" he cried out.

"To find Lem."

He reached out to grab her, but as his fingertips touched her sleeve, she broke into a run. "Stop! You can't—"

It was too late. In a blink, she vanished.

Shemi felt panic grip him. He raced forward, stopping just before her footprints ended. "Mariyah!" But there was no reply. Again and again he called out. It was hopeless. She was gone. "Fool girl." Shemi looked back over his shoulder in the direction of home. He shut his eyes and steadied his breathing. "Damn, damn, damn."

There was only one thing to do now. As he drew in a long, courage-building breath, a thought occurred. His whiskey. He had left it in the cupboard. An involuntary laugh burst forth. What a thing to worry over at a time like this! He shut his eyes and took a step. Then another. The next step he knew would put him beyond the border.

He was following not one but two reckless fools into the unknown.

As his boot touched the grass, he muttered, "And now there's *three* fools in Lamoria."

5

THE JOURNEY BEGINS

Knowledge is like the first step down a long road. All you can see is the ground at your feet. What lies ahead is shrouded in darkness until you find the courage to walk on.
Book of Kylor, Chapter One, Verse Fifty-Three

Lem stretched and yawned, seeking to work out the stiffness made worse by the bite of the chill morning air. He smacked his lips and scraped his tongue along his teeth. His mouth felt as if it were stuffed with sawdust. He glanced at the reason for this unpleasant sensation: the empty flask tossed aside a few feet away from his blanket. Why had he drunk the whole lot? A sip would have been plenty. All he had wanted was a proper night's rest. In the three days that had passed since leaving Vylari, he had barely slept for more than an hour or two at a time.

The fatigue from threading his way through forests and over hills together with the regular setting of traps for his food should have been more than enough to drag him into a deep slumber at the end of each day. But instead, he would simply stare up at the stars peeking through the treetops, thinking of home. He pictured Shemi sitting by the cottage fire, smoking his pipe and with some old book resting on his lap, lost in whatever tale he had chosen for his nightly entertainment.

THE BARD'S BLADE · 71

He imagined the children playing in the shallows of the Sunflow, giggling as they tried to catch the tiny lights scattered throughout the water. No matter how hard you tried, it was impossible. They slipped through your fingers or simply vanished, reappearing somewhere else a second or two later. No one really knew for sure what they were. *Spirits* was what Shemi had told him when he was a young lad. That might be true, but somehow he doubted it. If every one of them really represented a departed soul, there were far too many. Such a vast number of people could never have existed.

But beyond this, what captured his thoughts and kept him awake most of all was Mariyah. By now, she would have found out that he had crossed the border. That would force her to accept the situation. Her parents would never allow her to come looking for him, and she would prevent Shemi from doing the same. It was the only way. Now that he was no longer in Vylari, whatever evil threatened his home had no reason to come. Still, he had no idea how to proceed. Finding this Order of the Thaumas would certainly be on the agenda. But for now, his immediate concern was survival. He needed to find a town or village. As able a woodsman as he might be, he could not last forever on his own.

No one can survive alone, my boy. Shemi's words drifted through his mind. *Not forever. If I can imagine a fate worse than death it would be to live alone. People need one another as much as they need food and drink.*

But even if he did find other people, what would they be like? Would they recognize him as not being one of their own? It was speculated by some that there *were* no other beings beyond Vylari; that the reason no one had found them was less to do with the barrier and more to do with no one being there. Perhaps war and magic had destroyed them all, some would say. But the arrival of the stranger dispelled this possibility. There were others, and sooner or later he'd find them. He hoped sooner. His supplies would last him for a time yet, but not indefinitely. Trapping and hunting would slow progress as well, and so far he had yet to see anything larger than a squirrel.

He pulled his waterskin from under the foot of his bedroll. It was nearly empty. He needed to find somewhere to fill it again soon. The last spring he had happened across was a day's walk in the opposite direction.

The wild was no place to become weak, and he had heard the baleful cry of wolves in the far distance. So long as he was healthy and strong, they would not trouble him; people were not their natural prey, and he had never heard of anyone being attacked. All the same, he did not want to put it to the test. And no doubt there were more than wolves in the forest; plenty of beasts that would be more than happy to take advantage of an easy meal.

After a meager breakfast of berries and a small hunk of cheese, Lem gathered his belongings. To keep going south was the only thing he could think to do. He had considered changing direction, but that might lead him in circles. Better to choose a path and stick to it. There had to be an end to the forest somewhere.

With the ground more or less level and the trees not as dense as they had been the previous day, he set off at a leisurely pace. There wasn't much sense in hurrying when you didn't know your destination, and he wanted to preserve as much energy as possible. As he walked, the sun filtered down through the high branches in a thousand slender fingers, freckling the forest turf with light. It was fall back home, and it felt like fall here too. The leaves were beginning to turn, and the wind carried with it the chill that promised winter was on its way.

Somehow, though, it felt different here. The plants were

the same. The few creatures he had spotted were no different in either appearance or behavior. Yet there was something not right about this place. It lacked feeling. *Spirit* was the only word that came to mind as he sniffed the air and ran his hand over the bark of a pine he was passing.

In Vylari he could hear the land speak to him. Not so much in words, but as an essence carried on the breeze. One that made you understand that you were home . . . and safe. He had heard it as he was leaving, right up until the moment he crossed the border. Now there was nothing. It wasn't exactly an unsettling silence; more like a painful absence, as if a dear friend had died and you could no longer be in their company.

Lem huffed a self-chastising laugh. *You're just lonely,* he thought. *This place is no different than Vylari. Stop letting your imagination run wild.*

As the hours passed, the day became unseasonably warm and humid. Shemi detested the heat, though he had never allowed this to prevent him from taking his long walks. Lem, on the other hand, loved summer above all. Summer meant lively festivals and joyful nights spent along the Sunflow. And it meant more time with Mariyah. Her parents would reluctantly allow her to accompany him to a few of the various celebrations for which he was hired to play each year, but only on the condition that she would stay with relatives while they were away. He, of course, was expected to find accommodation elsewhere. Though her parents trusted him with their daughter, they would not, as her father put it, *allow young hearts to be needlessly tempted.*

As his mind drifted to seasons past, melancholy gradually crept back in. Summer would no longer hold the same meaning. It was yet another in a long list of things he was already starting to miss.

"Stop it!" he said. "It's done. You have to look ahead."

No sooner had these words left his mouth than he spotted a narrow road a few yards beyond the tree line. It was little more than a wagon trail, but this had to be what he was looking for. Straightening, he picked up his pace. His pulse quickened with anticipation as he tried to picture what the inhabitants would look like.

Well . . . they'll look like me, of course, he thought, stifling a laugh.

Before stepping out onto the road, Lem pulled the stranger's letter from his pocket and read it again. *The wind will guide you home.* What could this mean? He had asked himself this question at least a hundred times since leaving Vylari. His eyes scanned the letter again. The stranger declared himself a member of the Order of the Thaumas. Lem could only think to start by trying to find them and hope they could help decipher the rest.

Lem tried to settle his mind by paying attention to the various trees, bushes, and underbrush along the roadside. Most of it was familiar, though here and there he would see something unknown in Vylari, and his thoughts returned to the question of exactly how big the world really was. If you kept going, would everything be completely different? Or were some things always the same no matter how far you traveled? There were no maps in Vylari of Lamoria that he knew of, and the stories spoke only of its violence and brutality—nothing at all of how the people lived or what they ate.

A rustle in the brush off to his left snapped him out of his musings. At first, he could see no obvious source. Then he heard something most unexpected: a giggle that, from the timbre, came from a child. Lem paused, his pulse quickening, unsure what to do. Perhaps he should ignore it and keep walking?

Before he could decide, the source of the giggle leapt

out from its hiding place, arms raised above his head and fingers curved into what Lem assumed were meant to be claws. It was a young boy who looked no older than eight, with shaggy blond curls, plump cheeks, and a fair complexion. He roared as loud as his tiny lungs would allow, his face screwed up into a snarl.

Lem could not help but smile. Covering his heart with both hands, he stumbled back a pace, feigning shock. "My, oh my. You certainly scared me."

The youth smiled in return, looking most pleased with himself. "I'm not really a monster. It's just a game."

"Thank goodness," Lem replied, blowing out an embellished sigh of relief. "For a moment, I thought it was the end for me."

The boy laughed. "You're silly. I'm much too little to hurt you."

Lem crouched low and waved the boy over. "What's your name?"

The boy stood firm. "My mother said to never talk to strangers on the road."

"And what did she say about scaring them?" he asked, forcing a more serious tone.

The boy kicked at the ground, shifting from side to side, eyes downcast. "She wouldn't like it. You won't tell her, will you?"

In spite of his efforts to look stern, Lem's smile returned. "Only if you tell me your name."

The boy thought for a moment, then said: "Pauli. What's yours?"

"Lem."

Pauli crinkled his nose. "That's a funny name. Where are you from?"

"A long way from here," he replied. "Is there a town nearby?"

The child looked at him as if he had said something unusual. "Of course there is. That's where I live. Harver's Grove. It was named after my great-grandfather." This last bit of information was said with obvious pride.

"Can you take me there?"

Pauli took a step back. "No way. My mother will whip the hide off me if she finds out I'm talking to strangers. But if you keep going, you can't miss it."

Before Lem could say another word, the boy spun around and shot off into the thick of the woods.

Lem stood in the road until it was clear that the boy had no intention of returning. He felt a mild sense of relief. His first encounter with a Lamorian had gone far better than he could have imagined. He could only hope that the adults were equally friendly.

———

As Pauli had said, it wasn't long before he came to a faded sign hanging from a post by a rusted chain that read *Harver's Grove.* Initially, he could see only a few small wooden buildings. Though clearly not of solid construction and in serious need of repair, Lem was surprised to see that, apart from having larger windows and doors, their general design did not look much different from those back home.

It was then a brief spell of panic took hold of him as he paused by the sign. He gripped the post with trembling hands, his breath coming in rapid gasps, eyes fixed on the road a few hundred feet ahead. There they were. People. And not children . . . fully grown men and women. He'd thought that meeting the child had eased his trepidation, but it returned now in full force.

After a few seconds, he managed to steady his nerves sufficiently to press on.

Dozens of people were scattered about the walkways

and street. The buildings, though in poor condition, were not as ramshackle as those situated at the town's edge. Glancing through the windows, he could see that most of them were shops or other businesses. No one appeared to be in much of a hurry, moving along with expressions that bordered on despondency. They were dressed simply, in light shirts, pants, and leather shoes or boots. The women wore similar attire to the men, with only a few of them wearing dresses. As with the boy, everyone's features were comparable to his own, though most of the men appeared a touch narrower in the shoulders than himself and bore the obvious facial lines of maturity.

Just when he was starting to calm down, he saw something that took him completely aback. From out of a nearby shop stepped a man whose face was completely covered with thick black hair. Lem nearly tripped over his own feet in astonishment. On the opposite side of the avenue, he then spotted another man with the same strange growth. By the time he'd reached the next corner, he'd seen two more.

Are these men part beast? As near as he could tell, only men bore this trait. He touched his own face, wondering if it would one day happen to him. The idea was deeply disturbing.

At first glance, he thought them to be rather ungainly, the way the men lumbered about, and most were in dire need of a bath. While not exactly repulsive, they lacked the cheer and grace he was accustomed to seeing. They trudged about their business joylessly, oddly reminding him of a bear on its hind legs. Surely they would not believe he was one of them.

To his relief, only a few people took any notice of his passing, their eyes lingering mostly on the balisari across his back. But their faces were impassive and the interest fleeting. So far, he was blending in quite well. *Do I really look like them?* he wondered.

On either side of the main avenue were several more streets, all of which were flanked by buildings. The air carried a foul odor, cow dung mixed with . . . he didn't know what. But it was making his stomach churn.

Lem reached the far end of town in only a few minutes. Beyond, the road stretched on into the wilderness, though where it ended he had no idea. Without a notion of what to do next, he thought the best course of action would be to explore the town properly and learn as much as possible about his new surroundings. This didn't take long. Aside from the main avenue, in total there were about ten or so streets, and all but one of them appeared to be residential. The exception was the last street to his right. Here he found more shops, a tavern, one of two he had seen, and a blacksmith. It was also where his next surprise occurred. This one had him staring in slack-jawed wonder.

It was a massive, four-legged beast. Taller than a steer, and with a much longer face and snout, it had a sleek yet powerful-looking body, long pointed ears, and no horns. Thick hair sprouted from the back of its muscular neck, and where Lem would have expected to see a fairly smooth tail, it looked more like a wide splay of loose hair tied tightly at the base and reaching nearly to the ground. A man was astride a leather seat bound to the creature's back, and he was directing it with a strap affixed to a metal bar that had been shoved into its mouth.

"Spirits and fire! What in blazes is that?"

"You've never seen a horse before?"

Lem spun to see a young woman eyeing him curiously. He hadn't realized he'd spoken aloud. She was wearing a blue-and-white-striped shirt and tan pants, and carried a small basket over her left shoulder.

"Y-yes," he stammered. "Of course I have."

The woman cocked her head. "Where's your accent from? I've never heard onc like it before."

The hairs prickled on the back of his neck. This was it. Exposed in his very first hour. His mind raced, searching urgently for a response. "You wouldn't have heard of it. It's very far away."

"Fine," she said with a shrug. "Don't tell me. It's not like you're the first man to come to the frontier to hide. What did you do? Kill someone?" This suggestion was as shocking as her enquiry about his accent had been frightening. But at least she had moved away from his surprise at seeing the . . . *horse*.

"No. Of course not," he told her.

"Yeah. I guess you're too cute to be a killer," she remarked. "Better watch yourself, though. A pretty fella like you could get himself in trouble in this dung heap of a town." After one more admiring look, she turned to walk away.

"Wait," Lem called after her.

The woman stopped, her expression now one of impatience. "What?"

"Where can I find lodging?"

"Nowhere to stay? Well, you could try the Oak and Amber." She pointed a bit farther up the street and over to the right. "It's just a tavern. But they usually have a spare room to rent."

Lem bowed. "Thank you."

The woman shook her head, laughing. "Where do you think you are? A royal court?" Her voice then lowered a touch. "Look, if you *are* some sort of runaway noble, you'd better learn to act like us common folk pretty quick. If you don't, you'll stand out like a pig in a pastry shop."

Not knowing exactly what a 'noble' might be, he still caught her meaning. "Thank you for the advice."

With a heavy sigh, she rolled her eyes and continued on her way. Lem waited until she had entered a building a few yards farther down before setting off toward the tavern.

The sign above the door was covered in what appeared to be holes from a knife and barely legible. Even before opening the door, Lem was struck by the reek that seeped out through the cracks in the walls. He shuddered, covered his nose, and steeled himself. Did everything in Lamoria smell so bad? How did they stand it? *You had better learn,* he thought, forcing his hand back to his side.

As bad as it had been outside, the stench was immeasurably worse inside, causing his stomach to heave violently and his mouth to fill with saliva. The dimly lit interior made it impossible to see for several seconds.

"Close the bloody door, boy," called a harsh gravelly voice.

Lem took a small step forward, swallowing hard, and closed the door, as the voice had instructed.

As his eyes adjusted, he could make out a circular bar set in the center of a large room. Several tables of poor craftsmanship, looking as if they had been repeatedly broken and repaired, were scattered about on either side. An odd assortment of lamps hung on the walls and from the rafters above, though none of these were giving off enough light to see clearly. The patrons were all hunkered at their seats, mostly at the bar, though a few at the tables, mugs gripped in their hands and muttering to one another in slurred voices, eyes darting over to the new arrival.

A hulking figure of a man wearing dark trousers, a stained shirt, and an apron was leaning lazily against a support beam off to his right. "What do you want?" he barked, an uninviting scowl on his face.

"A room, please," Lem replied, doing his best not to retch. "A young lady told me you might have one available."

The man huffed. "A young lady? Some cheap strumpet, more like. What you need a room for, boy? You got business in these parts?"

"I . . . I'm just looking for a room, is all. And possibly, some information about . . . the Thaumas?" Not knowing what to say in the face of these gruff questions, Lem stuttered out something possibly too near the truth.

At that, the man's countenance turned even darker. "The Thaumas?" he snapped. "How about I guide you to the street, flat on your face."

With strides that were quite agile and quick for so large a man, he lunged forward. Lem shuffled back until he was pressed to the door, his heart thudding wildly. The man was a full head taller and, though it seemed impossible, smelled even worse than the tavern.

"I'll leave," Lem told him, praying that he was not about to receive a sound beating.

The man grabbed Lem's collar, his malicious grin displaying teeth as stained as his clothes. "That you will."

The power in the bartender's arms was fearsome, and Lem felt himself being lifted to the tips of his toes.

"Put him down, Durst," called a female voice from somewhere behind the man's massive frame.

Durst looked over his shoulder. "Just taking out the trash, is all."

"I said, *put him down*." She spat out each word slowly and distinctly.

Glowering with suppressed rage, Durst released his hold. "Yes, ma'am."

As the big man moved aside, Lem could see a woman standing in a doorway at the far left corner of the room. Her shoulder-length auburn hair was held back by a head scarf, and she was wearing a simple green cotton dress. She looked perhaps ten years his senior, her eyes not yet etched with the lines of middle age. After giving Durst one final scolding look, she smiled in Lem's direction and waved him over.

He hesitated for a moment. The few patrons who had bothered to look up had already lost interest and were concentrating again on their drinks.

"It's not polite to keep a lady waiting, young man," she added, one hand planted on her hip, the other holding a slender, long-stemmed glass.

Lem crossed the room with his head kept low, taking care not to glance at anyone directly.

Once he was standing in front of her, she slowly looked him over from head to toe, nodding with admiration. "Lovely. I suppose it's too much to hope that you're in need of a job. I could use another server."

"I am, actually," he replied, trying not to sound too eager. "But I was hoping . . . well . . . I've never served before."

"Let me guess. You're a musician."

Not much of a guess, given the balisari poking up from his back.

"Yes."

She inspected him once again, as one might a pig or a sheep before purchase. "Are you any good?"

Lem nodded. "At least, that's what I'm told."

"Haven't had a musician in a while," she said, to herself more than to Lem. "Might be worth a try. What's your name?"

"Lem," he replied, eyes still downcast.

"Well, Lem, I'm Zara."

He bowed, regretting the action immediately as he recalled what the woman outside had told him. "It's a pleasure to meet you."

"Good-looking *and* polite. I like that. And not from these parts, from the sound of you."

Thinking it best not to say anything on this score, Lem waited for her to continue. To his relief, she did.

"So long as you don't start playing hymns, I'll give you a chance. Folks who come in here don't like being reminded that they're sinners."

"I won't play hymns," he assured her. Not that he knew what a hymn was.

She took a sip from the glass, then gave him another long look. "You need somewhere to stay, you say? Well, I'll make you a bargain. Play for the customers each evening, and I'll give you room and board. Agreed?"

Lem nodded.

Assuming that the proposition needed no further discussion, she turned to the door. "Durst will help you get settled in."

As soon as she was gone, Lem had an uncomfortable feeling that the barman's eyes were boring into his back. Taking a deep breath and putting on a smile, he slowly turned to face him.

"I'm sorry if I've caused you any trouble."

Apparently this was the wrong approach. Where before Durst's scowl was merely unfriendly, it was now blatantly hostile.

"Is that right?" he snarled. "You're sorry?" He didn't wait on a reply. "Let me tell you something, boy. You're not the first pet Zara's had warming her bed. You won't be the last either. So you'd better watch yourself. Or you *will* be sorry."

His warning shook Lem. Pet? Bed? *Sweet spirits of the ancestors!* Was that what this offer was about? Surely, she didn't expect him to . . . what had he gotten himself into?

Durst reached under the bar and produced a small rusted key. "Come on, then. Move your sorry ass, before I plant my boot in it."

Lem followed him to a corridor off the far-right corner of the common room, then along this to the last door on the left. With a final look of contempt, Durst handed him the key and plodded back toward the bar.

"Supper is served in an hour," he called back. "Don't expect me to come get you."

Lem opened the door, careful not to break the key off in the lock. Unsurprisingly, there was little in the way of comforts: just a bed, a dresser, a washbasin, and a single lamp hanging in the corner. There was a window, but this had been heavily boarded up. Lem decided to leave it like this for the time being, lest there be some good reason for the measure.

At least it doesn't stink quite so badly back here, he thought, trying to keep up a positive attitude.

A closer inspection revealed the pillow and blanket to be covered in dust and badly worn. "It's still better than sleeping in the woods, I suppose," he muttered, unstrapping his pack and balisari.

This opinion was quickly revised as soon as he sat down on what he immediately felt must be the hardest and lumpiest mattress ever made. Even under his fairly light weight, the bed creaked and cracked in protest.

It was a start, albeit a rough one. He already had a place to live and employment. And while his first mention of the Thaumas hadn't been well received, Durst had seemed determined to dislike him from the moment he'd walked in. Perhaps the two reactions were unrelated. Whatever the case, he would need to be careful until he learned more about the ways here.

He decided to unpack later, after he'd had the chance to clean the room up a bit. As a start, he beat the dust from the blanket and pillow by hand before lying down. Staring up at the ceiling, he began to wonder how it had been for his mother. How had she managed? More than ever he wished that she had told him the truth before she died. Though on reflection, he doubted that anything she could have said would have adequately prepared him for this experience.

So far, the stories about the outside world were seeming quite plausible. If a mere barman could be that antagonistic, what would others be like?

Of course, the woman with the horse and the child on the road had been pleasant enough. And Zara was at least willing to help him. Then again, if what Durst had suggested was the case, her help might come at a steep price. It was unnerving that someone could be so aggressive with their desires. Vylarians were not like that. Passion certainly existed, but it was rarely so blatant and open, and never expressed on a first meeting.

After what he estimated to be an hour, urged on by the rumbling in his stomach, he left his room and returned to the bar. Only about half of the patrons remained, and most of these had moved away from the bar in favor of a table. A bent old woman with thin silver hair was carrying bowls of what Lem could only assume, given the aroma of meat and spices struggling to overcome the ever-present stench, was the evening meal.

Durst looked up from the bowl he was cradling. "*You* eat in the kitchen."

Lem wasn't going to argue.

The old woman clicked her tongue at Durst. "Don't be cruel. He's just a boy."

After passing out the remaining bowls, she took Lem's hand, smiling warmly. Her palms were rough and her grip surprisingly strong. "Come and eat with me. I could use the company. It's Lem, isn't it? I think that's what Zara told me."

He returned the smile and nodded. "Yes, that's right."

"Well, Lem, I'm Martha. And best you stay away from this lot. They can be a bad influence on a youngster."

She led him out through a side door and down a narrow alley at the rear. The kitchen was a completely separate structure from the main building. This was done in Vylari as well, mostly as a precaution against fire, but only at large banquet halls, never with anything as small as a tavern.

Inside, Lem was impressed by the scope of the place. Several ovens, only one of which was currently lit, and a long row of neatly organized tables ran along the right-hand side. Against the opposite wall stood a number of well-crafted cabinets, while to the rear were several doors, which, if the same as kitchens back home, would be rooms for dry storage.

"All this just to feed the tavern?" asked Lem.

Martha chuckled, patting him on his shoulder. "Don't be daft. At one time this kitchen served over half the town. Back in the days when it *was* a town." She pointed him to a table near the lit stove, then tottered over to a steaming pot.

Lem took a seat and waited for Martha to return with a pair of bowls and cups of wine. Though he was uncomfortably aware that it was rude of him, he was unable to prevent himself from staring suspiciously at the offering for a long moment before eventually scooping out a spoonful. A smile quickly formed. It wasn't as bad as he had feared—a simple beef stew. Not as good as Uncle Shemi's, but decent enough. The wine, on the other hand, had a bitter taste about it.

"What happened here?" he asked. "You know, to make things change."

Martha sighed. "Copper mines dried up. Nothing else worth coming this far out for. Most folks either moved back to the cities or went north, if they could get work at the new mines opening up." She shrugged and took a mouthful of stew. "Not much else to say. Same old story up and down the frontier. One day a town is filled with people, the next they're gone."

"Why did you stay?"

She let out a sad laugh. "It's my home. Where else could I go?" She straightened her back and blew a short breath, banishing her melancholy. "Besides, it's not so bad here. I have my own little patch of land. And the Archbishop doesn't bother us much; one of the perks of living in the ass end of nowhere."

The mention of the Archbishop got his attention.

Martha gave him a knowing look. "You don't have to worry. I can hear you're foreign. I won't judge you." She leaned in, her eyes darting around, as if to make sure no one could hear. "And don't let the others fool you. Most folks around here are about as pious as a viper. Still, if you don't follow the teachings of Kylor, you shouldn't go around advertising it."

"I won't. Thank you." Kylor? The Archbishop? One thing was certain—he would need to learn more about things before someone realized his complete ignorance. He shuddered to think where that could lead.

"So tell me," Martha continued, her face softening back to a kindly state. "What's a nice young man doing way out here in the middle of nowhere? You're far too well-mannered to be from Bulvidar. And you're definitely no miner." She scrutinized him for a moment. "If I had to guess, I'd say you're from . . . Lytonia?"

Lem decided to take a chance. "Is it that obvious?" Bulvidar? Lytonia? How many names did this world have that he would need to learn?

Martha laughed. "You mean I got it right? No wonder you look like a lost puppy."

"I feel like one," he admitted. "To answer your question, I left home so I could see the world. I guess I'm not ready to settle down just yet."

"And you chose Harver's Grove? Did you hit your head?"

"I . . . I figured it was as good a place to start as any."

"Well, you're brave, I'll give you that. Not too many folks from your parts care to visit Ralmarstad, let alone the outlands. And by yourself, no less."

"I was actually sort of curious about the Thaumas."

At once Martha's expression hardened. "Why would you want to know about them?"

He searched his mind for an answer, her sudden change in demeanor unsettling. "No reason. Just curious."

"The Thaumas aren't ones to go asking strangers about. They're no friends of the Archbishop, and too meddlesome for their own good, if you ask me."

"I'm sorry. I didn't mean to upset you."

"I'm not upset. And to be honest, their business is their business. But that doesn't mean I'd go around asking about it."

"Do any live here?" He knew he should let the matter drop, but he couldn't help himself. He had to know more. And at least, unlike Durst, she seemed willing to talk.

"Not here in Harver's Grove. Maybe in Lobin. But I doubt it. They stay clear of Ralmarstad." She had the stern look of a parent scolding an unruly child. "You take my advice and leave them be. Go shining a light on yourself and see what happens. You'll be in front of the Hedran as quick as that." She snapped her fingers.

Whatever the Hedran was, Martha's warning tone and dire expression said he didn't want to find out the hard way. "Don't worry. I was only curious. Last thing I want is to get in trouble."

This seemed to satisfy her. "You just keep your head down, and you'll be fine."

For the rest of their meal, Martha went on to tell him about Harver's Grove in the days before the mines closed. Nothing of particular interest or importance, but for Lem, each bit of information was crucial to his survival, and he knew his next objective must be to study the history and geography of Lamoria. Learning about it through short conversations would take a lifetime. So finding books would be a priority.

"Is there a library in town?" he asked, while helping her to clear the table and douse the stove.

"A library? We're lucky to have a place to buy cloth. You might find a few books around town in one of the shops. But that's about it."

This was disappointing. But he would not let it deter him. In fact, even from this short conversation, he felt more at ease.

After helping Lem gather together a few cleaning supplies, Martha took his arm and they exited the kitchen. No sooner were they beyond the door than a rumble of thunder in the far distance produced an irritated frown on the old woman. Lem could see the sky had already turned dark gray with the threat of heavy rain soon to come.

"I had better get home," she said. "And you had better get ready for your first performance. Storm's coming. The place will be filled tonight." She gave his hand a squeeze. "Good luck."

Lem returned to his room, ignoring the growled insults from Durst as he passed. He spent the next hour cleaning and putting his few things away in the dresser. By the time he was finished, he could hear intermittent thunderclaps and the rain pounding hard on the roof. There was a small leak in the far corner of the room, but the floorboards beneath this were rotted away, allowing the water to simply pass straight through to the ground below.

An easy fix, he thought, now set on making his accommodations as clean and comfortable as possible.

Seeing the fruits of his cleaning efforts lifted his spirits considerably. Sure, it was still shabby, but the smell was almost gone, and that alone was enough to elicit a smile. Perhaps he would find a way to make it here after all.

He was in need of a good cleaning himself, and was about to seek out some bathwater when a loud bang at the door and a shout from Durst to *Get your sorry ass out here and play* denied him the opportunity.

He had brought a few sets of clothes along with him, though nothing fine enough for a public performance; at least, not by his standards. Lem had always taken great pride in his appearance when he played, but in his hurry to leave, packing finery hadn't seemed practical. After a short consideration, he chose a well-fitted pair of black pants and a white, open-collared linen shirt. A groan slipped out on realizing that his only boots and belt were those in which he had traveled. Both were badly stained and worn. Nonetheless, they would have to do.

He unwrapped his balisari and made sure the strings were properly tuned, then set off toward the common area. As he walked, he felt his anxiety building. He was always nervous before a performance, though this was typically offset by excitement. He loved to play for an audience. The way they responded to the music, the joy he could see in their eyes and hear in their cheers, was intoxicating. Not this time. This time there was pure dread. Not that he doubted his abilities. But he had only ever played for his own people. He knew what kind of music they enjoyed. He could look at a crowd and tell what they were in the mood to hear. This would be different. What if they did not like Vylarian tunes?

As the door to the common room opened, he saw Martha had been correct in her forecast. The tavern was filled to bursting, with every table and every inch of space at the bar occupied. Still more customers were standing in the gaps between the tables, drinking and laughing. He could see Durst behind the bar, his face slick with sweat as he moved about, shoving mugs in front of thirsty customers. Three servers, two young men and a girl he had not seen earlier, were darting about carrying trays filled with mugs and pitchers. Lem was impressed at how even when twisting and turning their way through the dense crowd they managed to keep from dropping their cargo of spirits, setting each down and then nimbly darting back to the bar for more.

Zara appeared from behind a tall man who, with head thrown back and ale spilling grotesquely from the corners of his mouth, was attempting to drain his mug in one enormous swallow.

"Ah, there you are," she said. "Are you ready?"

Lem forced a smile, doing his best not to appear anxious. "Yes." He looked around but could see no obvious stage or dais. "Where do you want me?"

She flashed an impish grin. "That is a question I can answer later tonight."

Lem flushed. "I mean, where should I play?"

Zara laughed, amused by his embarrassment. "You *are* adorable. They're going to love you." She pointed to an area off to his right, where a few extra lamps had been hung from the rafters. "You'll be over there."

Before Lem could move, she let out a sharp whistle. "Durst! Get Lem a stool and clear him a space."

Lem wished she hadn't. Zara ordering the bartender about on his behalf was certain to deepen Durst's growing resentment.

Lem threaded his way through the crowd, hugging his balisari close. Durst had come from behind the bar and unceremoniously jerked a stool from beneath a young man, sending him crashing to the floor. The youth scrambled up, furious, but upon seeing who had robbed him of his seat, decided that standing was just fine. Durst clearly had a reputation.

"You had better be good," the big man remarked, shoving the stool near the wall. Lem could only nod, his throat dry.

Taking his seat, Lem placed the instrument between his knees. At first no one paid him any attention as he strummed a few chords. This was enough to realize that the jostling of the crowd had knocked it slightly out of tune. Straining his ears to hear over the clamor of voices, he made a few final adjustments.

"Play already!" someone shouted.

"Yeah, play!" another joined in.

As he considered what to play first, more jeers and taunts were directed his way from the increasingly impatient crowd, making it difficult to focus. Looking up, he saw Durst standing behind the bar, grinning with clear satisfaction at the crowd's reaction. He took a long breath. Rather than intimidating him further, the sight of the brute deriving so much pleasure from his situation had the opposite effect. Determined to wipe the grin off Durst's face, a quiet calm washed over him, settling his nerves to a manageable level.

Closing his eyes, he allowed his fingers to pluck out a tune that he had learned from the old man who had given him the last of his formal instruction. After all this time, he still enjoyed playing it, and the song was frequently requested when he and his friends were lazing beside the Sunflow.

The sound of the crowd faded as his hands glided freely over the strings. Before he realized it, he was smiling. He could picture home in his mind. Every detail was clear, from the flickering lights in the water darting about on their mysterious journey downriver, to the feet of his friends kicking at the sand as they twirled and jumped in time with the melody.

As if something within his soul commanded it, he began to sing. The words came out effortlessly, each syllable conjuring up feelings of bliss and merriment. The song swelled and ebbed, then swelled again, rising to a climax that had beads of sweat forming on his brow.

After the final note was struck, there was dead silence, broken only by the distant roll of thunder.

He opened his eyes, half expecting to see a host of mocking and angry faces glaring back at him. But to his relief, they were staring at him with uniformly dumbfounded expressions. And not only those nearby; every patron was turned in his direction. Even those on the far side of the tavern were giving him their complete attention.

Then, just one man sitting at the bar began hooting and clapping. At this prompting, the rest of the tavern erupted in wild cheers and whistles, the stomping of feet shaking the entire building.

More, they cried. *More. More.*

He glanced over to the bar. Durst sneered back at him, then spat demonstratively onto the floor. Lem, euphoric from the crowd's reaction, could only smile brightly back, triggering the man's face to flush crimson and lips to twist up into a snarl. Lem wasn't trying to provoke him, but for the first time since leaving Vylari, he felt truly confident.

It was the same feeling he had when he played back home. It was partially the reason he loved music: the way it connected with people, creating joy, sorrow, mirth, and every other emotion the heart could possibly hold. When he played, he was the shepherd and the people, his flock.

A groundswell of relief passed through him. He knew that wherever he went and whatever happened next, he could always find joy in his balisari. And maybe he would survive in this harsh world after all.

6

STRANGE MEETINGS

Beware those who would corrupt your spirit with false
gods. For their evil will lay claim to your soul and you will
be forever lost.

Book of Kylor, Chapter Six, Verse Ten

Mariyah sat bolt upright, trembling violently and
gasping for air. For a moment she could not remember where she was, the desire to flee nearly
overcoming her reason. The pop of an ember snatched her
attention.

"Again?"

On the far side of the smoldering embers, Shemi was
propped up on one elbow, his face awash with concern.

It took several seconds before she could form a reply.
"Yes."

The nightmares had begun the day they'd crossed the
border of Vylari and had become increasingly more vivid
and terrifying.

"Was it the man in the mist?" Shemi's joints cracked
in protest as he sat up, wincing from the stiffness in his
muscles.

"I . . . I think so. The worse it gets, the harder it is to
remember."

Shemi reached over to the pouch beside him and retrieved

a small piece of cloth. "This will help," he said, tossing it over.

Mariyah unwrapped a tiny brown-and-red root, about the size of the tip of a finger. Shemi had found it the day after they'd crossed the barrier. Topin root would relieve pain from overworked muscles but also served as a mild sedative. She had refused the offering initially, knowing Shemi would likely have the greater need for the remedy. But this time she popped it into her mouth, the bitter taste causing an involuntary grimace. Washing it down with a drink from her waterskin, she nodded to Shemi and lay back down.

"Thank you. I'm sorry I woke you."

Shemi smiled warmly. "It's all right, my dear. It's almost dawn anyway."

In truth, it was still a few hours away. "We should try to get some more sleep," she said, though unsure if it was possible.

Shemi, though quite fit for his years and extremely proud of this fact, was testing his limits on a daily basis. He settled back down on his blanket. "Maybe just a bit longer."

The stress of leaving Vylari was, of course, the likely culprit for the nightmares. Mile after mile of joyless travel, each step carrying them farther from Vylari, kept them wrapped in a cloak of despondency, exacerbating their fatigue and leaving them with a relentless edge of anxiety. Were there anyone to bear witness, their passing would have undoubtedly elicited pity. But there was no one. Not a soul. And no sign of Lem, either. They had tried to find his trail, looking for signs of his passing in every blade of grass or broken twig, but to no avail. Though in a forest so vast, it was soon apparent that they had little hope of this. And as the days came and went, her fears began to multiply that the forest stretched out forever, that they would never find Lem, that this had been all for nothing.

Was it a mistake? Perhaps Lem did not love her as much as she thought. Had she risked everything to find a man who did not want her?

Mariyah tried to cast aside these thoughts. She knew better. But they continued to plague her. Shemi would scold her for despairing should she speak it aloud, and he would be justified in doing so. Lem loved her unconditionally. He had left because of his love; not to hurt her, but to protect her. The part of herself that was rational understood this. But at night, under a foreign sky, surrounded by a world about which she knew nothing, being rational was difficult.

The topin root helped; the dreams did not return once she fell back asleep. But when the dawn came, a headache made the dim sunlight sifting through the trees feel like tiny bits of glass in her eyes.

Shemi was already up and humming an old tune her mother used to sing when she was young. Her eyes welled up with tears, and she turned hastily away, blinking rapidly to stop them falling.

"What's wrong?" asked Shemi. He held out a helping of dried fruits and a hunk of stale bread, the last of what was in his pack.

Mariyah gave him a fragile smile. "Nothing. I was just thinking about home."

"Don't you worry, lass. You'll see it again." Shemi plopped down beside her and placed his breakfast on his lap. "Once we find Lem, everything will be fine. Well . . . after I give him a good thrashing, it will."

Mariyah laughed for the first time since their departure. It felt good. "I get to beat him first."

Shemi put on an exaggerated frown. "You would deny an old man his simple pleasures?"

"Would you be so discourteous as to step ahead of a lady?"

Shemi snapped his fingers. "Like that."

This served to lighten the mood considerably. After finishing their breakfast and packing their few belongings, the two set out at a brisker than normal pace. Shemi pointed out several shrubs and wild berries neither had seen before, though they did not dare to taste them. Most of the small animals they ran across were nothing they hadn't seen before, which led Mariyah to wonder whether beasts were able to pass through the barrier.

By midday, the heat was becoming uncomfortable. Though for once, Shemi didn't appear to mind, being too distracted with finding new plants and speculating about their possible uses to notice. Mariyah was not as interested in wild things, though she had always enjoyed the forest. Her mother would occasionally take her on a hunt—her father, not caring for it, would stay home. It was a special time for just mother and daughter that until now she had never fully appreciated. She had gone with Lem a few times, but it wasn't the same. As much as she loved his company, and she did enjoy hunting with him, her mother's absence was keenly felt. And never more so than now.

The memory of fresh venison roasting over a fire was making her mouth water. She had seen tracks several times. It shouldn't be too hard to find one.

"There!" said Shemi in a whisper, pointing through the brush.

Mariyah had been so lost in thought that she had not noticed there was a road ahead. They ducked low and approached it cautiously.

"Do you think Lem would have come this way?" she asked.

Shemi knelt, examining the rough, deeply grooved surface. "No way to know."

"You told me the letter said the stranger was part of something called the Thaumas. Wouldn't he try to find them?"

"Probably," Shemi replied. "But he would need to find people first. If he did come through here, it's likely he would follow the road, hoping it leads to a town."

The road stretched out from east to west, vanishing in the distance with no indication of which way they should go. Certainly there was no way to know what direction Lem might have chosen.

Mariyah closed her eyes, and after several seconds opened them again and said, "East. If he came this way, he would have gone east."

Shemi cocked his head. "Why do you say that?"

"I know him," she replied, to herself as much as to Shemi. "Lem always chooses left when he gets lost."

"Then left it is."

Mariyah proceeded at a slow walk, daring to allow herself a touch of optimism. If they reached a town, surely Lem would be easy to find. The balisari he carried would make him recognizable. She knew he would not have left it behind. Someone would have noticed him. What to do then could be dealt with later. Should they find it impossible to go home, at least they would be together.

After about half an hour, the squeak and squeal of a wagon sent them scurrying back into the thick brush. From the west they could hear voices. One was deeper, probably male, and two were most certainly children. After a minute they could see a wagon drawn by two large animals that looked somewhat like cattle or oxen, though not as broad and lacking horns. Though the animals were an oddity, Mariyah's attention was on the figure driving. He was rather burly, with a square jaw and unkempt red hair. He wore brown trousers ripped at one knee and a soil-stained white shirt. Two children, a boy who looked to be no more than six years old and a girl who appeared slightly older, were bouncing and laughing beside the man, presumably their father. The wagon was empty, or seemed so from their vantage point.

"What should we do?" asked Shemi.

Mariyah was unaccustomed to Shemi being indecisive. But in this instance she could understand. What *should* they do?

When Mariyah didn't reply, Shemi added, "We could wait for them to pass and follow."

The wagon was still a hundred or so feet away. Mariyah took several long breaths, yet still her hands shook. "No. Sooner or later we'll have to talk to someone." *Better a man and his children,* she thought. Less likely to want a fight . . . or so she hoped. Still, she checked the knife attached to her belt before stepping onto the road, Shemi just behind her.

The man spotted them at once and pulled the wagon to a halt. There was a long tense moment of silence, only broken by the whispering of the two children.

"I have no gold," called the man. "And I'm unarmed."

Mariyah and Shemi exchanged glances. Gold?

"He thinks we're trying to rob him," said Shemi in a quiet voice.

Mariyah put on a friendly smile. "There's nothing to be afraid of," she called back. "We're looking for a friend. We were hoping you might have seen him."

The man looked confused. "A friend?"

"Yes. We think he passed by this way recently."

"No one has been on the road," he replied. "Not that I've seen." The man furrowed his brow. "By the sound of you, you're a long way from home, aren't you?"

"A very long way. Are you sure you've seen no one?"

The man seemed to be thinking about what he should do, eyes darting over to his children for a moment. Eventually, he said, "Positive."

"Is there a town where we might look?" she asked.

The man nodded. "But I wouldn't go looking there if I was you. Folks there aren't so friendly, if you catch my meaning."

She most certainly did not. "Can you tell me how to get there?"

"It's about a day's walk east. Straight down the road."

There was a town. Lem would almost certainly have found it. So that's where they would go. "Thank you," she said, with a slight bow.

"If you want, you could come with me to my house," he said, as they were turning to leave. "I'm going to Harver's Grove tomorrow anyway. I could ask about your friend for you."

"What do you think?" Mariyah asked Shemi.

Shemi eyed the man with suspicion. "I don't know." He stepped in front of Mariyah to speak. "Why would it be dangerous for us to go ourselves?"

The man looked at him incredulously. "You can't be serious?"

"Very."

"Are you one of the faithful?"

"Faithful?" replied Shemi. "What do you mean?"

"Where are you from not to know that?"

"What does it matter?"

"It matters a great deal. Harver's Grove might be filled with vagrants, drunks, and beggars, but strangers are not easily welcomed there. Especially if you're not of the faith."

Faith? thought Mariyah. Before Shemi could respond, she interjected, "We're from a long way from here. We don't know about these things."

The man scratched his chin. "Is that so? Must be a world away. Well, do as you like. But remember that I did warn you."

He snapped the reins and the odd beasts lumbered forward. The children's eyes never left them as they passed, whispering to one another with apprehensive expressions.

"Wait," Mariyah shouted.

The wagon stopped.

"Are you sure about this?" said Shemi.

Mariyah looked at the wagon, then back to Shemi. "No."

They hopped into the rear of the wagon, and a moment later the animals heaved forward.

"I'm Gersille," said the little girl, peeking her eyes just above the backrest.

The boy shoved himself up beside her. "I'm Bertal."

Mariyah smiled. "Those are nice names. Mine is Mariyah. And this is Shemi."

The man laughed. "It seems my fearless children have better manners than their father. I'm Tadrius Marcone."

"It's a pleasure to meet you, Tadrius," said Shemi.

Tadrius dipped his head in acknowledgment. "There's a bag of apples back there if you'd like."

Mariyah's stomach was rumbling, their breakfast having inadequately satisfied her hunger. But something made her wary about eating fruit grown by strangers.

"Thank you," she said, hunger winning out.

"Can I have an apple too, Papa?" asked Bertal.

"Me too," added Gersille.

Their father smiled down at them. "Just one each."

The two grabbed for the bag and traced a small circle in the air above the apples with their index and middle fingers before munching happily into them. Their eyes never left Mariyah and Shemi for more than a few seconds through each bite.

"Is it true you don't believe in Kylor?" asked the girl.

"Gersille," snapped her father. "You know better than that. What does Kylor teach us about strangers?"

Though the reprimand was not directed at him, Bertal lowered his eyes. "That we are to treat them as we would treat our own kin."

"But Mother says that heretics . . ." began Gersille, undeterred.

"I'm not Mother," said Tadrius, adding just enough force into his tone to silence her. He glanced over his shoulder. "Forgive my children. They forget their manners at times."

"It's all right," said Mariyah. "She's just curious. But I'm afraid I don't know who Kylor is. So I can't really give you a good answer."

At this, she noticed a curious expression come across Tadrius's face. "You really must be from far away. Good thing you ran into me."

"Why's that?" asked Shemi.

"Ignorance can get you killed in these parts. Bishop Ondreus puts bounties on heretics. But I suppose you don't know who that is."

"I'm afraid not," Mariyah admitted.

"Let's just say that he's not a man you want to meet. My advice is to stay away from Harver's Grove, or any other town this far west. People are not as . . . understanding as they are in the cities." He made the same sign the children had made over their apples. "Truth be told, you should probably forget this friend of yours and go home."

"I'm afraid we can't," said Mariyah.

Tadrius nodded. "I see. Well, if he came through here, he probably did end up in Harver's Grove. Lucky for you it's not a big place. They'd notice a stranger in town. If he's still there, I should be able to find him. Assuming he hasn't gotten himself in trouble. Anything you can tell me about him?"

"He's nineteen years old," she replied. "Thin build but with broad shoulders, about six feet tall, auburn hair down to here"—she placed her hand at the bottom of her shoulder—"and gray eyes."

"Gray eyes?" Tadrius repeated. "Not too many folks with gray eyes. Anything else that would help?"

"He's a musician," said Shemi. "He plays the balisari."

The man lowered his head. "A musician, you say? Egar Vaylin told me there was a musician at the Oak and Amber now. Couldn't say if it's your friend or not. Haven't been there in months. But it's worth a try."

Mariyah's earlier optimism now bordered on excitement. Conversely, Shemi was grim-faced, and his hand never drifted far from the small knife hidden under his shirt.

They continued for a few hours, the children eventually falling asleep on the seat beside Tadrius. They traversed open fields that had been recently harvested, passing by ramshackle buildings that appeared unoccupied. Small trails led away from the main road, snaking into the thick of the forest. *This is a farming community,* she thought. It was unexpectedly comforting. In a strange world of unknown perils, farming she understood.

The wagon turned north at a crossroads then east again, splitting a cotton field.

"This is mine," announced Tadrius, proudly. "My fields yield more cotton than any in west Bulvidar."

"Why do you leave so much unpicked?" asked Shemi.

Mariyah too had noticed that though the majority was picked clean, quite a bit still remained untouched. This would not be the case in Vylari.

Tadrius frowned over his shoulder. "We do our best. Can't get it all, you know."

Mariyah shot Shemi a warning look before he could say more. "How many fields do you have?" she asked.

"Six in all," he replied, still looking a bit irritated at Shemi. "The rest are twice as big as this one."

They passed a few small buildings and a large barn, and Mariyah noted that their construction was not unlike that back home. Then again, why would it be? Every house needed doors, windows, and a roof, after all. Most, however, were not painted; rather, some sort of dark lacquer had been applied. And the pitch of the roof was slightly steeper.

The house was nestled in the center of a grove of walnut trees. A modest dwelling, as were most farmhouses, it was sturdy, with a broad front porch where two rocking chairs were placed. A swing hung from the branches of a tree, and there was a small vegetable garden that still bore a few unripe gourds and a row of tomato plants.

Tadrius pulled the wagon up and gently woke the children. After lifting them to the ground, he whispered something into their ears and waited until they were inside before speaking to Mariyah and Shemi.

"I need to let my wife know we have guests," he said. "Don't want to startle her."

Mariyah and Shemi hopped off the wagon and stood at the back, not wanting to be too close to the peculiar beasts that pulled it.

"I don't like this," said Shemi, once Tadrius was inside.

"If he can find Lem, I'll like it just fine." She gave him a reassuring smile. "You heard him. There's a musician in the town."

Shemi did not look convinced. "The musician might not be Lem."

Mariyah didn't understand his pessimism. She was nervous too, and the idea of meeting people from Lamoria had frightened her to no end. But thus far, her fears had been unjustified. Tadrius had seemed more than happy to help them, not caring that they were perfect strangers. And the children were delightfully curious and friendly. In fact, aside from the mention of heretics and Kylor, they might have been riding in a wagon with a Vylarian family. Why then did Shemi look as if a bear were about to leap out from behind a tree and maul them?

A moment later Tadrius reappeared, waving them over. The children could be heard inside talking with excited voices about the two strangers coming to stay.

"Please excuse the mess," he said, inviting them in.

"Think nothing of it," said Mariyah.

Beyond the door was a small sitting room with a couch, and a few chairs and side tables scattered about. Several shelves hung from the walls stuffed with various odds and ends—figurines of people and animals, some familiar, others not. A bookshelf, though half empty, caught Shemi's eye. Mariyah noted the tiny paintings on the left wall, each depicting a face from the shoulders up. Family portraits, perhaps? The floor was covered with various rugs, none matching and all heavily worn and frayed around the edges.

They passed through a door to their right and down a short hallway. The scent of cooked meat and spices carried on the air, causing Mariyah's mouth to water.

The next room served as both kitchen and dining area, much like in Shemi's house, though considerably larger, with a table that could easily accommodate a dozen or more people. A woman was standing in front of the stove directly ahead, pouring soup into a tray of bowls on a flat cart beside her. She turned and wiped her hands on her apron and smiled.

"Welcome, friends," she said. "Blessings be upon you."

Her brown hair was tied neatly into several braids, and she looked about the same age as Mariyah's mother.

"Blessings to you," said Mariyah, hoping this was the greeting expected.

Shemi nodded politely. "Thank you for having us."

"Not at all," she said. "My husband told me that you were in need of aid. And you know what they say: The light of Kylor illuminates those who give of themselves." She stepped forward, wiping her hands once again with a rag. "I'm Noradeen. But you can call me Nora."

"I'm Mariyah, and this is Shemi. Your husband was very kind to help us. I hope we're not too much of an inconvenience."

"No, no, no," she said. "You make yourself at home. Sit. I was just finishing up here."

"Can we help?" asked Shemi.

Nora's smile vanished and her posture stiffened.

"They meant no insult, Nora," said Tadrius. He turned to Shemi. "Guests do not work."

Shemi lowered his head in an apologetic bow. "Please forgive my ignorance."

Gradually her pleasant demeanor returned. "You are forgiven. It's easy to forget that not everyone has found the way of our Lord."

Tadrius sighed and started to the door. "Excuse me. I need to put away the wagon."

Nora returned to the stove and continued filling the bowls. "If you would like to wash before dinner, there's a pump just outside. The soup will take time to cool." She nodded to a door off to their left.

"Thank you," said Mariyah.

The door led to the rear of the house where a small shed stood a few yards back, along with some disused plows and a broken wagon. At the corner stood what Mariyah hoped was the *pump*. A tub of water was placed beneath a spigot fixed to a metal rod that was protruding three feet from the ground, with a long curved handle attached at the top.

Mariyah looked to Shemi and shrugged. "Don't ask *me* how it works."

Shemi examined it for a time, arms folded over his chest, head tilted to the side. "I think . . ." He grabbed the handle and pulled. It took some effort, but he was able to lift it. But no water came out. He then pressed down. This time a tiny trickle spilled into the tub. Shemi grinned triumphantly and repeated the process. Soon water was pouring in a steady stream and continued for almost a minute even after he released the handle.

"Most clever," he remarked.

Shemi turned his back and allowed Mariyah to wash and then change into one of the two sets of spare clothes he kept in his travel pack, checking first that no one was about. Fortunately for Mariyah, she and Shemi were roughly the same size. Once finished, he did likewise.

"I'd forgotten what being clean feels like," Mariyah remarked, squeezing the excess water from her hair and tying it back into a ponytail.

"Now if only there's a bed," said Shemi.

Washing had indeed felt good and went a long way to lifting her spirits. And she too was looking forward to sleeping on something softer than a pile of pine needles.

Back inside, Nora had already set the table and was waiting in a chair by the stove.

"My husband will be along shortly," she said. "Let me show you where you'll be sleeping."

Nora then led them from the kitchen and down a short hallway.

"I'm afraid the bed is only big enough for one," she said.

"So one of you will have to sleep on the floor. Assuming you are all right with sharing a room."

"Mariyah is like a daughter to me," said Shemi. "So there's nothing improper."

"Excellent. I was afraid you might insist on sleeping outside. That would not speak well of our hospitality."

"I've had quite enough of outside for a while," said Shemi, grinning over at Mariyah. "A floor sounds fine, so long as there is a roof above it."

Mariyah gave him a reprimanding look. "If you think I'm taking the bed, you're wrong. Your old bones need it more than mine."

"Don't worry," Nora chipped in. "I have some thick blankets that will feel as if you are on a mattress too."

"I'm sure it will be fine," said Mariyah.

The room was not exactly spacious, and as Nora had said, the bed was far too narrow for them both to fit. A small dresser was shoved beside a closet door and a night-stand completed the furnishings. Clearly this was not a room used frequently.

After stowing Shemi's pack, they returned to the kitchen. Tadrius was seated at the table and Nora was passing out the bowls.

"Where are the children?" asked Mariyah.

Tadrius shifted in his seat, averting his eyes.

"They are being punished," said Nora, when her husband didn't reply. "I'm afraid my husband is a bit permissive when it comes to their upbringing."

Mariyah could see Tadrius's barely contained anger.

They took a seat, Nora joining them a minute later. Both Tadrius and Nora lowered their heads and closed their eyes.

"We ask for Kylor to bless this bounty provided for us," said Tadrius. "And we ask for your guidance so that we might face the coming days with courage and fortitude. As once it was, forever shall be."

"As once it was, forever shall be," repeated Nora.

As before, they traced the circle over the meal.

Mariyah exchanged a glance with Shemi. Some sort of ritual? She had guessed that Kylor was of great importance, though she had still not worked out if he or she was a living being, a spirit, or perhaps something else. And the hand gesture . . . it had to mean something. But what? She decided it was better not to ask too many questions.

She picked up the spoon, allowing it to hover above the bowl for a time. Aside from an apple, this would be her first experience with food from Lamoria.

"It's just tomato soup," said Nora, noticing her hesitation. "You *do* have tomatoes where you come from?"

Shemi was already on his second mouthful. "It's very good. I never thought to eat it cooled. I'll need to remember that."

The soup was tangy, more so than Mariyah had expected, with the hint of a spice that reminded her of wild onion, though not as strong. She smiled up at Nora. "It's good."

After they finished their soup, wine and bread was brought, along with a plate of roast meat that Mariyah hoped wasn't from one of the beasts she had seen earlier. She noticed that neither of their hosts spoke during the meal, which made it most uncomfortable. In Vylari, meals were as much a time to catch up on the day's events as to satisfy hunger. When the food was gone, they sat in equally uncomfortable silence while Tadrius cleared the table.

"I'll be leaving at first light," Tadrius informed them once the last dish was stacked and placed on a counter beside the door.

"How long will you be gone?" asked Shemi.

"Harver's Grove isn't far," he replied. "So I should be back before nightfall."

"I hate it when you go to that wretched town," said Nora. "Not a righteous soul among them."

He turned to Shemi and Mariyah. "My wife is convinced that any town with a tavern is a den of evil. That's why we're out here at the frontier. Though we do still need their trade at times, I'm afraid."

Nora sniffed. "One day they'll pay for their hedonistic ways." She quickly added with a contrite smile, "No offense intended."

"None taken," said Mariyah. "I've never been one for taverns either."

Nora looked surprised. "I would have thought . . . well, one assumes heretics—excuse me, non-believers—*enjoy* frequenting taverns."

"Not particularly. Too loud for my tastes. And the smell . . ." She crinkled her nose. "You go home stinking of stale whiskey and pipe smoke."

"It's not the smell that I mind," said Nora. "It's the way people behave. It's disgraceful."

"I met *you* in a tavern, Nora," said Tadrius. "You seemed to like them just fine then."

Nora's face turned red, her eyes darting from her husband to her guests. For a moment it looked as if she might strike him, but instead she spun on her heels and stormed out.

"She's really not that bad," said Tadrius. "Just a bit . . . enthusiastic when it comes to her faith. Don't get me wrong, I'm as devout as anyone. But Nora is . . . truly committed."

Without understanding what their faith was, Mariyah could only nod, feigning comprehension. "There's no need to explain."

They could hear the front door slam shut. Tadrius sighed, running his fingers through his hair.

"Shouldn't you go after her?" asked Shemi.

"When she's upset, she prefers to be alone to reflect and pray." He pushed himself up and retrieved a bottle from the cupboard. "Join me?" The scent of whiskey filled the kitchen.

"So whiskey is permissible?" asked Mariyah.

Tadrius shrugged while filling their cups. "It's not so much the whiskey as it is drunkenness. But even the Archbishop knows better than to expect people not to enjoy themselves. Strictly speaking, being drunk is against the law. But it's never enforced." He held up his cup and stared at it for a long moment. "Except in *my* house. There are times I envy non-believers." He finished the drink in a single gulp. "But don't tell Nora I said so."

"Your secret is safe," said Mariyah.

Tadrius grinned. "Then another cup, shall we?"

They sat and talked for a time, finishing most of the bottle. Mostly Tadrius spoke about his children and his wife and their life before moving from Lobin. Mariyah did not know where this might be, but from what she could gather, it was a large town, packed with people. Apparently, Nora had not always been so devout. Something had changed her, but what it was he did not say.

"I should be getting to bed," said Tadrius. It was nearing midnight and Nora had not returned. "Thank you for the conversation."

"It was our pleasure," said Mariyah.

"Indeed," added Shemi. "We are in your debt."

Tadrius stood, rubbing the back of his neck. "Only if I find your friend. Lem, was it?"

Mariyah nodded.

"Well, Harver's Grove is small. If he's there, I'll find

him." Apparently unaccustomed to having more than a cup or two of whiskey, he stumbled to the door. "You should stay inside while I'm gone. We don't want any trouble." Without further explanation, he exited the kitchen.

Mariyah and Shemi then retired to their room. Nora had left the blankets by the door, and to Mariyah's relief and delight they were every bit as thick and comfortable as promised.

"A strange folk," remarked Shemi as he settled in. "Not what I expected."

"Me either. I imagined them . . . more . . . I don't know. Just different, I suppose."

"Of course, we've only met two," Shemi pointed out. "Well, four if you count the children."

Mariyah tried to imagine Lobin as she stretched out on the floor. The way Tadrius had described it, it seemed impossible: mighty towers climbing high into the clouds; hundreds upon hundreds of people scurrying about, like an anthill that had been stepped on by a naughty child; markets containing such a variety of goods as to scarcely be believed. In a way she regretted that she would never see it. But once they found Lem, they would return to Vylari. Though she knew it was said to be impossible, Lem's mother had found a way. Surely they could too. And until it was proven otherwise, she would hold on to this hope.

Mariyah had never found it easy to fall asleep in a strange place. But this time, with the fatigue of travel, along with the sheer emotional stress of the past few days, she found herself falling into a deep slumber seconds after shutting her eyes.

7

THE ZARA TRAP

The deadliest blow is not dealt with a cry of fury but with a
smile and a song.
Book of Kylor, Chapter Thirty-Six, Verse Twelve

After that first night, Lem's reputation and popu-
larity grew. Soon he found himself playing to a
full house almost every night, storm or no storm.
People throughout Harver's Grove were talking about the
young master at the Oak and Amber who played music
equal to what could be heard at any royal palace. And
when he walked the streets, he was universally greeted
with smiles and compliments.

For obvious reasons, Zara was well pleased with the arrangement. The only other tavern in town, the Bull and
Quail, was now virtually empty most evenings. Such was
the establishment's decline that its desperate proprietor
had even ventured into the Oak and Amber a few times
in an attempt to lure Lem away. On each occasion he was
quickly—and roughly—thrown out before he could utter
more than a few words. It was the only task involving Lem
that Durst seemed to actually enjoy, and Lem was well
aware that the barman would far rather it be he on the
receiving end of his violence.

He had tried to make peace with the barman, even helping him clean the bar on a few occasions. But his efforts were futile; if anything, they seemed to fuel the man's animosity. Not that it mattered. Durst worked for Zara, and Zara would not allow Lem to be touched. At least not by Durst.

She had persisted with her advances, offering him a place in her bed where, as she put it, she could "look after him properly." It was an offer he invariably declined, explaining that he was betrothed and that his fiancée awaited his return. It was uncertain if she believed him, but to his relief she never pressed things beyond casual flirting and innuendos. As it was, even though the reason he gave for his reluctance was a lie—the betrothal having been broken the moment he left home—his heart did still genuinely belong to Mariyah. They could never be together, yet the idea of loving another was unimaginable. Not while his soul felt so empty. Perhaps never.

Although Lem had done his best to gather as much information as he could about this new world, he found that most people had little interest in life beyond their own front doors. Without pressing the issue, and thereby exposing a difficult-to-explain degree of ignorance, he found that even after speaking to dozens of the townsfolk, he still knew very little.

Not to say he'd learned nothing. From his conversations with Martha, he now understood that Archbishop Rupardo Trudoux V was head of the Church of Kylor in Ralmarstad. The king, Zolomy, controlled the government, but only with the consent and support of the Archbishop. He still hadn't entirely puzzled out the strange relationship between the church and the king, but it appeared to him that it was the Archbishop who held the true reins of power, his position ordained by their god, Kylor—about whom he still knew very little.

Lem thought this form of hierarchy quite strange indeed. Vylari was governed by a council of elders, each town independent of the other. When decisions for everyone had to be made, a special group was appointed. Aside from that, few laws were needed. A single person ruling over the whole of Vylari was a laughable prospect. No one would tolerate it. But here it was accepted as normal.

He'd also teased out of her that while the Order of the Thaumas was not exactly forbidden in Ralmarstad, they refused to bow to church authority, which in turn set them at odds with the king. The Order was quite powerful in its own right, having mastered most of the known magics, and they'd aligned themselves with every powerful nation beyond Ralmarstad borders. Lem now realized why asking questions about them was dangerous. He'd be viewed as a heretic, there to stir up trouble. And heretics were not tolerated.

Eventually, he became resigned to the fact that to learn more would mean leaving Harver's Grove. But that presented a difficulty. One thing he *had* quickly discovered was the need for gold. To leave, he needed a whole lot more than he currently possessed. Zara gave him a few coins here and there to purchase basic necessities, but beyond that, his entire wealth amounted to what little he'd had upon his arrival—two Vylarian copper coins and a silver, which would be recognized as foreign at once, so were of no use.

Another setback for his plan to move on was learning that the city of Lobin, the nearest major hub in Ralmarstad, was a two-week journey by foot. Though he could make it in half that time on horseback, there was no chance he would think about mounting one of those beasts. He'd tried to calculate how much gold he would need to set him on his way, but it was impossible to account for things of which he had no knowledge. From the few conversations he'd overheard, Lobin was an expensive place to live. At least in Harver's Grove he had food and shelter. So, for the time being, he was forced to stay put.

Regardless of how many people came to listen to him play each night, Zara always made a point of complaining about how little gold she was making. If she were to be believed, the tavern was on the verge of shutting down. Not that Lem *did* believe her. Though inexperienced in the ways of Lamoria, he'd had more than enough experience with dishonest people. It was one thing it had in common with Vylari. Only four months prior he had to threaten the mayor of Olian Springs with being brought before the council for refusing full payment after a performance in his home. And Mariyah was constantly chasing down those who would attempt to avoid paying for a wine shipment. Zara did not want Lem knowing how much he was increasing her wealth. And it was no mystery as to why.

A few patrons would toss him a spare copper now and again, but that was the limit. As much as he needed more, Lem could not hold it against them. They had nothing extra to give. What little coin they earned was spent on day-to-day survival. Well, that . . . and ale. Unless he intended on staying here permanently, he would need to find a way to earn more. He was at present playing for a room and meals. That had to change. It had been acceptable when there was nowhere else to turn, but that was no longer the case. If nothing else, there was always the Bull and Quail's offer. While he was grateful for Zara's help, fair was fair.

She was sitting at her desk reading through some papers when he finally screwed up enough courage to speak to her on the matter.

"Zara, I want you to know how grateful I am for all

you've done for me," he began, trying his best to not allow his anxiety to bleed into his tone.

She leaned back in her chair, expressionless as she tossed a paper onto the pile. "But?"

Lem took a courage-building breath. "But if I'm to continue playing here, I need to be paid in coin as well as room and board." He was about to launch into a well-rehearsed explanation of his merits and why his request was reasonable, but Zara's hand slamming on the desktop cut him short.

"I take you in. I give you food and shelter. I protect you from Durst—he'd have beaten you to death by now, you know. And you still want more?" Her face had turned crimson in an instant and her typically calm and measured voice was now piercing.

Lem had never seen her angry, certainly not to this degree. There had been a time or two when a patron got a bit too drunk or when Durst would irritate her. But nothing like this. The look in her eyes chilled his blood.

He wanted to retreat; to ask her to forget he mentioned it. But he knew that he couldn't. He had to find a way to leave. With nothing of value to sell, aside from his balisari and his locket, neither of which he was willing to part with, this was the only way. He was finding it impossible to speak in the face of Zara's wrath, yet he did not leave.

"Are you going to say something?" she demanded. "Or just stand there wasting my time?"

Lem shoved his hands into his pockets to hide that they were shaking. *You can do this*, he repeated in his mind until, in his calmest tone, he said, "I'm not ungrateful. I really do appreciate what you've done for me. All the same, I think I deserve at least something. The tavern is filled practically every night, and I don't have even a few coppers to buy myself a new pair of boots. I'm not asking for much. Just enough to take care of my own needs."

She shot from her chair, knuckles pressed to the desk. "You think I'm rich? You think just because we have bigger crowds that I'm awash with gold? You know how much ale I have to buy just to keep these sorry sods happy? How much food? Every drop they drink, I have to buy more. And it's not like I can raise my prices. Oh, no. The second I do that, they're off to the Bull and Quail. If you imagine you can sing them into staying, you've lost your mind. You're good, but you're not *that* good."

Had he retreated when first she raised her voice, the obvious attempt at intimidation and misdirection might have worked. But remaining firm and speaking out had bolstered his resolve. He detested confrontation, preferring to work out differences calmly and rationally. Shemi was the outspoken one in the family. But it was clear that to get what he wanted he would have to stand his ground. What's more, her blatant lies and selfish greed were stirring his anger. All the same, he knew he needed to be cautious. Zara was not prone to succumbing to pressure. Not to mention that at a snap of her fingers, Durst would be only too delighted for an opportunity to pound his head to a bloody pulp.

He considered his next words carefully. "The owner of the Bull and Quail said he'd give me four silvers a night."

Instead of another angry outburst, an expression of calm came over her, and the room fell ominously quiet. Reaching into the desk drawer, she removed a small dagger. For a dreadful moment, Lem thought he had miscalculated—fatally so.

A wicked smile eased its way up from the far corners of her lips. "Is that right?" she said, her voice barely above a whisper. "Four silvers a night? Is that what he offered? And I suppose you expect me to do better. Yes?"

Lem could not look away from the blade. He didn't really think she would use it; not unless he actually said he was leaving. *Stay calm,* he told himself. *She's just trying to scare you.* It was working, too.

He held up his palms. "I didn't say I was going to take it. But I *am* one of the reasons so many people are coming. Surely a few coins isn't asking too much."

Slowly, she sank back down into her seat and for a long, nail-biting moment said nothing. Then her practiced, welcoming expression was restored. Very deliberately, she returned the dagger to the drawer. "Of course you're right. You deserve something for all your hard work. I've been unfair to think otherwise. But four silvers is more than I can afford. And I promise you, that thief at the Bull and Quail has no intention of paying that much either. The minute you arrived, he'd go back on his word. So here's what I'll do. One silver a night when we're busy, and ten coppers on other nights."

Ten coppers? It took forty to make one silver, and forty silvers for one gold. It was well short of what he'd been hoping for. On the other hand, she was probably right in saying that the proprietor of the Bull and Quail would have changed the deal once Lem had committed himself. He was quickly learning that people in Lamoria often did not keep their word. Not that his own people were completely honest either. But a contract, even a verbal one, could be brought before the council if broken. Here, there seemed to be no consequences for dishonest dealing.

Though Zara's sudden change in tenor was sounding off warnings, he bowed his head. "Thank you. You are too kind."

"Yes, I am." She returned to her papers. "Now, shouldn't

you be getting ready? There's a storm coming tonight. You know what that means."

On the way out, just before closing the door, he caught a glimpse of Zara shooting him a dark look. He knew that he had stepped onto the precipice. But it was too late to turn back now.

Zara was a woman who needed to control everything around her, and she was accustomed to getting her own way. Durst would do whatever she said without question, as would everyone else who worked for her, apart from possibly Martha. Even the few townsfolk who did not frequent the taverns knew better than to cross her. Yet what else could he have done? He needed to be paid. Perhaps in time she might have thrown him a few extra coppers. But that could have been months from now . . . or maybe never. The real danger, he considered, was that she likely suspected his desire to leave Harver's Grove. Remembering the look on her face and the sound of her voice, he had serious doubts that she would just sit by and watch as he walked away. She might offer him more coin to stay. But then she might choose to do something more . . . drastic.

———

As expected, the rain brought in the crowd. The fall storms, he'd learned, were common in this region and could last for several days, though naturally Zara didn't mind this one bit. And according to Martha, the winter snows had much the same effect on business. "Of course, since you arrived, it's twice as busy as it used to be," she'd told him during one of their now-customary suppers together in the kitchen.

In truth, it was their conversations as much as anything else that had prompted his confrontation with Zara. Martha was fearless, with a strong sense of right and wrong. He would most assuredly miss her when he left. She had become his first real friend here, and the only reason he was not completely disgusted by Lamoria.

As he stared out over the common room, a sense of hopelessness closed in. When he had first arrived, the Oak and Amber had seemed like a haven and Zara his salvation. Now it was the exact opposite. It had become a prison and she his jailer. But he needed to keep moving forward. The vision the stranger had shown him burned always in the back of his mind. He required information, and to get it, he couldn't spend every day and night in some dilapidated tavern at the edge of nowhere. The dirt-covered faces he saw pouring cheap ale into their swollen bellies simply fed an urge to just grab his belongings and run out into the storm and never look back. Was there somewhere in this world that didn't reek of stale spirits, unwashed bodies, and urine? One could grow accustomed to most odors, or at least after a time find them tolerable. But this foul stench wasn't among them.

While strumming out the first song, he noticed Durst looking over at him. The man was smiling. Genuinely smiling. Never before had he regarded Lem with anything but undisguised contempt. An uneasy feeling rose in the pit of his stomach. *This can't be good.*

As the night wore on, so his sense of foreboding continued to increase, in part due to Durst's persistent smug looks in his direction. Had his hands not been so practiced, he would have made mistakes from sheer distraction.

He was preoccupied enough not to notice a new face among the patrons until well into the night. The man was sitting alone at a table just off to Lem's right, near a support beam. Dressed in a deep blue jacket with gold buttons, he had wavy, shoulder-length black hair, and his fingers sported several gold rings. His features were different from those of most of the townsfolk—angular jaw, with an aquiline nose and narrow, blue eyes—and his complexion was much darker than most. When Lem did finally notice him, the newcomer smiled and raised his mug, giving him an approving nod. Strangers in the tavern were not entirely uncommon, but the wealth displayed set him well apart from the dust-covered travelers Lem had seen previously.

Lem nodded in return, wondering if perhaps his gratuities for the evening might amount to more than the usual copper or two and a few drunken words of admiration. Zara emerged from the crowd, but rather than coming over to Lem, she sat down with the newcomer. The two of them began chatting, although it was clear that the man was more interested in listening to Lem than speaking to Zara.

By the time the last note was played, the tavern was still mostly full. Over the course of the evening, Zara had come and gone from the stranger's table several times. Lem could not help but notice that although the man always held a mug in his hand, he didn't appear to drink. Lem couldn't blame him. He had tried the ale once and very nearly emptied his stomach.

Normally, Lem made a point of returning to his room immediately after a performance. If he did not, he was sure to be goaded into one final song that invariably turned into five or six more. He preferred to be alone, anyway. This time, however, the man at the table waved him over. Lem considered ignoring the invitation—he was quite tired—but the prospect of extra coin compelled him.

"You have quite a talent," the man said, gesturing to the seat opposite.

"Thank you," Lem replied, giving a slight bow.

"My name is Farley. And you are Lem, correct? Or did that scamp Zara tell me wrong?"

"No. That's my name."

"That woman. I'm surprised she didn't have that oaf of a bartender throw me out."

Lem creased his brow. "Why would she do that?"

"Because I'm definitely not the kind of person she would want around someone like you."

"What do you mean?"

Leaning back in his chair, Farley clasped his hands behind his head, a broad smile splashed across his face. Even his bearing, with a level of confidence and ease unlike the customary slump-backed despondency exhibited by the locals, was unusual. "You really are about as naïve as they come, aren't you? Zara is making a fortune off you. The last thing she wants is for someone to snatch you away."

"And you are such a person?" Lem asked, just a hint of skepticism showing through.

Farley raised an eyebrow. "Maybe you're not quite as naïve as I thought. It's good to doubt. People are liars."

"So I've learned." Lem caught sight of Zara talking to a group of patrons. She had not yet noticed that he was sitting with Farley. Durst, however, *had* noticed and was watching them intently. "What can you offer me?"

"Straight to the point. I like that." Farley leaned forward, elbows on the table. "I own a small traveling theater troupe. I would like for you to come and work for me."

"As what?"

"As a musician, of course. What else? I have musicians in my employ. But no one with your talent. You see, people's tastes have changed over the past few years. They don't want long productions. The trend is for short skits, and we can manage three per night. But the intermissions are killing my business. I need someone who can keep the crowd entertained while we prepare the next play. And from what I heard tonight, I think you're perfect for the job."

Lem noticed that Durst had left the bar and was now whispering into Zara's ear. "How much will you pay me?"

"More than Zara, I can assure you."

At that moment, she looked over, her face contorted with anger.

"How much?" he pressed.

"Five silvers per night."

Before Lem could respond, Zara arrived at their table, wearing a tight-lipped smile.

"Now, now, Farley," she said, taking a chair and moving it protectively close to Lem. "You wouldn't by any chance be trying to steal away my prized musician, would you?"

"Of course not," he replied with a disarming smile. "You know me better than that. I was just curious about how he had come to be in this out-of-the-way little town of yours."

"Oh, I know you quite well," she responded. "Lem here is what you might call a foundling. He would be lost without me. Isn't that right, Lem?"

"Of course," he replied, then rose from his chair. "If you will excuse me, it's been a long night."

Zara took his hand, gripping it a bit too firmly. "Yes, do that. A young man needs his rest."

"It was a pleasure to meet you," Lem said, bowing to Farley.

"The pleasure was mine," he replied. "I'll be in town for another day or two. Perhaps I'll see you again."

"I would like that," said Lem. *Very much.*

Pulling free of Zara's hold, he threaded his way quickly through the crowd and back to his room. He felt a powerful urge to leave there and then, but that would likely cause a major commotion. Something to be avoided if at all possible. No, he would wait until morning. Zara was not an early riser. Neither was Durst. He regretted not finding out where Farley was staying. But a man like that should be easy enough to find.

Quickly packing his few belongings, he wrapped up his balisari and placed everything in readiness in the corner. His heart was pounding with a mixture of excitement and anxiety. Dimming the lantern, he stripped off his clothes and slipped under the blanket.

You should just pick up your things and walk right out, he told himself. *She has no right to keep you here.*

But the truth was, when Farley had mentioned "this little town of yours" to Zara, he was more accurate than he knew. This was *her* town. At least in the sense that she was as powerful a person as one could find here. Should she decide to kill him, there would be no one willing to stop her. Nor would anyone dare to challenge her motives. He would be dead, and nothing would happen to her as a result—not a single consequence or modicum of justice. Another lesson he had learned shortly after his arrival. A merchant, over-served with whiskey, had made the grievous error of placing his hand on Zara's backside without invitation. At the time she had appeared only mildly annoyed. But no one saw the man again, and his cart was found abandoned just outside of town. Rumors spread that Zara had watched while Durst chopped off the man's fingers one by one, allowing him to bleed until he was nearly dead before slitting his throat. Lem had been unsure as to the veracity of the story, though Durst had made an offhanded comment a few days later that should Lem step out of line, he would add ten more fingers to his growing collection.

It took about an hour before he was able to quiet his

mind enough to begin drifting off. The dawn could not come soon enough. Even if Farley were not being honest about the pay he offered—which was a distinct possibility—it was still a way out of Harver's Grove.

He started to wonder what life would be like amongst a traveling troupe of actors. A small group of his friends used to put on plays around Vylari each spring, and occasionally he would tag along with them for a week or so. Those had been quite enjoyable days, even though he was a terrible actor himself. He'd rarely taken part in anything onstage, content instead to simply watch their productions and help behind the scenes. This new adventure, he imagined, would be entirely different. He would now have the chance to really see and learn about his new world. Then, with a bit of luck, he could locate the Thaumas and help prevent the image he'd seen of burning lands and dying friends from becoming a reality. The prospect was sufficient to banish any fear he had of Zara's wrath.

A firm knock at the door startled him awake. A second, much louder thud had him sitting bolt upright, throwing off his blanket. Who in blazes could be at his door at this hour?

Durst's harsh voice gave him his answer. "You want your pay or not?" he shouted, banging hard enough to shake loose bits of wood from the doorframe.

Lem stumbled to the door and cracked it open. Durst was smiling again, setting off renewed warning signals. He thought to push it shut, but a thick powerful arm shot out, shoving the door fully open and throwing Lem several paces back.

"I've been waiting for this." Durst grinned, his massive hands clenched into fists.

Lem had no time to react. The first blow sent him flying over the bed and crashing into the far wall. Great waves of pain shot through his skull; for a moment he was completely blind. He could feel the floorboards shake as Durst rounded the bed. He tried to scramble to his feet, but another blow to the center of his back forced him down again. Initially he thought his back was broken. Only the realization that he could still move his legs told him otherwise.

"You're lucky," Durst snarled. Flipping Lem over, he gripped a handful of his hair. "I wanted to kill you. But Zara said no."

Lem was helpless as another punch thudded into his cheek, then yet another to his eye. And still they kept coming, blow after blow, each accompanied by a loud grunt of satisfaction. How many times Durst pummeled him before he finally lost consciousness was impossible to tell. The last thing Lem remembered was the taste of blood filling his mouth and the sound of heavy breathing before the mercy of unconsciousness took him.

8

BETRAYAL OF THE INNOCENT

No longer will the heresy of the non-believer be tolerated and looked upon as innocence. We must purge ourselves of the disease that has infected our souls. The heathen and the apostate are to be looked upon as enemies of the people. All shall be brought before the Hedran and tried. Should a citizen offer food or shelter, they shall be charged with crimes against Kylor and subject to imprisonment and stripped of property.

**Letter from Archbishop Rupardo Trudoux I
to the Ralmarstad nobles**

Mariyah woke, the vestiges of sleep still clinging to her eyes, making her surroundings appear out of focus. At first she thought she had been startled by a dream. But another loud bang at the front door said otherwise. Someone was there, and from the sound of it, determined to enter.

"What did you do?" shouted Tadrius, from outside in the hall. His voice was panicked.

"What you should have done the moment you saw them." Nora's tone was hard and cold.

Mariyah scrambled to her feet and shook Shemi awake. "Something's wrong," she said. "Grab your things."

Shemi sat bolt upright, hand reaching for his knife.

Realizing it was beside the bed, he rolled to the floor and snatched it up. "What's happening?"

"I don't know. But we need to go. Now."

Barely had they donned their packs and pulled on their boots when the clanking of steel and stomping feet shook the house. Seconds later the door burst open, and a man carrying a vicious curved blade stormed in. To Mariyah's eyes he was enormous, several inches taller than Tadrius, with lank black hair, leathery skin, and dark eyes that seemed to project malice and violence. Two more men were standing in the hallway, both armed with the same weapon. They wore tunics fashioned from steel ringlets, each with a gold eye within a black circle emblazoned on their chest.

Shemi shoved Mariyah behind him, knife at the ready.

"Unless you want to die where you stand, you'll drop it," said the man, his deep gravelly baritone sounding nastily like two rocks scraping together.

"What do you want with us?" demanded Shemi, unwilling to back down.

"You are to be brought before the Hedran," he replied, with no hint of emotion, which in itself was frightening. "To be tried as heretics under Kylorian law."

Mariyah knew she needed to act. Shemi would give his life to protect her. And from the look of the man, the fight would be swift and bloody.

"We will go with you peacefully," she said, pulling at Shemi's arm.

"We will not!" roared Shemi. "They have no right to take us anywhere."

Mariyah slipped between them. "Please. Otherwise they'll kill us."

"You'd better listen to her, heretic," said the man. "Or you both die."

Shemi glared for an anxious moment, then allowed the knife to slip from his grasp.

The other two men burst in, each carrying a pair of shackles. Shemi's pack was removed and their hands bound in front. The cold iron bit into Mariyah's flesh as they were pulled into the hall and shoved roughly to a quick walk.

Mariyah caught sight of Tadrius standing in the living room, unwilling to meet their eyes as they passed. Nora was waiting on the porch, looking most satisfied.

Why would she do this? Surely it wasn't because they did not worship their god? No one could be so cruel. But the venom in Nora's eyes told a different story.

Shemi was not as restrained. "What kind of person are you?" he shouted, struggling to make eye contact. "We trusted you." At this he was pushed forward, sending him face-first to the ground.

Mariyah could hear Shemi's joints pop as he was lifted to his feet by the shackles, unable to stifle a cry of pain.

"Stop it, please!" But her words were answered by a hard thrust to her back that almost sent her down as well.

A wagon awaited them on the path that led to the main avenue. The strength of the men was terrifying; they were each lifted off their feet and tossed inside as if they weighed no more than children.

"Bring the farmer, too," ordered one of the men.

"What?" cried Nora, her expression going from smug to outraged.

"Did he not offer them food and shelter?"

"Yes. But I explained this to your captain! He didn't know they were heretics. We only learned later. That's why I came to you. My husband has done nothing wrong."

"If that's true, then he'll have the chance to defend himself to the Hedran."

Nora threw herself in front of the door, hands pressed to the frame to bar their way. "You can't do this."

The man loomed over her. "You have children to look after, yes?" Nora nodded, her defiance melting away. "If you are taken, who will care for them?"

Nora lowered her head and stepped aside, allowing him to pass. Moments later he reemerged with Tadrius, hands also in shackles. Once he was loaded in, one of the men hopped into the driver's seat while the other two stood to the rear, with a direct view of their prisoners.

"I'm sorry," said Tadrius. "I truly am."

The reins snapped, and the wagon groaned slowly forward. Nora was on the porch, leaned against the doorframe, weeping into her hands.

"What will happen to us?" asked Mariyah.

"We are to be taken to the Hedran," Tadrius replied. "The court of the Archbishop. But I don't know what they will do to you . . . or to me."

"Why would your own wife do this?" asked Shemi.

Tadrius looked back at the men following. "I don't know."

Mariyah could tell he was afraid to speak. Obviously, Nora had not intended to put her husband in danger. Still, as the shackles dug into her wrists and she looked at Shemi, huddled up and in pain, she was finding it difficult to feel any pity for him.

"Do you know where we're going?"

"Keep quiet," ordered the guard. "Or I'll shove a gag down your throat."

Mariyah thought it best to do as they were told. But she had no intention of submitting to this Kylorian law. She eyed Shemi, who was shifting his back against the side of the wagon, still in pain from his harsh treatment. They would find an opportunity to escape. They would. She had to tell herself this. What sort of penalties would the so-called crime of heresy incur? In Vylari, theft could see you confined inside your home for a time, or perhaps forced to work off the value of what was stolen. More serious crimes could be punished with exile into the wild, the duration set according to the offense. But something told her that punishments this side of the barrier would be more severe. How much more, she had no intention of finding out.

———

They traveled for several hours, turning from the main road around midday onto a rough trail where the forest thickened. The uneven, pitted ground caused the wagon to jostle and bounce, battering poor Shemi relentlessly, who would wince and suck his teeth from the impact. Upon seeing Mariyah's concern, he forced a smile and winked. But the façade was unconvincing.

Just before sunset, they came to a wooden bridge that spanned a narrow river. On the far side, four more guards clad in the same uniforms awaited. After a brief exchange, two men reached in and dragged Tadrius out.

"You're a lucky man," said one guard, removing the shackles. "Your wife negotiated a settlement and made restitution."

"Restitution?" Tadrius repeated, rubbing his wrists. "With what?"

"Ten years of service," he replied. "You'll have yourself some lonely nights, I suppose. But you keep your land."

Tadrius was dumbstruck for several seconds before lowering his head and nodding in defeated acceptance. "Where are you taking me?"

The guard laughed. "It's not *you* who is serving. Your wife is. We just received the notice an hour ago. She must really love you. She would've had to ride hard to get to the bishop so quickly. I guess she didn't want you brought before the Hedran."

"What of my children? Where are they?"

"How should I know? At your farm, I would guess. So you should hurry back. Your wife is already gone." When Tadrius did not move, the guard grabbed his arm and pushed him toward the bridge. "Go on. Before I forget I received the notice."

Shoulders slumped, looking both stunned and utterly beaten, he glanced back a silent apology to Mariyah and Shemi before trudging away. Mariyah could not imagine what must be going through his mind. Betrayed by the same woman who had sacrificed herself to save him. It did not salve Mariyah's loathing or make up for what Nora had done, but in a small way Mariyah was glad for Tadrius. He had done nothing wrong—merely extended kindness to strangers. The idea of him losing his farm, not to mention his children, was heartbreaking. And while she was sad that the children would have to grow up stripped of their mother, perhaps it was best. Better no parent than one who would teach them to be disloyal to their own family.

A second later, the wagon moved onward. As they rounded a sharp curve, she caught the scent of a campfire and the sound of voices. Off to their right a few hundred feet from the trail was a small wooden building. Both windows were covered with boards, and two men stood near to the door clad in red robes and each carrying a long silver rod with a fist-sized onyx eye affixed to the end. In a clearing opposite, about two dozen men and women, some in similar robes, others in common attire, were standing around several small fires, talking and laughing casually. A few glanced over in their direction, looking as if disgusted by what they saw.

They pulled up in front of the building, and Mariyah

and Shemi were ordered out. The two men by the door approached and silently bowed to the guards, and then grabbed Mariyah and Shemi by the arm and led them inside.

The interior was an open room with a row of three benches to their right and a short platform in the center. To the left were five six-foot-tall cages, barely broad enough to fit a single person. A great red eye, like those atop the rods, had been sloppily painted on the rear wall.

They were locked inside two of the cages, and the men then took position on either side of the dais, facing the door.

This must be the Hedran, thought Mariyah. She could only assume those outside were to be their judges.

"What happens to us now?" she called out to the guards. But they did not so much as turn their heads.

Shemi slid down in the cage and tucked his knees to his chest. "Not very hospitable, are they?" he remarked, with a wince.

"We're going to be all right," she said, trying to convince herself of this as much as Shemi.

"Of course we are. You have the mighty Shemi to protect you."

The sheer ridiculousness of the statement had them both laughing. And for a few moments, it managed to dull her fear. She tried to tell herself that whatever happened, it wouldn't be that bad. How could it be? They hadn't stolen anything or hurt anyone. But no matter how many times she repeated it in her mind, she knew better. Tadrius hadn't hurt anyone either. And now his wife, vile creature that she was, had been pressed into service for ten years. Admittedly, Mariyah had no understanding what *service* meant. But if the brutality they had endured thus far was an indication, it wasn't something pleasant.

After a little more than an hour, the door opened, and the men and women outside began filing in and taking seats on the benches. Hushed whispers filled the room as all eyes fell upon the prisoners. Mariyah's heart raced madly. Though he looked calm, Shemi's fear was betrayed by his white-knuckled grip on the bars.

Last to enter was an older woman with shoulder-length dark brown hair. She was slightly hunched and wore the same robes as the others, only with gold borders around the sleeves and collar. She also held a similar rod, though longer so to be used as a walking stick. She mounted the dais and faced the assembly.

Spreading her arms wide, she intoned: "May the blessings of Kylor be upon you." Her voice was commanding and confident.

In unison they replied, "And also with you."

"We have come here as brothers and sisters to form the Hedran, as is our sacred duty," she continued. "If there is any among you who feels incapable of carrying out the will of Kylor, speak now." After a brief silence, she said, "Then let us mete out justice upon those who would defy our Lord."

The two robed men approached the cages and unlocked the doors. Mariyah's adrenaline coursed like fire through her veins. Their shackles were removed, and they were pointed to stand in front of the dais.

Mariyah's eyes darted over to Shemi, then to the unguarded exit. She thought he understood her intentions. If not, this would be a short and probably disastrous move. The men allowed them to pass, then returned to their positions.

Mariyah was struggling not to look anxious, clasping her hands together to prevent them from shaking. Shemi looked notably relaxed, though he was favoring his right leg. Hopefully it was little more than a temporary lack of blood flow. They would need to run fast enough to get outside of the guards' line of sight. If they managed that, shadow walk could keep them hidden until they were deep enough in the forest to shake any pursuit.

"You of course know why you're here?" said the woman.

"I'm not sure I do," Mariyah replied, sounding more defiant than she'd intended. *Keep them at ease. Make them think you're beaten.*

"Lying will only make matters worse," she said. Her eyes fell on Shemi. "You are the elder. What have you to say?"

Shemi folded his hands at his waist and bowed. "I am. But I'm afraid I'm not sure what you want to hear. We've done nothing wrong. A friend went missing, and we were merely trying to find him. We didn't intend to break any laws."

The woman huffed. "You do not live by the laws of Kylor, true?" A look passed between Mariyah and Shemi, then Shemi gave a small nod in answer to the judge's question. She then continued, "And yet you chose to trespass into his lands. That is more than enough to condemn you."

Mariyah could see that this was a formality, not a trial to ascertain guilt or innocence. She stole a glance at Shemi. He was still leaning slightly, but not as pronounced as a few seconds ago. It would have to do. From the look on the woman's face, time was running out.

She pictured the layout beyond the door. The surrounding area was heavily wooded. They would only need to make it about one hundred or so yards.

"If you will allow us to leave," said Shemi, "we promise never to return."

"You should have thought of that before coming here." She turned to the others. "As you have heard, the heretics have offered no defense. Does anyone wish to speak on their behalf?" Her words were met by more silence. "Then as lawful judge and anointed servant of Kylor, I find the two pitiful souls here before me to be guilty of heresy."

Mariyah's arm shot out and grabbed Shemi. "Run!"

Shemi did not hesitate, moving quickly to the door despite the pain in his leg. Mariyah expected at minimum for the two cloaked men to try to stop them. They were only a few feet away. But they did nothing. Nor did anyone else in the room.

Outside stood two guards. They spun, reaching for their blades, but Mariyah had anticipated this and let her foot fly. It sank into the nearest man's groin with a thump, and he doubled over. Shemi charged past and buried his shoulder into the second guard's chest, sending him stumbling back. His slight frame wasn't enough to topple the much heavier man, but a well-placed fist to the nose immobilized him.

"Hurry!" Mariyah shouted, forcing Shemi to the lead. His leg was clearly a hindrance, but he was able to run. They rounded the building just as the door opened.

"Leave them," called the voice of the woman.

Did they intend to just let them go? It seemed unlikely. The forest was closer than she'd thought, and even slowed by Shemi, they were into the trees and brush in seconds. The tingle of shadow walk itched in her belly.

"It only works if no one can see you," said Shemi, slightly out of breath.

At first she didn't understand, but then it dawned on her. Shemi was looking right at her. Shadow walk only worked if no one was looking directly at you.

"I don't want to get separated," Shemi said, his eyes still on hers.

"Just keep moving," she said. "It's dark anyway; we don't need to shadow walk."

And so far there was no sound of pursuit. Maybe they *were* going to let them escape.

They continued running until they were a bit deeper into the woods before Shemi halted and dropped to one knee. "We can't run aimlessly," he said. He lowered his head and closed his eyes, catching his breath.

Mariyah was not as skilled a hunter as Shemi, but still she drew up beside him and began to steady her breathing. It took almost a minute before she could hear anything over the thudding of her heartbeat. But gradually she was able to tune it out and listen to the rhythm of the forest. The earthy scent of dead leaves and rich soil filled her nostrils. Wind hissed through the high reaches of the pines, detaching weak limbs and pinecones that bounced off the lower branches and landed on the soft turf below. Small animals and insects chirped and squeaked, rustling about, feeding and avoiding predators, struggling for survival, unconcerned by the comings and goings of the human interlopers. Truly a world within a world.

She reached out with her senses. No one was coming from behind. And no one was in their path for at least a few hundred yards. It was said that hunt masters like Shemi, who had spent years wandering the forests of Vylari, could detect a mouse in the dark from a quarter mile away. Though this was a bit of an exaggeration, their skill was amazing.

As she opened her eyes, something caught her attention. Not a sound or a smell; something else. A . . . feeling. Shemi was already on his feet.

"Did you hear something?" he asked.

"No," she replied, dismissing it as fear-induced paranoia. "I think we're going to be all right."

"Strange they haven't come after us," Shemi remarked, rightly concerned.

"I'll take whatever luck comes along at this point."

"No argument from me," he replied.

They continued at a quick pace, but after another few yards, the strange feeling had markedly intensified. Something was out there, hidden in the dark. She stopped short and again listened, but heard nothing other than the natural sounds of the forest.

"What is it?" asked Shemi.

"I'm not sure."

They slowed their advance. In her heart she knew they were in danger. But it wasn't a *someone* waiting for them. And she felt certain no animals capable of harming them were in the vicinity. Of course, there might be beasts in this world she had never encountered.

Shemi kept close beside her, his experienced strides virtually silent on the leaf litter and underbrush. The feeling grew deep in her belly, waves of anxiety so strong it took all her willpower to not break into a panicked run.

She was about to tell him that there was nothing wrong and quicken their pace when she felt a warm sensation rising through her boots. A loud sizzle and what sounded like the cracking of a whip startled them to a halt. Before they could react, a blue light rose beneath their feet in a twenty-foot-diameter circle.

Both Mariyah and Shemi instinctively tried to leap back, but it was as if their feet were fastened to the ground.

"What's happening?" Mariyah cried. "What is this?"

Shemi pulled at Mariyah's arm, frantically attempting to free her. But his efforts were useless. Whatever had trapped them would not let go. There was a second sharp pop, and thin streams of white light shot upward, striking them both in the chest. Mariyah's entire body seized, pain ripping through her head and neck. She could barely hear Shemi's cries above her own. The acrid smell of burned hair and clothing assaulted her as the pain spread like a flame over dry grass, wrapping around every inch of her body.

She could feel her legs lose strength, though the pain was so excruciating she could not tell if she had fallen to the ground or was still held upright by whatever sinister force had caught them. A shock to the back of her head, like someone had stabbed her with a long needle, ended her torment, allowing darkness to claim her.

9

BATTERED BUT NOT BROKEN

Justice is the only vengeance worth seeking. Alone, it is wrath; hollow and devoid of virtue.

Book of Kylor, Chapter Two, Verse Five

Wave after wave of throbbing pain afflicted his entire body, forcing Lem from the blessed refuge of unconsciousness. As the world returned to the fore, so his agony increased. He tried to open his eyes but quickly realized that both were swollen almost entirely shut. Only a thin line of blurred light was able to penetrate his battered flesh. Reaching up, he touched his face. His skin felt unreal: the outer layer numb, yet stinging spitefully just beneath the surface.

"Don't try to move."

Though he couldn't see her, he recognized Zara's voice. A cool rag was pressed gently against his forehead.

"I'm so sorry," she said. "Durst can get out of hand at times. Particularly when it comes to me."

Lem attempted to sit up, but the pain increased unbearably. He fell back, blindly waving his arms to swat away Zara's touch.

"I know you're angry," she said, her tone soft and caring as if she were genuinely concerned about his condition. "But don't you worry. I'll be punishing Durst. You can count on that. Truth be told, he's very sorry about what he did."

"It's over," he managed to mumble through swollen lips. "I'm leaving."

Zara laughed. "Is that right? And just where do you think you'll go?"

He no longer cared what happened. Whatever fear he once had was overcome by rage. "I'm going with Farley."

"Farley? I'm sorry, Lem. I'm afraid Farley left town this morning. He was quite put out that he didn't get to hear you play again."

Lem strained to open his eyes a little further. He could now make out Zara sitting on the edge of the bed, her head tilted to one side and a bowl of water on her lap. "I don't care. I'm leaving anyway."

"And what will you do for coin?" she asked. "While you were unconscious, someone came in here and stole your instrument. They even took the coppers you had stashed away." She clicked her tongue. "Poor boy. But don't you worry. I'll get it back for you in a day or two, once you've had some time to heal . . . and to think about what's best for you." She leaned in close, her voice just above a whisper. "Durst will be watching your room, just in case anyone thinks you have more to steal. I'm even hiring a guard to stay with you when I'm not around . . . for safety's sake, naturally. We can't have this happening again, now can we?"

Hatred the like of which he had never felt flooded into Lem's heart as she exited the room. He was trapped. Without his balisari, he had no way to earn a living. And without the little coin he had brought with him, he could not even buy a lesser instrument. Even if he found a way to escape Harver's Grove, what would he do then? Starve, most likely. But at that point, anything was better than remaining under Zara's thumb. He swore that he would leave and never look back as soon as he was able, regardless of the outcome.

The problem was, Zara would be watching his every move. If she really intended to hire a guard to stay with him, which seemed likely, he would need to find a way of slipping out unnoticed. He could try to shadow walk, but the timing would have to be perfect.

Of course, before anything else, he had to heal sufficiently to travel. That would take at least a few days. Then maybe he could track Farley down. He allowed this hope to comfort him. Yes. That was the plan. Find a way to escape and then go after Farley. A troupe like his was sure to have a spare instrument he could use. In spite of this, the thought of leaving his precious balisari in the clutches of Zara rankled him to near madness. He could, he supposed, wait until it was returned; she would have to give it back at some point if she wanted him to continue playing. But if he waited too long, he might miss his chance of catching up with Farley.

Zara checked in on him a few times throughout the day, though when she brought him food he refused to eat. This feeble show of defiance elicited little more than a half-hearted scolding. Zara was in control, and she knew it. She had him right where she wanted him. Each time the door closed, he experienced the same feeling of helplessness that plagued him upon leaving Vylari, gnawing at his spirit like an infestation of termites. But unlike before, it was not joined by despair. Instead a rage was building—a murderous fury for which there was no salve and no respite.

———

The following day Martha brought him his food, gasping in shock at the sight of him.

"Look what that monster did to you," she said, quickly

placing a bowl of porridge on the nightstand and sitting on the bedside. "He should be whipped for this."

Lem smiled through the pain. He did not want her involved, and Martha was sure to insist upon it. "I'll be fine. It was just a misunderstanding. Nothing to be worried about."

"Misunderstanding, my foot. He had no right to do this. I'll have him before the magistrate by morning. You can count on that."

"Please," said Lem. "Leave it alone. I have it handled."

Martha was fearless. But being fearless would not protect her from Zara if she caused trouble. The *magistrate* was little more than an office above a clothing shop with a lone old man behind a desk. He had no real power, certainly not over someone like Zara. Martha would more than likely end up being beaten herself. Or worse.

"Promise me you won't do anything," he pressed.

She hesitated for a moment before nodding her compliance. "Have it your way," she said, anger bleeding into her voice. "But if he does it again, he'll answer to me."

Lem reached out and clasped her hand. "Thank you."

"Don't thank me yet. You need medicine. You can thank me when that swelling has gone down." She stood and slid the bowl on the nightstand closer. "Eat. I'll be back in a flash."

Sitting up as far as the soreness would allow, Lem ate his porridge. Not his favorite, but then chewing anything more substantial would have proven to be too much. Martha returned just as he finished, this time bearing a bottle of sweet-smelling salve that she applied liberally to each of his wounds. On contact it tingled warmly, drawing out much of the sting. She then retrieved a small red mushroom from the folds of her apron.

"Eat this," she said. "It will help you sleep."

Not taking no for an answer, she held it to his mouth

until he allowed her to pop it in. The taste was bitter and earthy, with a gritty texture uncharacteristic of any mushroom he'd had before.

Martha laughed. "Tastes bad, heals good." She crossed over to the door. "I'll check in on you in a few hours."

Within minutes, Lem felt his eyelids getting heavy and was soon in a deep dreamless sleep.

True to her word, Martha returned just as he was waking up. She had more food, and once again, after applying a second coating of salve, forced him to eat another foul-tasting mushroom. He was awake just long enough to see that it was evening and to realize that the salve had been quite effective in reducing the swelling on his face. Barely had he thanked her when he felt himself drifting back to sleep.

The next time he woke, it was Zara standing in the doorway. The sight of her smile renewed his anger.

"Looks like Martha is quite the nurse," she remarked. Her hair was up and she was wearing one of the blue cotton dresses she often wore when the bar was crowded. "The place isn't the same without you. People have been asking nonstop when you'll be back. It's good to know you're wanted, isn't it?"

Lem sniffed and rolled over on his side, refusing to look at her.

"I'll tell them you'll be back tomorrow."

Lem waited until hearing the door close before rolling onto his back and then shifting to a fully seated position. The hours of rest, along with the salve, had by now reduced his pain to a tolerable level. Cautiously, he placed his feet on the floor and pushed himself up.

No sooner had he risen than a wave of dizziness struck him, forcing him to grip the bedpost. Mercifully, the sensation quickly passed. Taking a few deep breaths, even though his legs felt weak and his back throbbed from where

Durst had punched him, he found himself able to walk to the other side of the room. As a test, it proved two things. He would probably be well enough to play tomorrow night; and if he had to run, he would need a little more time.

He returned to the bed, letting out a groan as he leaned back on his pillow. He could still see Durst's face as he let fly his punches. If he could find a way, Lem swore that he would make the vicious bully pay. The trouble was, as things stood, he knew that any attempt at revenge would more likely than not result in further injury. Durst was too strong, too big, too cruel. Lem had fought before on a few occasions, but that was when he was a young lad, and the consequences were never more severe than a few bruises and scrapes. What Durst was capable of doling out could certainly kill him. In all probability, the next time, if there *was* a next time, he would.

Lem closed his eyes for a bit, but without the aid of another mushroom, sleep was elusive. Minutes felt like hours as he stared up at the ceiling. He tried running over in his mind different scenarios for escape. A few of these involved hurting Durst quite severely, though these were more fantasies than actual plans. Whatever he did, with or without vengeance, he could not afford to get caught. Zara would not hesitate to kill him rather than allow him to leave. Of that he was certain.

You should have never left home, he thought. *Look at you. How can you protect all of Vylari when you can't even protect yourself?* If he was this vulnerable in a small nothing of a town, what would happen to him once he reached a city? When he found the Thaumas? If he met an enemy with more power than a lowly barman? From the conversations he'd had with Martha about life outside Harver's Grove, it seemed that danger lurked in every shadow. One misstep could leave you dead in the streets, victim of the countless predators hunting an easy mark. And that's what he was—an easy mark.

As depression and self-pity set in, a tiny voice in the back of his mind pierced the gloom—a faint flicker of light guiding him to his courage. He imagined his mother sitting at his bedside when he was a boy, when the summer storms came at night. The thunder would rattle the windows, sending him hiding beneath his blanket. She wouldn't say a word; her reassuring smile was enough to allay his fears. It was as if she passed her strength to him through the special bond only they shared. More than ever he needed her courage to bolster his own.

Finally, he managed to still his mind and close his eyes. Tomorrow he would start looking for a way out. Though Farley was probably long gone by now, it didn't matter. His time here would come to an end, one way or another.

———

He woke several times during the night, a result of too much rest, he assumed. He thought to search the kitchen to see if Martha had left a mushroom. Foul tasting or not, at least they allowed him to sleep soundly.

The door to his room creaked open just as he was about to rise. He fully expected to see Zara, but to his surprise it was Martha standing in the doorway. She was never at the tavern so late.

Her expression was an unreadable stone mask. "Gather your things," she said. "You're leaving."

Ignoring the pain in his back, Lem sprang up. "What . . . what are you doing here?"

"We haven't long," she responded, casting a glance over her shoulder down the hall. "If you want to go with Farley, now is the time."

Lem's belongings, Zara having neglected to unpack them, were still in the corner. He yanked out pants and a shirt, then pulled on his boots. "Zara took my balisari," he told her. "I have nothing to play."

"I have your instrument," she said, the urgency becoming more pronounced.

Pulling on his pack was especially painful, the weight pressing in where Durst had punched him, but he gritted his teeth and fought through the discomfort. "Where are Zara and Durst?" he asked.

Martha flashed a mischievous grin. "You'll see soon enough. But we need to hurry."

As fast as he could manage, Lem followed her into the common room. Dozens of empty mugs covered the tables and bar. No one had cleaned up yet, which was most strange. Zara always made sure the tavern was ready for the next day before allowing the staff to go home, sometimes even forcing a patron who had found himself short on coin for his bill to help Durst and the servers.

Just as they reached the front door, Lem spotted a body on the floor in the far corner. It was Zara. She was lying facedown in a puddle of spilled ale, hair splayed over her head and dress torn at the shoulder.

"Is she . . . dead?" Lem asked.

Martha laughed. "Dead drunk, that's all. She'll be fine in the morning, I promise. I added a bit of something special to her wine to make sure that we could leave without a problem."

Lem felt oddly relieved. Much as he despised the woman, he didn't want her killed. Not even after all that she had done to him.

The streets were empty aside from a pair of horses tied to the post in front. On one was lashed his precious balisari. Lem stifled a joyous cry. "Thank you," he whispered.

"Why are you whispering?" asked Martha. "No one is about. Now come on. We need to go before it's too late."

"Too late for what?"

Martha held out the reins for Lem. "A bit of justice, of course."

Lem stared at the beast with intense trepidation. "I . . . I don't know how to ride."

"Well, you had better learn fast."

Though Lem had seen it done many times since arriving in Harver's Grove, he'd never had the slightest desire to try riding on one of these strange-looking creatures himself. Now, however, the pressing look on Martha's face said that there could be no argument.

Steeling his nerves, he prepared to place one foot in the stirrup, as he had seen others do. But before he could, the door to the tavern flew open and Zara staggered out, a dagger in one hand, the other reaching for the frame for support.

"Where do you think you're going, you ungrateful son of a hound?" she demanded, her voice heavily slurred from the drug Martha had given her, drool dripping from one corner of her mouth.

In two rapid steps Martha moved in front of Lem. "Go back inside, Zara."

Zara squinted one eye, then sneered disdainfully. "Go home, old woman. I'll deal with you later." Taking a moment to gain her footing, she took a step onto the promenade.

"Don't make me hurt you," warned Martha.

Lem looked from Martha to Zara, who was still brandishing the dagger. He thought he could possibly disarm her. *Possibly.* He had heard Zara was deadly with a blade, but perhaps her inebriated state would give him the advantage. He grabbed at Martha's shoulder to pull her aside, but found that she was set firm and easily shrugged his hand away.

"Last chance," said Martha. Her arms shot out, extended to her sides, her fingers splayed apart.

Zara snarled. "I've had enough of you, old woman. Time you learned your place."

Fearing for Martha's life, Lem was about to lunge at Zara. But a dim glow surrounded Martha's hands. Startled, he moved a few paces back. Zara noticed as well and stopped at once.

"Thaumas," hissed Zara, pointing the tip of the dagger like an accusing finger.

"Not exactly," replied Martha.

A Thaumas? The shock and excitement of finding a Thaumas was almost enough to overcome the fear of the moment.

"I'll see you in front of the Hedran, you cow," said Zara.

Martha's head tilted slightly forward. "Is that right?"

In a flurry of motion, Zara charged in, blade held high to strike. With the speed of a much younger woman, Martha's arms flew forward, and thin blue strands of light leapt from each of her fingertips. They struck Zara in the chest and face, and she cried out, the dagger falling to the ground as she was thrown back into the wall beside the tavern door.

Without pause, Martha turned to Lem, who was staring in disbelief and horror at what he had witnessed. Magic. Real magic. Not like the barrier, unseen and abstract. This was blatant, unfettered power. The very evil he had been taught to fear and revile. And it had come from the only person to have shown him genuine kindness since arriving in Harver's Grove.

"Lem," said Martha. When he didn't respond, she snapped her fingers in front of his face. "Lem."

Lem blinked. "How . . . What did you do?"

"No time for questions. Drag her inside. Quickly, now, before someone sees us."

Lem hesitated, unable to move until Martha repeated the order. To his relief, as he drew near he could see that Zara was still breathing. Lifting her under her arms, he pulled the woman inside and laid her near the front wall, taking care not to let her head hit the floor too hard. By the time he was back outside, Martha was already astride her mount.

"Blast that damned woman," she said, angrily. "I swore I was done with all that."

Lem approached his horse, but did not mount it. "You're a Thaumas?"

"No," she replied, eyes fixed on the bar door. "I never made it past the third ascension. But I know enough to handle the likes of Zara. Now hurry. That Farley fellow is waiting."

The horse jerked its head and stomped, skittish from the turmoil. It took several tries before Lem was able to mount. Hands clasped tightly on the reins, he felt sure the beast was ready to bolt at any moment.

"Ease off," said Martha. "Just relax. Belle's a good mare. She won't throw you so long as you're gentle."

Lem loosened his hold, and a few seconds later Belle calmed considerably. He then watched closely as Martha pulled on the reins and urged her horse forward with a slight bump of the heels. Lem's stomach fluttered when, mimicking this, his own mount reacted in exactly the same way. After a few yards he was riding up alongside Martha, though the jostling of the beast's gait had caused the pain in his back to return in force.

———

They rode east out of town in silence for a time, Lem's eyes never leaving Martha for a moment. Finally he built up the courage to speak.

"You use magic?"

Martha, now riding a few feet ahead, looked back and smiled. "Surprised?"

"But magic . . . it's . . ." He didn't want to speak the word. It felt wrong to use when associated with the kind old woman.

"If you call me a heretic, I'll thump your head," she warned, though not in a way that made him think her displeasure was sincere. "You're from Lytonia. You know better."

"I wasn't going to say that." He had almost forgotten that she thought him from Lamoria. Now he was stuck in the lie. Part of him wanted to tell her everything. She had, after all, just rescued him from Zara. But he held back. She had also concealed that she was a wielder of magic. But then, why would she tell him this? He had no reason to know. There was no expectation of her to pass on intimate details about herself.

This debate continued in his mind until he heard her conspicuously clearing her throat. Belle had slowed to a walk, and was seemingly content to follow Martha with little guidance from Lem.

"I'm sorry. What did you say?"

"How is it you never learned to ride?"

Lem searched for a believable reply. "I just don't like horses."

Martha shook her head. "What's not to like about horses?" She waved a dismissive hand. "It doesn't matter. You know you can never come back here, right?"

"I don't intend to," he said. "But what about you? Surely you aren't going back? Not after what happened?"

Martha cocked her head and raised an eyebrow. "Me? Leave Harver's Grove? Young man, I was born there, and I'll die there."

"But what about Zara?" Zara had threatened to bring

her before the Hedran. Though he wasn't exactly certain how that worked, he had learned it to be a court controlled by the Archbishop.

"I can handle my niece," she said.

Lem's eyes widened. "Your niece?"

Martha gave him a guilty, rather apologetic smile. "I'm sorry to say it's true. I should have told you. But it's not something I'm particularly proud of."

"But she tried to kill you."

Martha sniffed. "She was out of her mind from the drug. It's doubtful she'll even remember tonight. And if she does, it won't be difficult to convince her to keep my secret. In a right state of mind, she'll remember that I'm still blood."

The mention of Martha's "secret" chilled him to the core. "How did you learn magic?"

"The same way anyone does," she replied, as if it were a common subject. "When I was younger, I left home to join the Order of the Thaumas. A silly thing to do. And I wasn't very good. What you saw back there was about as much as I know, other than a bit of glamor."

Lem nodded, pretending to understand. "I need to find them. Can you help me?"

Martha gave him a curious look. "Why would you need *my* help?"

Lem was afraid to respond.

Seeing his distress, Martha held up her hand and said, "It's fine. Keep your secrets."

"I'm . . . I'm not from Lytonia," he confessed, reluctantly.

She halted her mount, regarding Lem for a long moment. "Let me guess: You're a heretic. Do you worship the spirits of your ancestors or something like that?" Then in a flash of perception, her eyes widened, as a broad smile slowly stretched across her face. "Kylor's grace! Are you from the western tribes?" When he didn't correct her, she

THE BARD'S BLADE · 155

began to laugh, holding her side with one hand. "I should have known. Why else would you seem so out of place?" Her laughter continued as she spurred her horse forward. "Well, aren't we just a fine pair of liars. Here I am, pretending to be a good and righteous woman of the faith. You, a simple foreigner. When both of us are one slip of the tongue away from our heads being removed from our shoulders."

Not knowing who the western tribes were, he let the lie stand. "Please. I need to find the Thaumas. How do I do it?"

"I knew there was something different about you," she said, her amusement causing her to ignore his question. When she noticed Lem's serious expression, she quelled her laughter, though could not subdue her smile. "I'm sorry. But I can't help you. When I left the Order, I was bound. A spell prevents me from divulging their location. But if you leave Ralmarstad, you should be able to find them if you're determined enough."

Lem nodded, more than a bit disappointed. Still, the information was useful. They *could* be found. And he was most assuredly determined. "Thank you."

"Just be careful not to ask about them until you're beyond Ralmarstad borders," she said. "I know hiding who you are can be hard. Believe me, when you saw me loose the elemental magic on Zara, I was scared you would think I was a heretic and try to turn me in."

Lem furrowed his brow. "You saved me. Why would I do that?"

"Why does anyone do anything in this bloody world? I've seen children turn on parents. Husbands on wives. Just about every kind of betrayal imaginable. All for the love of Kylor."

"I promise, I'll never say anything to anyone about you," he assured her.

"I know that now. You're a kind young man. I can see

that. It's why I knew I had to get you out of that wretched tavern. Lucky for you I overheard Zara talking about Farley's offer just after Durst had his fun with you."

The mention of Durst's name brought on a swell of anger. "How did you find him?"

Martha chuckled. "That was easy. Zara told him you had refused his offer. Fortunately, he didn't believe her and decided he would stay in town a few extra nights until he could speak to you again. Someone who dresses as fancy as that isn't hard to find. I told him what happened and he agreed to take you with him. Actually, he seemed rather excited about it."

Lem now regretted not confiding more in Martha earlier. Had they more time, he might even now. But it was too late. Ahead he saw the silhouetted figure of a man against the light of the half-moon standing in the road, his horse a few feet away.

"This is as far as I go," said Martha, pulling up her mount. "You take care of yourself, Lem. And thank you."

"For what?"

"I haven't been able to . . . well . . . just be myself in a very long time. I'm glad you know what I am. It will make the days ahead more tolerable."

Lem smiled. "I'll never forget what you did for me."

Martha wheeled her horse around and moved up beside him close enough to touch his hand. "You keep your wits about you. This Farley fellow might be your way out of here. But I wouldn't trust him if I were you. Of course, these days, who *can* you trust?"

Before Lem could speak, she gave his hand a squeeze and spurred her horse to a quick trot. In seconds Martha had vanished into the night, and the beating of hooves was soon swallowed by the darkness.

"Strange woman."

Lem hadn't noticed Farley's approach. "Thank you for waiting," he said.

"You can thank me shortly," said Farley, with a grin that was slightly comical. "When Martha told me what had happened, I knew I couldn't just steal away with you in the night. Not without a bit of justice first."

Farley took the reins of his mount, and Lem climbed down. Though he was off balance for a second, he was relieved to be back on solid ground.

"Justice?"

Farley led the horse to where the other was tied to a felled limb. After securing it, he pointed to a narrow trail a few yards ahead. "It's waiting just down there."

The trail led a short distance to a small farmhouse situated between two large fields, though in the darkness, Lem could not tell what was being grown. It was a modest dwelling, though appeared well maintained when compared to the buildings in town. The windows were lit, and smoke drifted up from the stone chimney. However, Farley did not approach the front door. Instead, they rounded the right side to where a small wooden shed stood. Waiting beside this was a man in simple work clothes, a short wooden club in his left hand. Lem blinked in astonishment. Kneeling helplessly beside the farmer, with hands and feet tied and his mouth gagged, was Durst.

"About time," said the man, scowling. "A few more minutes and I was going to cut him loose. I got work in the morning, you know."

Farley reached into a pouch affixed to his belt and retrieved three copper coins. "You know what to do, don't you?"

The man stared at the coins, his scowl redoubling. "You said five."

"No, *you* said five," Farley corrected. "*I* said three."

The two men locked eyes for a tense moment. With a dissatisfied growl, the farmer then snatched the coins from Farley's hand and shoved them into his pocket.

"The pigs it is," he muttered before walking away.

Farley waited until he was well out of earshot before speaking. "Now, then. Here we all are."

Durst was struggling against his bonds, eyes wide, mumbling incoherently through the gag. Farley unsheathed his dagger and, with an inviting smile, held it out to Lem.

Lem stared at the blade in horror. Did Farley really expect him to kill Durst? In cold blood? This was what he meant by justice? The idea was repellant. And Martha . . . she knew. How could she have thought he would want this?

"I can't," he said, holding up his palms.

Farley cocked his head. "So you've never killed? Interesting." He reached out and grabbed Lem's wrist, pressing the dagger into his hand. "Well, it's time you did. After all, from the look of your face, he deserves it."

The dagger felt oddly heavy. He wanted to drop it, but he couldn't. He was paralyzed, transfixed, as if the steel had somehow captured his mind. Only with an enormous effort was he able to rip his eyes away from the weapon and look down at Durst. The man who had beaten him so mercilessly and with great joy was no longer menacing, with his muffled pleas and tears spilling down his cheeks.

Lem had imagined scenarios not unlike this one—Durst helpless and at his complete mercy. He wanted nothing more than for Durst to wake up in a cold sweat, as he had, shaking and weeping, brought low by the terror inflicted upon him. And now . . . here he was.

"Look at you. You're nothing but a coward."

"That's right," said Farley.

Lem hadn't realized that he had spoken aloud. He held out the dagger. "I can't do this."

"I'm afraid there's no choice," Farley told him. "If he's still alive when the farmer returns, he'll just cut him loose. And if that happens, you can count on Durst making a beeline for the magistrate. Then we'll really be in a fix. Especially that nice old lady. She was the one who caught him and gave him to me. Though how she managed to subdue the brute is beyond me. She must be tougher than she looks."

Durst was shaking his head vehemently, making desperate muted promises not to turn them in. Through the red-faced tears, Lem could still make out the crooked smile of the man who had beaten him until he could not move. A surge of fury rushed in, and before he realized what he had done, the toe of Lem's boot thudded into Durst's ribs and the bound man coughed through his gag and leaned forward, his head a few inches above the ground.

Lem took a short step back and kicked him solidly in the face, grunting heavily from the effort. Blood spewed from Durst's nose, his torso once again upright and his eyes wide with sheer terror. Lem paused a moment as the sight of his once-tormentor's blood sent desires through him that were both frightening and oddly exhilarating. He knelt back down, the blade in his hand extended, the tip hovering above Durst's heart. A firm thrust and it would be over. The barman recoiled, the grunts and cries becoming hysterical. Lem could feel his heart racing, the muscles in his arm begging to sink steel into flesh.

"That's it," urged Farley. "Do it."

Lem glanced over his shoulder to where Farley was grinning encouragingly. *What am I doing?* He had never imagined himself capable of this, or of any level of cruelty. Durst was a vile bully of a man, and in his entire life, Lem had never wanted to hurt anyone more. But to consider murdering him? That it had gone this far, that he had come so close, filled him with shame. Knowing that Durst would likely turn Martha in was still not enough to sway him. He cared for her, and dearly hoped nothing would happen as a result. She had saved him. But this was not the Vylarian way . . . not *his* way. A calm fell, sweeping away his anger and along with it, his thirst for revenge. "You're a foul person, Durst. I don't think I'll ever understand someone like you." He withdrew the dagger and stood. "And I won't let you make me into someone I'm not."

Durst's entire body bounced and jerked from his uncontainable sobs of relief.

Lem could see the disapproval in Farley's expression.

"Never allow the wickedness of others to dictate who you are." The words of his mother slipped out like a prayer.

Farley took the blade and regarded Lem for a time. "Are you sure about this?"

Lem nodded.

Farley let out a long sigh. "Very well. Then I suggest you wait by the horses. You might not want to see this."

"You mean you're going to kill him anyway?"

"I'm afraid I can't risk otherwise. Kidnapping is a serious offense, and you can be sure that the farmer won't be willing to take the blame. He'll tell them I forced him to do it. On the other hand, if there's a body, he'll just feed it to his pigs and be done with it. No body, no crime. No crime, no problem."

Durst began struggling to break free, thrashing and twisting until he fell over onto his side, as Farley's words told him that his fate was sealed. He was indeed a coward. Despite all the strength in his powerful limbs, he was in fact weak. Even so, Lem could not help but think this was wrong. Did he deserve death? Possibly. But something about this struck him to the depths of his spirit.

"Go on," said Farley, flicking the tip of his blade toward the road. "Unless you want to watch."

Lem started back to the horses, unsure how to feel. The anger was gone. But something else had been left in its place, something he could not quite define.

"You have it in you," Farley called after him, and Lem paused. "Somewhere in there is a killer. Your hands—they were steady as stone. Or didn't you notice?"

Lem held them out. Farley was right. Not even the slightest twitch. But what did it mean? The possible answer to this was even more disturbing than what was about to happen only a few yards away.

As he continued back to the waiting horses, Lem heard the muted begs for mercy suddenly turn into a series of panicked screams. He raised his hands to cover his ears, but before he could, the screams ended as abruptly as they had started.

At least it was quick, he thought. But he found this to be of little consolation. It was still murder. That Farley had wielded the blade did not matter. It had been done for revenge . . . *his* revenge. Farley had obviously believed this was something he would want, and so had Martha. Was this what it meant to live in Lamoria? Vengeance and blood? Was that the driving force here? The reason for living? Some perverse notion of justice? Lem had never felt more grateful to his elders, to the ancestors who had stolen away and founded Vylari. What a terrible world this was.

There was only one thing of which Lem was completely sure: He would never forget the sound of Durst's final cries.

Never.

10

THE BARGAIN

A person can wisely choose to slay a foe, fearing retribution. Or wisely choose to show mercy, hoping to have it one day returned. Which voice will you obey? It is this decision that will either guide you to happiness or cast you to the pit of sorrow.

Book of Kylor, Chapter Two, Verse Nine

The pain—it was gone. As consciousness returned, Mariyah found herself sitting upright, arms stretched above her head by chains, the manacles clamped tight around her wrists. She attempted to move her legs, but felt ropes wrapped securely around her ankles.

The room was pitch black and smelled of overripe fruit and stale beer. As her eyesight slowly adjusted, she could make out a few large cubes, presumably boxes, off to her left. The rest was filled with indiscernible forms of irregular mass, their details concealed by darkness. Some sort of storage building was her guess.

"Shemi?" she called out.

"Your friend is being held elsewhere," came a voice. It sounded like the woman from the trial, but she couldn't be sure.

A shadow moved directly ahead. Mariyah struggled uselessly against her bindings.

"What did you do to him?" she demanded, summoning as much command as she could to her voice.

"Nothing. But it is not what we *have* done to him that should concern you, but what we *will* do."

"Please. Don't hurt him. I'll do anything you want."

"Of that I'm sure. And as it happens, there is something you can do. You can confess."

There was the flash of a spark, and a lantern gradually came to life. As Mariyah had supposed, she was indeed in a storage room. The oddly shaped lumps turned out to be piles of cloth and a few barrels cast randomly about. Confirming her suspicions, the same woman from the trial was seated a short span away; only she had shed her robes and was dressed in a pair of black trousers and a blue blouse. In contrast to the passionate tone and expression she previously displayed, she looked stoic, her legs crossed as she placed a lantern on the floor and folded her hands in her lap.

"Confess to what?" said Mariyah, through gritted teeth.

"Murder. Specifically the murder of the poor guard you stabbed when you and your . . . companion? When you and he fled."

Mariyah stiffened. "That's a lie."

"Of course it's a lie. But you will confess nonetheless. Otherwise I will charge him with murder as well." Her mouth twitched, as if in an effort to smile. "He'll be taken to the mines and set to the most backbreaking labor imaginable. The young and healthy rarely live past three years. Someone as old as your friend . . . I would be surprised if he lasted a week."

With each word spoken, Mariyah could feel hope evaporating. "If I agree?"

"I'm afraid I can't simply let him go," she replied. "But I can reduce his charges to simple trespassing. For a heretic,

164 · BRIAN D. ANDERSON

that is a one-year sentence. And I can see that it is served out in a prison where he is much more likely to survive the ordeal. And afterward, he will be free to return home."

"What will happen to me?"

"You, my dear, will be the jewel in my crown. One so young and pretty will certainly find a noble willing to pay. And a life sentence will fetch a goodly sum."

"I . . . I don't understand. You plan to sell me?"

She waved a hand. "No. Not really. But your sentence can be commuted to indenture. Which means you will be in the service of whoever is willing to pay for your freedom." A soft, almost inaudible laugh slipped out. "'Freedom' being a word used liberally, I suppose. As your sentence will be for life, so will be the term of indenture."

The words sent a shiver through Mariyah's spine as the reality of her situation sank in. "Why would you do this?"

"My dear, there is only one reason anyone does anything: personal gain. Once your case is settled, I can adjourn the Hedran and go home. It's important to me, for reasons you needn't concern yourself with, that this happen as quickly as possible.

"I could, of course, report that you murdered the guard, with or without a confession, and you would certainly be convicted. But that would take time. Though I have influence, I must adhere to the law . . . at least publicly. And I have no desire to spend any more time in this wretched place than necessary." She ended with a wry grin. "It's far easier if you simply confess and be done with it. I get what I want, and you save the life of your companion. A good deal, if you ask me."

Everything about this woman was vile; the very embodiment of the evil she had been told existed in Lamoria. The obvious pleasure she took in the suffering of others, the way having power over the life of a complete stranger

THE BARD'S BLADE · 165

pushed her mouth into a satisfied smile . . . Mariyah had thought she understood fury when Nora had betrayed them. She hadn't. Not until this moment. "How do I know you'll keep your word?"

The woman's smile grew as she leaned forward, steepling her hands to her chin. Had she been able, Mariyah would have ripped her apart.

"You don't. But I promise that he will suffer greatly before he dies should you say no. And *that* you can believe."

Mariyah refused to sob openly, though could not stop tears from falling. She was defeated in every way imaginable. All choices were gone. "I agree."

The woman stood. "I knew you would see reason."

As she turned to leave, Mariyah couldn't stop herself from asking, "What was that . . . *thing* that caught us?"

"I'm sure you noticed we did not chase after you. There are wards throughout the forest that prevent any unauthorized passage in or out. The magic is quite effective. And as you are now aware, quite painful. I actually was surprised you ran. It's common knowledge that Hedran courts are protected this way. Not many are stupid enough to think they can escape." She started toward the door, pausing when she touched the knob. "You were never going to get away, my dear. Your fate was sealed the second you were put in shackles."

Mariyah let out a scream the moment the door slammed shut. Why was this happening? How could people be so cruel? The probability was high that the woman would not keep her promise. Shemi would die, and she would spend the rest of her days in misery. And there wasn't a damn thing she could do about it.

A short time later another woman, a bit younger, entered bearing a thin gold circlet in one hand and a knife in the other.

"Hold still and I'll let you out of your bonds," she instructed.

For a brief second Mariyah thought of escape. But she knew that the wards would prevent it. And even were that not the case, her cooperation was the only thing keeping Shemi alive. She nodded her acquiescence.

The woman bent down and fastened the circlet around her left ankle. She then cut the ropes and, retrieving a key from the folds of her sleeve, unlocked the shackles. Mariyah rubbed her shoulders, trying to relieve the burning from the hours of the constant stressed position. The woman did not look worried in the slightest that Mariyah was now free and close enough to assault her. Though no murderer, Mariyah was not beyond a fight when the situation called for it. And this was absolutely one of those situations.

But the moment her muscles tensed to lash out, white-hot pain stabbed into her belly, nearly as excruciating as the ward had been. Helpless and screaming, she curled up, writhing on the floor.

"Thinking about escape, are you?" said the woman. "Or were you thinking about perhaps hurting me?" She clicked her tongue. "I'm afraid we can't have that."

"What have you done to me?" Mariyah said, once the pain had lessened enough for her to speak.

"Not a thing. You did it to yourself." The woman pulled out a blue orb about the size of the end of her thumb, attached to a chain around her neck. "The anklet you wear prevents you from running or from hurting anyone. And this controls the anklet. The mere thought will produce a severe punishment . . . as you just experienced."

The pain dissipated, allowing Mariyah to push herself up and lean heavily against the wall. Her eyes were fixed on the anklet. More magic, this as sinister as the wards. "Where's Shemi?"

"You should rest now," she said, disregarding the question. "It's a long journey to Lobin."

The woman exited, leaving the door slightly ajar. Mariyah leaned down to examine the anklet. It was outwardly unremarkable. How could something so common cause so much torment? She slipped the tip of her finger between the metal and her flesh, but this produced a sharp pain in her head that made her eyes twitch, so she quickly withdrew.

Mariyah could hear voices from outside. She thought to look, but feared what might happen. Even the desire to know what they had done to Shemi was not enough to test the power it held over her.

She rummaged around until she found a sack of grain to use as a pillow, and lay in the corner farthest from the door. Tiny spiteful reminders nagged at her each time her mind drifted to thoughts of escape, which also served to prevent her from sleeping. After a time, helplessness overwhelmed her until she could not hold back the tears and began sobbing fitfully. Her life was over. Hope was gone. And she would never see home . . . or Lem again.

11

LOBIN

It is impossible to stay clean when dwelling among swine.
Book of Kylor, Chapter Four, Verse Eight

So badly did the memory of Durst's screams plague Lem's conscience that he had still not spoken a word by the time morning broke. Equally disturbing was the fact that Farley appeared to be entirely comfortable with the act of murder. Had he simply traded one prison for another? Zara was a bad person by any standards Lem could imagine, but Farley might turn out to be just as bad, if not worse. For now, he would try not to dwell on the possibility. He was away from Harver's Grove, and Farley had informed him that they were bound for Lobin, a city situated on the coast of the Sea of Mannan. Other than that, Lem had little idea what to expect—only that it was sure to be a far cry from anything he had seen before.

"So tell me," said Farley. "How exactly did you end up in Harver's Grove?"

With the previous night's events still weighing on his mind, Lem only became fully aware of the question after it had been repeated.

"I thought to do some traveling," he replied. This had been his standard answer to any of the townsfolk who asked. Knowing this would not be sufficient for Farley, he added, "If it's all the same to you, I'd rather not talk about my past."

Farley smiled. "I understand. Many a young man seeks to reinvent his life. Take me, for example. I'm the son of a brickmason. By the time I was fifteen, I'd watched my father work himself so hard he walked like a decrepit old man. When I left home, I swore an oath that I would not repeat his mistakes."

"So that's why you became an actor?"

Farley laughed. "That's why I became a thief." Spotting Lem's startled reaction, he hastily added, "No longer, mind you. But as a lad, I thought it better than working myself to death like my father had."

"How does one become a thief?"

"By stealing. How else? Oh, I thought about joining a guild, but I was never much for taking orders. Turned out I wasn't very good at it anyway. So after a short but most unpleasant time in a Sylerian prison, I chanced upon the former owner of the troupe."

"So you didn't start it yourself?"

"No. A man named Chen Lumroy put it together many years before I arrived. I bought it from him when he was ready to retire."

Given Farley's apparent openness, Lem felt a touch guilty about not being able to share details of his own life. It did not seem to bother Farley in the slightest to talk of being held in prison. Or, as the conversation went on, about virtually any other aspect of his past. An open book was how Shemi would have described him: someone comfortable with who he was and where he was going. What's more, he didn't press Lem to talk about awkward subjects, which consisted more or less of anything to do with his own past. He did, though, insist on knowing one thing.

Looking Lem directly in the eye, Farley said, "For

someone so young, you don't say much about yourself. Which makes me think I might be in dangerous company. So I have to ask if you have people pursuing you or if you're in trouble of some kind. I need to know before I take you in. I have a responsibility to those in my employ."

"There is no one after me," Lem said, though as he spoke, he saw again the dark vision the stranger had shared and recalled the note in his pocket that predicted Lem would bring danger to all he loved. "You have my word on that." Maybe it was a lie, but Lem would have to stomach that for now.

Farley nodded. "Fair enough. Then your secrets are your own."

By the end of the day, Lem learned that Farley had left his troupe in Lobin while he came to settle some old business with a former associate in Harver's Grove. What precisely that business might be, he carefully omitted. It was probably better not to know.

Lem had quickly grown accustomed to being on horseback, even rather enjoying it at times. It gave him a better perspective of his surroundings, for one thing. After a while he started to notice many similarities to his home, though it was still the differences that were most eye-catching. There were several species of flower and a few thorny shrubs that were new, along with a few sightings of a tiny squirrel with black fur scampering busily about. Those in Vylari were either red or gray and twice as large.

By late afternoon, they were beyond any houses or farms. On either side of the road, the forest was dense with gnarled oaks and towering pines, broken occasionally by clearings that, from the burned twigs and much trampled-down grass, were used by travelers as campsites.

Farley told him that if they pressed on, they could reach an inn. However, Lem said that he preferred to sleep under the stars. The stench of Harver's Grove was at last gone, and the earthy aroma of the wild felt as cleansing as a hot bath.

After building a fire, Farley gave him a hunk of flat bread with tiny, unfamiliar nuts baked within, along with a few strips of jerky and a pear. After they had eaten, he asked Lem to play, and he was more than willing to do so, plucking out a half dozen tunes while Farley smiled with appreciation.

"You are going to be a real asset to the troupe," Farley told him, as Lem put his balisari away. "They're going to love you in Lobin."

The week-long journey saw them pass through several small towns. Though most were not much bigger than Harver's Grove, their streets had been paved with cobblestone and the buildings kept in much better repair. Also, the people themselves seemed cleaner and lacked the downtrodden quality Lem had come to think was typical in Lamoria.

By the fourth day, the relative wealth of Bulvidar was obvious. A good number of people were dressed in extravagant finery, their hands and necks festooned with jewelry, and were conveyed about in elegantly designed horse-drawn carriages.

Martha, Farley explained, had been unable to recover Lem's coin from Durst, who had probably spent it the day he took it. Nonetheless, he was happy to pay for their rooms and meals.

"Call it an advance," he said.

———

The night before they were due to arrive in Lobin, they stayed at a small trading post. There were only a few buildings, mostly large warehouses, together with a livery and an inn. Farley explained that it was primarily a place where merchants sold their wares at a discount to avoid paying city tax or purchasing a vendor's license. Lem pretended to understand what he was talking about, though from the grin on Farley's face it was clear he'd seen right through him.

That evening, after procuring rooms and eating a hearty meal of lamb and grilled vegetables, they enjoyed a few mugs of ale in the common room. Compared to the swill served at the Oak and Amber, the brew was smooth and refreshing. Even so, Lem preferred wine and switched after his second mug. While they drank, a flautist on a small dais near a brightly burning hearth entertained the patrons. Though the musician was not one whom Lem would consider masterful, he listened carefully, paying special attention to which tunes the crowd enjoyed and those they ignored. Some of them were similar to Vylarian melodies, though not as complex.

Farley tipped the flautist a few coppers before they turned in for the night. Lem noticed there were at least forty or so of these coins in the jar near his feet—about a silver's worth. This set him wondering. If a musician could make a whole silver over the course of a single evening in a place like this, how much might one be able to make in a large city? Of course, with Farley, he would only be required to play for about an hour each night to clear five silvers. In a tavern he would have to play markedly longer. Though never one to be motivated by wealth, he found himself increasingly eager to get to Lobin. It felt as if it would be the next step to his goal: finding the Thaumas and uncovering the truth behind the dark warning the stranger had issued in Vylari. And while the dream of returning home was little more than a fantasy, the idea could not be set aside as impossible. Nor could seeing Mariyah again.

He recalled experiencing similar feelings when first arriving at Zara's tavern. But back then he had been completely ignorant of the outside world. He had learned much in a short time, though; enough to temper his anxiety. For now, Farley had been kind to him—perhaps he had even saved his life as much as had Martha. But Lem didn't know enough about the man to fully trust him yet. After all, most people he had encountered so far, with Martha as a notable exception, were to his mind entirely self-serving. Ultimately, Farley might not prove to be any different.

Lem dismissed these thoughts as a waste of time. He would know soon enough. For now, he was just happy to be away from Harver's Grove and have a chance to move on. He wondered how Zara had reacted on realizing that he was gone. He hoped Martha had been correct in saying she would not likely remember a thing. Which meant Zara would think Lem had escaped her clutches on his own. A vision of her screaming obscenities and vowing revenge drew a smile.

The night passed quickly by, and he awoke with the tingle of anticipation in his belly.

The trading post was only half a day's ride from the city. Soon the forest gave way to flat grassland, enabling him to catch his first glimpse of Lobin.

Even when more than an hour away, he could see the buildings rising from behind a long wall spanning well over a mile from east to west. Five colossal black towers capped by gleaming silver domes climbed impossibly high, like fingers reaching up to the heavens from within a mountain of lesser but still impressively tall structures of white and gray.

"You've never seen the watchtowers before?" Farley asked, laughing at his opened-mouthed expression.

"I had no idea anything could be so tall."

174 · BRIAN D. ANDERSON

Farley simply nodded, offering no further explanation as to their function.

After passing through several intersections, the road broadened enough to accommodate six wagons abreast. Which was just as well, as the way ahead was now packed with hundreds of people traveling in both directions by wagon, carriage, horseback, and foot.

If this many people were outside the city, Lem thought, his excitement mounting, how many must there be within?

A few paved roads shot off from the main highway here and there, along which were built massive two- and three-story houses surrounded by elaborate iron gates. Nearly all boasted spectacular trimmed hedges, neatly manicured lawns, and flower beds that were a riot of color. Dozens of men and women could be seen laboring within the grounds.

"Maybe you can earn enough to buy yourself one," said Farley, seeing Lem's interest, though from his tone, he was not being serious.

"I would never need so big a house," he replied. "How many people live there?"

Farley shrugged. "Depends on the size of the family, I suppose. I guess you could ride up and ask, but I doubt the servants would tell you anything. These are private estates owned by the wealthy and powerful of Lobin. This time of year, the owners mostly stay in the city until the end of the trading season."

"Trading season?"

Farley laughed. "Were you sheltered as a child? From spring until late fall is when the markets open. The seas are too rough in winter." Farley gave Lem a long, considering look. "You really *were* sheltered, weren't you? Don't go about saying things like this, or people will start to wonder where you're from."

"How do I know what's the wrong thing to say?"

"If you don't know, then best say nothing. I don't mean to frighten you, Lem. Not everyone is a fanatic. But you never know who is. That's the Archbishop's power." He relaxed his posture and smiled. "Just keep to yourself and to the troupe and you won't have to worry. But if you're really curious about Lobin, you could go to the library while we're here."

"That would be wonderful." Realizing he sounded a bit too enthusiastic, he added, "I've always been interested in history."

"And yet you seem to know so little about it."

Lem averted his gaze. Farley seemed a man not easily duped. Surely, he must suspect that there was something different about him. Of course, no one in Harver's Grove had considered for a moment that he might not be from this world. Thus far he had been thought a noble in hiding; a runaway from the north; from some tribe in the west; plus a few other far-fetched things. And as much as he would have liked to tell Farley the truth, for now he thought it best to stay silent.

The main city gate was flung wide and guarded by half a dozen men dressed in yellow-and-green uniforms, carrying short spears. Three of these were checking random wagons as they passed, though as they were allowing entry after just a quick glance and a few short words, this did not appear to be a particularly stringent process.

Beyond the gate, the street was oddly narrow. The buildings on either side had been built on slightly higher ground, with a low retaining wall placed between the pavement and the promenade. Shops with huge glass windows, their wares hung neatly on display to attract the attention of passersby, were in abundance. On the second floors were narrow balconies with wrought-iron railings, many of which were occupied by people sitting at tables, talking or eating.

"Apartments, mostly," said Farley, gesturing upward.

Lem realized that he was craning his neck, ignoring the road ahead. "Yes. Of course."

He needed to stop behaving as if seeing a city for the first time—even if that were the case. The truth was, he had never seen anywhere near so many people in one place. The entire population of Harver's Grove could not amount to a small fraction of the crowd packing this single avenue.

The dress in Lobin was much more colorful and diverse than the villagers' had been, mainly greens and reds, though some had shirts and dresses of gold and glimmering silver. Women wore wide-brimmed hats decorated with long plumes, together with sleek form-fitting dresses that had elaborate stitching all along the sides and back. For the men, waist-length jackets and baggy trousers appeared to be the predominant fashion. The residents' skin ranged as much in variety as did their clothing—some as dark as tree bark, others as pale as milk, and there were a few who had intricate designs painted across their face and hands. These wore bright blue-and-silver silks, with gold ringlet chains draped over their shoulders and hung around their waists.

Farley laughed over at Lem's childlike fascination. "Men from the southeast. Nivania, mostly. The markings tell who their family is. Excellent bow-makers. And their wine isn't bad either." He pointed to a window of a clothing shop, where a pair of the loose-fitting trousers was hung along with a blue-and-red jacket. "You like those?"

"No," he admitted. "I prefer my clothes to be better fitted."

This caused Farley to laugh even harder. "If I was built like you, I would too. Don't worry, we'll get you some decent attire tomorrow. Just don't be wooing the girls in the troupe. Business and romance don't mix."

Lem forced a smile. "Don't worry. I won't."

They threaded their way through the streets, guiding their mounts carefully between the wagons and the multitude of pedestrians. Lem continued to stare around him in wonder, though he tried to keep the gawking subtle at least. As he passed new sight after new sight, he found himself overwhelmed to near tears. There was so much beauty that he had never known, so many people in the world—and it made the stranger's warning even more dire. Surely the warning was not meant only for Vylari. Which meant this would all be ash if he didn't find the Thaumas, if they couldn't stop whatever it was that lay ahead.

Farley cursed, pulling him from his thoughts, as he shouted angrily to those on foot that they should stay on the sidewalk. Most ignored him, though a few shouted obscenities back.

After half an hour, Lem felt completely lost. The buildings started to look the same, and the street signs on the corners meant as a guide were useless without a frame of reference. Ahead, the avenue curved left around a tall bronze statue of a man clad in nothing but a pair of short pants and high boots. In one hand he carried a sword, in the other an axe. His thick wavy beard fell down to the center of his chest as he gazed at the northern sky, mouth twisted into a ferocious snarl. Around the statue's base had been placed myriad flowers along with offerings of various fruits and nuts.

"Who's that?" Lem asked.

Farley had not so much as looked up. "Mannan, Lord of the Sea. Don't tell me you've never heard of Mannan?"

"Of course I have," he lied. "I've just never seen a statue of him."

"Bloody sailors still worship the old man, if you can believe it. The Archbishop tried to have it removed a few years back. Nearly caused a riot." He shook his head. "You can force them to pray to Kylor all you want, but they won't let go of some superstitions."

A few minutes later they entered a square with borders stretching for several hundred feet. Various tents and pavilions were lined in neat rows from east to west, each filled with a countless array of goods, everything from food and clothing to jewelry and weapons. To Lem it looked like a miniature city unto itself. At the farthest end of the square, towering above, was a pair of stone pillars of polished black marble.

"That's where we're going," Farley told him. He dismounted and began to lead his horse through the tents.

Lem did the same, trying to keep his bearings while at the same time marveling at the sheer variety of goods for sale.

On nearing the pillars, he saw that a stage had been erected between them, behind which stood several covered wagons and an assortment of tents. Above the stage, a banner proudly proclaiming that it belonged to *The Lumroy Company* had been hung. Apparently, Farley had chosen to keep the former owner's name.

"Best spot in the city," he announced, with a broad smile.

They led the horses around to the back of the wagons, where a gangly young boy was kneeling over a washtub, elbow deep in soapy water as he vigorously scrubbed a shirt against a washboard.

The moment he saw them coming, he beamed a smile and leapt up, shaking dry his hands. "Mister Farley! You're back. I was starting to think something terrible might have happened."

Farley gave him a warm smile. "You worry too much for someone so young, Finn."

The boy eyed Lem for a second before taking both mounts and pulling them toward the last wagon.

Just as he set off, the flap to the nearest tent opened, and a woman with straight red hair tied into a ponytail, her mouth twisted to a frown, stepped out to bar their way. Tall and slender, she looked to be in her early forties and was wrapped up in a white silk robe with matching slippers. She planted her hands on her hips, tapping one foot as she regarded Farley.

"So, you've finally decided to come back, have you? You know the *douan* has come by twice about their fees. You were supposed to pay them before you left."

He held up a hand, nodding. "I know, I know. I forgot. I'll see to it in the morning."

The woman gave a snort and then looked over at Lem. "Who's this, then?"

With a sweeping wave of his arm, Farley said, "Lem, might I present Vilanda Morsette. Vilanda, this is our new musician, Lem."

She let out a humorless laugh. "Musician? Like we need another bloody musician. Well, I hope he was worth it. Crowds have been lousy. Can't even get them to stay for the second play half the bloody time."

"I think young Lem here can help us with that."

"Well, he's pretty enough, I'll give him that. But it'll take more than good looks to please this lot. When are we going east?"

"When I say so." Farley's tone had become firm.

Vilanda looked unimpressed. "Well, you'd better *say so* pretty damn soon, or I'm bloody gone. You hear me?"

"I hear you quite clearly. Now, shouldn't you be getting ready? Or are you taking a holiday?"

After shooting Farley a furious look, she turned back to Lem. "Careful around him, boy. A real snake's arse that one is."

"Charming as always," said Farley.

With a final angry look and a dramatic exhalation, Vilanda returned to her tent.

"That, my boy, is the leading lady of this fine troupe," Farley said. "Don't let her foul mood put you off. She's really quite good. Now, let's get you introduced to the others."

He led Lem from tent to tent, making introductions and explaining the general layout—which wagon held supplies, costumes, provisions, and so forth. The interiors were without exception a disheveled mess, with wooden chests, cots, and piles of clothing shoved into every corner. There were ten other members in all—seven actors and three musicians.

Lem was shocked and embarrassed to see that not only did both men and women live together, they appeared to have no sense of modesty whatsoever. Lem tried to avert his eyes from actors in various states of undress, but found it impossible without stumbling into the stacks of boxes scattered about.

On the way to the musician's tent, Farley clapped him on the shoulder. "Life is different around actors." He was clearly enjoying Lem's embarrassment. "They're a . . . how should I put it? A free-spirited lot."

"Do they always run around like . . . that?"

"I asked the same question back when old Lumroy still owned the troupe," said Farley. "Sadly, the answer was no. If it bothers you, best stay out of their tents when they're getting ready for a performance."

"I will."

To Lem's great relief, all three musicians were men. Not

to say that he cared about playing with women, but the thought of living the way the actors did made his stomach churn with anxiety.

In contrast to the dismissive way he had been greeted thus far, the musicians displayed mild displeasure when he was introduced. There was Clovis, a short, stocky fellow who played a stringed instrument similar to Lem's bal-isari, only with six strings and a bigger body; Quinn, a narrow-shouldered percussionist; and Hallis, a tall, spindly flautist.

The trio were sitting around a table playing a dice game. Clovis regarded Lem closely, sizing him up. "Don't need him," he declared.

"Not a problem," Farley responded. "He's not playing with you. He'll be entertaining during intermissions."

Hearing this, Quinn and Hallis relaxed their posture and gave Lem a polite nod.

But Clovis shot up from his chair. "That's *my* job. You can't do that. I won't stand for it."

Farley turned to Lem with a smile. "How would you like to double your pay? It seems there might be another opening."

This was enough to cow the man back into his seat.

"I expect you all to make Lem feel at home," Farley said. "Am I understood?"

Quinn and Hallis both nodded, while Clovis folded his arms over his chest and sulked, refusing to so much as look at Lem.

"I have to attend to a few things," said Farley. "I'll be back before the first show ends."

Once Farley was gone, Lem gauged his new surroundings. It was as cluttered and disorganized as the other tents, with barely an empty space to be found. "Where should I put my things?"

"Wherever you want," snapped Clovis, flicking his wrist and returning his attention to the game.

With a half-hearted smile, Hallis stood. "Come on. I'll show you where you'll be sleeping." Crossing over to a stack of boxes, he pulled out a cot. "Just clear out a spot wherever you want. I'll have Finn bring you a pillow and blanket after the show tonight."

Clovis flung the dice at the tent wall. "I swear to Kylor, soon as I can find another job, I'm good as gone."

"What's your problem?" asked Hallis. "The boy didn't do anything to you."

"No? He just cost me two silvers a night. That's not nothing."

Lem thought it best not to mention that he was being paid more than twice as much. "I'm sorry. I had no idea."

"As if it would have made any difference if you did," Clovis retorted. "Well, you'd better be able to play the blazes out of . . . whatever that thing is that you're carrying."

"It's a balisari."

Clovis snorted. "Who cares? All I'm saying is, you'd better be good."

"You think Farley would have hired him if he wasn't?" Quinn chipped in. "I mean, it's not like *you've* been able to hold the crowd."

Clovis glared down at him, red-faced and hands balled into fists. For a moment Lem thought it would come to blows. But after letting out a loud growl, Clovis slammed his knuckles on the table and stormed out.

"You shouldn't push him like that," cautioned Hallis.

"What's he going to do?" Quinn responded. "What I said is true. He can't hold the crowd. What good is two silvers if the troupe goes out of business? Then we're all buggered." He stretched his arms, clasping his hands behind his head. "I hope you're as good as Farley thinks you are, Lem."

Me too, he thought.

Clovis returned a few minutes later, ignoring everyone and throwing himself down onto a cot at the far side of the tent. The young boy who had taken the horses, Finn, arrived a short time later with a tray of roasted pork and bread. Lem joined the others at the table, eating in silence. Clovis made a point of casting him angry looks every time he thought Lem would notice.

At least he's not as big as Durst.

Lem spent the rest of his time sitting on his cot, tuning his balisari. Clovis threw across a few cutting remarks every now and then—mostly centered around the fact that no one would know what instrument he was playing. Obviously a balisari was uncommon.

By the time the evening arrived, Lem could hear the clamor of expectant voices outside. Finn came to call them to the stage moments after the other three had finished changing their clothes. With a slight touch of surprise, he saw they were not wearing anything as fine as he would have anticipated for a public performance. This made him feel a little less awkward about his own shabby attire; not that it stopped Clovis from hurling a final insult.

"You're playing music, not feeding hogs," he chided. "Next time dress for the occasion."

The other two musicians rolled their eyes.

Lem followed them to the left-hand side of the stage. Where the market had been earlier was now completely empty of tents, and in their place was what he guessed to be nearly a thousand people milling about. He hadn't noticed earlier, but the buildings surrounding the square were mostly taverns, inns, and a few eateries. More people

184 · BRIAN D. ANDERSON

were gathered on the second- and third-story balconies, laughing and drinking as street performers below put their talents on display. It reminded him of the Harvest Festival back home.

"Is it this crowded every night?" he asked Hallis.

"Most nights. But if you can't hold them, they'll pack themselves into the taverns ten minutes after the first play ends. Too many times, and we'll lose our license." He paused, noting the look on Lem's face that said he had no idea what he was talking about. "I suppose this is your first time in a troupe."

"Yes," he admitted.

"It's not too complicated. The city pays us to play, and we pay the king's douan for the license. Of course, if the people don't like us, no one will have us back. Or worse, the mayor will complain to the king and we'll be removed from the registry. Understand?"

"I think so." The point was clear—they were expecting him to keep the crowd interested. And it was vital that he do so.

The actors, led by Vilanda, arrived a few minutes later. With faces covered in white powder, they wore an elaborate assortment of attire. The women were dressed in gowns that flared out just below the knee. Two of the men had on armor, though it looked to be made from flimsy metal that offered no real protection. The other two were in long leather coats with tall conical hats perched atop their heads.

Clovis, Hallis, and Quinn moved to a corner just off the stage where Finn had set up their instruments. This was why they didn't need to dress so well, Lem realized. No one was able to see them.

Vilanda climbed onto the stage and clapped her hands twice. On cue, the music started. It was a lively albeit simple tune. Lem's initial opinion was that they were competent enough as musicians, though unremarkable. The leading lady strode to center stage, her steps long and graceful and her arms spread wide, inviting the spectators to give her their full attention. After a few seconds they quieted down and pressed in closer.

"Thank you, gentle ladies and kind lords," Vilanda began in a much different accent than the one she'd displayed at their initial meeting. Each syllable was pronounced precisely and projected with force. "It is so very good of you to come. It will be my pleasure to show you something quite new on this fine evening."

"Good!" called a voice from within the crowd. "Last night was awful."

This was met by laughter and shouts of agreement.

Vilanda gave no hint of a reaction to the heckle. "Many a late night we have spent preparing for this production. And now, at long last, we are ready. The Lumroy Company proudly presents *A Midnight Encounter with Fate*."

As she spoke the final word, the musicians switched to a bouncing little tune that Lem quite enjoyed. With the crowd cheering enthusiastically, the entire troupe hopped onto the stage.

It was short, as Farley had told him, lasting no more than twenty minutes or so, and with its witty dialogue and well-choreographed movements, Lem found it enjoyable to watch. Once the play ended and the actors were taking their bows, he caught sight of Farley standing just in front of the stage. Clovis and the other musicians stood and started toward Lem, leaving Finn to stand guard over their instruments. By now the audience had doubled, but only seconds after the actors' departure, most of them were already showing signs of impatience.

"Good luck," said Hallis.

186 · BRIAN D. ANDERSON

"You'll need it," added Clovis.

Quinn shook his head and sighed. "Don't be an ass, Clovis." He looked to Lem. "You'd better get up there."

All at once, Lem felt his stomach flutter with anxiety, not uncommon when playing at a new venue. And this was by far the largest number of people he had ever played for, and without doubt one of the most important performances of his life. Climbing onto the stage, he walked to the center. No stool. It would have to be a standing performance.

"Not again," a heckler called out. "I bet he's no better than the last bloke."

"Is that a woman?" shouted another. "Or just a pretty man?"

"I'll take him either way."

Gales of laughter struck into him, setting his nerves slightly on edge. Slowly, he looked up to face the audience, and placed his hands on the strings. Glancing quickly over to the side of the stage he saw Clovis wearing a wide grin, thoroughly enjoying his discomfort. He took a deep breath and imagined he was back in Vylari, playing for Mariyah for the first time. No performance could have been more nerve-racking—or more important—than that one. He pictured her smile as she sat by the Sunflow and watched him play, and he felt his nerves settle.

"Dance of the Dragonfly" was by far the most compli-cated tune he knew. Most Vylarian musicians could not even begin to play it. Even with his talent and skill it had taken months to learn properly. Under normal circum-stances Lem would never have tried something so complex without a few days of practice first. But from the smug look on Clovis's face and the impatient mutterings from the crowd, he knew he would need his most impressive routine if he hoped to win them over.

Slow and tranquil in the beginning, the melody gradually increased in tempo, with short bursts of atonal scales serving as markers for the building rhythm. Faster and faster he played, his hands soon a blur over the strings; faster and faster until beads of sweat formed on his brow and dripped from his nose. Faster and faster; by now he could see the colorful creature clearly in his mind, darting from leaf to leaf, zigzagging this way and that before shooting skyward. It was as though the dragonfly were actually speaking through his balisari, each note called out in its voice. The scales and chords melded together, sounding for all the world as if they were being played simultaneously. Lost in the moment of sublime creation, for a time Lem had no sense whatsoever of where he was or why he was playing.

Finally, as they inevitably do, the dragonfly flew off into the distance, leaving behind the forest Lem had imaged in his thoughts. The melody diminished until only a single note called out, lingering in the air as if to say a heartfelt farewell.

He looked up. The crowd was slack-jawed in astonishment. Not a single person had moved a muscle toward the tavern. Then, as if everyone recovered their wits in the same instant, a booming applause rose up, striking Lem with an almost physical force. People were whistling and waving their arms above their heads, shouting for more. He spotted Farley standing dead center, arms folded over his chest and smiling broadly. Lem bowed several times before turning to leave the stage. By now the actors had changed into new costumes and were ready for the next play. Clovis was nowhere to be seen.

As he stepped down, Vilanda caught his arm and whispered into his ear. "Who in blazes *are* you?" He could barely hear her over the roaring cheers, begging him to play again.

"No one," he replied. "I'm just Lem."

"Hog turds," she shot back. "No one pops up out of no-where and does that."

Lem shrugged, not knowing what she expected him to say. He pulled free and stepped to the rear of the stage. The actors gave him praise as he passed, and a few slapped him fondly on the back.

"We'll keep our license now for sure," he heard one of them say.

Clovis had returned to his instrument and was gazing down with a defeated expression. Hallis, conversely, was staring over at Lem with a puzzled look, while Quinn was chuckling into his hand.

Lem played once more that evening, the second time singing as well, and just like the first time, was met with tumultuous applause. When the last play ended, Finn hurried to gather the instruments and then began sweeping off the stage. Lem started to help, but Farley arrived and called him over.

"You really are amazing," he said. "I thought you were good at the tavern, but what you did up there tonight . . . no words can describe." Holding out his hand, he passed Lem six silvers.

"I thought I was being paid five," he said.

"If you don't want the extra, I'd be glad to take it back."

Lem quickly shoved the coins into his pocket. "Thank you."

"You more than earned it," Farley said, giving his arm a squeeze. "Now get some rest. Tomorrow I'll show you around Lobin."

Lem gave him an appreciative nod and then returned to his tent. He could hear the actors hooting and talking as he passed, clearly thrilled with how things had gone.

Ducking inside, he saw Hallis lying on his cot, reading,

and Quinn sitting at the table with a bottle of wine gripped in one hand. There was no sign of Clovis.

"There he is," said Quinn, raising the bottle above his head. "The master has returned."

Lem blushed. "I'm no master."

Hallis looked over the top of his book. "You could have fooled me."

"Where's Clovis?" Lem asked.

"Sulking, most likely," Quinn replied with a grin. "I don't think I've ever seen him so upset. You really put him in his place tonight."

A sting of guilt struck. "I didn't mean to."

"The way he treated you, he deserved it. Old boy needed to be taken down a peg or two. I should know. He's my cousin."

"I should go find him," said Lem.

"Don't bother. He'll be fine by morning," Quinn said. "A few drinks and a fight or two, and you'll see . . . right as rain he'll be." He waved Lem over to join him. "Come on. Have a drink with me."

"Quinn," said Hallis, shooting a warning look.

"I know, I know," he replied. After Lem sat down, he leaned in and said in a whisper, "Farley left orders. One: don't get you drunk. And two: don't ask you about your past."

Lem thought this strange. Why would Farley care about them asking him questions? Unless . . .

No, he was being paranoid. There was no way Farley could have discovered his secret. "I can get *myself* drunk," he said. "So don't worry."

Quinn peeked over at Hallis to check that he had returned to his reading, then bent low to the table. His voice was noticeably quieter. "I know I'm not supposed to ask this, but who in Kylor's creation taught you to play?"

"My mother."

He blinked hard. "Are you joking? Your *mother* taught you to play the . . . what did you call it? A balisundy?"

"Balisari," Lem corrected. "She was my first teacher. I had two others after her, but mostly I taught myself."

"Horse crap," said Quinn. "Only a master plays like that. A full-fledged bard. And I don't think there are more than ten in the whole world."

From the way Quinn spoke, Lem sensed the title of "bard" meant more here than just a musician of notable skill. Yet another thing to look up. The list of things to do in the library was getting long.

"I don't know what to say other than I mostly taught myself."

Quinn sputtered a hard breath. "You'd better not tell Clovis that. You know he studied to become a bard when he was young? Didn't have the talent, though. Not like you. But then again, most don't. With your skill, you really should apply."

Lem furrowed his brow. "Apply for what?"

"For a bardship, of course. Normally you have to go through years of school and training. But I bet they'd accept you right away."

"What would that do for me?"

Quinn cocked his head. "Don't you know anything? If they name you a bard, you can say goodbye to all this squalor and hard work. You'll be playing for kings and queens. I'm talking whole bags of gold. Not the few coins Farley is willing to hand out."

"That's an interesting idea. But I think for now, I'd like to stay where I am."

"Well, that's good news for us. Now that you're here, we might be able to stay in business. Crowds are getting a lot harder to please nowadays."

After a few minutes of further talk, Hallis put aside his book and joined them. Occasionally Quinn asked Lem something about where he came from, but the flautist quickly jumped in and reminded him of the rule. It was still puzzling to Lem why Farley would impose such a measure, but as it avoided uncomfortable topics, he decided not to question it.

By the time two bottles of wine had been consumed among them, Lem was yawning and beginning to doze. He'd not been expecting to start playing on his first evening and was still road weary, not to mention a bit overwhelmed by the sights of Lobin. Just as they were about to each go to their cots, Clovis staggered into the tent, undoubtedly drunk and with his shirt torn at the collar. After firing Lem a hate-filled look, he threw himself face-first onto a pile of boxes.

"You see?" Quinn remarked while covering his cousin with a blanket. "I told you he'd be fine."

Lem did not want another conflict in his life; the last one had ended in blood. He resolved to find a way to make peace with Clovis if at all possible.

As he lay on his cot, he felt a smile form. The thunder of applause was still echoing in his head. He had no desire to play for kings and queens, nor for fame or praise. The spirit of the audience that evening had filled him completely; their energy and joy had become his own. Whatever a bard was, he didn't care. For the first time since the day the stranger had entered Vylari, he felt a respite from the fear and doubt that had consumed nearly every waking moment.

He could only hope this feeling lasted . . . at least for a while.

12

HARSH REALITY

Injustice is the garden in which the seed of misery is sown.
Book of Kylor, Chapter Three, Verse Twenty-Eight

Lem woke to the sound of clanking metal and a cacophony of voices outside the tent. Sometime in the night Clovis had crawled to his cot and was sprawled out facedown, his head hanging over the edge. Hallis and Quinn were sitting at the table eating a breakfast of ham, eggs, and bread.

"Look who's up," remarked Quinn. "Better get dressed. Farley said he wants you to go to his tent the minute you wake."

Lem rubbed his eyes and smacked his lips. His mouth felt dry, and his muscles ached. Though usually well able to deal with a single bottle of wine, his body felt as if he had consumed an entire bottle of whiskey by himself.

"Where can I get cleaned up?" he asked, rolling off the cot onto his feet.

"There's a public bath not far from here," Hallis informed him. "But you don't have time for that. Farley wants to get you some decent clothes for tonight. From what Vilanda said, word's already spreading about you. As I understand it, people are saying a bard's come to Lobin."

Both men chuckled.

Stumbling over to the table, Lem poured himself a cup of water. It did little for his aching joints, but at least his mouth didn't feel like it was filled with sawdust.

Just then, the tent flap opened and Farley poked his head inside. "About time you woke up." He eyed Hallis and Quinn. "I thought I told you two not to get him drunk."

"They didn't," said Lem.

Farley frowned over at Clovis. "I see your cousin behaved as predictably as ever."

Quinn spread his hands. "What can I say? At least he made it back this time."

Farley sniffed. "Well, he'd better watch himself. I'm not getting him out of jail again." He waved to Lem. "Come on. We have much to do today."

"Give me just a minute to change clothes," Lem said.

"You can change later. I've a few matters to attend while we're out and about, so we need to get going."

Lem quickly pulled on his boots and slung his balisari over his back.

"No need to bring that," said Farley. "No one here would dare touch it. And you wouldn't want it to get damaged—the city will be quite crowded."

Reluctantly, he placed his instrument on top of his cot.

"I'll look after it for you," Quinn told him. "Don't give it a thought." He noticed Lem eyeing the still-unconscious Clovis. "He might be an arse, but he would never harm a musical instrument, no matter how he felt about its owner. Go on. Get out of here."

"Thank you," said Lem.

He followed Farley from the tent and into the market square. Once again it was filled to bursting with pavilions crammed with goods. It was impressive how quickly they managed to take them down each evening just to set them up again a few hours later.

"We'll be heading north, near the docks," Farley said. "That's where the best clothes are. And I can show you where the library is, assuming you still want to see it."

"Yes, very much."

Lem jingled the coins in his pocket. How much would new clothes cost? More than six silvers, he presumed. This meant Farley likely intended to buy them. He didn't want to be too deep in the man's debt, but he certainly was in need of appropriate attire.

"You've caused quite the stir," Farley continued, as they squeezed past a fruit vendor. "People are saying there's a bard in Lobin."

"Yes. Quinn told me."

"That's ludicrous, of course. A bard would never come here."

"Why not?"

"They don't get along with the Archbishop, not since he publicly accused one of them of being a heretic. The entire order declared themselves apostates in solidarity." He let out a short laugh. "Thirty years and two Archbishops later, the bards still won't come. Not until they receive an apology. And you can be sure that will never happen."

Suddenly, being thought of as a bard sounded dangerous. "Should I be worried?"

"Not at all. No one cares about that anymore. At least not the folks who come to watch us. The church might send someone to check on you, just to be sure. But I'll deal with that. Strange that you wouldn't know this, given your talent."

Lem ignored the last comment. And as always, Farley didn't press the subject.

"I'll tell you this," he added. "No one would miss the chance of hearing a bard play. It should be a big crowd tonight."

"So you've encouraged the rumor?"

Farley grinned. "Of course."

It took almost an hour to reach the northern section. Lem tried to keep pace but found himself craning his neck and staring up in wonder at the massive buildings along the way. Many bore elaborate frescoes and were adorned with colorful banners and beads. Eventually, they drew close to one of the mighty towers he had seen when first arriving. He halted in his tracks, straining his eyes to view the top, but it was obscured by low clouds.

"Built by ancient gods," said Farley, tugging at his sleeve to keep walking. "At least, that's what they say. No one knows who really built them."

It seemed impossible, something so tall. "How old are they?"

"Like I said, no one knows. They were here long before Lobin was settled. Aside from being an attraction, they don't actually serve much purpose. King Zolomy keeps the treasury in one of them, but the others are empty. If you're really interested, for a few coppers you can take a tour inside. Be warned, though; it's a beast of a climb."

"You've been?" Lem was trying to imagine what the world would look like from such an enormous height.

"Once. Damn near killed me. Beautiful view, though. It's just so exhausting getting up there to see it."

It took a great effort for Lem to look away. What kind of people could build a thing like that? Let alone five of them. They had been hugely impressive at a distance. Now, up so close . . . they boggled his mind.

A bit farther along, the street widened, and traffic flowed more freely. They had kept to the promenade for the most part, making him feel somewhat trapped by the closeness of the other pedestrians. He could understand why some chose to walk in the avenue, even if it meant dodging the horses and wagons.

They arrived at a small shop just as Lem caught the tang of salt in the air. He heard bells ringing above the constant background noise of the city.

"The docks are just around the next corner," Farley informed him. "We can go see the ships once we've finished getting your clothes, if you'd like."

Lem nodded enthusiastically. "I'd like that very much." He had heard stories of massive vessels capable of traversing endless expanses of water so enormous that one could not see the far shore. In Vylari, other than the Sunflow, there were a few small lakes and narrow streams, and the boats held no more than six or so people. These were said to carry hundreds.

Inside the shop hanging on the walls were a variety of jackets, pants, shirts, and various small accessories. Several rows of shelves placed in the center of the floor held heavy bolts of cloth, all of them looking to be of the highest quality. At the rear stood an older man with a round face and a balding head. His right arm was fully extended, holding out a red jacket, which he was regarding with a scowl. In his mouth were several pins and in his free hand a pair of shears.

"What's wrong?" called Farley. "Not happy with your own work?"

Upon seeing Farley, his frown deepened. "What do you want?" he mumbled, still managing to grip the pins in the corner of his mouth. "I'm busy."

Farley clicked his tongue. "Now, now. You're not too busy for paying customers, are you?"

Removing the pins, the man placed the jacket on a nearby table. "Paying this time, are you? That would be a pleasant surprise."

Farley chuckled. "Can I help it if you're a poor gambler? Lem, this is Verin, the finest tailor in Lobin."

The man grunted, then turned his attention to Lem. "Being that you already have more clothes than the king himself, I can only assume this visit is for your young friend."

Lem nodded. "I need something decent for tonight's performance."

Verin lifted his brow. "So, you're the bard I've been hearing about today. A bit young for such acclaim, aren't you?"

"I'm—"

"A prodigy," Farley cut in. "One in need of your best work."

"Indeed." Rubbing his chin, he studied Lem closely. "A touch thin in the waist. Strong shoulders." He muttered incoherently while reaching out to squeeze Lem's arms and then his legs. Finally, he declared: "Two days. Best I can do."

"That will be fine," said Farley. "But we'll need something for tonight."

With a sigh, the tailor heaved his ample girth toward a door at the back wall. He returned a few minutes later carrying a small bundle tied with thin twine. "This will have to do for now."

When Lem began to unwrap it, Farley stopped him, then turned to Verin.

"Thank you, old friend. I'm sure it will do nicely." He reached in his pouch and produced a handful of silver coins. "Ten?"

"Fifteen." Verin's finger shot up. "Another word and it's twenty."

After a brief pause, Farley decided not to test the tailor's resolve and handed over the coins. "Now, for our other arrangement, I expect three full ensembles."

198 · BRIAN D. ANDERSON

"You'll have them."

"For two gold," added Farley.

"In advance."

"When you deliver," he countered.

"Half now."

"Come on, Lem." Farley turned to the exit. "I know another shop nearby."

Verin threw up his hands. "Very well, you old thief. On delivery. But you had better not try to cheat me."

Farley affected a deeply offended expression. "You must know by now that I would never be anything but totally honest with you."

After giving vent to his feelings with a loud snort of derision, Verin walked over to the table and picked up a ball of yellow string. He proceeded to hold lengths of this up to various parts of Lem's body, cutting them to size and then laying them on the table. The process took only a few minutes.

"Two days," Verin said. "Assuming the magistrate hasn't locked up half your troupe and driven you from the city, I'll see you then."

Farley winked and started to the door.

Once outside, Lem again caught the scent of salt on the air, and his excitement over seeing the ships returned. Scarcely had they set off when a horn blasted from just beyond the next corner; then a second blast sent people scurrying from the street and onto the sidewalk.

"What's happening?" asked Lem.

"Prisoners bound for the mines," Farley replied darkly, his lip curled in disgust. "Or worse."

From the south appeared a large wagon pulled by a team of six horses. Seconds later, another rumbled up behind it. This was followed by more of the same until there were six in all. The wheels squealed and creaked as the beasts strained under the weight of their burdens. As they drew closer, Lem could see that these were not wagons but wheeled cages with thick iron bars. But it was what the cages held that had his chest tight and eyes wide: men packed in so tightly that not even one more soul could possibly fit, their flesh pressed against the bars. Many of the faces were beaten, and all were clad in ragged clothes stained with blood and filth.

"Poor bastards," remarked Farley. "Even convicts should be given room to sit."

Lem covered his nose as the stench of feces, urine, and unwashed bodies reached him. What could these people have done to deserve such treatment? He wished he could do something to help, to give them some sort of comfort, but teams of guards armed with short clubs walking alongside each cage prevented anyone from coming near.

Tears welled as he looked upon their sunken eyes and grimy flesh. They were defeated and without hope. Unable to bear the sight, he started to turn his back. Then something caught the corner of his eye. A face. A familiar face. Bruised and caked with mud, it was still unmistakable.

"Shemi!" he cried, leaping over the retaining wall and running headlong for the wagon.

He did not make it halfway before a guard moved into his path and let his club fly. Although only a glancing blow, it was enough to send him down hard in the street. Blood trickling from his forehead, he struggled to regain his feet, but the crushing pain from a boot to the ribs quickly had him flat down once again.

He heard Farley's voice behind him. "That's enough."

"Your friend's lost his mind," the guard growled. "Get him out of here before I crush his damned skull."

A pair of hands lifted Lem up and pulled him away from the cages.

"Are you insane?" Farley demanded. "Or are you wanting to get yourself killed? What's gotten into you?"

Lem, still trying to catch his breath from the brutal kick, was for the moment incapable of speech. He could do nothing but watch helplessly as the cage containing his uncle slowly trundled out of sight around the next corner. With all the strength drained from his body, he staggered back until he sat down heavily on the retaining wall, his head in his hands.

Shemi! How?

There was only one possible answer. His uncle must have followed him.

"You need to tell me what's wrong."

Lem had almost forgotten that Farley was still standing beside him. He wiped his eyes and looked up. "I need your help."

Farley regarded him for a long moment and then nodded. "I'll help if I can. You can tell me about it when we get back to the troupe. But right now we need to leave. Your display has attracted quite a lot of attention."

He lifted Lem to his feet, and they made their way through the throng of onlookers. While moving along, Lem could hear numerous mutterings thrown in their direction, mostly along the lines of *heretic* and *northern scum*. Each voice fueled equal measures of his despair and anger. He wanted to strike out . . . to throttle each and every person that spoke.

The walk back to the troupe felt as if it took hours. Farley led him into his own tent and sat him down at a small table near the bed. Unlike the others', his living space was neat and had decent furnishings. Not luxurious, but certainly comfortable.

After pouring Lem a cup of wine, he sat in the chair

opposite. His voice was sympathetic, his expression kind. "Now, then, why don't you tell me what's going on?"

With unsteady hands, Lem drained the cup, wine spilling from the corners of his mouth. He slammed the cup on the table, puffing and gasping from drinking too fast, yet repeating this once Farley poured him a second.

"I need you to help me free one of the prisoners," said Lem, once calm enough to speak.

Farley blinked several times. "You want me to do *what*?"

"Please. I'll do anything you ask." His tears returned.

"Why?"

Lem nearly confessed everything. Only a tiny voice in the back of his mind stopped him. "I know one of them. He . . . he's family. My uncle. He's like a father to me."

Farley steepled his fingers under his bottom lip. "I see. And this uncle . . . does he have a name?"

"Shemi."

"Shemi," he repeated in a low voice. "And he is dear to you, you say?"

Lem nodded.

"Without knowing his crime, I can't say for sure I can do anything. If it's severe, it will cost a substantial amount of gold to buy his freedom. Perhaps more than I can afford."

That buying Shemi's freedom was even a possibility caused Lem's heart to leap in his chest. "Please. Will you try?" He sobbed with relief. "He was the old man in the middle. With long gray hair."

Farley nodded and rose to his feet. "I'll see what I can do. No promises, though. I'm not making myself a pauper over this. And you'll work off every copper."

"I will. You have my word." Hope swelled. "Thank you. I will never forget this."

"Don't thank me yet." He handed Lem his new clothes.

202 · BRIAN D. ANDERSON

"I may not be back before the show starts. This sort of business takes time. And I expect you to match last night's performance. So get your head on straight. You hear me?"

Lem nodded vigorously. "Yes. I promise. It will be even better tonight."

Farley heaved a sigh. "Very well. Now get going. I need to see how much gold I have to spend."

Lem stood and started toward the exit.

"You do realize that you'll owe me a big favor," Farley called after him.

Lem nodded over his shoulder. "I'll owe you two."

While heading back to his tent, his mind was barely able to contain what had occurred. Not for a moment had he considered that Shemi might follow him. Why would the old fool do such a thing? It was madness. He knew that Shemi loved him. But to leave Vylari?

Clovis was sitting at the table, his instrument in his lap, plucking out a simple melody. Still wearing the same clothes from the previous night and with bloodshot eyes, he was not exactly looking his best. The moment he saw Lem enter, he stopped playing.

Lem couldn't fathom facing a confrontation with Clovis right now. As it was, the torrent of emotions had him barely able to form a coherent thought. "That was pretty," was all he managed to say. "What was it?"

Clovis shrugged. "Just something I wrote a few days ago."

"I was never much of a composer myself. I guess we all have our talents, though, right?"

Clovis sneered. "Don't try to make me feel better. I know Quinn told you about my failure at the Bard's College. But I recognize true talent when I hear it. Even if I don't have it myself."

"My mother once told me that music isn't about how well you play. It's about how it makes you feel when you play it."

"That's easy for you to say. One night in Lobin and you're famous straightaway." He glanced down at his instrument with contempt. "I've been practicing most of my life. All I ever wanted was to play like you. Look at you— half my age and already as good as any of the bards."

"I've never heard the bards, so I couldn't say. But I wasn't lying when I said I liked your song."

"I'm sure you've written a thousand that make mine sound like a baying mule."

A laugh that Lem was unable to contain burst forth.

"That's right," Clovis responded, shoulders sagging. "Mock me. I deserve it."

Lem held up a hand. "No. It's not that. Quite the opposite, in fact. Where I'm from, it's true that I'm well known for my playing. It's also well known that I'm unable to write music of any worth. Believe me, I've tried. Many times. Yes, I could probably take your song and create variations on it. But that's a long way from writing original tunes. Believe it or not, I envy your ability."

"I wish I could believe that."

"Why would I lie?"

"To make me feel better."

Lem moved over to his cot and sat down. "I have to admit I was looking for a way to make peace with you. The last thing I want is to have problems here. But I'm not a liar. At least, not when it comes to music. If you asked me what I think of you as a player, I'd tell you that you are good. Not great, but definitely good. Do I think you could match me? No. Not if you practiced all day, every day, for the rest of your life. But the song I heard when I came in was better than anything I could write. *That's* the truth."

Clovis looked again at his instrument, this time with affection. "Thank you. I believe you mean it. It's just that you have no idea how hard I worked, only to fail. I've spent the last twenty years reliving the moment they expelled me from the Bard's College. Twenty long years. I knew I wasn't good enough. I'd watched others . . . like you . . . move on to heights I would never reach. I should have given up long before they made me leave. But I couldn't accept the truth. I couldn't accept my own limitations."

"But your compositions . . . surely they recognized your ability?"

Clovis ran his fingers gingerly over the strings, a sad little smile on his lips. "I wasn't interested in composing then. I didn't write my first tune until I joined the troupe. That was five years ago." He looked up, his sorrow fading. "You know, I write all the music for our plays."

"Is that right?" Lem was truly impressed by this. He had not been merely trying to reconcile with Clovis—he genuinely had no talent for composition. "How long does it take?"

"For each song? Not long. A day or two. Writing the melody is the easy part. It's orchestrating the piece for the flute and percussion that's the challenge."

Lem needed a distraction while awaiting Farley's return, so he was happy to listen as Clovis explained how he would watch the actors rehearse, trying out different melodies until chancing upon one that fit the scene. Later on, he would think about how to incorporate the other instruments into the piece.

"Of course," he remarked with a grin, "trying to get Quinn and Hallis to learn the new tunes is even harder than writing them. You think *I'm* hard to deal with? Try teaching anything to those two."

They talked on for an hour. Although skirting the subject of his home, Lem did reveal that his mother was his first instructor and that he was self-taught for the most part after that. On hearing this, Clovis had let out a frustrated moan, though it was without anger or jealousy. All he did was roll his eyes and say, "Of course, you taught yourself. You know, yesterday I would have really hated you for that."

Eventually, Hallis and Quinn arrived. Seeing the pair of them talking as friends at the table drew a soft laugh from both men.

"I see you've decided to stop hating our young bard," remarked Quinn. "That's good."

"Sounds like Farley's been spreading the word about you, Lem," added Hallis. "Should be a big night."

The mention of Farley brought Lem's thoughts rushing back to his uncle, and immediately his mood darkened. Quinn and Hallis joined them at the table, but he was no longer wanting conversation and had to force himself to seem interested.

He glanced toward the tent entrance and frowned. It was still hours before sundown. Hours before he would know Shemi's fate. At last he excused himself, saying that he needed to rest.

"I'm still tired from last night," he explained over their objections.

"Come on, lads," said Quinn, rising from his seat. "Let's give the young bard some quiet."

After they exited, Quinn shot back inside for a moment on the pretense that he had forgotten something.

"Whatever you said to Clovis, thank you," he told Lem.

Lem responded with a weak smile, then stretched out on his cot.

He tried to close his eyes, but whenever he did, the image of Shemi's battered face appeared. His mother would pray to the ancestors from time to time for help or guidance. Lem's own prayers were rare, and when he did pray, he did not expect an answer. But now, he would try anything to save his uncle.

By the time the sun was waning, the clamor of an eager audience waiting near the stage was so loud that it sounded as if they were right outside his tent. Clovis and the others returned just as he was unwrapping his new clothing. Within was a blue shirt with ruffled collar and matching trousers. Silver stitching and buttons were sewn down the side of each trouser leg and on the front of the shirt. The material was soft and bore a sheen that reflected the light, lending a faint aura to the outfit. Unfortunately, his old boots would be sure to diminish the overall allure, but left with no better option, all he could do was clean them up as best he could.

By the time Lem stepped outside, his nerves were frayed, and he was desperate for news about Shemi. His eyes darted around, searching without success for a sign of Farley. As he continued to peer into the audience—which was at least twice the size of the previous night—he felt a hand touch his shoulder.

An impatient Vilanda was standing behind him. For this performance she was wearing a black dress with a lace scarf tossed over her shoulder and another just like it tied as a sash around her waist.

"Have you seen Farley?" she asked. "I know he was with you this morning."

"No. He left hours ago."

"Well, he had better get his arse back here soon."

As with every encounter so far, she seemed angry about something. And the way she spoke to Farley . . . it was as if she were the one in charge.

"I'll let him know you're looking for him."

She flicked her wrist. "Don't bother. He knows he'd better find me."

Following the same routine as the previous night, once the musicians were in place and the actors lined up beside the stage, she clapped her hands twice and the music started. This time Lem listened with more interest. Clovis was in fact very adept at setting a mood with his compositions. This one was dark and ominous, matching the slow and deliberate strides of Vilanda as she made her way to center stage.

Tonight's first play, *Murder by Starlight*, was a gripping mystery about a woman who had killed her husband after discovering his infidelity. Lem tried to pay attention, but could not stop himself from regularly searching the crowd for Farley. Knowing that it could be well into the night before he returned did not help his patience.

You need to calm down, he scolded himself. *You promised Farley a great performance. And you had better deliver.*

As the first play ended and the actors were taking their bows, the word *bard* could be heard floating throughout the crowd. The call was quickly taken up by more and more until thousands of people were crying it out in unison. The sound was deafening. Lem could feel it resounding in his chest as he stepped up onto the stage, balisari hanging over his shoulder. As loud as the audience's chanting had just been seconds ago, it was nothing compared to the thunderous roar that now erupted in response to his appearance.

He shut his eyes, waiting for the fervor to subside. It took more than a minute before they finally settled. Lem then opened his eyes, and at once his heart seized in his chest. Farley was standing right in front of him. What's more, he was smiling. Lem felt as if an enormous weight had been lifted from his back, and for a moment he forgot the audience altogether.

"Do you have him?" he called down.

Farley nodded with a laugh, then gestured for him to begin playing.

Lem wanted to jump from the stage and embrace the man. Farley had done it! He had saved Shemi.

"Go on, then," called a voice, snatching him back into the moment.

Lem strummed out the first few notes. He had intended to play an old Vylarian lullaby. But it didn't feel right. Not now; not when his heart was so joyful. He stopped playing midway through the lullaby's introduction, and for a moment, Shemi was the only thing in his mind. There was no prophecy, no burning land, no fear. He was fishing with Shemi along the banks of the Sunflow, watching the stars pop out one by one until the entire sky was filled to bursting with celestial light.

A single note rang out. Then a chord. A simple, almost childish introduction. It was a song he had learned only the year before. Its simplicity was due to its composer: a young student named Girald, who, while not very talented when it came to playing the balisari, like Clovis possessed a definite creative gift.

Lem continued, improvising an intricate web around the basic melody, each note seeming to dance around the one before it until inevitably giving way to the next. By the time the song ended, he realized he was smiling from ear to ear. The crowd shared his joy, cheering and calling for more. But Lem was intent on only one thing. Not bothering to take a bow, he rushed from the stage, speeding past the actors, continuing at full tilt until he reached his tent.

There, lying on his cot, was Shemi. Farley had disposed of his filthy rags and put him into a long nightshirt. But although Farley had also cleaned Shemi's face of grime, the bruises were still quite pronounced. Shemi's eyes were only half open as Lem knelt beside him.

"Am I dreaming?" he asked, his voice barely audible.

"No, uncle," Lem replied, brushing back the hair from

his face. Tears gathered in his eyes. He had never seen Shemi so helpless and weak. What had they done to him? "It's me. I'm here. You can rest now. Everything is going to be fine."

"Mariyah," the old man croaked.

"Don't worry about her," Lem said. "Her parents will look after her."

Shemi shook his head. "No. You have to save Mariyah. Don't let them take her."

It was as if cold steel had stabbed him in the gut. "What are you saying? Where is Mariyah?" Without realizing it, he had grabbed his uncle's arms and was shaking him. "Answer me. Where is Mariyah?"

"I couldn't stop her," he said. His eyes fluttered. "They took her. They . . ." His voice faded to nothing, and a second later his body went completely limp.

Lem shook him again. "Shemi. Wake up. Tell me where she is."

It was pointless. The old man was unconscious.

The tent flap opened, and Farley stepped inside. "You see? Everything worked out just fine."

Lem stood, pale faced and quivering.

"This *is* the one you wanted?" asked Farley, confused by Lem's distress.

"Yes. This is Shemi."

"Then what's wrong? You look upset." He glanced over to the sleeping man. "Don't worry. He'll be fine. They beat him, but the healer I brought him to said it was nothing too serious. The tonic he was given will keep him groggy for a while. But he'll be all right."

"I know I have no right to ask," said Lem. "But I need your help again."

Farley gave him a sour look. "If it involves more coin, you can forget it. That old man cost me ten gold pieces.

Good thing I got there before the ships docked or it would have cost me twice as much."

"Please. There is a girl. They have her."

Farley knitted his brow. "A girl? What girl?"

"Her name is Mariyah. She's being held as well."

"Not anymore, she isn't. Most of the prisoners were shipped away this afternoon. If she was there, she's already gone by now."

Lem felt dizzy. "No. I have to save her."

Farley crossed over and helped him to the table. "I think it's about time you told me what's going on here. Your uncle was imprisoned by the Hedran. So that's what we're talking about, right? A heretic? An apostate? Tell me when I'm close."

Lem's mind was in bits. All he could think about was Mariyah, caged and beaten like an animal. "I love her," he said. "I have to help her."

Farley leaned back, looking stunned.

"I'm begging you," Lem continued. "Help me save her. I'll do anything you ask. Anything."

Farley regarded him in silence for almost a minute. He then rose sharply to his feet. "Wait here. I'll be back in a moment."

Lem waited, barely able to contain his desperation. Why had Shemi brought her along? What was he thinking? If she died, he would . . .

No. There had to be a good reason why she was here too. He would wait until Shemi had the chance to explain.

When Farley returned, he rubbed his temples and plopped wearily into the chair. "Do you have any idea what you just cost me?"

"I'm sorry," said Lem. "I promise to make it up to you."

"I'm not talking about the girl. I mean tonight. Forgetting the ten gold I've already spent, I've had to tell Clovis that he'll be playing the second intermission this evening. I can't have you onstage in your condition."

"So you'll help me?"

"I can't." His hand shot up before Lem could object. "Even if she was still here, my purse is already stretched too thin."

Lem's heart sank. "Is there nothing you can do?"

"Perhaps. I'll go back to the magistrate in the morning and see if I can find out what she was convicted of and where she was taken. But you're going to have to face the truth. There's a good chance you'll never see her again."

"Please. Just do whatever you can. If I can find her, I'll get her free."

Farley looked at him with warning eyes. "I know what you're thinking. Forget it. Prisoners cannot be taken."

Farley rose and crossed over to Shemi, then lifted the nightshirt to reveal a thin gold band around his ankle. "You see this? The magic it holds will kill him if he tries to flee or if anyone tries to take him away. His sentence was one year. So that's how long he's indentured to me. And only *I* can release him before then."

He reached inside his shirt to pull out a tiny blue glass orb attached to a silver chain. "So long as I have this, he's mine. And before you ask, the answer is no. Until I recover my losses, it stays with me. I like you, Lem, but I can't let that rob me of my common sense."

He returned to his seat. "I'll do what I can to find this girl for you. All the same, I think it's best you try to forget about her. Wherever she is, she's beyond your reach now. Just be thankful I was able to save your uncle."

Lem nodded slowly. But it was far from being a gesture of agreement. Mariyah was here because of him. He would not abandon her. He would find out where she was. And if it took him the rest of his life, he *would* set her free.

13

PROMISES OF THE HOPELESS

There are two lives we lead: one within, the other existing beyond our corporeal selves. Should sorrow dominate both, peace will be forever out of reach.

Book of Kylor, Chapter Ten, Verse Four

Mariyah stared down at the foul hunk of metal wrapped around her ankle. More than anything she yearned to rip it free and smash it into a thousand pieces. Well, maybe not more than *anything*. The heartless monster of a woman who had forced her into a confession . . . if only Mariyah could have the chance to wrap her hands around the woman's throat, that might bring her even greater satisfaction.

The tiny ship's cabin in which she had been placed was dark, moldy, and caked with slime. On top of this, the way everything constantly swayed back and forth with the motion of the sea had made her violently sick for the first day. Or was it two? It was impossible to tell without so much as the tiniest glimmer of sunlight. Sleep had come sporadically, and when she did manage to drift off she was plagued by nightmares of her journey. The beatings and cruelty she and others had endured on their way to Lobin would be scarred into her memory forever. At least whoever held her now had yet to beat her, though that was likely to change before much longer.

In spite of the bargain she had made, poor Shemi was probably dead by now—or had been sent to the mines or something equally horrific. From the brief conversations she'd had with other prisoners on the journey to the coast, she knew she was in Ralmarstad. She still had no idea what this meant. And as talking among prisoners was strictly forbidden and brutally enforced, she had been unable to learn much more. One thing was certain: The stories about Lamoria were true. Every one of them. It was not only heretics who were abused, either. Just before being packed onto the ship, she had witnessed three large men beat a young boy without mercy, simply for the crime of begging for a few coins to buy food. They had left him bleeding and unconscious in a pool of his own filth.

Looking around the tiny room, her hand drifted down to the anklet. Its reality was unavoidable. She was trapped, and had been since the moment she crossed the bridge in the back of the wagon. No; even before that. From the first word she'd spoken to Tadrius, her fate was set. This was her life now . . . for however long it lasted. Even should the opportunity present itself, the anklet excluded any chance of escape. The woman who had handed her over to the captain had been sure to reinforce what could happen should she try. Though the lesson was unwarranted.

She leaned back and closed her eyes. A hatred had taken root in her heart. At its core: Kylor. And while it was true that not everyone she had encountered was evil or cruel, they had done nothing to change their own world. *Inaction is complicity*. This was a saying she remembered Shemi using on several occasions. Not that he'd been referring to anything like this. Theft and shady dealing were the evils he'd been speaking of. Nonetheless, his words were equally true in these most dreadful of circumstances.

Thinking about Shemi brought back a horrible memory. She had seen him screaming to her, waving his arms frantically through the bars of his cage until a guard beat him back. She tried not to picture this when remembering him, instead calling up the image of the sweet old man sitting in his favorite chair, pipe clamped between his teeth, reading one of his books that delighted him to no end. But it was the pitiless scene that was burned into her memory and would invariably force itself to the fore, no matter how hard she tried to keep it away. A small part of her hoped that he had died before being subjected to the cruelty of the mines.

The cabin door opened and light flooded in, forcing her to shield her eyes.

"Are you ready to eat?" a voice asked.

After a moment, her sight adjusted, and she saw the same woman who had come to her twice before. She was older than Mariyah, perhaps twice as old. Her brown hair was cut short above her collar and her round face bore a sour expression.

Mariyah turned away. She would not speak, nor would she eat. Death would be her release. Had she a blade, her life would already have ended.

"They won't allow you to starve yourself," the woman said. "Lady Camdon has spent far too much. So you might as well eat now before they order you to."

Mariyah was fully aware that the magic of the anklet could be used to compel her obedience. But she would be damned before obeying any command of her own free will.

The woman sighed. "This is why bull-headed people like you end up in prison."

Rage overcame Mariyah and she swung around, glaring hatefully. "No. They end up there because of Kylorian savagery."

"Ah, she speaks. I thought that might get a reaction." The woman smiled, banishing the almost-permanent frown that Mariyah had seen thus far. "Since you do have a voice, will you tell me your name?"

Mariyah turned away once again, arms wrapped around her knees.

"I thought not. But you should know that you're quite fortunate, more than you could possibly know. Ralmarstad prisons are a nightmare, from what I've heard. And as I understand it, you were convicted of murder. I can't even imagine a life sentence in a place like that. At least now you'll be able to live a decent life."

Mariyah felt the pain of the magic creeping through her leg, as her thoughts of violence threatened a punishment. "You dare to stand there and say I'm fortunate? Get out!"

"I know it doesn't feel like it. But I promise, things aren't as bad as they seem."

"If it means I'm to live among your kind, it's worse," she said, hoping that the insult would have some impact.

There was a long pause before the woman spoke again. "Give it time. You'll see that I'm right. Until then, I'll keep bringing your meals like I'm told. You can depend on that."

The clack of a lock was enough to send more rage, along with the punishment of searing hot pain, through her extremities. This time she was able to bear it without crying out. *Fortunate? Take off this anklet and I'll show you fortunate.* She remained still for several minutes before picking up the plate and placing it in the corner on top of the others. Servants fed by servants. Is that what this world really was? A society populated by powerless masses born to serve the few who had the strength to control them?

Those able to instill sufficient fear to keep them docile? It certainly seemed to be that way. Why would Lem have chosen to come to this terrible place?

Lem.

She hadn't thought his name in days. When she had, she'd wept uncontrollably. She hoped he had not fallen prey to the same fate. She told herself that he was safe somewhere and getting by. She could not allow thoughts of him being beaten and imprisoned to drag her to even greater depths of despair. If only he had come to her first and told her the truth! She could have talked some sense into him; convinced him to stay. Or at least forced him to bring her along. Her refusal to be left behind might have been enough to make him reconsider.

As her mind retrod the familiar path, a stray thought entered. By now her parents would have guessed what she had done. But for them, life would continue as it always had. In time, their grief would diminish. Mother would be the most affected. Father would put on a brave face and do his best to convince her that their daughter had found happiness in Lamoria. Whether or not he truly believed it, one immutable fact of existence could not be ignored: Their daughter was gone, and could never come home.

When she'd left Vylari, the choice hadn't felt real. Surely there must be a way back, she'd reasoned. And if not, she would find the courage to accept it. Finding Lem was all that mattered. Now, as the moldy stench of the cabin assaulted her, the creaking of the timbers sounding like the whispers of death and pestilence sneaking up from the darkness, she was oddly grateful that they would never know her fate. At least they would be spared that pain.

Usually thoughts of home brought tears, but not this time. This time there was only more anger. Anger at herself, at Shemi . . . and at Lem. This was *his* fault. Shemi was either dead or soon would be, and she was destined to live out her days in bondage. In her fury, she wanted to hate him. But it seemed there was room within her for both love and anger. As much as one threatened to drown out the other, they were each painfully alive.

As promised, the woman returned again and again, bearing food and drink until the stack of plates was nearly as tall as Mariyah herself. Her hunger was growing and her strength waning with each meal she refused, but her will would not crumble. One hope drove her. Perhaps if she was defiant enough, they would simply decide to kill her and be done with it.

On this latest visit, that hope was dashed.

"They told me they're going to make you eat later today," the woman informed her. "So all this has been for nothing."

"It's not for nothing," she replied, her voice barely above a whisper. She had become so weak and dehydrated that she could do little more than sit on the floor, slumped against the wall. "They can make me obey. But I will never do anything they say willingly."

"Let me speak to her," came another female voice from outside the room.

The servant woman glanced over her shoulder. After a momentary pause, she gave a nod and then stepped outside to wait in the passage.

The woman who stepped forward was tall and slender, with neatly combed red hair that fell halfway down her back and was held away from her face by a silver band on her brow. She wore a green cotton blouse, loose trousers, and a pair of cloth shoes. Not the attire of a servant, Mariyah considered.

The newcomer smiled sympathetically, her head slightly tilted and hands folded at her waist. "I understand what you are going through."

"Who are you? Another servant? I have nothing to say to you."

"Indeed I *was* a servant. But no longer." She knelt beside Mariyah. "I was much like you in the beginning. Now I am free to make my own choices. And if you listen to me, you can be too."

"Say what you came to say. Then leave me alone."

"Though I am not permitted to explain everything, I can tell you that you should not be afraid. I know things seem hopeless. But they're not. You were chosen for a reason, Mariyah." She touched Mariyah's cheek, and Mariyah recoiled, albeit weakly. "You are special. More than you realize."

The woman knew her name. "I was not chosen. I was captured."

"True," she conceded. "And I'm sorry for the pain you've suffered. But when I say you were chosen, I don't mean by the brutes in Ralmarstad. You, Mariyah, were chosen by destiny. I admit to playing a small part in this. But then we must play the parts we are given."

"You're insane." Mariyah felt woozy. "Leave me alone."

"Gertrude tells me you are refusing to eat."

Gertrude. The other woman had never given her name. "I will not submit." She was now having trouble keeping her eyes open, and the pain of hunger sharpened.

The woman smiled. "Are all the people of Vylari this stubborn? Or are you unique?"

This *did* get Mariyah's attention. "How do you know—" she began.

"Your captors questioned you prior to your indenture, though I am sure you have no memory of this. An effect of the anklet, I'm afraid."

Mariyah tried to remember but could not recall being

asked anything. But she would have never revealed where she was really from, at least not willingly.

"It was what brought you to my attention." She laughed softly. "If I didn't know better, I would say Kylor brought you to me."

"To the pits with you . . . and Kylor."

"If you think to make me angry, you've missed the mark. Insult him, and me, all you want."

"Then tell me what will. If it will make you leave, I'll say it."

"I know that your pride tells you to be defiant. But if you trust me, and do as I say, I swear that one day you'll be free. Who knows? Maybe you can even return to Vylari."

"You're a liar." If she'd still possessed the strength, she would have lashed out. The anklet sent a wave of pain through her, but it was dulled by starvation.

"Why would I lie? I could simply make you obey. But I won't. In fact, if you really want to die, I will not force you to eat. You can sit here and throw your life away. I won't lift a finger to stop you."

Mariyah regarded her suspiciously. This must be a trick of some kind, one designed to condition her into obedience. Yet with the power of the anklet at their disposal, why would they bother with subtle means?

"How can I trust you?" she demanded. "Someone could be forcing you to lie."

In response, the woman lifted the legs of her trousers. On her left ankle, there was a slight discoloration where an anklet had been. "My name is Trysilia. Like you, I was once falsely convicted. On the spirits of my ancestors, you have my word that I am telling you the truth."

Mariyah gazed up at the woman. She wanted to believe her. More than anything, she needed hope. Part of her rejected the idea that it still existed. But Trysilia knelt down and slipped her arm around her like a mother consoling a frightened child. Mariyah wanted to feel relief, to give in to this embrace, but the memory of Tadrius's initial kindness, so welcome and so false, held her back.

She had no idea how long they remained like this. Trysilia held her, gently rubbing her back until Mariyah felt her body relaxing, despite the anger and fear that still burned within her, her jaw and fists unclenching for the first time in what felt like an eternity.

"Come. You will stay with me in my quarters until we arrive," said Trysilia.

"But what about the Captain?" asked Gertrude, who was still standing outside the door. "He won't allow it. You weren't even supposed to come down here."

"I'll speak with him."

"You know good and well Lady Camdon would not approve."

"Lady Camdon is not here. And I am no longer her servant. Don't worry—you won't be held responsible. I promise."

Whether from a lack of food or the overwhelming torrent of emotion, Mariyah felt suddenly light-headed. She opened her mouth to protest, but nothing came out. She wanted to stay here in the dark, where she could remain hidden. Where she would not be forced to look upon the foulness and horror of this wretched world, and where it could not look upon her. The dizziness increased, and her eyes fluttered as she struggled to keep them open. Her attempts to pull away as Trysilia lifted her to her feet were only in her mind, though; her body no longer had the strength to resist. A moment later everything around her drifted into a faraway haze as darkness enveloped her completely.

14

A SEA OF BLOOD

*Only the hand of the faithful should carry steel meant for
blood. Such a hand is blessed with the gift of righteousness.*
Book of Kylor, **Chapter One Hundred and Two,**
Verse Sixty-Four

L em had heard the boos and hisses from the audience
when they realized the bard they'd all come to see
would not be playing again that evening. He didn't
care. All the same, he pretended to be asleep when Clovis
and the others entered the tent. He was in no mood to explain to them what had happened. In truth, he wasn't even
sure what he would say.

"Well, what do you make of that?" he heard Clovis ask.

"No idea," said Hallis. "You don't think Farley has
hired himself a servant, do you?"

"Could be," said Quinn. "But it doesn't explain why
Lem didn't finish the night. Or why he's sleeping on the
bloody floor."

"Should I wake him?" asked Hallis.

"No, let him sleep. Whatever it is, it can wait until
morning."

"I'm not sure I like the idea of sharing a tent with a
stranger," Clovis said.

"What do you think he'll do?" mocked Quinn. "Look at him. Poor bloke is beaten half to death. He couldn't hurt you if he wanted to."

They talked for a short while longer before going to bed, speaking in whispers and taking care not to make too much noise as they moved around the tent. Lem could only lie there with his eyes shut, unable to banish the awful thought of Mariyah trapped in Lamoria—a world where bartenders hurt you for no reason other than for the sport of it, where someone as old and kind as Shemi was imprisoned and beaten nearly to death. He imagined these horrors and more befalling Mariyah. He wanted to cry out, but resigned himself to silently begging the spirits for help. *You can't save her if your mind is gone,* he told himself repeatedly. *Stay strong. You must. For her sake.*

Somehow, he had to hold onto the belief that Farley was wrong. That there was a way. Even if it ultimately cost him his life, he would never give up. Mariyah had found the courage to come after him. He would not shame her by losing himself to despair.

It was close to dawn before he finally fell asleep, waking only a few hours later. Shemi was still on the cot, eyes now open and gazing at him with an agonized expression. Lem didn't speak for a few moments. He already knew what his uncle wanted to explain. What had happened was written clearly in his eyes, vanquishing all trace of Lem's anger from the night before.

"You couldn't stop her, could you?" he whispered.

"I wanted to," Shemi answered. "But she loves you so much. I could only do my best to keep her safe. And in that I failed. I will never forgive myself."

Sitting up, Lem took his uncle's hand. "I'm the one at fault. I should never have left. I thought I was doing the right thing. I wanted to save Vylari. But I was a coward.

I didn't even have the courage to say goodbye. And now Mariyah is paying for my mistake. Both of you are."

"No, don't think that," Shemi insisted, his voice rising. "You only did what you thought you had to do. It's my fault for not telling you about your father years ago. I just hoped you'd never need to find out."

Lem glanced to check that the others were still sleeping. "We should talk quietly," he warned. "Until I know more about this world, I don't want people knowing about me."

Shemi's voice dropped accordingly. "I understand. Farley asked me about you when he took me to the healer. But I pretended to be too weak to talk."

Lem was coming to realize that he would need a more believable story. That he was a quiet traveler who didn't like to speak of his past had been sufficient when he was on his own, but now that his uncle had been found a prisoner in the Hedran jail, he would have to expand on his story with a few details at least. It was either that or be completely honest. Farley wasn't from Ralmarstad, and so far as Lem could tell had no strong feelings one way or the other about non-believers. But that could change if he thought their presence were a danger to the troupe.

"How did you end up a prisoner?" he asked.

Shemi's expression became grim at the memory. He recounted the events leading to their capture. "The poor man who took us in was not at fault. I still can't believe his own wife betrayed him. What kind of people are these?"

"What happened to Mariyah?"

"I . . . I don't know. We moved around for a while, picking up more prisoners. But we were kept separated." His tears fell uncontrollably and it was almost a full minute before he could speak again. "You have to save her. She was sentenced to life. Some of the others told me how horrible the prisons are. You can't leave her there."

Lem pressed his forehead to Shemi's. "I won't. We'll find her. And if I have to tear down the prison with my bare hands, I'll get her out. Farley's seeing about it now."

"I wouldn't trust him. He's up to something. I saw it in his eyes."

"For now I don't have a choice." Quinn stirred, and they stopped talking for a moment. "You get some more sleep."

Shemi wiped his eyes and settled back into the cot. "Wake me if you learn something."

Lem stood over Shemi and gave him a warm smile. "I promise."

The aroma of porridge and fresh bread drifted in, which meant breakfast was on the way. Finn would be along shortly. Lem checked Farley's tent, but he had already left. On turning back, he found Vilanda standing in his way, both hands planted firmly on her hips.

"I suppose you think you're fooling everyone," she told him.

"I don't know what you mean."

"You think you're going to replace me? Well, you just try it and see what happens."

"I have no idea what you're talking about. I can't act, and I have no desire to try."

She stepped so close their noses were almost touching. "Don't think you can play games with me, boy. I'll watch as your blood stains the ground, and I won't lose a wink of sleep over it. Do you understand me? My husband taught me everything he knew. I can kill you a hundred different ways and no one will suspect a thing."

Lem stepped back a pace. She was serious. But why was she so angry? "I have nothing against you," he said, trying to sound reassuring. "And I'm sure your husband was a fine man. Whatever you think is going on, I promise you're wrong. I'm just here to play music. That's all."

She snorted, then spun on her heels. "You tell that son of a pig he had better come see me. And I mean today."

Lem stood there dumbstruck as Vilanda strode away and ducked inside her tent. What was that all about? He'd never so much as had a conversation with Vilanda that lasted for more than a few seconds. What did she imagine he was doing? As much as he racked his brain, no answers were forthcoming.

Back in his tent, Clovis and Quinn were sitting at the table, waiting for Finn to arrive. Hallis was sitting on his cot, thumbing through a book.

Clovis eyed him curiously. "So now that you're back, do you mind telling us why you left last night? And who is that on your cot?"

Shemi had fallen back to sleep.

"He's my uncle," Lem explained, taking a seat at the table. "He came looking for me and got himself into a bit of trouble. Farley helped me free him."

Clovis looked at him incredulously. "*Farley* helped you? You're not serious."

"Of course I am."

"Farley doesn't help anyone," said Hallis. "You can bet whatever he did, he'll expect ten times more in return."

"Hey. Maybe he really is a bard," offered Quinn, smirking. "Farley might be trying to get into his good graces."

"If I were a bard, would I need his help?" Lem pointed out. "I *will* say that I understand why they refuse to come here."

"You won't get any argument on that from me," agreed Quinn. "I'd pray to Kylor to get us the blazes out of here, but I might get arrested for blasphemy."

"Don't start," said Hallis.

Quinn chuckled. "What? If you think it's so great, why did you leave?"

Hallis stiffened. "That's enough."

Lem could see that the exchange was upsetting Hallis. But Quinn seemed to enjoy it.

"Don't worry," said Clovis, joining in. "We won't turn you in."

"Turn him in?" said Lem.

"Our dear friend Hallis," Clovis explained. "A while back he had the temerity to wed a woman from . . . where was it again?"

"Ur Minosa," said Quinn, before Hallis could reply.

Clovis raised a finger and gave an exaggerated nod. "That's right. Ur Minosa. Left the church for her, yes?"

"This isn't funny," snapped Hallis.

He looked worried, though Lem had no idea why. "Why should that matter?" he asked.

"Are you serious?" laughed Clovis. "You know what they do to apostates?"

Hallis leaned in, his voice a hissing whisper. "Are you wanting to get me killed? *Shut your mouth.*"

"Young Lem won't turn you in," said Quinn. "Will you?"

"Of course not," he replied, smiling over to Hallis. "I think you should be free to marry whoever you want."

"Spoken like a true heretic," said Clovis, rocking back and slapping his knees. "He hates it when we make sport of his blasphemous union."

"Then you shouldn't," said Lem. "Not if he's your friend."

Quinn cocked his head. "Aren't you the considerate one?" After a moment, his posture deflated. "I suppose you're right. We'll just have to pick on him for being an insufferable bookworm."

Hallis still looked agitated, but this only lasted a short time.

"You should be careful not to stay in Farley's debt," said Clovis, returning to their original topic. "I know you think he's your friend, but I've known the man for five years. He never does anything from kindness alone. If he's helping you, there's a reason."

"I'll remember that," said Lem.

Lem was not so naïve as to think that Farley was acting from pure altruism. He was offering his help because he knew it would earn him gold in the end. Of that there was no doubt. Even so, it was surprising to hear the others speak so harshly. Why did they have such a low opinion of their employer?

Finn arrived a short time later with their breakfast. He looked fearfully at Shemi, staying as far away from the cot as possible.

"It's okay," Lem assured him. "He's my friend."

Finn was eyeing Shemi's exposed ankle. "Is he . . . you know . . . a prisoner? From the Hedran?"

Lem frowned. The others were taking notice of the anklet as well.

"My father says anyone brought in front of the Hedran should be killed."

"Then your father is an idiot," said Lem.

"Easy, Lem," said Clovis. "You can't blame the boy for believing what his father tells him."

Calming himself, Lem looked Finn in the eye. "I want you to listen to me carefully. Shemi wouldn't harm a soul. He's as kind and gentle as anyone you're ever likely to meet. Understand?" He shooed the boy to the exit. "Now bring another bowl and more bread. He'll be hungry when he wakes up."

With a final suspicious glance at Shemi, Finn scampered away.

"It's going to be like that until we leave Ralmarstad, so

you'd better get used to it," said Quinn. "But I do have to ask, what did your uncle do to get arrested? And by the Hedran, no less."

"His only crime is not being a follower of Kylor," Lem said defiantly.

Quinn nodded. "Well, around here that would do it." Seeing Lem's rising anger, he held up his palms. "Makes no difference to me. Believe in whatever you want. I don't see how it's any of the Archbishop's business what people do in their own homes anyway."

"If it makes no difference, then why ask?"

"What he means is," Clovis chipped in, "things are not the same here. Look, Lem. I know your past is some big secret. But it's obvious you're not from Ralmarstad. Just be careful. The Archbishop tolerates us because we provide something the people want. But make no mistake—cause any problems and they'd lock you up in an instant. The Hedran is not a thing to be taken lightly."

Lem had no idea why people would hate someone else for their beliefs, or lack thereof. Clearly he didn't fully understand Ralmarstad ways. But one thing was certain—he wanted to leave it behind as soon as possible. "Why come here at all, then?"

"Are you kidding?" said Hallis. "Gold. You make twice as much here as you can in the north."

Gold. Everything in Lamoria revolved around it. It seemed to Lem fouler than magic. And yet without it, nothing he wanted could happen. Mariyah could not be saved. Shemi would still be in prison. And he would still be trapped in Harver's Grove.

Conversation turned to more mundane topics while they finished breakfast, though Hallis did make a point to once more impress upon Lem the importance of not revealing that he had left the church.

Clovis told Lem that they would be spending the day shopping for a few personal items, and invited him to come along. Lem politely refused, explaining that he needed to be there when Shemi woke. It was good to see their accepting attitudes, though. It was becoming increasingly apparent that the primary dispute among people had to do with the worship of Kylor and little else. More than ever, he felt the urgency to educate himself on the subject.

Shemi stirred just as Finn appeared with the additional breakfast, still with a wary look in his eye. Lem groaned in frustration when the boy was unwilling to come within a few feet of his uncle.

"You'd think one that young wouldn't be so afraid of unfamiliar things," Shemi remarked under his breath, once Finn was gone.

"Youthful ignorance," said Lem.

Shemi rolled over on his side. "I don't think that's the reason. People in this world have strange ideas. More and more I think the stories we were taught are true. That the barrier was created for our own protection."

"From what I've seen, so do I."

Shemi's face was still badly bruised, and his arms and hands were riddled with cuts and scrapes. But he was at least able to stand and walk.

For a few hours they sat and talked. Lem spoke about what had happened to him since departing Vylari, leaving out most of his experiences with Durst. He didn't want Shemi knowing how close he had come to cold-blooded murder. But as always, his uncle could see straight through him and knew he was holding something back.

"I suppose you'll have to tell me everything that happened another time," he said.

Lem felt guilty for not confiding in the old man. But with everything else happening around him, his heart

230 · BRIAN D. ANDERSON

could not bear more. He did tell him the vision the stranger had shown him, which helped Shemi better understand his reason for leaving.

"Strange," said Shemi. "Shortly after crossing the barrier, Mariyah began having nightmares. She couldn't remember many details, but she did say there was fire and death all around her. And a voice."

This was indeed curious, but if it was important, there was no way of knowing. The questions continued to mount, but no answers were forthcoming. It was maddening.

"Do you have any idea where they would have taken her?"

"No." Shemi's mouth twitched as if the memory caused him physical pain. "None of us were told where we were going."

They both sat in despondent, hopeless silence for a time.

Shemi eventually reached over and placed his hand on Lem's. "Maybe the Thaumas can help us. They wield magic, after all."

"Yes," agreed Lem. "Maybe they can help."

It was early afternoon when Farley appeared, his expression grim.

Lem leapt from his seat. "Did you find her?"

"Yes and no," Farley responded. "The girl you're after was indentured to a wealthy noble. But I couldn't find out to whom or where she was taken."

"Indentured?" cried Lem.

"It gets worse. Her sentence was life. Which means someone paid an enormous amount of gold for her release. Even if you find out where she is, it would take a king's fortune to free her." Seeing Lem's growing despair, he placed a hand on his shoulder. "She was spared prison. Wherever she ended up, it's better than that. Mostly they become household staff and the like, serving out their sentences in relative comfort. Believe me, it's far better than a filthy cell and back-breaking labor."

"Is there any way to find out where she is?" asked Lem.

"None that I know of," replied Farley. "Records are kept with the city magistrate only for a few days, then turned over to the church. Unless you have connections within the clergy, you won't get far. And the last thing a foreigner wants is to start poking around, drawing attention to themselves. I hope you can appreciate the risk I took just making a simple inquiry."

"I'm sorry," said Lem. "I don't mean to sound ungrateful. But I can't just forget about her. Whatever I have to do to find her, I'll do it. There has to be a way."

Farley stepped back, head bowed in thought. "There might be." He turned to Shemi. "Wait for me in my tent."

Without the slightest hesitation or objection, Shemi did as instructed. Lem watched him go, stunned by his compliance. Particularly considering they were discussing Mariyah's fate.

"He has no choice but to obey," said Farley, noticing his reaction. "The magic of the anklet compels him. And what I have to say, you might wish to be kept private."

The idea of Shemi being forced into submission by magic was deeply disturbing. He thought of the lore he'd been taught growing up—that Lamorians had taken magic and twisted it, that they'd become greedy with power and used it for unnatural horrors. Compelling others through an anklet certainly qualified as an unnatural horror in Lem's book.

Farley took a seat, waiting for Lem to do the same before he continued. "As I told you before, even if you find her, the cost would be enormous. Much more than you could afford, I'm afraid. And the more time that passes, the more expensive it will be. Ralmarstad nobles take great pride in the way their servants are trained. The longer she's

232 · BRIAN D. ANDERSON

there and the more she learns, the more valuable she'll be. And before you go thinking you can somehow sneak away with her, remember the anklet. Any attempt to flee will kill her. And I hear it's an extremely painful way to die."

"There has to be some way to remove it."

"Sure there is. Convince the owner of the anklet to take it off. Other than that, no."

Lem's despondency was increasing with each word Farley spoke. "But you said there *was* a way to free her."

"Yes, perhaps. Now, understand I still have no idea how to find her. But I might at least have a way you could make enough gold to pay the debt." He leaned back in his chair, his expression becoming unsettlingly dark. "But it depends on what you're willing to do."

"If it means saving Mariyah, I'll do anything."

"Even kill?"

For a moment Lem thought he had misheard. "Kill?" he repeated. "Who?"

"Whoever I tell you to," Farley replied flatly. "It's all perfectly legal, I assure you. I have a license from the Order of the Red Star."

"You mean it's legal to murder?" Never could he imagine such a fiendish thing.

Farley sighed. "Seeing as how you seem so determined to keep your past a secret from me, I was hoping to avoid this. But if you're going to keep up the deception, you really do need to learn more about our ways. This isn't Vylari."

A violent spasm of fear ran through Lem, triggering an involuntary cough. His eyes darted to the exit.

"Calm down," said Farley. "Your secret is safe with me."

"H-how did you find out?"

"You can thank dear Uncle Shemi for that. And before you blame him, know that he didn't have any choice but to tell me. And he doesn't even remember doing it. Fantastic magic, I have to admit. I can even order him to forget, and he does it instantly."

Lem took a moment to compose himself. Farley had known the entire time about Mariyah. Even before bringing Shemi to the tent, he had already been crafting a plan. The rest was nothing but an act: the surprised way he'd reacted to Lem's professed love, the way he'd pretended to not know who Shemi really was. All of it. What else did he know? Mariyah's location, perhaps? His desperation was steadily being offset by anger. Had he been duped from the very beginning? As impossible as it seemed, he began to wonder if this was the whole reason behind Farley's efforts to save him from the clutches of Zara. And Durst's murder . . . a test to see if he would kill? If so, he had failed. "And if I refuse?"

Farley flicked his hand dismissively. "Then you play music for the rest of your life, and your fiancée remains bound to serve whoever it was that paid for her release." His tone then changed, taking on a sinister quality. "But you won't say no. Shemi told me that too. He says you'd do anything to free her. You would navigate across a sea of blood to save your precious love. Oh, you'll do it all right. And I'll be your guiding star."

With a rush, Lem could understand why the others had been so adamant about not trusting their employer. "Why me?"

"Why not you?"

"Because I'm not a killer."

At this, a smile slowly stretched across Farley's face. "Not yet. But like I told you back in Harver's Grove: There's one in you somewhere. I can feel it."

Lem lowered his head, hands folded on the table. Could he do this? Was Farley right about him? "How could such a thing be legal?"

"It's a gray area, more like. But in most kingdoms, it's not the assassin who is held accountable, it's whoever paid the contract. Of course, should an assassin be caught, they must either provide proof of the contract or accept responsibility. This is where groups like the Order of the Red Star come in. To be a member means you're willing to sacrifice yourself for the good of the Order."

"What happens if you're caught and you show them the contract?"

He gave Lem a tight-lipped grin. "Let's just say it doesn't turn out well for the assassin. Trust and discretion are the foundations upon which the Order was built. People come to us because they know their identity is secure. Otherwise, it would all fall to pieces. And I promise you, that will *not* be permitted to happen."

The memory of Durst kneeling helpless on the ground, begging for his life invaded Lem's thoughts. He had come close, admittedly. But that was in the heat of anger. This would be different. This would be murder for gold. He would be killing someone who had done him no harm. It was hard to imagine a more wicked deed.

"How would it work?" Was he really going to go through with it? With each question he asked, the answer was coming closer to yes.

"I'm a member of the Order," said Farley. "You're not. So the contracts will come through me, and I in turn give them to you. It's much safer that way."

Safer for whom? he wondered. "There's something I want to know. When you came to me that night in Harver's Grove, was this what you had planned?"

"It was a thought," admitted Farley. "I'm in need of a replacement. So my eyes have been open. But with you I was genuinely interested in your talent as a musician. The troupe was not doing as well as I liked. For me to conduct my . . . other business, I need it to thrive."

Replacement? Suddenly it all fell into place. "Vilanda," he said. "That's why she accused me of trying to replace her."

"Very perceptive," replied Farley, his usual friendly manner returning in a blink. "Her husband worked for me for a few years, and after he died, she took over. But I'm afraid she's not as careful as he was. The last few times it's nearly come back to me. I can't have that."

"So she was right."

Farley nodded. "You could say that. I was going to replace her regardless, though. So fortune seems to have smiled on me. On both of us, in fact."

"And Shemi? What about him?"

Farley shrugged. "My interest is in you. Once his debt is paid, you can do whatever you want with him."

"If I agree, he's never to know."

"I understand completely. You think I'd want my mother knowing the things *I've* done?"

Lem ran his fingers through his hair. The tempest of emotions raging through him—doubt, fear, anger—made him want to flee from the tent and never look back. But there was a hard truth to face. What Shemi told Farley was right: There was nothing he wouldn't do to save Mariyah. Like Farley said, he *would* navigate over a sea of blood . . . even if it was one he had created himself. His love for her overcame all other considerations, even his own soul.

"I'll do it." The words came out as if spoken by someone else. The consequences of his choice were unknowable, though he was certain it would lead him down a path that would irrevocably change him.

Farley reached over and gave his arm a fond slap. "I

knew you would. Trust me, you've made the right decision."

"What about Vilanda?"

"Let me worry about her. For now, just continue playing for the crowd and keep them entertained. I'll let you know when it's time." He stood and turned to the exit. "Oh, and one more thing, Lem. I was being serious about needing to learn our ways."

Lem stared after him, the panic of discovery still churning in his stomach. The look he had seen in Farley's eyes increased his unease. It suggested that he was more than a little pleased about learning his secret, and the reason was not hard to guess. This knowledge gave Farley power. Lem was now under his control every bit as much as if he too were wearing an anklet.

Shemi returned a short time later. "I hate this thing," he remarked, rubbing his ankle. "You have no idea what it's like to not be in control."

Yes, I do, Lem thought bitterly.

15

HOPE AND PORRIDGE

It takes not a firm hand but a gentle touch and a soft kiss to
bring the hopeless back into the light.
Book of Kylor, Chapter Five, Verse Twenty-Six

The sweet scent of wine mingling with the salty air
invited Mariyah to open her eyes. She had been
having that dream again, of the man and the mist.
He had been saying something that had seemed quite urgent, though what it might have been was lost in a groggy
haze.

Her vision was blurred as she woke, and she was conscious only of the soft warmth of a proper bed—a sensation she had thought she'd never feel again. As the world
came more into focus, she could see that she was in a small
cabin, not much larger than the one she had previously
occupied, although that was where any similarity between
them ended. A square table to her left had been positioned
beside a round window that let in glorious daylight. There
was a wooden chest and a dresser, though this was all the
room could hold and still allow for free movement. Trysilia
was sitting beside the bed, sipping on a glass of wine while
reading a book. She smiled when she noticed that Mariyah
had awakened.

"I assume you're hungry?" she said.

Mariyah nodded, then tried to rise.

Trysilia gestured for her to be still. "Not until you've recovered your strength. We still have a week before we arrive."

"Where are we going?"

"Ubania."

Mariyah noticed a bowl and cup on the nightstand. As she reached out, she found her hand trembling.

Taking the bowl, Trysilia fed Mariyah a spoonful of thick porridge. "Not the best fare, but I was afraid you wouldn't be able to handle anything too rich after starving yourself for so long. Though the cuisine aboard ship, even at its best, is somewhat lacking."

Mariyah said nothing, though she allowed Trysilia to feed her the entire bowl. While it was not by any standards appetizing, Mariyah felt some of her strength return.

"I have to ask that you remain in the cabin unless I'm with you," Trysilia said. "The captain is not the most understanding of men. I paid him well for you to be housed in my quarters, but he would be quite upset if you were to wander around the ship alone. Strictly speaking, you're still a prisoner of the Hedran until we arrive."

Mariyah slowly nodded her acceptance of this condition. What other choice did she have? "Can you tell me something about where we're going?"

"Ubania is one of two city-states that are controlled by the Archbishop."

"Is it true the laws are different elsewhere?"

"Yes. Beyond Ralmarstad, Kylorian law is only enforced in Ubania and Gothmora. The Archbishop has no power over other nations."

"But where we're going, he does?"

"Yes. But Lady Camdon is far too powerful a noble to

be intimidated. You'll live more or less a normal life, free to worship as you choose."

"I don't worship anything."

"Is that right? Interesting."

"Why is that interesting?"

"Little is known about Vylari," she explained. "Most don't believe it exists."

"Vylari was created to protect us from the evils of Lamoria." Mariyah chose not to mention the barrier. She was not ready to give this woman her trust, despite her apparent kindness. It was possible, she knew, that those who imprisoned her had found out when she was questioned. Either way, best to say nothing, at least for now.

"I think it's important you know that what you've seen is not representative of most of the world. Only in Ralmarstad are the cruelties you've experienced permitted. But there will be time for weighty subjects once you've regained your strength. For now, please rest. We can talk more later."

Mariyah wanted to protest. The time for weighty subjects was right now, as far as she was concerned. But her stomach was full for the first time in quite a while, and her eyes felt impossibly heavy. Everything Trysilia was saying might be a lie, of course. She might be playing some vicious game. There was no way to know for certain. But for now, at least, she felt safe. She closed her eyes, and for the first time since leaving Vylari, sleep came easily.

16

A NEAR MISS

As Kylor stood atop the stone, a wrathful man threw himself on the ground before him and wept. "I have committed evil deeds. Made others suffer. Is there no redemption?"

Kylor looked upon the man and his soul was revealed. "Your regret is without conviction. Should I release you of your pain, you would only cause harm again. Evil absent repentance is beyond redemption."

Book of Kylor, Chapter Thirty-Seven,
Verses Seven and Eight

Taking Farley's advice, Lem sought out the library the following day. Located not far from the tailor's shop, it was set along one side of a massive, busy square that was tiled with red stone and featured two marble fountains near the center between which were benches large enough for four people to sit comfortably. The square was teeming with people, some congregating in small groups, others streaming in or passing through from all directions.

The library building itself was equally impressive—gleaming white marble with a broad colonnade stretching across its face. Lem could not fail to notice an enormous, all-seeing eye surrounded by a host of strange symbols carved into the façade directly overhead. Runes of some sort, he speculated, though where they came from or what they said was a mystery.

Beyond the threshold, Lem found himself in a large foyer. Here the vaulted ceiling had been painted to resemble the night sky, with a crystal chandelier affixed to a silver base where one would expect the moon to be. The floor was of green-and-red marble and boasted a number of elaborately woven carpets. On the wall hung various paintings and tapestries, the scenes and people depicted entirely unfamiliar. Lem assumed they were Lobin events and citizens of some importance. At the rear stood an oblong table where a young woman in light blue robes with a pair of silver chevrons on each sleeve was seated.

Only days ago, he would have been totally awed by the magnificence of the décor; now it held nothing more than a passing interest. Not even the great towers had caught his eye on the way here. His mind was fixed on one thing.

The woman at the table barely looked up while directing him to the main library, without giving so much as a nod of acknowledgment when he thanked her for the assistance.

The halls he passed along were as wide as some streets, all of them cleaned and polished to a mirror shine. More art hung from the walls, though again the imagery was foreign. Most people he encountered were clad in robes similar to that of the woman in the foyer, the chevrons on their sleeves varying in number and a few with a silver star stitched over the left side of their chest—a sign of rank or position, Lem presumed.

The scale of the building was tremendous. The thought that a library could be this massive was dizzying. But upon making a wrong turn and finding himself in the Office of Licensing and Commerce, he realized that this was more than just a library. It housed the entire bureaucracy of Lobin.

After a few more wrong turns he reached a tall archway. Passing through, in spite of his single-minded purpose, Lem caught his breath. To his right was a large oak desk, where an older woman was running her finger across the pages of a heavy leather tome. But it was what lay beyond that left him in stunned amazement. Row after row of shelves climbed nearly to the ceiling, all of them packed with books. Thousands of them. Tens of thousands. And two levels of mezzanine gave access to still more shelves against the wall.

Men and women, some wearing the same official robes he'd seen before, others in common attire, were seated at small round tables at the end of each row. Lem smiled. His uncle would break down weeping at the sight of this, he thought. If he ever brought Shemi here, he doubted he could convince him to leave. There were more books in this one room than there were in the whole of Vylari. The sum of knowledge they contained must be staggering.

"Can I help you?" The woman at the desk had folded her hands and was smiling over to him.

"Yes, please. I need books on history."

The woman lifted her brow. "History? I'm afraid you'll need to be a little more specific."

Lem thought for a moment. "I suppose something that you would use to teach a child."

She gave an understanding nod. "Trying to educate your little ones?"

"Yes," he lied. "I thought this would be the best place to start."

"Wonderful. Are you a scholar?"

"No. But I enjoy reading." This was also a lie.

Reaching into a drawer, the woman produced a slip of

paper and began writing. "It's good to see a parent wanting better for their children," she said. "There's far too much ignorance in the world. The Lord of Creation gave us minds as a gift, you know. It's a pity people rarely use them." She held out the paper. "These should be good for a child. Assuming they can read."

"Oh, yes. Quite well, in fact."

"That's definitely a step in the right direction."

On the paper she had written five titles, each with a series of numbers beside it. Lem frowned at these. "Please forgive me, but I've never been in a library before. What does this mean?"

The woman laughed softly. "It can be daunting the first time, particularly for the poorly educated. No insult intended. I think it's grand what you are doing for your . . . son?"

Lem nodded.

She explained that each number signified a row, a subject, and the book's position on the shelf.

"This one will be ten rows down on the left," she told him, pointing to the first book on the list. "I'll let you figure it out from there. When you're finished, don't put them back. Just bring them to the desk."

"Thank you," said Lem.

As he was turning to leave, she remarked, "You know, it's never too late to start learning. Your son isn't the only one who could benefit from knowledge."

Lem smiled back at her. "I'll remember that."

Every shelf was fitted with a ladder attached to a rod at the top spanning its entire length. He watched as people slid these along from side to side to obtain those books out of reach. Brilliant, he thought. And the numbering system was inspired. It took him only a few minutes after reaching the correct row to find the first volume: *A History of Ralmarstad*.

244 · BRIAN D. ANDERSON

After retrieving everything on the list, he found an empty chair at one of the tables and began sifting through the pages. He could see why the woman would recommend these for a child. The language was rudimentary and the details thin. Nevertheless, they were perfect for giving him a better understanding of the world he was now in.

After several hours he felt his back ache, and his vision started to blur. He had made it through one book and was halfway through a second: *Lobin through the Ages*. Shemi would have been able to read them all in a single sitting. A great pity he wasn't able to bring him along.

When it was time to return to the troupe, he did as instructed and brought the books to the desk, thanked the woman for her help, and started to the exit.

"I hope you'll come back," the woman called after him.

"I will," he promised. "First thing tomorrow."

He was as good as his word, and over the next week fell into a routine. After breakfast each day he would spend a few hours at the library, then return to the troupe to tell Shemi what he had learned. His uncle had become quite excited on being told how many books the library held, even suggesting that he might go there himself. However, after approaching Farley on the matter, the idea was quickly squashed as being too risky.

"Indentures don't walk about freely," Farley explained. "We'll be leaving Ralmarstad in a few months. He'll be able to do as he pleases then."

Aside from all manner of mundane tasks, Shemi's regular duties involved helping Finn to keep the troupe fed and their clothes washed. He didn't seem to resent this. Indeed, he said that he wanted to contribute so not to be a burden. And after a few days, Finn had stopped looking at Shemi as if he were liable to launch an attack at any moment.

Lem's fame in Lobin had spread, and now the square was filled to capacity every night. Such was the size of the crowds that the city guard was sent to keep order, though there had not yet been any serious disturbances. And though he did nothing to encourage it, most of the citizens genuinely believed him to be a bard, a fact that Farley relished.

"I'll have enough gold to free Shemi in no time," Lem told him after a particularly good night.

"You'll have to wait until we leave Ralmarstad for that," Farley responded. "There's no sense in freeing him until then. It's not like he can just wander around. Don't worry, we'll sort it out. Besides, he's not begging to leave, so what difference does it make?"

"I think it makes a difference to Shemi," Lem countered. "And I know it does to me." This was the first time he had argued with Farley. He was expecting him to be put out, but all he did was smile.

"I understand how you feel. But think about this. By the time you have the gold, we'll be out of Ralmarstad, or at least very nearly. If I free Shemi, all I can do is pass over control of the anklet. Otherwise there will be an inquiry as to why he's being released early. Too much attention. Do you really want to *control* your uncle?" Farley slapped him on the shoulder. "Just be patient, lad."

Lem wasn't entirely convinced that what Farley said was true. At the same time, he didn't yet understand the laws well enough to contradict him. He was a slow reader, and given the vast amount of information he was still wading through each morning, it could be some time yet before he could accumulate enough knowledge to fully understand the laws that governed the land.

He had learned that beyond the provinces of Bulvidar, Dumora, Galidor, Thrisia, and Ur Gathswan, which

246 · BRIAN D. ANDERSON

made up Ralmarstad, as well as two of the Trudonian city-states, Ubania and Gothmora, on the north shores of the Sea of Mannan, those who did not follow Kylor were not looked upon as heretics. The High Cleric did not possess the same power and influence as did the Archbishop. Beyond Ralmarstad, the church was subject to the rule of the monarchy and courts of the land. Not to say that the High Cleric was not powerful, being considered by the faithful to be the manifestation of Kylor's voice and will, but very limited by comparison.

Where the Church of Kylor had once been a single entity, this was changed during the Ralmarstad civil war, which broke out in the midst of a long and brutal famine. The High Cleric, helpless to do anything to alleviate the suffering, begged the people to have faith that Kylor would help them. He promised that soon the rains would return, and the crops would grow once again. Each day he would kneel in front of the temple steps for all to see and pray for mercy.

But as time passed and more people perished, it became clear that the High Cleric's prayers had gone unheeded. It was in this most desperate of hours that an ambitious cleric named Rupardo Trudoux declared the state of suffering to be an act of Kylor, a punishment on Ralmarstad for the kingdom's heretical ways. Moreover, he blamed the High Cleric directly for allowing the heresy to fester. Thousands flocked to his banner. The result was a bloody uprising, and the queen and High Cleric were both exiled. The High Cleric retreated to Xancartha, establishing it as a new holy city where he continued to guide the religion of Kylor in peaceful worship. The queen, sadly, was later captured and executed by the Hedran.

The more Lem read, the more he came to realize that everything led back to the Archbishop. Nothing was done without church approval. Most books on the subject Lem read incessantly praised the Archbishop, claiming the True Church was chiefly responsible for the peace enjoyed since the war that shattered the kingdom, though to call it peace was misleading. Several wars had been waged against the nations who refused to, as it was phrased in one particularly biased volume, *give themselves over to the true word of Kylor*. Which basically included any kingdom outside of Ralmarstad. Each war ended in stalemate, the most recent being fifty years past.

As far as information on the current High Cleric, Lem had yet to find anything significant. Though the reason for this could have been that he had simply not found it yet among the thousands of books and it was still waiting to be discovered, he thought it likely that, given the way the histories were written to be favorable to the Archbishop, they had been omitted from the library entirely.

Shemi had been appalled by this when Lem told him. The thought of burying knowledge was unimaginable. But when he mentioned it to Farley, his reaction was predictably dismissive.

"What do you expect? The Archbishop doesn't tolerate dissent. And nothing fosters rebellion like knowledge. Keep them ignorant. No easier way to stay in power."

The truth of his words was inescapable, and ultimately Lem resigned himself to the fact that what he learned would be strongly biased until they left Ralmarstad behind.

He and Vilanda had barely spoken since Shemi's arrival. Whether this was due to Farley interceding or her dismissing the notion that she was being replaced, he didn't know. Though he caught her staring at him with clear disdain from time to time, he was too overcome with concern about Mariyah and the Thaumas to spare any energy toward worrying about her as well.

It was the end of Lem's second week in Lobin when things changed. He had just finished his performance and was in his tent when Farley arrived, carrying a folded parchment with a wax seal bearing the imprint of a five-pointed star. The symbol of the Order of the Red Star. The final play was still in progress, and Shemi, as had become a usual routine, was gathering up the brooms and brushes for cleaning the stage. They were alone.

"It's time," Farley said, handing over the parchment. "Once you break the seal, there's no turning back. The contract is yours, and only you can fulfill it."

Lem looked down at the lump of wax as if it might leap up and bite him. "What happens if I don't open it?"

"Then I'll give it to Vilanda."

"And if I fail?"

"That would be unfortunate. For both of us."

Lem held the document up to the lamp, but could not see what was written. "What do you mean by *only I can fulfill it*?"

"Precisely that. Once the seal is broken, you are bound."

"You mean I have no choice in the matter?"

"None other than death. Should you change your mind about accepting the assignment after breaking the seal, you will die."

More magic, Lem thought. And magic just as malevolent and cruel as the anklet. He was coming to understand why those who had founded Vylari had shunned its use. That the people of Lamoria could so easily embrace it was a testament to their brutality.

"On the bright side, not all contracts are like this," Farley added. "It's just that seeing as how you're untested, the client insisted. It costs more, but it guarantees success. Once you've established a reputation, it won't be necessary. Vilanda's husband, Travis, rarely had to do these kind of assignments. Though he didn't mind, given that they pay more."

Lem took a deep, cleansing breath. He had already come to terms with the fact that he would become a killer, so why should this deadly clause make any difference? But it did, all the same. He had already lost so much control over his own life. This was giving up even more.

As if to firm his resolve, an image of Mariyah rose in his mind. She was alone, she was being held captive, and it was his fault. If he didn't do this, he would be sealing her fate. That was more than enough to press him on.

Holding up the contract, he gripped the seal between his thumb and forefinger. There was a loud pop as he applied pressure, followed by a soft hiss. The seal dissolved into a small puff of red smoke that shot straight up into Lem's nostrils. He tried to turn away, but it was too late. The bargain was made. He sat there for a long moment, rubbing his nose. Though odorless, the smoke had caused a terrible itching. But this only lasted for a few seconds.

"I know how hard that was for you," said Farley. "But you made the right decision. In the end, you'll see."

"How long do I have?"

"As long as you need. The binding spell isn't set to a specific time. However, it knows your intent. If you change your mind and decide to let the target live, it will know."

Lem frowned. Farley made it sound as if magic had a mind of its own. Perhaps it did. Perhaps magic was nothing more than some evil spirit sent to plague the world, used by sinister forces to bend others to their purpose. But then again, was it not also a kind of magic that protected Vylari? Suddenly, he felt very small and weak, helpless against the ferocious malice of the world. All those around him seemed to know so much, while he knew next to nothing.

He opened the parchment and looked at its contents. *Lord Brismar Gulan*. Beneath the name was written: *4371 King's Crown. North Lobin.*

"A noble lord on your first kill," remarked Farley. He could not see what was written from his vantage point, so obviously he already knew the contents of the contract. "A real stroke of luck. You get two gold for your share."

A surge of disappointment rose. "Only two? I thought you said . . ."

"You work under me," Farley explained. "And before you start thinking to get your own contracts and cut me out, remember two things. One: Your uncle is indentured to me. And two: I know who you are . . . and where you're from."

Lem's sense of disappointment was overcome by a flash of anger. "If you tell anyone about Vylari, I'll . . ." His voice trailed off. What would he—no—what *could* he do? Farley had hinted that Vylari's location would be of great interest to the Archbishop. Lem had repeatedly explained that it could not be found, to which Farley would shrug and say that it wouldn't prevent them from trying to pry the information out of him in a most excruciating way.

"Don't worry, lad. I'm sure I'll never need to reveal your secrets. Just do your part and all will be well."

The friendly smile on his face; the kindness he showed by rescuing him from Zara; even his help releasing Shemi—it had all been leading to this. Despite Farley's denials, Lem felt certain that this was what he'd intended all along. From the moment he walked into Zara's tavern, the wheels had been set in motion.

"What do I do now?" he asked.

Farley spread his hands. "How should I know? You're the assassin. But I suggest that you acquaint yourself with where he lives. That seems like a logical place to start." He stood and moved toward the exit.

"Can I ask you a question?" called Lem.

Farley paused. "Of course."

"How did Vilanda's husband die?"

Farley did not answer immediately, head downturned, a barely noticeable smile twitching at the corners of his mouth. "Maybe you should ask *her* that. She was there when it happened. She can tell you all about it."

Once alone, Lem looked at the contract again. He ran his finger over the name. *Lord Brismar Gulan.* Though he said it aloud a few times, it didn't feel as if he were talking about a real person, someone whose fate was sealed. What had he done to deserve death . . . to be murdered?

Shemi arrived a few minutes later, his back bent and looking utterly exhausted.

"That bloody Finn has the energy of ten festival dancers," he said.

Lem jumped up and helped him over to his cot. "What happened?"

"Oh, nothing really. It's just that ever since he got over his fear of me, he insists on us playing every game he knows. It wouldn't be that bad if I didn't have to work so late. But by the time we finish with the stage, I feel like I've been working all day in my garden." His joints cracked in protest as he stretched out. "The boy needs friends his own age, that much I can tell you. Sooner or later, my old bones are going to give out."

"You want me to talk to him?"

"No. I can handle it. He's just lonely. I'll set him straight in a day or so. Anyway, from what Clovis said, we'll be leaving soon." He pulled up the blanket. "And then Finn will be heading back home to his parents."

Lem had been surprised to discover that Finn was not a regular part of the troupe. It turned out that Farley had hired him when they arrived in Lobin. Apparently, it was a habit of his to hire a local child in each city they visited in order to help with the upkeep.

"Farley doesn't like attachments," Quinn had explained. "Particularly when it comes to children. In his mind, it's better to find someone new each time we move on."

Shemi was soon in a deep sleep, allowing Lem to move back to the table. After taking another long look at the name on his contract, he retrieved a knife from his belongings and fastened it to his belt. By now the crowds outside had dispersed. That Clovis, Quinn, and Hallis were not there meant they had decided to go to the tavern.

Stepping from the tent into the night, he heard the sound of shoes scraping against the pavement off to his right.

"So he *did* give it to you. I knew he would."

Standing in the shadows between the tents was Vilanda.

She moved closer, allowing Lem to see her more clearly. Her face was not powdered, and she had already changed out of her stage costume. She was not one for the night life, generally retiring directly to her tent after a performance.

"I'm leaving," she told him.

"I'm sorry to hear that," was all he could think to say.

Vilanda sniffed. "No, you're not. But you should be. You have no idea what you're getting yourself into."

He tried to affect a confused look. "What are you talking about?"

"No need to lie," she said. She didn't appear angry, as he would have expected. In fact, he could swear there was pity in her eyes. "Farley told me he was giving you the contract. I guess I'm not as good as Travis was."

The reference to her husband rekindled Lem's curiosity.

Without thinking, he asked, "How did he die? Farley told me that you were there."

"Of course I was there. I needed to be sure it was done right."

"You're saying that *you* killed him?" he asked, horrified.

"Not with my own hand, no. But I was the one who paid for the contract." She sneered at Lem's reaction. "You think I wanted it? You think I wanted to kill my own husband?"

"Then why?"

Though her expression did not change, a single tear slipped down her cheek. "So that Farley couldn't. I loved my husband too much to let him suffer. I had to know it would be quick and painless. That's why I paid the contract. And that's why I had to be there."

"I don't understand. Why did Farley want him dead?"

"Does it matter? All you need to know is that Farley is not the man you think he is. If you stay with him, he'll eventually kill you."

"Is that why you're leaving? Because he wants you dead?"

"I doubt he cares enough to bother killing me," she replied. "No, I'm leaving because I can't watch it happen again." She stepped in close and placed a hand against his cheek. "So young. So many experiences ahead. Don't let him take it from you. Get out while you still can."

She turned and began walking away, but stopped after a few steps. "You could leave with me if you wanted. You could pack your things and forget all about this place. There are other troupes. Better than this one."

The offer took him aback. The sincerity in her voice was genuine. "I'm sorry," he said. "I can't."

She let out a mirthless laugh. "You've already broken the seal, haven't you? Too bad. You have a true gift. If you

254 · BRIAN D. ANDERSON

want to know the real reason I'm leaving, it's so I don't have to watch you become like Travis. *He* was gifted too." She removed something from the folds of her sleeve and placed it on the ground. "This was my husband's vysix blade. I considered using it on you tonight." She started once more to walk away. "One day you might wish that I had."

This time she did not stop. Lem watched as she vanished around the last tent, her words seizing him to the core. She had come to kill him. What had changed her mind? Why had Farley wanted her husband dead? And if what she said was true, why had she chosen to take his place?

So many questions were rattling around inside Lem's head, but he knew it was pointless to dwell on them. He could not have gone with Vilanda even if she had told him the answers. It didn't make any difference if Farley was the wickedest man alive. No matter what she revealed to him, it would not have released him from Farley's influence. Nor would it have freed Shemi . . . or saved Mariyah.

He picked up the blade she had left. The scabbard was made from dull black leather with no ornamentation whatsoever. The handle was black also, and when he pulled it free, so was the blade. This was the weapon of an assassin. Of that there was no question. Returning it to the scabbard, he shoved it into his belt. Unlike the knife he had brought with him, this was a blade that had taken lives. It made his skin crawl to have it pressed against his waist. How many had already felt its touch? Yet another question without an answer. One thing was certain: However many it was, that number would be increasing by one.

Finding Lord Brismar Gulan's home proved to be a simple matter of merely asking a bartender near the north end of the city. He thought perhaps this was not the best idea, given that he was about to murder him, but he had timed it quite well. The bartender answered his question while in a rush to serve an unhappy patron on the other end and only glanced at Lem for the briefest of moments. If asked about it later, it was highly unlikely that he would be able to accurately describe who had made the inquiry. Still, there had to be a better way of locating future targets, one that didn't risk exposure.

From the shadows on the other side of the street, Lem regarded the three-story building to which he had been directed, where Gulan resided on the top floor. At ground level there were several shops and on the second floor another residence. A narrow stairwell situated between a jeweler and a haberdashery led to the upper levels, though this was blocked off by an iron gate and guarded by two surly-looking men wearing swords. A balcony spanned the front and right sides of the top two floors, the lights in the windows of which were all dimmed. A narrow alley to the right of the building was barred by a tall fence, but another on the left was open.

The guards were leaning casually on the wall, passing a bottle between them. Though they didn't seem to be particularly vigilant about their duty, Lem did not want to risk being seen. Instinctively, he felt the tingle of the shadow walk. Only a few people were about. Nonetheless, he needed to time it carefully. If someone happened to look directly at him, the guards might notice his crossing.

His heart felt like it was trying to pound its way out through his ribs. Only by tightly gripping the hilts of his knife and the vysix blade was he able to keep his hands from trembling. *You should wait,* he warned himself. *Find out something about this man first.* The desire to have this over and done with was making him act impulsively. Gulan might not even be at home. Or there might not be a way in, even if he did succeed in getting past the guards.

He started to turn back. After all, there was no set time. He could wait. He *should* wait.

But you're not going to.

Stupid, stupid, stupid!

In a sudden rush, he burst into a dead run, straight for the open alley. The guards did not look up. To their eyes he was nothing but the dimmest shade, gone before it was noticed. Once out of their view, he pressed his back to the wall and gulped for air, his head swimming.

Don't pass out. Keep moving.

A part of him hoped he wouldn't find a way into the top apartment and that he would be forced to turn back. But a drainpipe on the far corner dashed this hope. It was an easy climb. And just a short distance from the pipe, he could see a window. Perhaps it was locked? If so, he would then have the perfect reason to call things off for the night.

The slick surface of the pipe made for a harder climb than he'd anticipated. Even so, and to his disappointment, it was not so difficult as to stop him from drawing level with his objective.

He stepped warily onto the ledge. The window opened outward and had no handle to grip, and white curtains prevented him from seeing inside. Very carefully, he removed the knife from his belt and pushed it between the edge of the window and the frame. At first there was no movement. He pressed harder on the knife handle, his other hand still wrapped around the drainpipe for balance. Such was the pressure he was exerting, the blade bent under the force. He heard tiny pops and cracks as the wood started to splinter. Encouraged, he pressed harder still.

All at once the window flew open. Surprised, he let the knife slip from his grasp, and he felt himself teetering precariously backward. Only by some marvel of balance did he manage to snag hold of the frame's upper lip, preventing what would have likely been a fatal fall. The clatter of steel hitting the hard slates below echoed loudly through the alley.

Knowing this might draw the guards to investigate, panic seized him, and abandoning all caution, he threw himself inside. Curtains quickly wrapped themselves around his body and over his head, leaving him totally blind. With a bone-jarring impact, he crashed down onto the floor.

To his ears, the screeching tear of the curtain's supporting rods being ripped free combined with the resounding thud of his body hitting the boards might well have been a herd of cattle stampeding through the room. For a moment, he lay completely still. Even his breathing seemed loud enough to be heard by anyone within fifty yards. But as the seconds ticked by, he realized that no one had been alerted. No voices came from outside, and none from the room he was in. Aside from the faint sound of hoofbeats on cobblestone drifting up from the street, all was silent.

After a few more seconds, he calmed enough to notice a pain in his ribs. The handle of the vysix dagger was pressing nastily up against the bone. Shifting his weight to relieve the pressure, a stray thought flashed through his mind. Had Vilanda not given him this blade, he would now be weaponless and unable to go on. It was as if some unseen force were demanding that he continue, removing the obstacles . . . and his own objections.

Pulling away the curtains, he could now see that he was in what looked to be an office or den. There was a small desk in the far corner, a few bookcases, a tall cabinet, and a round table in the center where several bottles and a few half-empty glasses had been left. The furnishings were more austere than he would have expected to see in the home of a lord. Maybe not all nobles were wealthy, he considered.

Or perhaps Gulan had simple tastes. He shook his head, cursing inwardly. None of this mattered. He had to concentrate.

There were two doors, one directly ahead and another to the right of the desk. The first turned out to be a closet containing nothing but a few boxes and a folded leather coat stuffed onto a high shelf. The second led into another room of similar size, with walls covered with wine racks, most of them well stocked. There were also three barrels, each stamped with an eagle holding a rose in its beak, stacked at the far end beside yet another door. Whoever Lord Brismar Gulan was, he certainly liked his spirits.

Lem pressed his ear to the door. Hearing nothing, he eased it open just enough to see a hallway, its floor covered in blue carpet and rooms spaced evenly on either side. He would need to search the entire dwelling.

You don't even know what Gulan looks like, you idiot. He shook his head at his own foolhardiness. He could easily end up killing the wrong person. But if he turned back now, the broken window was sure to be discovered and his target alerted. A man with enemies who were willing to pay to have him assassinated was sure to suspect the worst. Then he would employ extra protection. This could seriously complicate matters. No, it was too late. Lem knew that his path was fixed.

He pulled the door open another inch.

Just then, a man emerged from two rooms down. He was dressed in a loose-fitting white silk shirt, black pants flared at the cuff, and a smooth-edged hat studded with gems around the brim. His hands were planted firmly on his hips as he talked angrily to an unseen person still inside.

"I've already told you, Brismar, your wife cannot do as she pleases just because she's the king's cousin. So either stand up for yourself or I'll do it for you."

Quickly Lem pushed the door shut again, leaving just a narrow crack to see what was happening.

"I will," a voice replicd. "But you have to understand that she's not one to take bad news well. You don't know what she's capable of. She'll never allow me to be free of her."

The man in the hall threw up his hands. "You're a weakling and a coward. You should simply tell her you don't love her."

"You think she doesn't know that? She's always known."

"But if you tell her about us . . ."

"I already have. She doesn't care. I can have all the lovers I want, but she will not be divorced. She said she would see me dead first. I promise you, she meant it. And if you confront her, she'll kill you."

"I won't keep living like this."

A hand reached out through the doorway and touched the man's face. "You won't have to. Not forever. But you have to give me time. She fears the disgrace of divorce and the disapproval of the king. I'm working on a way she can leave me without ruining her name."

He slapped the hand away, glaring furiously. "You said that a year ago."

"And I meant it. You're a merchant; you don't understand what's involved. If I left her for a low-born, her reputation would be severely damaged."

"So what will you do? Make me a noble?"

"If I could arrange that, would you want it? That way we could be together, and her precious reputation would remain intact."

The man's posture relaxed for a moment, then stiffened once again. "No. You're dreaming. I'm first-generation merchant class. The son of a farmer. The king would never elevate me to lord."

"You're a self-made man with a flawless reputation. Just give me more time. I'm sure I can make the king understand."

The man in the hallway took a small step back. "I'm sorry. The answer is no. Either leave her or forget about me." Having delivered his ultimatum, he turned away and strode off down the hall, disappearing around a corner.

"Damned fool," said the voice from inside the room. "He had better not do what I think he's planning."

Lord Brismar Gulan then stepped into the hall. A stout, broad-shouldered man with thin blond curls and a long face, he looked to be in his late forties. He was dressed in a yellow satin robe embroidered with a pattern of black-and-red thorn bushes. Lem could see the consternation in his eyes as he began walking toward him.

Lem felt the tingle of shadow walk, this time made more pronounced by a massive rush of adrenaline. He raced back into the adjoining room, closing the door as quietly as possible. He hoped that maybe Gulan was just coming to collect a bottle of wine and would not continue to the office. This notion was crushed only seconds later when he heard the clack of the doorknob. Lem pressed his back to the wall near the desk, desperately trying to control his breathing. Lord Gulan stepped inside, taking a moment to turn up a lamp set on a sconce to his right.

"What in the name of creation?" he gasped as his eyes fell on the broken window and fallen curtains. Rushing to the ledge, he leaned over to look outside. "Damned thieves."

Gulan hurried over to the desk, passing mere inches from where Lem was standing. He pulled open the drawers, hastily sifting through the contents. His eyes then shot to the closet. Removing a small knife from the desk, he crept over and, ready to strike, threw open the door. Finding no one inside, he let out a relieved sigh.

"At least they were incompetent thieves," he muttered almost silently. Had Lem not been standing so very close by, he would not have heard these words at all.

Mumbling curses, Gulan gathered up the curtains and tossed them into the closet. While the man's back was turned, Lem reached to his belt and drew the dagger. With a feeling of both curiosity and revulsion, he noticed that though his heart was racing madly, his hands, just as Farley had said, were steady as stone. Gulan took out a clean glass from the cabinet that he filled from one of the bottles sitting on the table. After draining the contents in a single gulp, he poured himself another, this time plopping down in a chair and leaning back with a frustrated groan.

Lem had never been so close to someone while shadow walking. It felt strange. He had been near enough to smell the man's perfume. And now, less than ten feet away, Gulan was completely oblivious to his presence. Lem had hunted deer this way and had avoided bears once or twice. But this . . . it was as if he were truly invisible. As slowly as he could, he took a step to the side, still pressed to the wall. Gulan did not look up. He took another step. Then three more. When directly behind his victim, he moved silently away from the wall. By then Gulan was on his third glass.

Now, mere seconds before committing the deed, the doubts he'd stifled again flooded his brain, weakening his already faltering resolve. Could he really go through with this? From the conversation he'd heard, all the man wanted was to be happy. And for this, he deserved death? Though he was not certain that Gulan's wife had paid for the contract, it seemed likely. It was incredible that a selfish, vain woman was able to sentence him to his end without so much as a trial. What kind of society would allow this to happen? What justified cold-blooded murder?

Lem lowered the blade. No. He could not do this. He would have to find another way to save Mariyah.

The thought had barely formed when a searing pain shot through his stomach, then spread throughout his entire body. He dropped to his knees, issuing a half-suppressed cry while doubling over with both arms wrapped tight to his body.

Gulan sprang up from his chair, clearly bewildered by Lem's inexplicable and sudden appearance. "Who the hell are you?" he demanded. "How did you get in here? Are you the one who broke my window?"

Lem could neither move nor respond. He could only watch as Gulan ran over to the cabinet and pulled out a long, curved knife. He tried to stand, but the pain was paralyzing. All he could do was lie there in helpless agony as the snarling man charged, blade held high to strike. At the very last moment—more from instinct than any real attempt at defending himself—he managed to raise his arms, though to little effect. The bite of steel overcame the pain in his stomach as Gulan's blade sank into his left shoulder. He fell onto his back, feeling the blood pouring from the wound. Gulan's knife was again raised, poised for a second strike that would undoubtedly end his life. Astonishingly, it did not come. Instead, the man began staggering from side to side, with eyes wide and mouth open, issuing short sputtering coughs.

"What the . . ." These were the only two words he managed to utter before keeling over, motionless, with the unmistakable vacant eyes of death.

All at once the pain in Lem's stomach vanished. Not a trace of it lingered. It was then he noticed the small rip on the sleeve of Gulan's robe.

He scrambled to his feet, wondering what in the name of the ancestors had just happened. He should be dead. With heart still pounding furiously, he knelt down to examine his victim. A tiny scratch on Gulan's arm directly beneath the tear in the robe was the only obvious wound. *Surely that couldn't have been enough to kill him.* But the results were undeniable. Upon inspecting his knife, he spotted a tiny droplet of blood on the blade. He must have inadvertently nicked Gulan when raising his arms in self-defense. Incredible as it seemed, this had to be the cause. There was no other explanation. Lem regarded the weapon with both wonder and disgust. Perhaps the blade was poisoned? Of course, there was always another, more repugnant possibility . . . magic. Either way, it had saved his life.

With great care, he sheathed the vysix dagger and tucked it back into his belt. Gulan's attack had wounded him badly. Blood soaked his shirt and was dripping from his fingertips onto the carpet. Not that he felt overly concerned about this at the moment. All he could really grasp was the fact that he had done it. It didn't matter that it had been sheer luck, or that Gulan would have likely killed him. He had murdered. Something compelled him to look his victim in the eyes. The terror and confusion of the man's final moment were frozen in place, the violence of his end written for all to see.

Guilt threatened to see him collapsed on the floor weeping. He had tried to imagine what he would feel; tried to convince himself that he would be able to reconcile this evil by focusing on the good he was doing by rescuing Mariyah from a lifetime of captivity. The wet squish of his foot in the blood pooling at his feet snatched him back. More hoofbeats clopping on stone, echoing in through the window drew his attention. It was then the pain of his injury pushed its way to the fore. He had never been stabbed before. In fact, the savage beating he'd received at the hands of Durst caused the first significant wounds he had ever suffered. This was different; sharper and more pronounced.

What have I done? He stumbled back, hand clutching his shoulder, until he struck the table, toppling several glasses as well as an open bottle of wine that rolled onto the floor, its contents splattering across the rug, adding purple patches to the dark red bloodstains. How could he face Mariyah now? How could he tell her the price he had paid for her freedom?

You may not have known exactly what to expect. But you knew what you were doing. Lying to yourself won't help.

However, truth and reason did not expel the feeling that something dark had invaded his spirit, a taint that would cling to him forever.

After two attempts, he finally spurred himself into action. Removing the sash from Gulan's robe, he bound this around his wound. The way the body jostled limply when he tugged the cloth from the dead man's waist caused his stomach to knot and boil. This, however, was quickly overcome by a growing sense of urgency. He needed to leave. Not from fear of discovery, but because he couldn't bear being near Gulan's body a second longer.

The pain of his injury continued to plague him as he descended the drainpipe and made his way to the corner of the alley. The guards were exactly where they had been before, totally unaware that inside the building they were meant to be safeguarding, only minutes ago an innocent man had been unjustly slain. Using shadow walk with a bit more confidence now, Lem crossed to the other side of the avenue and ducked around the next corner.

He paused to look back in the direction of the apartment. It was odd. He could see Durst kneeling in the dirt,

pleading for his life as clearly as if it had happened that
night. But already Gulan's face was blurred in his memory.
What did that mean? Perhaps it was a blessing. Or perhaps
it meant that Farley had been right—that there had been a
killer inside him all along. And now it was free.

He kept to the more dimly lit areas on his way back to
the troupe. Although the binding had helped to slow the
bleeding, the pain in his shoulder was increasing with
every step. Shemi would demand to know what had happened to him. Attacked by robbers was an easy enough
lie to tell, but what about Farley? Would he be pleased or
angry? Anyone with half a brain would know that Gulan
had been murdered. The trail of blood he had left at the
scene was more than enough to establish foul play. The
most important question was, how hard would the authorities look for the killer? Being that Gulan's wife was the
king's cousin and the likely source of the contract, perhaps
he could hope that they wouldn't bother very much at all.

Upon reaching his tent he found Shemi, Clovis, and
the others already asleep. Knowing that he needed to treat
and bandage his wound properly, he considered waking his
uncle to help. But the idea of lying to the old man was
more than his heart could hold at the moment. His body
felt weary, his legs heavy and sluggish. Again he tried to
picture Gulan, and still the image was elusive. It was as
if it had been plucked from his memory. Driven away by
guilt, no doubt. It would pass.

He went to Farley's tent, dragging his feet with each
step.

Farley was still awake, sitting at his table reading a book.
He looked up as Lem entered and hurried to his side.

"What happened?" he asked, sounding genuinely concerned.

"He's dead," was all Lem could manage initially.

After helping him to a chair, Farley began stripping away his shirt. "You idiot. What possessed you to go there tonight?"

"I had to get it over with," Lem replied weakly. "I . . . I just had to. That's all."

"Tell me exactly what happened," Farley instructed. He crossed over to a chest at the foot of his bed and removed a wooden box containing needle, thread, bandages, and various other healing supplies. "Don't leave out a single detail."

While his wound was being cleaned and stitched shut, Lem recounted the events, including the conversation between Gulan and his lover. He hardly felt Farley's needle passing through his flesh. He had obviously done this before.

"And no one saw you enter or leave?" he asked.

Lem shook his head.

"Are you sure?"

"I would have known. Shadow walking only works if someone is not looking directly at you. If I'd been seen, I would have felt it."

Farley raised an eyebrow. "Shadow walking?"

Lem had not intended to reveal this ability and silently scolded himself for carelessness. "It doesn't matter. I'm positive no one saw me."

Farley regarded him closely as he took out a bandage and secured it with a strip of cloth. If he understood what shadow walking was, he didn't say, and he didn't press the matter further.

"So Vilanda gave you Travis's old dagger, did she? That woman never ceases to amaze me. A pity she decided to leave. A dreadful assassin, but a fine actress. She could certainly charm an audience."

"It doesn't look like I'm any better at killing than she

was," Lem remarked, in a way hoping that Farley would agree with this assessment.

"Oh, I don't know." He counted the points off on his fingers. "One: The target is dead. Two: You're alive. Three: No one saw you. And four: Unintentional or not, you made it look like a failed burglary."

"I was lucky."

Farley laughed. "I'll take luck over skill anytime. After all, wasn't it luck that helped me find you in the first place?"

A sigh slipped from Lem's mouth. "It doesn't matter anymore. I'm a murderer now. Gulan didn't deserve to die. All he wanted was to be happy."

His remark immediately drew a mocking scowl. "Don't be so gullible, Lem. You didn't believe that tripe he told his lover, did you? Lady Gulan doesn't care if he divorces her any more than she cares whom he beds. She *is* the king's cousin, after all. And not just any cousin—she's his *favorite* cousin. No one would dare to criticize her, not even if her husband left her for a stable boy. Gulan just told his lover those lies to placate him. He'd never leave her; he'd be ruined if he did. No, the truth is, the only reason she had him killed is because he tried to do the same to her . . . twice, in fact. With his wife dead, he would inherit her quite considerable wealth."

Lem was now caught in two minds. He knew Farley might be lying, that Gulan might not be the deceptive scoundrel now being put forth. But then again, he wanted to believe Farley was telling the truth—that Gulan had fully deserved his fate. If that were true, he had not so much murdered someone as meted out a measure of justice.

"Next time will be easier," Farley told him. "You'll see."

Next time.

The two simple words seized Lem by the throat. There *would* be a next time. There would be many next times.

There was no longer any doubt about that. He would have to find a way of living with this new person he'd been forced to become. Memories of happy days teaching children to play the balisari, singing with his friends beside the Sun-flow, and most treasured of all, counting the stars with Mariyah—these were all now distant dreams about someone he had once known but to whom he had said farewell a lifetime ago.

He rose to leave, no longer wanting to look at Farley's smile lest he lose himself and double the number of deaths he had caused this night.

"Do take care with the dagger," Farley warned. "The death magic is very strong. A scratch is enough to kill. But then, you already knew that, didn't you?"

Lem did not so much as acknowledge that he had spoken. The whirlwind of emotion he'd felt only moments ago had already calmed, as if something had shattered within his spirit. He wanted to weep, to cry out, something . . . anything that made him feel like the same person he had been when this day began. But perhaps the vysix dagger's magic had killed more than one person tonight. He held out his hand; still steady as stone.

As he entered the tent, his thoughts turned to Mariyah. He *would* save her. More than ever he was sure of this. But this certainty also posed a new and heartrending question. Would he still be the man she loved once she was free?

17
―――

WARM BEDS AND COLD GREETINGS

Be grateful for times of peace. They are fleeting.
Book of Kylor, Chapter Two, Verse Nine

The following day, Trysilia explained to Mariyah that she was to be the personal assistant of Lady Loria Camdon and laid out the duties she would be expected to perform.

Mariyah listened attentively for more than an hour. The sheer number of tasks was enough to make her head ache.

"It's not easy," Trysilia acknowledged, sensing Mariyah's increasing anxiety. "But once you settle into a routine, you'll find you have a great deal of free time. Life at the manor rarely changes."

"It sounds dull."

"I can assure you, it's anything but. And if you become restless, the grounds are enormous. Though I think you'll find plenty inside the manor to entertain yourself with."

"And Lady Camdon. What's she like?"

Trysilia thought for a long moment before answering. "Not the warmest of people, though never cruel or uncaring. A difficult woman to truly know. I've been with her for ten years, and there are times when she still seems like a complete stranger to me."

Mariyah pressed her about how she'd come to be in the

Lady's service and how she had been freed, but Trysilia quite forcefully told her that she would have to wait. Lady Camdon would make clear all she needed to know about her situation when the time came. As for her own past . . . she preferred not to speak of it.

"It's for your own good," she explained. "And for Lady Camdon's as well. Just be patient. There's nothing to worry about."

Mariyah was still considering the possibility that everything Trysilia was telling her might be part of an elaborate ruse to lure her into a false sense of security, but such a ploy seemed pointless. Why go through all this trouble simply for the sake of petty cruelty? There were easier ways to make someone suffer. And if it really were the case, what could she do about it?

Mariyah soon found herself becoming rather fond of Gertrude as well, who often came to visit during the times Trysilia was otherwise occupied. She was good-natured and free with her humor, and she did not govern her tongue with as much discipline as Trysilia—letting slip that Trysilia had been until recently Lady Camdon's personal assistant, and that she had journeyed to Lobin to find her own replacement. Mariyah guessed that this was perhaps the reason for the lack of an anklet—she had been freed and trusted to return. That alone was enough to inspire more optimism.

She considered pressing for more information, but thought this might anger Trysilia and perhaps get Gertrude in trouble with her mistress. However, she did learn that Gertrude had not been indentured, but had served the Lady's family for most of her life. Because of this she had finally saved enough gold to ensure that her daughter, Ellabeth, could attend school to become a scholar. She was eager to boast about how clever she was.

"Ellabeth was accepted to the Halls of Kylor last year," she told Mariyah, grinning broadly. "She wants to study something to do with plants. Grows the best greens I've ever seen in my life. Creation knows how she does it. They grow so big you'd think it was magic."

Mariyah responded by describing her parents' vineyard and the wine they made each year. "Best wine in Vylari. Well, if you ask my father it is."

As always, mentioning her father caused a pang of sorrow and guilt that would last for hours. Not having said goodbye to her parents had plagued her conscience ever since she'd crossed the barrier. She had done it impulsively, with no regard for the consequences. The worst of it was the pain she had caused her family . . . and poor Shemi. All from one stupid mistake. Her love for Lem had exacted a high price. Was it too high? The selfish part of her heart, the one that charged forth blindly into Lamoria, said no. But the part of her who loved her mother and father, who loved Shemi, said differently.

That night, Trysilia handed her a piece of parchment with a list of strange phrases.

"You need to memorize each one," she said.

"What are they?"

"They will allow you to pass through the magical wards protecting the estate." She smiled at Mariyah's obvious revulsion. "I'm afraid magic is something you'll have to learn to live with."

"I . . ." She bowed her head. "If I must."

"Not all magic is foul. In fact, some is quite beautiful, not to mention useful. All the floors throughout the manor stay clean without a single brush or drop of water. And every room remains lit without the need for lamp or candle."

"Lady Camdon is a sorceress?"

Trysilia smiled. "Lady Camdon is a remarkable woman.

Magic is not often practiced by the nobility. The sorcerer class typically comes from the low-borns."

"Why is that?"

"Very few possess the natural gift," Trysilia replied. "One cannot simply decide to learn magic. The fact is there are far more low-borns than nobles. So of course more low-borns will have the gift. Most nobles look upon the practice as beneath them. Or at least that's what they say rather than admit a low-born possesses talents they do not. Childish, really."

She went on to describe some of the various magical devices and charmed implements with which Mariyah would need to become familiar. Most were unremarkable and used for everyday tasks, such as maintaining a constant temperature within the manor or keeping insects and vermin away, though a few others were more elaborate.

"Do all people here have such things?" Mariyah asked.

"Only those who can afford them." She stood and started to the door. "I'll leave you to look this over."

"Why did you choose me to take your place?" Mariyah called after her. "Was it just because of where I'm from?"

Trysilia turned, frowning. "Gertrude should learn to mind what she says. She confessed that she let slip about you being my replacement. As for my reasons: No, it wasn't just because of where you are from. There's a light inside you; a strength of spirit. Even now, I can feel it. I knew I had to get you out of that horrible place. I was . . . compelled, I guess you could say." There was a long pause before she spoke again. "There is something I must ask."

"Of course."

"Can you tell me how to find Vylari?"

Mariyah drew a breath. This was a question she had been expecting to hear. And a question she knew she could not answer. "I'm sorry. But I can't."

Trysilia nodded. She didn't look angry. She looked . . . sad. "I see. I had to try. My people are running out of places to where they can retreat. A land so well hidden as yours . . ." She forced a smile. "It doesn't matter. I understand why you can't say. Forgive me for asking."

This was the first time she had seen a crack in Trysilia's confident façade. Mariyah wanted to give her a few words of comfort, tell her something that might assuage her sadness. But she had sworn never to reveal how to find her home. Not that she really knew herself; but the stranger had found it. And Lem's mother had returned there also. Mariyah could certainly find the general area, even if the barrier prevented finding its exact location. That could be enough. And as much as she wanted to trust Trysilia, she couldn't. Not with information that could potentially harm her people.

As a relief from confinement, Trysilia took her above deck on a few occasions. She had caught her first glimpse of the sea when being brought aboard, but it had been late in the evening and all she could see were a few yards of pitch black broken by a reflection of moonlight across its surface. Now the sea was truly revealed, leaving her awestruck. Nothing could have prepared her for its absolute enormity and splendor, especially set against the warm light of the setting sun. The swells lifted the great ship effortlessly, setting it back down only to rise again in a gentle yet almighty cadence. No matter how hard she tried, she could not see even a tiny speck of land on the horizon. It was both beautiful and terrifying.

"I never imagined anything could be so big," she said, gripping tightly onto the rail near the bow.

Trysilia sighed. "Yes. It is the one thing I will truly miss."

The millions of tiny reflections across its surface reminded her in a way of the Sunflow, only infinitely vaster. It made the sky on a clear winter night appear to be empty by comparison. The gradually sinking sun was like a giant fireball boiling away at the edge of the world, the sea reaching up with delicate ribbons of light to spirit it down into some unfathomable depth. The reds and lavenders of the darkening sky formed a tapestry of glory that only the soul of creation could possibly have been capable of producing.

The captain, a man of sour disposition with a thick, salt-and-pepper beard, bald head, and a weather-beaten face, was staring down at them from the main wheel.

"Why can't all people be like Gertrude?" mused Mariyah, glancing over her shoulder at him.

"For the most part, your experience is limited to the worst among the people of this world," Trysilia told her. "They brutalized you and stole your freedom. Gertrude is no different than most, really; she was simply not crippled from youth by hatred. It's not just to do with where she was born. I would wager that even the people of Vylari could act out of fear under the right circumstances."

"My people may not be perfect," Mariyah snapped back, a bit more forcefully than she'd intended, "but they would never do to anyone what was done to me."

"Perhaps. But I think when you see the rest of Lamoria, away from the ugliness, you might view things differently."

"I'm not sure I *care* to see it," she remarked, casting a disdainful look at the captain.

Trysilia wrapped an arm around Mariyah's shoulder. "You remind me so much of myself—thinking in absolutes and feeling every moment with intensity. One day, though, you'll start to understand that life comes in many hues, and that not all canvases are painted with the same brush."

Mariyah knew she was right. And going home was seeming more impossible with every day that passed. If the rest of the world was really as different as Trysilia claimed, perhaps she might learn to live in it. Right at this moment, though, she wished that they could remain on the ship indefinitely. Each day brought her closer to the unknown—to Lady Camdon, a woman who, despite the fact that Trysilia was free, was complicit in her servitude.

The morning of their arrival, Mariyah's nerves were as much on edge as ever. Gertrude had brought her a flowing blue silk dress with intricate gold swirls stitched up the left side. The neckline swooped low, and there was a white sash tied into a large bow around her waist. Her hair was brushed and wrapped into a bun on the back of her head, though a good portion was left loose and decorated with silver threads. The shoes were covered in silk to match the gown and studded with tiny blue and white stones that scratched the tops of her feet.

"Do I have to dress like this all the time?" she asked, shifting and tugging at the shoulders.

Gertrude laughed. "Only in public. You'll get used to it. I'll teach you how to fix your hair properly as well."

Trysilia arrived, bearing a sorrowful expression. "We dock within the hour," she informed them.

"What's wrong?" asked Mariyah.

"This is goodbye."

"You're not coming?"

She smiled. "My time is over. I'm going home now."

"But I thought you were going to teach me what I'm supposed to do."

"I've shown you all you need to know for now. As for the details, Lady Camdon insists upon teaching those herself. It was the same when I arrived." She regarded Mariyah's dress. "You look marvelous, by the way."

A lump formed in her throat. Against all the odds, she had made a friend. Now, already, she had to say farewell. "Can't you at least stay for a short while?" she asked.

"I've stayed long past what was required of me. There is

nothing for me here, though I do mean it when I say that I'll miss you. Perhaps one day we'll see each other again." She looked over to Gertrude. "Take care of her . . . and your-self."

Gertrude was stoic. "I will. And mind you keep well clear of Ralmarstad."

"I'll do my best," she promised. She leaned in as she took Mariyah's hand. "I have always believed that things happen for a purpose, even if we can't see what it is straightaway. I was meant to find you. Which means you are meant to be here. So be strong. And remember, there *is* beauty in this world, even though it's sometimes hard to see."

"Goodbye," said Mariyah, feeling an unexpected rush of gratitude toward Trysilia. "And good luck."

With a final nod to Gertrude, Trysilia left them.

"Damn that woman," muttered Gertrude a few seconds after she was gone.

Mariyah was perplexed. "What's wrong?"

Her question raised a sigh. "Trysilia could go anywhere she wants, yet still she's determined to return to the same pit she came from."

"Isn't she going to be with her family?"

"Yes, and that's the problem. She's from the western tribes. They live in lands close to the Ralmarstad border—a most dangerous place. I tried to convince her to remain in the north, where she'd be safe. I could even visit her from time to time. But she wouldn't have any of it. Stubborn damned woman."

Mariyah didn't know who the western tribes were. But she recalled Trysilia's statement about her people running out of places to retreat. "Maybe she misses her family."

"To blazes with her family." This time Gertrude could not hold back her emotion. "For all she knows, they're dead. After all, it's been ten years. At least here she was safe from those bloody Ralmarstad demons."

"I can understand why she would want to know," said Mariyah. "My parents don't even know if I'm dead or alive. Maybe it's the same with hers. I would risk anything to see them again, if only to let them know I'm all right. Just a chance to say . . ." The sight of Gertrude's tears caused her own to fall. "A chance to say I'm sorry."

Dabbing her eyes on her sleeve and wiping her nose, Gertrude smiled. "Look at us, blubbering away like this. You have an impression to make. We can't have you all red-eyed and puffy. Lady Camdon would be most put out."

For the next several minutes Gertrude took great care in applying various colored powders to Mariyah's face and around her eyes. Once finished, she held up a small mirror, looking most pleased with her handiwork.

Mariyah gasped at what she saw. "I look . . ."

"Beautiful. You look absolutely beautiful."

"No! I look like a . . . Oh, I don't know what to call it."

The soft reds around her cheekbones and the deep purple around her eyes were ghastly. It was as if someone had attempted to paint her after drinking too much wine.

Gertrude laughed. "Trysilia reacted the same way the first time. But I'm afraid it's the style in Ubania."

"Do all women paint themselves here?" She had to resist the urge to wipe it off.

"The men too," she replied. "You'll need to learn how to do it yourself eventually."

The jostling of the ship and the peal of its bells snatched their attention. They had arrived. Mariyah realized that she had forgotten to pack her belongings—mostly a few items of clothing Trysilia had given to her along with some other odds and ends.

"I'll pack for you," Gertrude said. "You need to get

going. There will be a carriage waiting at the end of the dock." When Mariyah hesitated, she added, "Go on. I'll be there shortly."

On her way above deck, she hoped to see Trysilia one last time, but was disappointed to encounter only the captain and a few deckhands. The ship was being tied to a long wooden dock, beyond which, as Gertrude had stated, was a white carriage pulled by a team of four horses. Instead of seeing the expected buildings and a bustling city, there was nothing but a road that wound its way over a steep rise. A man in a long black-and-red coat, a white ruffled shirt, black trousers, and a tall, flat-topped cylindrical hat was awaiting them.

Mariyah's heart raced as the crew extended the gangplank, allowing the man to board the ship. He walked straight up to her. "You are the new assistant?" His accent was odd, with long vowels, hard *t*'s, and rolling *r*'s.

Mariyah nodded. "That's what I—"

"Yes or no will do fine," he said sharply.

"Yes."

He turned to where the captain was standing near the entrance to the main cabin. With a snap of the fingers, he held out his hand. "If you please."

The captain scowled, clearly not liking being ordered about. He removed a chain with a blue orb attached from around his neck and handed it over. "Here. Now get off my ship."

"You do understand what you are meant to do?" he said, unmoved by the captain's words and aggressive posture.

"I know. You don't have to tell me."

"Should anything befall her, you will be held accountable. Am I understood? She is to arrive safely and precisely where she tells you."

"I said I did, didn't I?"

"Then I hope you will not object to accepting this?" Reaching into his jacket, the man pulled out a sealed parchment. When the captain didn't take it, he added, "If you are forthright, and intend on delivering Trysilia home safely, this should not be a problem. However, if you choose to say no . . . as I understand it, my mistress holds the bond owed on this vessel, does she not? A small delay. But I'm sure we could find another willing to do as she requires."

The captain fumed, veins bulging from his forehead. "You can tell Lady Camdon that"—his shoulders sagged as he finally forced himself to take the parchment—"that I accept." Without further ado, he broke the wax seal. This produced a popping sound along with a flash of red light. A puff of smoke hovered over where the seal had been, then drifted up into the captain's nostrils.

"Satisfied?" he spat.

"Quite." The man turned to Mariyah. "Now, if you will follow me, the Lady awaits."

Although confused by his exchange with the captain, Mariyah thought it best not to ask any questions. Stepping onto the dock, a new problem arose as she stumbled forward, only just preventing herself from falling to her knees. It had taken her days to grow accustomed to walking on a surface that was in constant motion. Now back on solid ground, she found herself having to deal with the same predicament in reverse.

"Is this Ubania?" she asked, after steadying her footing.

"This is Lady Camdon's private dock," he replied. "And you would do well to keep your questions to yourself until you have been evaluated."

Aside from a few trees and some small bushes, nothing about her surroundings appeared in the least remarkable. Only the carriage stood out, elegantly decorated with a gold-and-blue pattern painted on the doors and around the windows. The driver was equally resplendent in a bright red suit with gold buttons up the front and polished black boots.

Mariyah turned back to the ship. "Where's Gertrude?"

"My wife will be along shortly," he replied.

"Your wife?"

"Yes." He gestured to the carriage. "Now, if you are finished . . ."

Mariyah was startled to see the door open on its own when they drew near, though the man seemed to accept this as being perfectly normal. Inside were two seats facing each other, both spanning the entire width of the coach. They were soft, and warm to the touch, and the scent of oiled leather was pleasing.

Just as it had opened, the door closed spontaneously. Mariyah sat facing the front, the man in the seat opposite. A moment later there was a sharp crack of a whip, and the carriage lurched forward.

"My name is Marison," he announced, with what to Mariyah sounded like exaggerated formality. "I am in charge of staff and maintenance. Privately, you will address me by my name. Publicly, I am to be called *sir*. Is that clear?" Not waiting for a reply, he continued. "As for other servants and staff, you are not to address them publicly unless it pertains to your duties. Privately, you may speak freely."

"How many others like me are there?"

"Was I not clear when I said to keep your questions for later?"

Mariyah nodded. She was not liking this man. Not one bit.

"As for Lady Camdon, you will follow her directives to the letter and will not speak until given leave. She will explain in detail what is expected of you and how you are to behave." He folded his hands in his lap.

When he said nothing more, she asked, "Is there anything else?"

Without a reply, Marison reached beneath his seat and produced a bound notebook, which he placed in his lap. Shifting slightly and crossing his legs, he opened it and ran his finger across the page, his lips moving ever so slightly as he read.

Mariyah frowned but held her tongue. Looking out the window, she could see that they were now passing through a thinly wooded area. The road was paved with red bricks and was bordered by a white fence on either side. They passed a few small houses—each one virtually identical in their single-story design, well-kept lawns, and flower gardens planted beneath the windows and along the base of the porch. She wanted to ask who lived there, if for no other reason than to irritate Marison. The impulse was resisted. Until she knew more about Lady Camdon, it would be foolish to tempt fate. And there was the not inconsiderable fact that the man was currently holding the charm that controlled her anklet.

After a time, the forest gave way and the sea reappeared in the southern-facing window. From this vantage point she could see that they were near a high bluff, although how high exactly was impossible to tell. The carriage slowed, and she heard the squeaking of metal hinges. A moment later they passed through a tall gate made from what appeared to be pure silver, though given its untarnished surface, she thought it must actually be steel.

At this point she could glimpse only a corner of the manor, but even this restricted view was sufficient to make her catch her breath: four stories of the purest white marble that even at a distance shimmered with gold veins running throughout. As for the road, this was made from a black stone with gold bricks along both edges. The front garden was equally spectacular, with hedges shaped into the forms of great birds and beasts, some looking as if they were doing battle, surrounding tall crystal fountains shooting thin streams of water dozens of feet into the air. Flowers of an uncountable variety were spread about everywhere, at first seeming random in their placement. However, the more Mariyah gazed at them, the more purposeful and exact their design appeared.

As the carriage curved to the right, the full splendor and scope of the manor came into view. A colonnade on either side of a promenade ended at a staircase atop which was a pair of silver doors as tall and broad as the gate. The top floor boasted several balconies with carved balustrades, all of them easily able to accommodate a dozen or more people. For Mariyah, the amount of labor, time, and wealth it must have taken to build a home of this magnitude was almost impossible to comprehend.

The carriage halted and the door opened. Marison stepped out first and extended his arm toward the manor doors.

"Lady Camdon awaits. You will be taken to her immediately."

Mariyah stepped out, eyes wandering about in awe.

"Did you hear me?"

"Yes."

"*Sir.* We are in public."

"Yes, sir." Taking a deep breath, she started toward the front entrance.

"One more thing," Marison called after her, his softened tone barely noticeable. "Good luck."

Mariyah gave him a slight bow. "Thank you . . . sir."

She wasn't certain what to make of Marison. Was he as cold as he presented himself? While passing through the colonnade, she could hear him telling the driver of the coach to go back to the dock for his wife. It was difficult to imagine someone as good-natured as Gertrude being married to such a man. They seemed an unlikely match. Of course, after only one meeting, how could she really know? She hadn't thought very much of Gertrude in the beginning, either.

Upon reaching the top of the stairs, just as with the coach, the doors opened spontaneously. Beyond the threshold, once again Mariyah was struck by what she saw. The ceiling of the foyer was at least thirty feet high, with delicate crystal threads suspended from what appeared to be fist-sized rubies. The floor was polished white tiles embedded with emeralds and veined with weblike gold strands that twisted and crossed in a way similar to the flowers in the garden: at first sight random, and yet within a larger deliberate pattern. A pair of winding staircases were situated straight ahead, and on either side of these as well as in between were tall archways. Directly above the center arch hung a great banner on which was painted a gold brazier with black fire rising from within.

A woman appeared from the archway on the left, her blouse, knee-length skirt, and shoes all black. In contrast to this was a white belt with a gold buckle cinched around her waist. She appeared young, in her late twenties perhaps, and her dark brown hair was wrapped in a swirling bun on top of her head. Like Marison, her expression was blank.

"You will come with me," she said in a flat tone. Without waiting for a response, she spun around and disappeared down a hallway to Mariyah's right.

Mariyah had to run to catch up, causing the gems in her shoes to dig into her feet. At a quick clip they continued on through a long series of massive chambers, all lavishly decorated and each clearly designed to be as awe-inspiring as possible. The furnishings were finer than

anything Mariyah had ever seen. Not even the best crafts-
men in Vylari would have been capable of creating such
masterpieces. There were also tapestries, paintings, and
sculptures of extraordinary detail and vivid colors set on
display in a way that made them impossible to ignore as
one passed by. To Mariyah's mind, there was little doubt
that this show of wealth and power was intended to deliberately humble and intimidate anyone who visited.

After what seemed like a mile of walking, they stopped
in front of a set of double doors.

"Were you taught how to pass through the wards?" the
woman asked.

"I was given a list of words. But I don't know how to use
them yet."

"I see." She faced the door. *"Unorium anon."* The doors
swung outward. "Lady Camdon is inside." She then
started back the way they had come.

Mariyah's heart pounded furiously as she entered. With
several couches and chairs together with an assortment of
tables between them, the room was clearly a parlor of some
kind. On her left was an unlit hearth, above which hung
a painting bearing the same symbol she had seen on the
banner in the foyer. It wasn't as extravagant as the other
chambers; the impression was one of comfort rather than
opulence.

Sitting with legs crossed near a bookshelf opposite the
hearth was a woman dressed in a plain white silk blouse and
a pair of loose-fitting black pants decorated with a bright
red floral pattern. Her ice-blue eyes contrasted strikingly
with her dark complexion and straight black hair, which was
accented with streaks of white and fell around her shoulders. Even sitting, Mariyah could see that she was tall, and
although thin, did not appear frail. Despite the gray of age
in her hair, she looked to be no more than in her forties.

"Come," she said in a smooth but authoritative tone, gesturing to a chair placed in front of her. "Sit." She wore the same indifferent expression as everyone else Mariyah had met thus far.

Trying not to look nervous, she did as instructed, knees and feet together, hands folded in her lap and her eyes fixed on the floor.

"You're not timid, are you?" asked Lady Camdon.

"No, my lady," she replied.

"Then look me in the eye."

Mariyah looked up.

"Are you afraid?"

"No, my lady."

"Good. Now tell me about yourself. I need to know what I have to work with before you're welcome here. Where are you from?"

"I am from Vylari, my lady. My parents own a vineyard. Most of my life I have helped them maintain it."

Lady Camdon leaned an elbow against the arm of the chair, her chin resting on the tips of her slender fingers. "Did Trysilia send me a simpleton? Or do you think *I* am one? Vylari is a legend, girl. Nothing more. Now, I'll ask you once again. Where are you from? Lie and you can go back to where Trysilia found you."

"I'm not lying," she insisted, her tone a touch too aggressive. "I *am* from Vylari."

With poise and grace Mariyah had rarely seen, Lady Camdon rose and crossed over to a chifforobe, from the top drawer of which she removed an onyx box. Very deliberately, she lifted the lid, casting Mariyah a sideways smile as she did so.

"I do not abide liars to live in my home. And as I gave you a second chance to tell me the truth . . ."

She removed a marble-sized red gem, which she held up

to her lips and whispered to softly, too softly for Mariyah to hear the words clearly. The gem emitted a pulsing light from within its facets. "You should know that, had you been honest, this would not be required."

Fear gripped Mariyah as Lady Camdon approached, the gem pinched between her thumb and index finger. "I swear that I've told you the truth," she insisted.

"We shall see. Hold out your hand." When Mariyah hesitated, she frowned. "I said hold out your hand. This will not hurt."

Reluctantly, Mariyah did as instructed. "What is it?"

The gem was pressed firmly against her flesh. "It guarantees honesty, though not in the coarse and painful way that the anklet you wear does. You see, Trysilia was told to find me someone very special. And someone from the mythical land of Vylari would be special indeed. But I have to ask myself, did she do as I said? Or did she take a particular liking to you and fall for this story of yours unwittingly?"

She returned to her chair. "My responsibilities demand that I be selective when it comes to my household, and the position I need filled is one of great complexity and significance."

The gem felt warm. It had occurred to Mariyah that Lady Camdon could have easily commanded her to speak by making use of the anklet. Why then would she go to the trouble of using this gem instead? Was she really concerned that the anklet was painful? She didn't come across as being a caring or considerate woman.

"I am from Vylari," Mariyah reasserted.

Lady Camdon sighed. "I have not asked you a question yet. Until I do, be silent." She pressed her finger to her bottom lip. "Let me see, now . . . how do you feel about Ralmarstad?"

Mariyah spoke before she could think about the words. "I hate it. Nothing but cruelty and corruption."

"And me? How do you feel about me?"

"I think you are a cold woman who enjoys belittling others. I understand why Trysilia chose to leave."

"Perhaps a bit *too* honest. Next question: Where are you from?"

"Vylari. I grew up on my parents' vineyard."

Lady Camdon raised an eyebrow. "Well, then. That *is* special. Though whether *you* are remains to be seen. Still, I would like to hear about your home. But there will be time for that later. For now, tell me, why did you leave Vylari?"

"To find Lem."

"And who is Lem?"

"He is my betrothed."

"I see. And did you succeed?"

"No. We were captured shortly after crossing the border."

"We? Who else was with you?"

"Shemi, Lem's uncle." Mariyah could not stop herself from answering plainly and truthfully.

For nearly an hour the questioning continued, right up until Mariyah began her account of being sentenced to life in prison. At this point Lady Camdon removed the gem from her hand and returned it to the drawer.

"That you can tell me about Vylari is enough for me to keep you here, though I am not yet certain you're right for the position I have in mind. You will have to prove to me you can handle the responsibility. Judging from the look of you, that will be quite a challenge."

As if he had been silently summoned, the door opened and Marison entered, bowing low before approaching Lady Camdon. He passed over the orb that controlled the anklet and then, nodding curtly to Mariyah, quickly exited.

"Hold out your left hand," she ordered.

This time she did so at once.

Without a word of explanation, Lady Camdon removed a thin silver ring from her own little finger and placed it on Mariyah's. It was slightly too big, but a moment later contracted to make a tight fit. Lady Camdon then grasped the orb in her palm and closed her eyes. A scent arose that reminded Mariyah of burned timbers. When Lady Camdon opened her hand, the orb was nothing but a tiny portion of black dust.

"You may remove the anklet now," she said, wiping her hand so that the dust fell onto the floor. It sparkled for an instant as it struck the tiles, then vanished without a trace.

Mariyah's jaw went slack. She could feel that the magic was gone. She was . . . free. As if afraid Lady Camdon might change her mind, she quickly ripped the anklet away and tossed it across the room.

"You will pick that up on your way out," said Camdon. "And you must keep it with you at all times."

Mariyah was utterly confused. But knowing that she was no longer under the control of the despised anklet caused her to let out a stifled sob. "Thank you. I'm sorry about what I said."

"I asked for the truth. I do not fault you for rudeness when you had no choice. However, if you speak that way to me again, I will send you away."

"Why . . . why did you destroy the anklet?" was all she could choke out.

"I cannot abide injustice. And I will not abet it. However, I hold a certain position in Ubania that forces me to make others believe I do. The truth is, you are free to leave at any time. The ring only prevents you from trying to harm me, nothing more. I bear you no ill will, but at the same time I am not foolish enough to leave myself vulnerable."

"So I can leave?"

"Of course. Now, if you want; though you should be aware that it is unlikely you would make it very far from my estate. I am forced to register you as indentured to me. The Archbishop has all noble houses closely watched, more so here than in Ralmarstad proper even, as he rightly suspects we're more likely to cause him trouble. Step beyond my lands and they will catch and imprison you as a runaway."

"So I am little more than your property. Even without the anklet."

"No. You're a prisoner at worst. I will not force you to work. My lands are extensive. I might expel you from my home, but I would never turn anyone who has fallen prey to Ralmarstad treachery over to the authorities. You are free to hunt and forage within my borders. I will not deny you that right. Just be aware that you will need to dwell there for the rest of your life, with no aid or kindness from me." She flicked her wrist. "Perhaps you might find such a life preferable."

"It depends on the alternative . . . my lady."

"Fair enough. I spent a substantial amount of gold to bring you here. Serve me for six years and I will see you are brought safely to wherever you want to go, no matter where it is or how far away. In that time, you will have repaid the cost and I will be satisfied. Given the conditions of the prisons, I think it a suitable alternative."

"Is that why you free the condemned?"

"My reasons are my own." Her tone had sharpened. "You will not question me or anything I do. Just because I would see an end to injustice, do not think me soft-hearted or sentimental. Trysilia served me four years beyond the time she could have left. In spite of that, I promise you that I do not miss her company in the least. If I found that she ran afoul of Kylorian law again, I would not lift a finger to save her.

You, child, are even less important to me. As of now, your only value is in the stories you can tell me about Vylari. Now leave me. Gertrude will show you to your quarters."

As if on cue, the door opened and Gertrude entered, bowing low.

"What about my duties?" asked Mariyah. "When should I—"

"Another word and you can leave my house this instant," she snapped.

Mariyah bowed her head and turned to leave. Gertrude, looking flushed, waved for her to hurry.

"The anklet," Lady Camdon's stern voice reminded. "I thought I was clear that you are to keep it with you at all times."

Not daring to speak, Mariyah searched the floor in what she thought was the right area, eventually finding it beneath one of the chairs near the hearth. To her dismay, the metal was twisted and half melted, as if someone had placed the anklet in a fire. She held it up.

At the sight of this, Lady Camdon shot up from her chair, spanning the room with long, deliberate strides, and snatched the anklet from her grasp. "What did you do?" she demanded. "You may speak."

"I don't know," Mariyah replied, a tremor in her voice. "I just threw it. I don't know how this happened."

After examining the anklet for a moment, Lady Camdon leaned in close so that she was almost nose to nose with Mariyah, peering into her eyes. With a rapid jerk, she then stepped back and shoved the anklet into her pocket. "Gertrude, remove this girl from my sight. Then find a suitable replacement."

"Yes, my lady. Right away."

Lady Camdon returned to her chair and took a sip from

a glass of wine, her eyes directed downward as if in deep thought.

Mariyah's mind was a whirl. A suitable replacement? Was she to be cast aside so quickly? She noticed Gertrude again waving for her to hurry. Once back in the corridor, she leaned against the wall and slid down.

Gertrude knelt beside her. "Are you all right, dear?"

She didn't know what to feel. She was free. And yet still trapped. To live on the estate grounds would certainly be preferable to a life of harsh confinement. But to be completely alone for the rest of her life was a daunting prospect, to say the least.

"How long do I have?" she asked.

"I don't understand. How long for what?"

"She said you need to find a replacement. How long until I have to leave the manor?"

Gertrude reached out and lifted her chin, smiling. "Not for you, silly. For the anklet. You'll have to wear a fake one to avoid any unwanted questions." She stood, hand extended. "Come. Let's find your room. There's hot water and a meal waiting."

Mariyah allowed herself to be helped up. "Thank you. I thought that . . ."

"What? That I was about to get on another bloody ship and go back to that rathole of a city? I'd resign first. Actually, she was quite taken with you, I think."

Mariyah cocked her head. "Taken? She threatened to throw me out."

"She does that to every new arrival. So don't take it to heart. The Lady is a hard woman, but she's fair."

"She said I could live on the estate if I wanted. Was she telling the truth?"

Gertrude's face twisted, as if she'd tasted something

foul. "Live in the woods? Scrounging for food and covered in dirt? You wouldn't want to do that."

"But I could?"

"Yes."

"Has anyone ever done it?"

"Once. And he didn't last long. He ended up coming back to the manor in less than a week."

"Lady Camdon let him back in?"

Gertrude laughed. "She's not as heartless as she wants people to think."

Along the way they ran across two more servants: a younger woman with copper skin and bright eyes and an older man with a pale, chalky complexion and a narrow build who was busy arranging books in what looked to be the library. Both nodded to Mariyah as the women passed and gave her a welcoming smile.

Gertrude told her their names were Kylanda and Rastimar.

"We're really not supposed to speak to one another while we're working," she said, "unless it's something to do with our duties. But don't worry. You'll meet everyone properly later tonight. All the household staff eats together."

"How many are there?"

"Not as many as you'd think. The manor more or less cleans itself. Fifteen of us take care of the rest. Of course, more temporary staff are brought in during parties and other social functions. Not that you need to worry about that right now. You'll have a day or two before being expected to start work. Not even the Iron Lady expects new arrivals to jump in on their first day." She bent low to whisper in her ear. "That's what we call her when she's not around."

Most of the staff were housed in rooms in the east wing of the manor, close to the kitchens. Mariyah, however, was

given a suite across from Lady Camdon's personal bedchamber. It was quite spacious, though not as elegantly
furnished as the rest of the manor. The bed was twice the
size as the one she'd had back home, and it looked warm
and inviting. The mere sight of it reminded her that she
had just finished a long journey. The dressers, wardrobes,
and closets were filled with apparel of varying styles and
sizes.

"You'll need to find what fits you," Gertrude told her.
"Once Lady Camdon officially appoints you as her personal assistant, you'll have a proper fitting."

"And if she doesn't?"

"It *has* happened once or twice. But I'm sure you'll be
fine. Have a look around, and I'll come get you when it's
time to eat." She turned to leave, pausing at the door. "Oh,
I almost forgot. We have running water here. Have you
had any experience with it?"

"Running water?"

Gertrude tittered, then pointed to the door in the right
corner. "In there. I would show you, but I think it would
be fun for you to learn about it on your own."

As it turned out, *fun* was not exactly how Mariyah would
have described her first experience with running water.
Hot running water. The huge ceramic basin, large enough
for her to fit her entire body inside, had two knobs and a
spigot. She scalded her hand twice before figuring out how
to combine cold and hot water to a pleasing temperature,
and another few minutes pondering how to prevent the
water from running away straight down the drain. However, once she finally worked out that she simply needed to
pull up a knob affixed to the spigot, she found a warm bath
to be a most pleasant experience.

In the same way the dust had disappeared when Lady
Camdon brushed it onto the floor, the droplets of water

from her body when she stepped from the tub vanished the moment they struck the tiles. As useful and benign as it was, she found even this kind of practical magic to be unsettling. That she would be forced to walk upon it at all times made her skin crawl.

There was one other room in her suite, apparently a parlor, though with only a small table, four chairs, and a single empty cabinet against the near wall. From the thick layer of dust, it looked as if it had not been used in some time. *At least the furniture isn't magic,* she thought. Though it was entirely possible that it was throughout the rest of the manor. With only fifteen servants, keeping the dust at bay by hand in a place so enormous would be nearly impossible.

The clothes were mostly formal dresses and gowns, along with a variety of bejeweled accessories and shoes. To her relief, she did ultimately find a few casual and far more comfortable outfits, as well as a beautifully soft nightgown.

The warmth of the water had been soothing, to be sure; it had also made her keenly aware that she had not slept in some time. The bed was practically begging her to test its quality, and she had no desire to reject its allure. After slipping beneath the cool sheets and pulling the thick blanket up to her chin, she instantly became drowsy. Lady Camdon might throw her out to fend for herself come morning; in this moment, however, she felt secure. Considering all the turmoil and uncertainty that was now prevalent in her life, why shouldn't she enjoy whatever small time she could? Her troubles would still be there when she opened her eyes once again.

Sadly, the respite proved to be temporary. It felt like she had barely drifted off when the door opened and Gertrude hurried in.

"Lady Camdon wants you to dine with her this evening,

I'm afraid." She bore a look of severe consternation. "So we'd better start getting you ready."

Mariyah yawned and stretched. Gertrude was already sifting through her wardrobe. "How long was I asleep?" she asked.

"About two hours."

It hadn't seemed that long. "I thought I was supposed to eat with the other servants."

"You are," Gertrude replied, holding up a cream-colored dress. "Trysilia almost never ate with the mistress. Except when there were guests, that is."

"And are there any tonight? Guests, I mean." She stretched once more then sat up on the edge of the bed.

"No. Lady Camdon canceled all invitations until her new assistant arrived."

Mariyah crossed over to the wardrobe and pointed out a few similar dresses that would fit. The one Gertrude had picked was too small. "Why do you think she wants me there?"

Gertrude selected a green dress with black borders and laid it out on the bed. "Who knows why the Lady does the things she does? It's best not to question her." Motioning for Mariyah to sit in front of a vanity next to the wardrobe, she retrieved several brushes and hairpins from its drawer.

A moment later the door opened, and the girl named Kylanda whom they had seen earlier entered. She was carrying a tray with a ceramic pot and a cup.

"I thought some tea might help," she said. "Gertrude told me that you were sleeping."

"Thank you," Mariyah said, nodding politely. "I'm still quite tired."

"I would think so, after all you've been through." She set the tray down and began preparing the tea.

The girl's gracious demeanor and welcoming smile went

far to assuage Mariyah's anxiety. "You went through the same thing, didn't you?"

"Eight years ago," she affirmed. "Feels like a lifetime since I left Lobin."

Mariyah glanced down to see she was not wearing an anklet. "So you're free now?"

"For three years."

"Don't you want to go home?"

She gave a wide-eyed shake of her head. "Not a chance. Too dangerous. There's nothing for me there, anyway. Most of my family are dead. Besides, I was barely in my teens when I arrived at the manor. Home . . . well . . . it isn't home anymore."

"But why stay?"

Kylanda smiled and handed her the cup. "Oh, I'll go in a few years, once I've saved enough gold. If I left now, I'd still need to find work. Lady Camdon pays well. Better than most. Besides, I have friends here that I love very much." She tilted her head and shrugged. "I guess it's hard to leave a place when it's all you really know."

Mariyah could not fathom staying somewhere she had once been a prisoner. "Where will you go?"

Kylanda pulled up a chair to sit in front of Mariyah while Gertrude proceeded to brush her hair. "I haven't decided yet. Near the mountains, maybe."

"You've never been to the mountains," Gertrude chipped in. "And you hate the cold."

Kylanda frowned. "You just want me to stay put." She leaned in and took Mariyah's hands. "I hear you were sentenced to life. Lady Camdon must have really wanted you, to let Trysilia spend so much."

"Lady Camdon knows talent when she sees it," said Gertrude lightly. "Which is why Mariyah is Trysilia's replacement . . . and you aren't."

Kylanda huffed. "Who says I wanted to replace her?"

This was clearly a well-worn topic between the two of them.

"So it *wasn't* you screaming at the top of your lungs when Lady Camdon announced she was sending Trysilia to Lobin?"

"I was not screaming," Kylanda insisted, looking a bit flustered. After a brief moment, she regained her composure. "The position pays more. That's the only reason I wanted it. To be honest, the thought of being in the Iron Lady's company all day and night . . ." She exaggerated a shudder. "I'm better off where I am."

"How many indentures live here?" asked Mariyah, thinking it best to change the subject.

"Other than you, only two," Kylanda replied.

"So few?" For some reason Mariyah had expected the entire house to be filled with them.

"I think you might have the wrong idea about Lady Camdon," said Gertrude. "If she could, she would have none. The mistress despises the practice. But appearances must be kept up, particularly among the nobility. A person of her wealth and status without at least a few indentures would be noticed."

"I don't understand," said Mariyah. "She buys the freedom of prisoners for the sake of propriety?"

"It's more than that," said Gertrude. "Well . . . it *is* that. But more too. I've known the Lady since she was a young girl. I've watched as she outsmarted every noble who tried to bring her down. I don't pretend to understand the ins and outs of politics, but I know that here in Ubania, a single mistake can be disastrous."

Mariyah was still unsure if she understood. But then, there was very little about this world that made sense to her.

"Where are you from?" asked Kylanda.

"She's from Vylari," said Gertrude, before Mariyah could speak.

Kylanda fell back in her chair, mouth agape. "Vylari? But that's . . . that's not a real place."

Mariyah shot Gertrude an irritated look. She had not intended to make it known where she was from. Gertrude's eyes widened, realizing her mistake.

"I'm sorry," said Gertrude.

"It's all right." She turned back to Kylanda. "Yes. It's a real place."

"But how . . . I mean why . . ." She leaned forward as if trying to see if there was a lie in her eyes. "Vylari? Are you having fun with me?"

Mariyah thought for a second to say yes, that it was just a joke. "No. It's true."

"Why would you ever leave?"

Mariyah sighed. "It's a long story."

"One you don't have time to tell," added Gertrude. "Lady Camdon doesn't like to be kept waiting."

Mariyah could see that Kylanda was bursting with questions. "Don't worry. There's plenty of time for me to tell you all about it."

"Please," said Kylanda, grabbing Mariyah's arm as she stood. "Come see me the moment you're done."

"I'm tired," said Mariyah. "But I promise to come see you tomorrow."

Gertrude cleared her throat when Kylanda did not release her hold, eventually reaching over to pry her hand loose. "Now then, shall we?"

They exited the room, leaving Kylanda sitting in the chair, staring after them.

"She'll never leave you alone now," remarked Gertrude. "I'm so sorry."

"Really, it's all right," said Mariyah. "It would have come out sooner or later."

"There is something else," said Gertrude. "Lady Camdon insists upon good table manners. I think it's why she doesn't allow us to dine with her. Nobles are a prudish lot, prim and proper from head to toe. Low-borns are too coarse for their taste."

She led Mariyah to a parlor similar to the one in which she had initially met Lady Camdon, though this one had a round table placed beneath a window overlooking a courtyard. The Lady was sitting in a chair, tapping her foot.

"I thought I told you right away," she said.

"Forgive me, my lady," Gertrude responded.

Lady Camdon sighed with a displeased expression. "I don't need apologies. I'm hungry and I need to eat."

With a formal bow, Gertrude exited. Mariyah was unsure if she should speak or sit. Was this woman ever polite?

"Don't just stand there looking lost," Lady Camdon remarked, rising to her feet. "I said I'm hungry."

She sat at the table where two plates and glasses of wine awaited them. Mariyah sat across from her with hands folded in her lap. The food was unfamiliar—six long green vegetables placed neatly side by side and a fist-sized chunk of what she thought to be bread, the top of which was split into a star-like pattern. Two strips of meat, from the look of it almost raw, completed the offering.

"I'm sure you have been told that you typically dine with the rest of the staff."

Mariyah nodded.

"This will no longer be the case. You will dine with me each night."

Mariyah felt a pang of disappointment, but tried not to let it show. "As you wish, my lady."

"Don't you want to know why?"

"Yes."

"Because you are a timid little mouse. Unfortunately, you are also a very expensive little mouse, and I have no desire to spend more time and gold on another. So you will dine each evening with me. Does that please you?"

Mariyah considered her words carefully. "If it brings me closer to my freedom, then yes."

"You are free now. I've already explained this. Perhaps you are simple-minded."

"I am not simple-minded. Nor am I timid."

"What *are* you, then?"

"Alone. Alone and afraid."

Mariyah thought she saw the hint of a smile, but couldn't be sure.

"Fear serves nothing. The strong feed on fear. They use it to keep the weak servile. Is that what you are? Weak and helpless?"

Mariyah could feel her anger boiling up, threatening to surface. "No, my lady. I'm not."

"I'm not so sure. I think maybe you are." Lady Camdon paused, regarding her closely. "You didn't like that, did you? Being looked upon as weak."

"No," came a tight-jawed reply. "I didn't."

"I can tell. Look at you. Flushed and trembling. Ready to lash out." She gave a derisive laugh. "You think *my* words are harsh? Let me teach you a lesson, child, one that could save your life."

Mariyah met her eyes firmly.

"Words are powerful," Lady Camdon continued. "There is no denying that. The wise and the strong use them both to heal and to cause great harm. Their meaning and their intent can be mightier than the keenest blade or the straightest arrow. Just look at what they've done to you in the short time you've been sitting at this table. A few seconds longer and you'd have thrown away your life for the fleeting pleasure of telling me to go to the depths. Why? Because of an insult? So answer me this: Are you weak and helpless?"

"No."

"Then why care if I say you are? What changes? Do I have the power to make it true, when it is not?" She didn't wait for Mariyah to respond. "You may find me cold, even cruel at times. You may even come to hate me. Just know that I do not care. The weight of responsibility I bear would crush you. And yet it's my hope you will prove capable of helping me bear it. Trysilia did this quite well. Do you think you will be able to take her place?"

"Yes, my lady."

Lady Camdon locked unblinking eyes with Mariyah. "We shall see. Let us begin. It took Trysilia a full week to learn proper dining etiquette. You have two days." She picked up her cutlery, the fork in her left hand with prongs facing downward, the knife held in the right between her thumb, index, and middle fingers.

Mariyah watched as she carved off a tiny slice of meat with the tip of her knife, then slid it to the right side of the plate. She followed this by doing the same to one of the vegetable spears, only this time sliding the severed portion to the left.

Mariyah mirrored her movements precisely, repeating this procedure three times before eventually taking a bite— meat first and then vegetable. A sip of wine was then deemed permissible. The bread was for last, the fork pressed to the center as the edges were carefully cut into thin slices. When all else was done, these were picked up with the fork and dipped into the wine. It took nearly an hour to finish the meal.

"What is your opinion of the food?" asked Lady Camdon.

302 · BRIAN D. ANDERSON

Mariyah had been so involved with imitating her movements that she hadn't paid much attention to the taste. Though upon reflection, it was bland. "It was fine," she said.

Her caution drew a frown. "No. It was tasteless and plain. When we are alone, you will speak honestly, and I will return the courtesy. I will begin by saying that you fumble around with utensils like a drunken beggar. Naturally, that is to be expected, as I assume you have never used utensils before."

"I've used them."

"Then you should have done better." She paused for a moment. "How do *you* think you did?"

"I think I did well," she replied. "In fact, I feel the dexterity in my hands was far better. You nearly dropped your fork twice. *I* did not."

This time Lady Camdon's smile was unmistakable, though it only lasted for a brief second. "Very good. That you noticed is a step in the right direction. Perhaps there's hope for you after all." She waved a dismissive hand. "Now, leave me. In the morning you will report to the library. You have much to learn before you're ready to be seen."

Mariyah exited the parlor unsure of her feelings. Lady Camdon was as she herself described: *cold.* Though not exactly cruel. Mariyah had never felt as intimidated as she did in her presence. For some reason the memory of Tamion and the nervous way he'd looked at her after dropping the crate of wine entered her thoughts. The fear in his expression that she would tell her father. Mariyah resolved never to seem timid or clumsy like this in Lady Camdon's eyes again. She would learn all that she could about this place and the Lady's needs as quickly as possible.

While passing through the halls and chambers, she noticed that the lights had dimmed. It was only then she realized that there was not a single lamp or brazier anywhere. It was as if light shone from nowhere in particular and yet everywhere at once. She hugged her arms to her chest at the thought that magic was in the very air she was breathing, touching every inch of her body.

Back in her room, she quickly removed her formal attire and put on the nightgown still draped over the chair. This time sleep did not come right away. Her mind continued to dwell on the way Lady Camdon held her fork and knife, how she sliced the bread, and even how much wine she took with each sip. She could not keep herself from going over it again and again. She was positive that there had been no difference between their carefully calculated movements. Or *had* there? Gradually, uncertainty wormed its way in. Even knowing it was a silly thing to think about, she could not prevent it.

It was almost dawn before Mariyah was able to keep her eyes shut and finally drift off to sleep. By then, her head was aching badly, plagued with thoughts of the days to come, stoking her anxiety to near madness.

No. Six years was too long, she decided. Far too long.

18

DECEPTION AND SALVATION

Beware those who choose the shadows as their home.
Book of Kylor, Chapter Three, Verse Fifty-Nine

Lem crept along the inner edge of the courtyard, avoiding the dim, flickering light from the braziers placed in each corner. This time the guards would be ready for him; the target had been alerted in advance of his arrival, a careless mistake by the client. But then, here in Ur Minosa, the incompetence was staggering.

Moreover, with very little in the way of natural resources to trade and farmland that could barely feed their own small population, it was amazing it had ever become a kingdom in the first place. Even here in the capital, the only city of any significant size, most of the buildings were in desperately poor condition and the streets riddled with holes.

The archway at the north end was being watched by three bowmen just above where he was now standing. But these mercenaries were of low quality. With none of the trio barely bothering to glance down, getting past them would be easy.

His soft leather shoes, custom made to fit perfectly, didn't make a sound as he waited for the right moment. Expensive, but worth it. The tingle of shadow walk that he had once felt keenly was now only just noticeable. Sometimes it felt as if he spent all of his waking hours in this state. How many had it been? Twenty-three? No. Twenty-four. Sir Marrish Pollack, protector of Lake Folstoy, personal aide and brother-in-law to King Brilian, would make twenty-five.

He walked through the archway at a brisk pace, then ducked behind the corner. Never run until you were forced to; this was a lesson well learned. No one could see him unless they were looking straight in his direction, but they *could* hear him. Even with his special footwear, there was always the danger that a slight scraping of leather on stone might give him away.

The long hallway was tiled with polished marble. This tended to make things go faster. Less noise, so he could increase his pace. He needed to finish this quickly; Shemi was waiting and would worry if he didn't make it back before the first play ended. Not to mention that Clovis would have to fill in for him during the interlude, and that was sure to irritate Farley.

"What is it you do when you go off on your own like that?"

Shemi had asked him that question yet again only the night before. Lem had no answer. At least, not a believable one. But on the positive side, his uncle was a lot easier to distract since leaving Ralmarstad. He was now free to explore the cities and towns without fear. When Farley had reluctantly removed the anklet, he'd practically danced with joy. From Shemi's perspective, they had gold, a secure place to live—even if it did move constantly—and, in the larger cities, libraries within which he could lose himself.

Lem focused his eyes on the third room along on the left. Two men clad in leather armor and carrying short

306 · BRIAN D. ANDERSON

spears were guarding the door, one on either side. Unlike those on the roof, they were vigilant in their duties. Not that it would stop him.

Reaching into the small pouch hanging on his belt, Lem retrieved a silver needle. After removing the protective cap, he crept up to the first guard, and with a well-practiced flick of his wrist, sank the tip into the man's left leg. It was perfectly placed, allowing the needle to effortlessly penetrate the unprotected cloth of his pants. Objective accomplished, Lem stepped quickly back.

"Damned bugs," cursed the guard, swatting at the point of impact. Seconds later he stumbled back, the spear falling from his hand as he collapsed to the floor.

"What's wrong?" asked his startled comrade, moving closer.

Lem waited until the second guard was crouched low and completely focused on the now-unconscious man before darting in, this time striking at the back of the neck. Like the first guard, he slapped at an imagined biting insect, and like the first man was unconscious in seconds, sprawled facedown across his fellow guard's lap. It was a comical scene to be sure, drawing a tiny smile from Lem. Just for a second he imagined that it would not have looked out of place in one of Farley's more humorous plays.

Stepping over the bodies, he pressed an ear to the door. The voices inside erased his smile in a flash. There were two. One was unquestionably his target. A chill ran through him, knowing good and well to whom the second voice belonged.

Taking a breath, he pushed the door open. The small antechamber was far enough away from the rest of the room for him to pass through without attracting attention. Though by now, it really didn't matter if Sir Marrish saw him or not. Still, he at least wanted to *try* being decent about this.

He could see Sir Marrish relaxing in an armchair beside a lit hearth. He had a book in one hand and a young girl of around six years old with raven curls and a bright smile sitting on his lap, giggling with delight as her father read her a story. He hadn't noticed the door open. Why would he? Who would be fool enough to try and get in here? Not even the finest assassin could pass through without detection. As for anyone fighting their way in, well, if the arrows didn't get you, the spearmen surely would.

Lem crossed the room and pressed his back to the corner. This appeared to be a study or an office, though a bed had been brought in and shoved awkwardly between the desk and a bookcase. His target had obviously decided to barricade himself in. A wise move under normal circumstances. Much easier to protect one room than an entire house; less expensive too. Sir Marrish was not a wealthy man. Not exactly poor, either, but to hire the dozen or more mercenaries necessary to protect his house properly would have stretched his purse to its limits. He had no more than five hundred gold in his personal account at the King's Treasury, and the rents on the two homes he owned did not earn all that much. He had a few other assets scattered about Ur Minosa as well, but nothing substantial. Some fields and orchards, none of which were very fertile.

As Lem watched the man read to his daughter, he recounted the information he had gathered. It was astonishing how simple it was to learn every aspect of a person's life with a few coppers and a little patience. It was the number one rule for assassins: Know everything you can about your target. No one had taught him this lesson; he'd had to work it out for himself. Assassins did not advertise. You could know one all your life and be completely oblivious as to their occupation. Most stayed in one place, taking contracts near their home as they became available. Not many made an actual living from it. But there were a few like Lem, according to Farley—men and women who wandered from kingdom to kingdom, ever in the shadows and never stopping anywhere long enough to put down roots. They were the *real* professionals. And now, Lem was among those counted few.

The story was a comedy about a bear and a wolf arguing over who would eat a cornered rabbit. The clever rabbit goaded each of them in turn, whispering that the other one was plotting against them, and that if he was going to be eaten by anyone, he preferred them. In the end, driven by suspicion and greed, the bear and the wolf resorted to fighting each other while the rabbit hopped merrily away.

Sir Marrish closed the book. "I think it's time for bed now."

The girl put on her best sad face. "But I'm not tired," she protested. "One more. Please? Then I promise I'll go right to sleep."

Lem drew his vysix dagger. He would make it swift and painless. The girl would see the unconscious guards on her way out of the room, and her cries were sure to quickly alert the bowmen. This was not a problem. By the time they descended the roof, Sir Marrish would be dead and he would be well away.

"I've already read three," the target said. "Now off with you." Placing the book on the table, he lifted his daughter to the floor and gave her a playful swat on the backside to hurry her along.

"But Father," she complained through pouting lips. "It's so dark in the rest of the house. Can't I stay here with you?"

He tilted his head and rubbed his chin. "Well . . . I suppose. If you promise not to snore this time."

She crinkled her tiny nose. "I don't snore. *You* do."

Placing a hand to his chest, he huffed loudly as if the mere suggestion was unfathomable. "Me? Snore? Never."

Without another word the girl skipped over to the bed and dove under the blanket. Sir Marrish smiled at his daughter for a moment, then retrieved another book from a nearby shelf—likely something more interesting for an adult.

Lem felt a touch of guilt, a feeling he rarely experienced of late. The happy little girl snuggling down in her father's bed would wake in the morning to find herself an orphan. The guilt was fleeting, however. She would be placed in the care of the man who had put out the contract: the brother of Sir Marrish's late wife—the wife he'd had murdered so as to be with another woman. Revenge, Lem found, was by far the most common motive for his contracts. It still bothered him that the Order of the Red Star had apparently gained favor through bribes and intimidation with almost every king and queen in every nation they had thus far traveled. It amounted in a real way to government-sanctioned assassination. But so long as he was careful, risk of discovery was nominal. And he was always careful.

He waited until the girl was sleeping soundly before stepping out of the corner. Sir Marrish was so engrossed in his reading that he did not feel the gentle touch of the blade's edge on the back of his scalp. Lem had discovered quite early in his new career that, when used properly, the vysix dagger could be virtually painless. Just the tiniest scratch was enough to end a life. He had by now become rather good at gauging precisely the correct amount of pressure to use if he wanted to leave the victim unaware that they had just been killed.

He paused long enough to see the man's eyes close and his body slump down in the chair before exiting the room. The guards outside were still unconscious, and would be for another few hours. No one would know how he had done it. An examination of the body would turn up nothing. In the end it would just be put down as yet another example of the Shade's deadly work.

Hearing that people were calling him—a mysterious and deadly new assassin—the Shade did not fill him with any sense of pride. However, he had to admit that it was fitting. After the first debacle, it quickly became obvious he had a real talent for this type of work. Yes, shadow walk gave him a marked advantage, but beyond that he had also become a master of learning when, where, and exactly how to strike. He had developed a nearly infinite degree of patience. And perhaps most importantly, he had learned to ignore any feelings of fear.

He waited until the bowmen looked away before hurrying out of their line of sight. Once in the street, he glanced back at Sir Marrish's house, his face a mask of indifference. *Twenty-five*, he thought. He wondered how many more there would be. After paying Farley what he was owed, and a few odds and ends for Shemi, he had managed to save seventy-five gold pieces. Not nearly enough to save Mariyah. An indenture with a life sentence could cost a hundred times that. But it was a start.

The rumble of an approaching thunderhead spurred him to move on. He walked at a leisurely pace, with those he passed along the way taking little or no notice of him. He had stopped dressing in all-black attire some months ago. It didn't help; if anything, it drew attention, especially in the immediate aftermath of the contract being fulfilled. Walking about dressed like he was up to no good was not a clever thing to do.

Lightning split the sky, followed a few seconds later by a sheet of rain that drenched him to the skin within moments. He smiled. No show tonight. He could relax for the evening, probably by playing some dice with Quinn and Clovis. Hallis didn't care for games and would instead lie on his cot reading until dropping off to sleep. Shemi often joined in as well, especially if there was no time to make it to a bookseller after finishing his duties.

Despite Lem's objections, his uncle insisted on earning his keep by washing the troupe's costumes and cooking their meals. Farley paid him a copper per day, even though the cheap bastard normally paid the lads he hired twice that amount. But Shemi didn't mind. And in truth, the extra coppers wouldn't have had any great impact on their relative wealth. At the same time, Shemi's pay was enough to keep him well stocked with reading material. Occasionally he would need to ask Lem for a little more if a volume were of particular value. But he never complained. After all, it was usually only a few coppers, and it made his uncle happy.

A young couple raced by, jackets held up against the downpour. Lem stepped onto the street to allow them to pass. He noticed the young man wore a silver bracelet with several moon-shaped charms attached by tiny chains. A follower of the Moon Goddess, Nephitiri. As he watched them walk on, he thought of how different life here was from that in Ralmarstad. People who worshiped Kylor lived side by side with those who did not. There was no Hedran to persecute heretics. Living by Kylorian law was a personal choice, rather than something to be enforced. And while the High Cleric was a person of tremendous influence and power, the church could not throw anyone in prison without the consent of the ruling monarch.

In fact, he'd been amazed at just how many gods and

goddesses there were. Some, like Nephitiri and Mannan, Lord of the Sea, had substantial followings, with several temples spread throughout Lamoria. But there were myriad other lesser-known deities, with only a handful of worshipers. The Church of Kylor was by far the largest and most influential, with more followers than all the other faiths combined. And yet not a single conflict had arisen among them.

Lem had not realized he had stopped in the middle of the street, continuing to watch the couple until they disappeared around the next corner. He lowered his head, and the rain poured from his chin and the tip of his nose. He wondered where they were going. Somewhere warm and dry, probably. Somewhere that death wasn't a part of their every waking moment. Somewhere they could sit and simply love one another.

He stood there for a time, trying to picture home. The image was becoming increasingly difficult to call forth, which was troubling. That he killed was a thing he had come to accept. But he could always lose himself in the memory of the life he left behind. His mind had become something of a sanctuary, one that was slowly fading from view.

Just before reaching their tents, the rain increased to a full-blown torrent. He passed by Farley's without so much as a sideways glance. He would tell him tomorrow about the contract. No rush.

On entering his tent, he saw Shemi drying his hair beside his cot. A smiling Quinn was already rolling the dice, and, as he often did, taunting Hallis for not playing. In contrast, Clovis was looking decidedly sour, the stack of coins in front of him considerably smaller than Quinn's.

"Ah, another sheep ready to be fleeced," Quinn called.

Lem smiled. "We'll see who gets fleeced tonight."

"You say that every time," he countered. "How much have you lost? Four silvers? No, five."

"I'm feeling lucky tonight."

While changing into some dry clothes, he noticed Shemi had a grave expression. "What's wrong?" he asked.

His uncle replied in a whisper. "I saw Vilanda today. I was just about to go into a bookshop when she caught my arm."

"What did she want?"

"She said only that I should give you this." He produced a folded parchment from a small box under his cot. "I opened it. I'm sorry, but curiosity got the better of me."

Lem quickly unfolded the letter and read its contents. It was brief. Two sentences.

Farley lied to you. He knows where she is.

The words stabbed into his heart, and rage threatened to overtake his mind.

"Do you think she's telling the truth?" Shemi asked.

"I don't know. But I'm damn sure going to find out."

Storming outside, he headed straight into Farley's tent, finding him with a glass of wine in one hand and whispering into the ear of a young woman sitting on his lap.

Farley looked up, a frown rapidly forming. "Do you mind? I have a guest."

"I don't care. Shemi saw Vilanda today, and she sent me a message. Would you like to know what it said?"

Farley shrugged. "Why not? Oh, wait . . . is it about the girl? What was her name? Mariyah, I think. Now I suppose you're here to find out if what Vilanda said is true. Well, I'm afraid it is." He sighed. "I thought that damn woman might do something stupid."

Lem's hand tightened around the handle of his dagger. "I should kill you here and now."

The woman in his lap sprang up and scuttled rapidly away to the rear of the tent.

Farley remained unmoved. "I wouldn't do that if I were you. Especially as I know where she is and you do not."

"I'll find her, with or without you." Lem took a menacing step forward.

"I'm sure you would." He turned to his guest. "You should leave. My friend and I need to speak privately."

She did not need a second prompting and scurried out without a word.

"I'll have to make it up to her later," Farley remarked offhandedly. "Anyway. You were saying something about wanting to kill me."

Lem drew his dagger. "Our association has come to an end."

Farley pursed his lips and squinted through one eye. "Oh, I think not. Not if you want to see your beloved again. And if you're in prison, that's not very likely. I suppose you could wait until you're released, but you'd be quite old by then. That's always assuming they didn't execute you for murder in the first place."

"The contracts are sanctioned by the Order. You'd never turn them over."

"Are you sure about that?"

"What are you saying?"

"Only that you get the contracts directly from me. Correct me if I'm wrong, but you're not yet a member. I am. All I have to say is that you were the one who betrayed us. I'd surely get reprimanded for putting my trust in you. But you, lad . . . you would suffer a far crueler fate. Then who would save your love?"

"You're bluffing." But Farley's confident expression said otherwise.

Farley laughed. "You think? Perhaps; perhaps not. There's one way to find out."

Lem took another step. "You can't tell anyone anything if you're dead."

"This is true," he conceded, though without a hint of fear. "You could kill me, I suppose. Or you could listen first. It so happens, I see a way out of this for both of us. One final contract—one so big that we can both get what we want. Complete it and I'll tell you where to find your precious Mariyah."

This was enough to give Lem pause. "Who's the client?"

"The King of Garmathia."

This floored Lem, but he maintained a steady appearance in front of Farley. Who had drawn the wrath of Garmathia's king?

"And the target?"

"The High Cleric."

Lem blinked hard. "Have you lost your mind?"

"Not at all. King Tribos wants to install his brother as the next High Cleric. Sadly, this means the old one has to die. And you, my lad, are the only one with the skill to accomplish such a task. The king says he'll pay ten thousand gold . . . to each of us."

"Ten thousand?" Lem could hardly believe his ears. Slowly, he put the dagger away.

Noting this, Farley smiled. "Enough to buy her freedom, I would imagine."

As tempting as this sounded, Lem was no longer the ignorant outsider he once had been. He had studied the world around him. "It can't be done," he stated, flatly. "The High Cleric is too well protected. And even if I could get close enough, I would never make it out alive."

"But if you did, just think about it. You could be with

your love again. Isn't that why you've been doing all this killing in the first place? Twenty-five, isn't it? You—a man who at one time could not so much as entertain the thought of killing even someone who almost beat you to death. Now one of the finest assassins in all the kingdoms. You can't tell me it isn't worth the risk."

Lem's mind was reeling. On its face, killing the High Cleric sounded impossible. But was it? "I need time to think." He turned to leave, pausing at the exit. "Just know, if I do this and you betray me, you'll regret the day you ever set foot in Harver's Grove."

The rain was being blown sideways by a strong westerly wind as he started back to his tent. The droplets stung his face. Much as he hated to admit it, Farley was right. Saving Mariyah was the sole reason he had set out on this path. It was how he reconciled it in his heart; how he could live with the evil that clung to his life like a noxious mist.

But to kill the High Cleric . . . that was suicide. Wasn't it? Could there be a way? He had penetrated tight security before, but nothing like what he would face if he undertook this contract. And then there was the fact that it was most definitely not an assignment coming through the Order. Not even *they* would accept something so dangerous. It would be a killing of enormous significance and with wide-ranging consequences. There would be an investigation; a *real* investigation. Blame would need to be allocated. The clergy would not accept the crime to go unsolved, and he sure as hell didn't trust Farley to protect him. Likely as not, the man would turn him in for the reward and get himself paid twice for one crime. In fact, it was quite possible that was already the plan.

Lem had never felt so conflicted and unsure. There was only one person he could talk to; one person who could help him make the right decision. But how would Shemi take the news that his dear nephew had become an instrument of death? Not well; that was a certainty. He would be deeply hurt and disappointed. All the same, Lem needed to talk to someone. This was too much for him to take on alone. He entered the tent with head hanging low.

Shemi was sitting on his cot, wringing his hands anxiously. "Is it true?" he whispered as soon as Lem drew close.

He shot a glance over to where Quinn and Clovis were playing dice. Hallis was still reading, as usual unwilling to be coaxed into joining them. "It's true," he replied somberly.

"The bastard."

Lem knew he couldn't discuss anything here, not with the others so close by. And he didn't want to risk Shemi getting sick by dragging him back out into the rain.

"We need to talk," he said. "But it will have to wait until morning."

"Talk about what?"

Lem stripped off his clothes and put on a pair of cotton pants. "Tomorrow."

Hearing the gravity in his tone, Shemi nodded his acceptance. "Very well. But first thing."

Lem ignored the calls for him to join the game. He was in no mood. Tomorrow he would decide just how far he was willing to go to save Mariyah. Surely there had to be a way forward that didn't involve getting killed.

He glanced over at Shemi, who was now stretched out on the cot a few feet away. Dread filled his heart just thinking about the moment when he would tell his uncle what he had become. But what other choice was there? If he did decide to risk everything, Shemi at least deserved to know why. In truth, he deserved to know regardless. The old man's love and determination to risk all in a bid to save him had already caused him immeasurable suffering.

He hated the thought of causing Shemi more pain. But as had become his life, he had to do things he knew he might regret. He had come to understand one immutable truth about himself: It was a lack of options that he hated most. And his continued to dwindle.

19

THE LESSONS AND TRIALS
OF THE IRON LADY

Toil without intent holds no virtue. Do not waste your labors on frivolous pursuits. Time ill spent cannot be recovered.

Book of Kylor, Chapter One, Verse Seventy-Three

Gertrude came to wake Mariyah early on her first morning, just after sunrise. Although still exhausted, Mariyah felt a bit better after a cup of hot tea and a piece of sweet, crunchy bread that Gertrude called a jarmin biscuit.

"Poor dear," she said. "You mustn't let yourself worry so much. You look like you haven't slept a wink."

"I'll be fine." Mariyah rubbed the back of her neck.

"I hope so. Because I hear there's a stack of books as tall as I am waiting for you in the library. And the Lady has canceled all appointments and guests for the next month."

Mariyah wasn't sure if this was good news or bad. She noticed that Gertrude's hair was neatly wrapped in a bun and that she was wearing a formal-looking dress with a silk scarf tied around her neck. "Is there something special happening today?" she asked.

Gertrude grinned with obvious excitement. "Lady Camdon has given me and Marison leave to see my cousin for our anniversary. I thought I'd dress up for the occasion."

The idea of Gertrude's absence produced a mild sense of unease. "How long will you be gone?"

"Two weeks," she replied. "But don't worry. Kylanda has told everyone about you being from Vylari, so you won't lack for company. That's assuming Lady Camdon gives you a moment to yourself. From what I see, she has your plate rather full."

The turn of phrase brought back memories of the previous night's dinner. Before she realized it, she had let out a loud and quite lengthy groan.

"Now, now. We'll have none of that," Gertrude scolded gently. "It's like Trysilia told you. Once you learn how things are done here, you'll have plenty of free time."

She laid out a few dresses on the bed along with some shoes and a few bits of jewelry, then pointed to each set of attire individually. "Morning . . . afternoon . . . evening. You'll be given time to change before each meal." That done, she gave Mariyah a firm embrace. "You'll be fine. Just keep your wits about you. And don't let the others keep you up late. You need your rest."

After she departed, Mariyah dressed and made her way to the library. As Gertrude had said, a tall pile of books was waiting, along with a note from Lady Camdon.

It listed the books in the order she was to read, stating that she would be tested before dinner each evening. This was not too daunting. Mariyah was a fast reader and had always been quick to assimilate knowledge. Even Shemi had remarked on this.

The first book was entitled *The Art of the Silver Tongue* and dealt mostly with divining meaning behind the banter of the nobility. Many of the references she did not understand, and the way in which the social order was described was often confusing. Nonetheless, she found it an interesting read overall.

She had just closed the book when a different, much older woman with short brown hair and dark eyes ushered her wordlessly back to her chambers. *No speaking in public areas.* At that moment it felt like a particularly silly rule.

"Lady Camdon says that you're to join her for lunch in the parlor," the woman revealed once they were inside the bedroom. "And you're to wear this." She placed a gold anklet on the nightstand.

"Thank you," said Mariyah. "What is your name?"

"Sanji," she replied. "You should hurry. The Lady's not in a good mood."

Mariyah was loath to put on the anklet, even if it was nothing more than a piece of lifeless metal. Still, it was something that had to be done. She dressed as quickly as she could and hurried to the parlor.

Lady Camdon did indeed look to be in a foul mood. As before, Mariyah watched closely while she ate, mimicking her movements precisely. This time, there were no criticisms. Instead, she was questioned for the next half an hour on what she had just read.

"At least you're not as dimwitted as I feared," Lady Camdon remarked at the end, then dismissed her with a brusque wave.

Mariyah returned to the library, grateful to no longer be in the Lady's company. She wished Trysilia had been more forthcoming about the woman. Not that it would have made a great deal of difference. Of course, after spending ten years in her company, perhaps Trysilia no longer noticed her ill temper and rude behavior, or possibly she simply had not wanted to frighten her too much in advance of their meeting.

This routine continued for two weeks. After Mariyah

completed the first stack of books, she found a fresh stack awaiting her the following day. The subjects ranged from politics, etiquette, and history right through to much more unexpected topics such as botany and metallurgy. She didn't mind the reading, nor even the twice daily tests of her retention. What troubled her was that none of the staff had come to see her during this time, and when she tried to go to them, they turned her away without any hint of an explanation.

By the time Gertrude and her husband returned, Mariyah was feeling isolated and desperate for friendly company. At night, she found herself near weeping, overcome with inexplicable sorrow. It became so pronounced that when Gertrude came to see her, she rushed straight into the woman's arms, embracing her tightly for more than a minute, refusing to let go.

Gertrude walked her over to the bed and sat down beside her. "Now calm yourself, dear. It's not as bad as all that. I heard that you're to be officially made Lady Camdon's personal assistant later this week."

"Am I supposed to be excited?" Mariyah responded hotly. "She's nothing but a cold-hearted sow." Regretting the sharp response, she took a deep breath. "I'm sorry. But it's been two weeks and I haven't spoken to anyone other than Lady Camdon since you left. She won't even allow the others to visit me at night."

Gertrude furrowed her brow. "No one? Perhaps they've just been busy."

"No. It's her doing, I know it is. It's like . . . she's trying to break me. And I don't know why."

Gertrude regarded her for a long moment. "I don't think she wants to break you. Though I admit, it's strange she's kept you from the others. Stranger that no one has said anything to me about it. If I'd known, I would have

THE BARD'S BLADE · 323

come to see you soon as we arrived this morning." She removed a handkerchief from her sleeve and dabbed Mariyah's cheeks. "You rest easy. I'll find out what's going on."

Mariyah felt embarrassed that she had put on such an emotional display. "Thank you. I guess I'm just lonely."

Gertrude pushed the hair from her face. "Don't think on it. It's perfectly normal. I can't even imagine what this must be like for you. And if it makes you feel any better, Trysilia cried every night for a month when she first arrived. And *she* had the others to keep her company. In the end, she made it through. And so will you."

Gertrude's kind words helped considerably. So too did the thought that no matter how confident and strong Trysilia appeared, she had coped no better in the beginning.

Gertrude kissed her cheek. "Now you get to sleep. Tomorrow will be better. You'll see."

That night she slept soundly, waking in the morning feeling refreshed and filled with renewed confidence. She had just finished dressing and was preparing to set off for yet another day of study in the library when the door opened. It was Lady Camdon. This was the first time she had come to her room.

"Gertrude and Marison are no longer in my employ," she stated flatly. "And you will not attempt to speak with the rest of the staff again. Not at any time. Understood?"

Mariyah's newfound confidence vanished. The anger that had been simmering over the course of the last two weeks rose in a rush, and she spoke without thinking. "No, I do *not* understand. So either explain it to me or I'm leaving."

Lady Camdon's calm demeanor didn't change. "I owe you no explanation. But as you seem determined, I will tell you this: By trying to intercede on your behalf, Gertrude jeopardized both my plans and your future. As Marison is her husband, he chose to resign."

"Plans? What plans?"

"My plans are not your concern."

"If they involve me, I think they are."

"You presume to . . ."

"Yes . . . my lady. I presume to question you."

Though her aspect did not soften, for an instant there was the tiniest hint of something akin to approval in her eyes. "It's about time. I was beginning to think you too weak to stand up for yourself."

Mariyah was stunned into a confused silence.

"Do you really think I care what you know about metallurgy? Granted, if you have ambitions to be a blacksmith once you leave here, I can certainly find you more material on the subject. And why would I care about gardening? I was thinking that you were either the stupidest person in all creation, or possibly just stubborn beyond belief."

"It was a test?"

"In a way, yes. Soon you will need to become my eyes, ears, and occasionally my voice. The world in which I dwell does not suffer the weak. Trysilia was strong and clever; clever enough to recognize in you the qualities I require. But I had to be sure." She opened the door. "Come. Walk with me."

After a brief hesitation, Mariyah recovered her wits and followed Lady Camdon from the room. They walked toward the east wing in silence for a time, Lady Camdon wearing a thoughtful expression, as if having an inner debate.

"If I did leave, would you really let me live on your estate?" asked Mariyah.

"No," she said at length. "I would see you safely to the border of Ubania."

At this, Mariyah felt a surge of joy that threatened to make her cry out.

"I can see this pleases you. Now you understand that you are not a prisoner, not in any true sense of the word. You can leave here without fear of recapture. And once outside Ubania you will be as safe and secure as any other person. This is one choice you can make."

"And the other?"

"That is what I'll show you. But once I have done so and your choice is made, there is no turning back."

As they wound their way through the manor, Mariyah was already certain what she would choose: freedom. Real freedom, not the illusion within which she was now trapped.

They arrived at an elegant dining room with a table more than thirty feet long, at the end of which was seated an elderly man wearing a simple tan shirt. He had short, curly gray hair and a dark brown complexion, and was reading a thick, leather-bound book. From a pipe gripped between his teeth, a thin line of acrid smoke drifted up to the high ceiling. Mariyah thought him peculiar as he muttered incoherently, not seeming to notice as they drew near.

"Master Felistal," said Lady Camdon. When he did not look up, she cleared her throat with conspicuous intensity.

"What do you want?" he replied, eyes still fixated on his book. "I'm not in the mood for idle banter today."

Mariyah stifled a laugh on hearing someone speak to Lady Camdon so tersely.

"Master Felistal, please remember in whose house you are staying," she shot back, with poorly masked annoyance.

"I haven't forgotten. Though I think you need reminding to whom *you* are speaking."

"Must we go through this every time?"

The man looked up, chuckling. "If it means watching you become flustered, then yes." Seeing her anger growing, he waved a hand. "Forgive me. I should not amuse myself at your expense."

"If you were not so old and frail, you might find other ways to entertain yourself."

This made him chuckle even harder. "And you wonder why they call you the Iron Lady?" His gaze fell on Mariyah. "And this must be the one you were telling me about."

"Yes," she replied.

"I never thought I would meet someone from Vylari," he said, beaming a smile. "Please sit."

Mariyah sat to the right of the old man. Lady Camdon took a chair opposite.

"So . . . Loria here says you are extremely bright. That's high praise indeed from one as difficult as she."

"Thank you," Mariyah replied. Sneaking a look across the table, she saw that Lady Camdon was scowling.

"Have you enjoyed your time here?"

"No. I can't say that I have."

Felistal let out a hearty laugh. "Then Loria's reputation remains intact. Though I would think it is still preferable to Lobin." When Mariyah did not answer, he added, "You should feel free to speak your mind here, particularly when talking to me."

Lady Camdon nodded her approval.

"I think a prison is still a prison," Mariyah said. "One may be more brutal than another, but that does not make it more moral. I was captured, falsely accused of a crime, imprisoned, and then brought here against my will. Just because no one beats me doesn't make me less a prisoner."

"Did Loria not explain that you are free to leave?"

"She can still change her mind. Until I'm outside Ubania, I'm subject to her whims. You can call a wolf a rabbit. That doesn't mean it won't bite you."

Felistal nodded. "So true. I can see why she brought you to me." He placed his pipe on the table. "You're absolutely right, of course. What has been done to you, even by the Lady's hand, however gentle by comparison, is still an atrocity. I wish I could say there are better days ahead, but at my age lies are too difficult to remember." Pausing, he reached into his pocket and produced the anklet she had worn upon her arrival. "What can you tell me about this?"

Mariyah shrugged. "I don't know what you mean. It was the anklet they forced on me."

"I'm aware of that. What I'm asking is, do you know how it came to be in this condition?"

She shook her head. "I pulled it off and threw it across the room. How it got to be like that I couldn't say. Maybe the spell that cleans the floor did something to it?"

"No. That's not possible. In fact, there is only one possibility. But we'll come to that in a moment." He turned the book so that she could see the opened page properly and pointed to a single word. *Belkar.* "Have you seen or heard of this before?"

Mariyah thought she recalled a song Lem would play occasionally in which it was mentioned, though she wasn't sure. "Perhaps," she said. "I can't place it."

"Belkar was a man who reputedly lived ages ago," he explained. "A legend to most. A dark legend."

"Are you sure you should be telling her this?" Loria cut in. "I thought we were going to . . . limit the discussion."

"I will reveal only what she needs to know in order to make her decision."

Loria tightened her jaw, hands clasped on the table.

Felistal returned his attention to Mariyah. "As I was saying, Belkar was a powerful sorcerer, the most powerful the world has ever known. So powerful, in fact, he uncovered the secret to immortality."

Mariyah's eyes lit up. "I *do* remember. Belkar the Undying. It was a song my betrothed would sing. I forget the words—something about a war and being trapped inside a stone, swearing one day to return?"

Felistal scratched at his chin. "Interesting that his name survives in your land."

"Interesting is not the word I would use," said Loria.

"No. I'm sure you would prefer to use *dangerous*. Or *suspicious*, perhaps. But don't be so quick to judge."

"What's dangerous or suspicious about an old song?" asked Mariyah.

"In itself, nothing," Felistal replied. "And you should not think on it. However, the truth remains that ages ago, Belkar and his army of followers nearly conquered all of Lamoria. He was eventually defeated and driven beyond the mountains, but not before millions had perished. When it was over, his very name was considered a crime to speak aloud."

"Are you telling me that he's real?" Mariyah asked.

"Not necessarily. But the legend says that one day he will return, to bring darkness and death to all those unwilling to kneel before him. And real or myth, there are those who still believe it. At least to the extent that they're using Belkar's name to advance their own influence and power." He leaned forward a little. "This is why you're needed. Magical ability is rare, and even when someone has it, it's usually limited."

"You are saying I possess this . . . ability?" The thought was repugnant, and she could not prevent it from showing clearly in her expression.

"I do not *think* so; I know so. And in you it is strong. Quite strong in fact." He touched the ruined anklet. "*You*

THE BARD'S BLADE · 329

did this. And by sheer instinct, no less. It's the only explanation. Somehow, the magic in Lady Camdon's manor
must have unlocked your abilities. At least, that's my guess.
But how it happened doesn't matter. That it *did* happen,
and that it happened *now*, when things are growing ever
dark, that is what really counts."

"So you want me to learn magic?" Mariyah pushed back
her chair. "I won't do it."

"Do you believe in fate?" Felistal asked.

"No," she responded coldly.

He smiled. "Why not? Because you're here? Because
your life has taken an ill turn? My sweet girl, fate is often
cruel. That doesn't mean it isn't real."

"Prove it."

"Mariyah!" snapped Loria. "Mind your tongue. Don't
forget where you are."

"I haven't forgotten. But if you think I'll be cowed a
minute longer and fed nonsense to trick me into learning
to wield the same power that was used to keep me imprisoned, then you should just hand me over now. I refuse."

"As would I, were that the case," said Felistal. "But it
isn't. Neither Loria nor I will hand you over to anyone. On
my word. Please—just hear me out before passing judgment. Should you want to leave afterward, I will take you
to the border this very day, with enough gold to see that
you can live quite comfortably for many years."

The offer stunned Mariyah. She glanced over to Lady
Camdon, who was looking uncharacteristically anxious.
"I'll listen."

"Thank you," he said, with a look of genuine appreciation. "As I told you, there are those who will use the name
of Belkar to further their own ambitions. Whether or not
he actually exists is irrelevant. It's what people are doing in
his name that is the true threat. The disease is spreading,

and I fear it will afflict us all before long. I say fate brought you here because we are losing the battle. Our enemies multiply while our allies dwindle. Soon they will have control over Ubania, Gothmora, and most of Ralmarstad."

"Why should I care?" Mariyah cut in. "If you ask me, they deserve it."

"Perhaps," Felistal conceded. "But they won't stop there. Once Ralmarstad is under their control, they will wage war on the rest of Lamoria. And though I know you have little reason to care about that either, think of your home. Vylari is known to us. Which means it is probably known to our enemies."

"Vylari is protected," she countered.

"Yes, I know. The Thaumas have been trying to find it for more than five years. To warn you."

Mariyah felt her flesh prickle. The *stranger*.

"What's wrong?" asked Felistal.

It took a moment before Mariyah could form a reply. "The reason I left home."

"Your betrothed," said Camdon. "Lem, I think you called him. What of him?"

"This can't be mere chance," said Mariyah, in a half-whisper.

Felistal placed his hand on Mariyah's. "Why don't you tell me your story? Perhaps we can help one another sort this out."

Mariyah looked up, a torrent of conflicting thoughts and emotions tearing through her. Could this be precisely what Felistal had said it was? Fate? In a nearly languid daze, she began recounting the events leading to her departure from Vylari.

Both Felistal and Lady Camdon listened with intensity to every word, often glancing over to each other with apprehensive expressions. When she was done, Felistal stood and turned to the wall, head tilted forward.

"So he's dead," he muttered. "The fool. He was only to *locate* Vylari. Not enter. He wasn't ready."

"So it's true?"

"Yes. But it was not your betrothed he sought, it would seem. It was you. Tragically, there was no way for him to know this." He let slip a long sigh. "His father will be devastated."

"Me? But Lem's mother . . . she lived with the Thaumas, right? Doesn't that mean it has to be Lem you need?"

He turned to face her with a sad smile. "I didn't know her well, but yes, Illorial did live among us for a time. But it was *you* who came to be here. And it is *you* who possesses the gift. I have no idea what forces control our destiny. But I would have to be blind not to see that you have been guided here for a purpose."

The enormity of what he was saying was making her dizzy. She could neither move nor speak. *Lem.* He had left home to save Vylari . . . to save her. For nothing.

"I know this is all a bit much to accept," said Felistal. "And I know how afraid you must be."

"I'm not afraid," she managed to whisper. She wasn't. But what *was* she feeling? Anger? Misery? Desperation? It was all of these and more. But fear? No. Definitely not fear.

"So you'll stay?" asked Lady Camdon.

Mariyah did not answer for several seconds. She then locked eyes with Lady Camdon. "Yes. But only under my own terms. I want to be free to leave anytime I want. If I change my mind, you must agree to take me home. And I mean *my* home."

"I told you before we got here," Lady Camdon said, not

attempting to conceal her annoyance. "If you choose to stay, that decision is set. You cannot leave."

"I know what you said. And now you need to hear what *I'm* saying. If what you tell me is true, having seen Ralmarstad cruelty for myself, I would most assuredly wish to protect Vylari. In fact, were I a trusting child, I would probably not question it. But the fact remains, I do not know you . . . either of you. The first Lamorians I met in this world seemed kind. Then one of them turned us over to evil people. You ask for my help, then make threats. How are you better than those you say are the enemy?" She rose from her chair. "I will stay. And I will learn what you have to teach me. Should I find you're telling the truth, I will even fight. But I will be a servant no longer." She held out the hand bearing Lady Camdon's ring. "You ask me to trust you, yet you do not trust me."

Felistal looked over to Lady Camdon, an amused grin spread across his lips. "She makes a valid point, Loria."

Lady Camdon shot up from her chair, cheeks crimson and fists clenched. "I will . . . I will . . ."

Mariyah stood her ground, eyes fixed, arm extended. "Yes or no?"

For a tense moment it looked as if Lady Camdon would attempt to throttle her. However, after Felistal emitted a particularly contrived-sounding cough, she gradually relaxed her posture and met Mariyah's gaze squarely. "You will not disrespect me in my home. You will not tell the others what we do. And you will behave as if things are just as they were before. Otherwise you can leave. I'll not jeopardize everything simply to make you feel better."

Mariyah nodded. "Agreed."

Lady Camdon rounded the table and removed the ring.

"There is one more thing I would ask," Mariyah said, rubbing the spot where the ring had been. She saw a flash of anger appear on the Lady's face. "It's not a demand. I agreed to respect you, and where I'm from we never disrespect someone in their own home. If you say no, I won't ask again. But I will make this request just once: Please bring Gertrude back."

"Gertrude never left," she said. "I only told you that to force you into confrontation."

Mariyah glared. "Why would you do that?"

"I told you. I needed to know your limits."

"Personally," Felistal chipped in, "I thought it was a stupid idea."

"It was," Mariyah agreed, still simmering.

This drew a smile from the old man. "I like her, Loria. She reminds me of you. Well . . . before you were the Iron Lady."

Camdon was not amused. "I'll thank you not to mock me in my own home."

"You're right, of course," said Felistal. "I say let us leave the past in the past. It is time we move forward. Our foes are advancing, and we must be prepared."

"Yes," said Lady Camdon, her indifferent demeanor returning. "Quite right. I've sent out invitations for a ball to be held in three weeks' time. I expect you to be ready, Mariyah. And if you think I was difficult before . . ." A wicked grin appeared. "Well . . . you should get some sleep."

"What about the staff?" asked Mariyah. "Are they permitted to speak to me now?"

"I don't see why not. There's no further need to keep you from them. But I think you'll find your time quite fully occupied with other matters."

Felistal pushed himself up, groaning from the effort. "Now that all that's settled, if you don't mind, I too have business that requires my attention. However, I would appreciate your company, Mariyah, at least until we reach your chambers." He tottered over to Mariyah and held out his arm. "If it pleases you, of course."

Mariyah glanced over at Lady Camdon while taking his arm. The woman's expression was unreadable—a practiced and perfected mask. Had she enjoyed her little torments? It was hard to say. Mariyah didn't want to think so. Though now that things were different, she would find out soon enough. One thing Mariyah did know was that when she looked at the tall, regal frame and proud bearing, she did not see Lady Loria Camdon. She saw the Iron Lady.

With Loria already departed and way ahead of them, at first Felistal appeared deep in thought and did not speak as they walked slowly through the manor.

"You should not judge her too harshly," he finally said. "Loria Camdon is a remarkable woman. Everything you see around you is from her own labor. The Camdon family, though nobility, was of low status before she came into her inheritance. It was only through her shrewd dealings and outthinking of those who would see her fall that she's become one of the most powerful nobles in Ubania."

"Power doesn't make you a good person," Mariyah countered.

"No, it doesn't. Unfortunately, society is not kind to women like Loria. At least not in Ubania."

"What do you mean, *like her*?"

"Unmarried. And unlikely to ever be."

Mariyah frowned. "Why should that matter?"

"If she were not a noble, it wouldn't. But as part of the nobility she is expected to create alliances, and the most common way is through marriage."

"Maybe she hasn't met the right person."

Felistal shook his head, laughing. "The right person? How wonderful life must be in Vylari. The right person is the one who has the most wealth and influence. Love is not a consideration."

"How awful."

"Indeed. But it is the way of things. And for Loria, her challenges are compounded by a lack of an heir. If they could, her enemies would destroy her. But Loria is too clever for them by far. She may seem hard and uncaring, but that's how she must be in order to survive."

"That's still no reason to be hateful to others."

He sighed and patted her hand. "It has made her callous, I admit. But the young girl I knew is still in there somewhere."

"How do you know her?"

"I was her instructor in magic."

"So she's a sorcerer?"

He tilted his head, a grin forming. "If that's the term you choose to use, then yes. We referred to ourselves as the Thaumas, but *sorcerer* is the more commonly known name. And you, young lady, have the potential to be a truly great one."

"I still don't understand why you say that. I accidentally melted an anklet. Nothing more."

"It wasn't *just* an anklet. The metal used in their construction is quite unique and virtually indestructible by normal means. And as a Thaumas ages we become increasingly sensitive to the magic of others. Being near you is more than enough for me to know what you are capable of achieving."

"You should know I was raised to think magic is evil. And I have seen nothing yet to convince me otherwise."

Felistal chuckled. "I understand. And given that you have witnessed only its dark side, I understand why you might feel that way. The anklets are a terrible misuse. You have yet to see the beauty magic can create. Take your home, for example. It's magic that protects Vylari, not swords and spears. I think if you keep an open mind, you too will soon begin to see magic as I do: an instrument for good."

In spite of his words, Mariyah was finding it a hard struggle to imagine magic as benign. Even before being subjected to the anklet, she had always been told it was corrupt. That was why the people of Vylari had abandoned the practice long ago. For her to cast aside a lifetime of belief on the word of a stranger in such a short space of time was impossible.

"I'll try to keep an open mind," she said after a lengthy period of thought. "That's all I can promise."

"I can ask for no more."

When they reached her door, Felistal took her by the hands. "Do take care. You may not believe it yet, but you can trust Loria. Difficult as she is, if you listen carefully to her instructions, you will never again be a victim. She can show you how to triumph over those who would seek to harm you. That alone must be worth staying here for a time."

She dearly wanted to trust the old man. His kindly eyes and warm bearing reminded her of Shemi. So too did the way he'd been lost in his reading when she'd first seen him. But that wasn't enough. She simply could not give him her trust. Not completely . . . not yet.

"Thank you," she said. "I'll remember everything you've told me."

"I'm sure you will."

She waited until he had rounded the corner before entering her room.

Lying in her bed, she recounted the events of the day. She felt in control—not just for the first time since leaving home, but in a strange way, for the first time in her life. She had stood up to those who had power over her, and she had taken that power back. Yes, Lady Camdon could still make her life miserable if she chose to—possibly send her to prison. That wasn't the point.

She had shed her fear. And never would she allow it to regain its hold.

20

HOW TO KILL A HIGH CLERIC

Though the war has at last ended, peace remains elusive. Skirmishes continue to spring up along the border, though it doesn't appear likely to rekindle into a full-blown conflict. For that, at least, I am thankful. I doubt I will ever be forgiven for allowing the Archbishop to retain power in Gothmora and Ubania. I can only hope that one day people will understand why it was necessary; that I did it to stop the fighting and end the bloodshed. May Kylor forgive me.

Letter from High Cleric Marli Brume
to Queen Lyn Malferos of Lytonia

Shemi's face conveyed no emotion as he looked across the table. The small café where Lem had brought him for breakfast and to reveal his secret was empty aside from themselves and a few staff. It wasn't a popular place; the decidedly mediocre fare explained why.

His uncle's tone was as indecipherable as his expression. "Is that what you've been doing when you disappear at night? Murdering people?"

"Yes. Well, not *every* time. I have to learn as much as I can about the target first. I follow them around for a few days before completing the contract."

"You say *target* as if you were hunting a deer or a rabbit.

These are people." The old man's eyes drifted down to the table. "How about women? Or children?"

"No."

"Would you?"

"I would never harm a child. As for women, I've been lucky not to have had to make that choice."

"But you would."

Lem nodded. "Yes. I think so."

"And you claim all this is to save Mariyah. That's the only reason you've become a paid killer?"

Lem recounted in some detail how he had come to this pass.

"So it's Farley's doing . . ."

His uncle's eyes were pleading, and Lem knew he was searching for a way to absolve him, a way that wouldn't force him to face what his nephew had become. Reaching over, Lem took Shemi's hand. "I was the one who agreed to it. All Farley did was provide me with the means."

Shemi jerked his hand back. "Don't defend that pig."

"I'm not defending him. Believe me, if I could, I would leave him right now."

"So why don't you? There's nothing holding you here. Ralmarstad is hundreds of miles to our backs. And if that's not far enough, we could keep going."

Lem shook his head. "I need to earn enough gold to buy Mariyah's freedom once I've found her. I'd never be able to do that on a musician's wages."

"But why do you need Farley?"

He checked to be certain none of the staff could hear. "He's a member of the Order. I'm not. I work under him."

Shemi took a long breath. Rather than the anger and disappointment Lem expected, he saw pity. "I know you were afraid to tell me this. Now that you have, to be honest, I'm not sure how to feel about it. I've known you all your life, and I just can't picture you harming a soul. But I know how much you love Mariyah. I love her too. But there must be another way."

"There might be." Lem told him of the contract for the High Cleric. Shemi's reaction was predictable.

"Are you completely mad?"

"That's why I needed to talk to you. If I succeed, I'll have enough gold to free Mariyah."

"And if you fail, you'll be dead. Then who will save her?" He threw up his hands. "How could Farley even suggest it?"

The answer to that was easy to state. "Greed, pure and simple. But leave Farley out of it for now. Isn't it worth the risk? Isn't this the chance that would make every horrible thing I've done worth it? I'd be able to free Mariyah, and the three of us could find somewhere up north to settle down. I can earn enough playing the balisari. I might even see about becoming a bard." Even as he said it, he knew it was a fantasy. When he and Mariyah were reunited—and they would be, he had to believe it was true—there was still the stranger's dark vision to face.

Shemi regarded him for a long moment. "I *am* glad you told me. If you hadn't, you might have actually convinced yourself of the nonsense coming out of your mouth."

"How is it nonsense?"

"Because killing someone like the High Cleric is impossible. What do you think I do in the library? I've read all about him. The High Cleric is as powerful as any king or queen and twice as wealthy. You think someone like that isn't well protected? Not to mention that Farley is sure to betray you. For all you know, he's just using you to suit some other scheme."

Lem had already considered this possibility and put it aside.

Shemi's brow suddenly creased and his eyes narrowed. "Tell me again exactly what he said to you. Leave nothing out."

Lem did as requested. He could see that his uncle was working something out. Gradually, a smile formed on the old man's face.

"So King Tribos wants to install his own brother, does he? And to achieve this, he's willing to risk his throne if he fails?" He leaned back in his chair and took a bite of his less-than-tasty eggs. "I have an idea."

———

Lem's hands were trembling. Never before had he seen a structure of such unimaginable size and splendor. Not even the watchtowers in Lobin could compare with what stood before him.

Massive silver columns, untarnished by the weather, spanned the building's five-hundred-foot-wide façade. The edifice reached to an almost impossible height. At its apex, Lem could just make out a relief depicting the heavens shining down on a field of tall grass, in the center of which was a lone man kneeling with arms outstretched and head thrown back as rays of celestial light rained down around him. A staircase, also spanning the building's entire breadth, climbed up to a dozen evenly spaced archways, each watched by a pair of guards. Fifty more were standing at the bottom of the stairs, clad in crisp uniforms of a deep blue, matching the color of the dusk sky, golden helms, and each carrying a long spear with a hooked tip. The square, twice as large as any Lem had seen before, was home to a vast multitude of statues and fountains of such delicate beauty it was hard to believe they existed. Hundreds of people were walking about. Some, probably pilgrims, were unable to do anything but gaze in wonder. Others were knelt in prayer.

This was the true heart of clerical power, and it was clear that the church wanted everyone to know it. Lem shoved his hands into his pockets and did his best to steady his breathing. His legs felt like they were filled with wet sand as he took his first step. The second step was no easier. Nor was the third. By the time he reached the line of guards, he felt as if he would empty his stomach. Since becoming an assassin, fear was a thing he thought he could control. He was wrong.

At the top of the stairs, Lem paused. He had read as much as he could on his way to the Holy City of Xancartha, a two-day ride from Ur Minosa where the troupe was still located. Information was abundant, yet even drawings of what was referred to as simply *the Temple* had not adequately prepared him for its reality. Though anyone was permitted to enter, only those members of the order assigned here were permitted to worship within its walls. Everyone else prayed in the square, which would fill to capacity each night when the High Cleric's Light Giver would deliver the daily blessing. Just once a year, on the official first day of fall, the High Cleric himself would perform this rite. Not that fall ever came to the Holy City. Here, it was eternally springtime. The faithful believed this phenomenon to be the work of their god, but Lem suspected magic was involved—though how magic could be used to alter the seasons was incomprehensible. Winter had come and gone, and yet not a single flake of snow had fallen. Here there were only warm breezes carrying the pleasing fragrances of the gardens throughout the city and gentle rains that could be counted on falling at the same time each week without fail.

A hand touched his arm. "Are you all right?"

Lem looked across to see an old woman dressed in the blue robes of the clergy. She was smiling up at him.

"You look ill," she said. "Perhaps you should sit down?"

"I'm fine. Thank you."

"Don't be silly. You're as pale as milk. Come. There's a bench just inside."

Lem allowed himself to be led through one of the archways and into a large gallery that was also filled with pilgrims, clerics, and all manner of other people. It was as opulent as he expected. He was surrounded by more statues of masterful design, and gilded ornaments and relics in glass cases were on display for visitors and scholars to view at their leisure. As for the walls, though there were various artworks and tapestries, they were completely dominated by the life-sized portraits of past High Clerics. Each painting was so realistic, Lem could almost imagine that whenever he glanced at one, it was looking right back at him.

As promised, a row of wooden benches flanked a six-foot-tall crystal spire with the great eye of Kylor emblazoned in gold at its summit. The woman shooed away two young men chatting with each other and gestured for Lem to sit.

"Better?" she asked.

"Yes. Thank you." He did feel better, actually. His hands had stopped shaking, and his stomach was not churning quite so badly.

She patted his leg. "Now, why don't you tell me what has you in such a terrible state?"

"I was just a bit dizzy. Really. I'm fine now."

"Then if you won't tell me what's wrong, why don't you tell me why you're here?" She regarded him closely. "Not a pilgrim, I presume. And I can't place your accent."

"I'm here to see someone," he replied.

"Aren't we all? If you tell me who it is, perhaps I can help."

"Thank you again, but I doubt you can help me."

The woman frowned. "Young man, you should not underestimate the elderly. I've been walking these halls for more than fifty years. There isn't a soul here that I don't know."

"Forgive me. I didn't mean to insult you. But I think you would laugh if I told you who I'm here to see."

"Is it the High Cleric?"

Lem stiffened. "How did you know that?"

The woman's smile returned. "You're not the first to come here hoping to see him. At least a hundred people every day try to gain an audience, all with what they think to be urgent business."

"Do any get to see him?"

"Not a single one, I'm afraid," she replied, her tone sympathetic. "You could try to make an appointment. Though it could be quite some time before you see him."

"How long?"

"Three years. Two, if your business is truly urgent."

His heart sank. "I can't wait that long. It's vital I speak with him now."

She met his eyes for an extended moment. "I can see your determination. But sadly, it won't do you any good."

"There must be a way. Surely if it's important enough they'd allow it."

After another pause, she sighed. "Very well. There might be. It depends entirely on your reason. Tell me what it is, and I'll see what can be done."

"I can't."

"Then I can't help you. Believe me when I say that no one else will either."

After a moment of silence, she took his hand. "Nobody is going to just take your word for it that your business is important enough to grant you an audience. You'll have to explain it to someone. Why shouldn't it be to an old lady who's willing to listen? Better that than an uncaring bureaucrat who will more likely than not throw you out on your ear before you've spoken two words."

She had a good point. He would eventually need to explain to *someone* why he was so desperate for an audience. And if this woman had been here for as long as she claimed, she might very well be just the person he needed.

Lem drew a breath. "Someone is trying to kill the High Cleric."

The woman raised an eyebrow. "You don't say? And who might that be?"

"The King of Garmathia."

This prompted a short laugh. "Tribos? That rascal? What's he up to this time?"

Lem was more than a little taken aback by her casual reaction. "This is serious. He's already hired someone to do it."

"Really? He found someone stupid enough to make the attempt? I don't suppose you know whom he hired?"

Lem drew the contract from his shirt pocket. "Yes, I do."

The woman took the parchment and looked it over. "Astounding," she muttered. "Simply astounding." She handed it back. "And seeing as it's in your possession, I take it that you are the assassin in question?"

He nodded his affirmation. "The man I work for thinks I'm here to carry it out."

"But you decided to warn the High Cleric instead. Am I right?"

"Yes."

"And the man you work for . . . Where is he now?"

"In Ur Minosa."

"And you would be willing to testify against him?"

Lem's hope was increasing. "Absolutely. But I need to speak with the High Cleric first."

346 · BRIAN D. ANDERSON

The woman leaned back on the bench, eyes downcast in thought. "I suppose there's something you want in exchange. Yes?" Before he could answer, she said, "Not that it matters. I'm sure whatever small reward you ask for will be well earned and easily provided."

"Then you'll help me?"

"I will. But you must tell no one else why you've come." She stood with surprising verve for one so old. "You say that your employer is in Ur Minosa?"

"Yes," Lem replied. "Just across the border in Daris."

"What is his name?"

"Farley. He owns an acting troupe called the Lumroy Company."

"Would your return arouse suspicion?"

Lem creased his brow. "Why would I go back? I thought you were going to help me see the High Cleric." He also needed to strike a bargain that would shield him from anything Farley could say. Without that, he could find himself in prison or worse.

"If you're concerned about your own safety, don't be." Her tone had leveled and she appeared less frail than she had only moments before. "Whatever you've done in the past can be forgiven. That's why you want to see him, yes?"

Her insight was startling. Lem found himself feeling very small and vulnerable under the gaze of her bright blue eyes. He felt a sudden urge to run.

"Don't be afraid," she said. "You just might have saved the High Cleric's life. What do you think he would do, regardless of your offenses? I'm just happy it was me you found and not some mindless acolyte who was too ignorant to recognize the signature and seal of King Tribos as authentic."

Lem stood, still feeling a bit cornered. "What are you going to do?"

"The High Cleric returns tomorrow," she explained.

"But it will take time for me to see him. I would prefer that you give me the contract as evidence, but were I in your position, I would be reluctant to give it up. So I won't ask you to."

"Will he believe you?"

"Without question. And when the time comes, *you* can show him the contract. Then he will believe you too."

"How long should I wait?"

"Until you hear from me," she replied. "I'll send word with instructions."

"I don't even know your name."

"Dorina. Sister Dorina. Now be off with you. I have much to do if I'm to see His Holiness. You wouldn't believe the number of people involved in an audience, even for someone who's been here as long as I have. It will take me all day and probably most of tomorrow."

"Thank you. You have no idea what this means to me."

"It is I who should thank you. King Tribos has been a thorn in our side for some time. But thanks to the proof you showed me, we can finally rid ourselves of him." She caught the arm of a passing woman in cleric's robes and whispered something into her ear.

Lem noticed the way she bowed exceptionally low to the older woman and then immediately left with urgent steps to do her bidding. Apparently, Sister Dorina was someone of considerable importance. This was encouraging. Perhaps she really could help.

Dorina watched until the woman she had sent off vanished down a narrow corridor on the left of the gallery before turning back to Lem. "Now remember, not a word to anyone until you hear from me."

"I understand," he assured her. "And thank you again. I was afraid I had come here for nothing."

After bowing, he started toward the exit, feeling as if a

great pressure had been released. Fortune had smiled on him for the first time in a while. For once, he was saving a life rather than taking one. Soon he would be free of Farley and reunited with Mariyah. Then, perhaps, the future would not appear so utterly bleak. Who could tell? In time, maybe he really would become a bard.

The two-day ride back to the troupe was spent in daydreams about his future with Mariyah. He imagined her cries of joy upon seeing him, the look on her face when he freed her, and most of all, the way she would feel in his arms as he held her for the first time in what felt like years.

Though it would be wonderful for them to find a way back to Vylari, in all his and Shemi's research they had found nothing about their home that did not refer to it as mere myth—fantastical tales told to children about a land with rivers of starlight and fields of gold, where its people who dwelled in shimmering halls of spiritual light never aged and could call upon the rains to fall at a whim. A few mentioned the barrier, but only in passing, as a way to explain why it could never be found. Children's tales or no, there were certain truths buried within the fiction. Several had described the Sunflow River with surprising accuracy. And while not immortal, the people in Vylari did live considerably longer. But from what he could tell, this didn't become apparent until later in life. Most people could guess at Lem's age, but Shemi was taken for a man at least thirty years younger. Why this was, and why Vylarian men could not grow beards, Lem had yet to discover. But he did derive some pleasure from the knowledge that there were differences, as did Shemi. Still, a life outside of Ralmarstad would not be the worst of fates. It would never replace home, but he was confident they could carve out a good life for themselves.

By the time he reached Ur Minosa, he was feeling as if

he had arrived at the end of a long and difficult road. He had to keep reminding himself that the end, however close, was not there yet. Farley was troubled by his early return, but Lem quickly explained this away by stating that the High Cleric was not in the Holy City, and that accommodations there were very expensive.

"No need to spend gold needlessly," he said. "Unless *you* want to pay."

"Did you figure out a way to do it?"

"Of course I did. I've worked out everything. Don't worry."

Betrayal was not in Lem's character. But betraying Farley . . . that was different. He had to force back a smile whenever he thought about it.

Shemi was delighted that things had unfolded as planned. Well, maybe not *exactly* as planned. Even after many hours of careful consideration, they had not been able to work out how he would manage to gain an audience with the High Cleric. Initially, this seemingly unsolvable problem had made Lem want to abandon the idea. But Shemi had insisted that it would work out; that Lem would find a way.

"You see?" said Shemi. "I told you. Good always triumphs eventually."

"I'm not sure how *good* I am," Lem responded. "But I have to admit, you were right."

And I was lucky, he added inwardly.

Farley continued to look at him with mild displeasure, remarking several times that he should just go back to Xancartha and wait.

"This is a dangerous contract," Lem told him. "I will not charge in until I think it's time."

"And how will you know when that is unless you're there?" countered Farley.

"I'll leave in a few days. Calm down."

The troupe had a license to perform for three more days. After that, they would be forced to move on, at which point Lem would have to go back to Xancartha to inform Sister Dorina of their new location. Farley was already suspicious. If Lem were to leave the troupe and return for a second time without having fulfilled the contract, it would probably push Farley's suspicions into outright certainty that something was amiss.

By the time their last night in Ur Minosa arrived, it was Lem who was growing suspicious. Had Sister Dorina lied? Had she simply told him what he wanted to hear in order to make him leave? He thought she had believed him. Now it was starting to look like he might have to go through with it after all.

"Don't worry," Shemi said as they were bedding down. "She'll send word."

Lem was not convinced. He knew that by the time the sun was past the horizon the following day, the troupe would be on their way to the next town.

Unable to sleep, he was still mulling over what he should do next when the scraping of boots on stone and the clanking of metal had him sitting bolt upright. Shemi heard it as well and was scrambling from his cot.

"Hide the contract," Shemi whispered urgently.

Lem had been keeping it in his pocket, unwilling to let it out of his possession. His eyes now darted about for a place to conceal the document, but it was too late. The tent flap flew open and four members of the Clerical Guard rushed in, their short blades drawn.

Clovis and the others leapt from their cots, looking confused and frightened.

"What is this?" Clovis demanded, though with very little authority and backing away as he spoke.

"Which one of you is Lem?" responded the guard, the additional chevron on her sleeve denoting she was in charge.

Lem stepped forward, with Shemi rushing to his side. "I am."

The lead guard gave a sharp nod in his direction. The others searched him thoroughly, quickly finding the contract and handing it to their commander.

"Take him," she ordered.

"You can't do this," shouted Shemi.

"No. Stay out of it," Lem told him.

Ignoring Lem's plea, Shemi tried to follow as they shoved him toward the tent exit. Only a strong hand to his chest and the threat of a blade kept him at bay.

Once outside, Lem saw Farley in his nightclothes being forced from his tent by three more guards. He cast Lem a hate-filled stare. "You think to betray me?" he raged while struggling uselessly against his captors. "We'll see whose head ends up beneath the executioner's axe."

In response, Lem simply smiled.

Six more guards marched past. Three entered Farley's tent, while the other three headed toward Lem's. Two caged wagons were waiting in the city square where the troupe had been performing. Farley, thrashing wildly and shouting obscenities, was being led to the first. Fed up with his resistance, one of the guards struck him sharply on the back of the head with the pommel of his sword. Farley promptly went limp and was thrown unceremoniously through the cage door.

Lem had no intention of resisting. It was over. His plan had failed. Sister Dorina had betrayed him. It was his own fault; he should have just taken Shemi and made a run for it the moment he was told about the contract. That the guards had no interest in his uncle was a small consolation.

He could only hope that Shemi didn't do something stupid and get himself locked up as well. The thought of Shemi being alone was troubling. But for the time being, he at least had Lem's gold. That would be enough to keep him safe and fed for a fair while. Hopefully he would find work well before it ran out.

They bundled Lem roughly into the second cage and the door slammed shut with an ominous boom. There was a finality to this that he had never before experienced. He should have been afraid, but for some strange reason he wasn't. On his way back from the Holy City, he had imagined coming to the end of a long road. He had been right. It just wasn't the end he'd been anticipating.

As the wagon carrying him to his death pulled away, he began to laugh softly at the irony of it all. He had thought that if anyone were to be the instrument of his undoing, it would be Farley. How he hated the man! At least he'd had the opportunity to savor his downfall. More than that, he'd wanted Farley to know that he was the cause—the smile given when their eyes met was to let him know that it was he who had betrayed him to the High Cleric. After all, Farley had deceived and lied to him from the moment they met. Why shouldn't he have done the same in return? Of course, *that* was the irony. In the end it was not Farley but a kind old cleric who had brought him to his knees.

With the cage rumbling away from the square, looking back he could see the troupe gathering near the stage and staring after him. Clovis and Hallis were holding onto Shemi, preventing him from giving chase.

Lem turned away. Yes. The road had indeed ended.

21

GLAMOR, SECRETS, AND POLITICS

A noble rarely says what they mean directly, and never means what they say exactly. The art of diplomacy is centered in deception. It is cloaked in rumor, shielded in innuendo, and armed with lies.

The Art of the Silver Tongue

Mariyah opened her eyes and let out a startled gasp. She was home. The sun was shining onto the porch where her mother and father sat each evening after a hard day's work. But it was too early yet, and their chairs were empty. Birds sang joyously while flitting about the apple trees that she had delighted in climbing as a girl. The apples were not yet ripe, though it wouldn't be long. And when they were ready, the air would be filled with the aroma of her mother's pie. Hot cider would fill her glass, warming her belly to drive away the chill of the night.

The garden was in bloom, with bees buzzing from flower to flower in a capricious dance that ensured new life each spring. Their labor would soon be enjoyed by all; honey was a particular favorite. As a child she would wait with gleeful anticipation as mother unpacked her shopping basket.

"I don't know what you're so happy about," she'd tease, making a point of removing all the other items first. "They were sold out."

"Don't say that," Mariyah would respond, folding her arms over her chest. "It's not funny."

Invariably, right at the end, her mother would produce not one, but two large jars of the golden treat—the first for making breads and other delectable sweets, and the other Mariyah was given to keep for herself.

At this time of day, she knew that Father would be tending the vines and Mother would be at the market buying fresh vegetables for dinner. Mariyah hoped she didn't forget to pick up some strawberries. She loved to drop them into her wine; the tastes blended perfectly. Father was not keen on her doing this, actually looking offended at the mere suggestion that his wine needed anything to better the taste. Never had a man been born who took more pride in his labor. A pride well deserved. The grapes he grew were coveted by every winery in Vylari—of which there were quite a few.

The front door of the house opened, and Mariyah's heart fluttered. Was Father taking a day off? Or perhaps Mother had bought enough food on her last trip to the market and did not need to go today? The figure who stepped onto the porch was unclear—out of focus, as if she were looking at it through warped glass. One thing was sure: It was neither of her parents.

"Who are you?" she shouted. "What are you doing in my house?"

Gradually the image cleared. All at once her legs gave way and she fell to her knees. "Lem," she cried out.

He was wearing the shirt she had given him on his birthday, his face alight with a warm smile. He walked toward her with long confident strides, shoulders squared and back straight, hair blown away from his face by a stiff breeze. He was . . . beautiful.

"Is that the one you were looking for?"

The voice was an intrusion, one that Mariyah wanted more than anything to ignore.

But the voice persisted. "Quite a handsome young man."

In a blink, the world she had called forth vanished, leaving her kneeling in the round chamber where she had recently spent each day from early afternoon until the sun set.

"So that was Vylari," remarked Lady Camdon, seeming to care little that Mariyah was shaking from the emotions the scene had wrought. "A bit . . . rustic. But cozy, I suppose." She looked down at Mariyah and frowned. "Are you crying? You did well. *Very* well, in fact. To recreate your home in such detail usually takes many years to accomplish. And I can see why you miss the young man so much. He's a scrumptious little morsel."

"Don't talk about Lem like that," Mariyah snapped.

Lady Camdon cocked her head. "And why not? Should I not recognize beauty? I'm not so old as to have lost my passion. And that one . . . yes. I definitely see why you went running after him."

Mariyah had never been so close to striking her. Of course, now that she wasn't wearing the ring, nothing prevented it. But that would only make a difficult situation worse.

True to her word, Lady Camdon was an even more relentless taskmaster than before. The insults and petty slights had ceased, but that was of little consolation. As a person, she was even more infuriating to be around. Her compliments came across as disingenuous, even awkward; she was entirely emotionally inaccessible. In fact, the only emotion she was sure Lady Camdon possessed was anger. Not once had Mariyah heard her laugh, and her smiles were reserved for the balls and formal dinner gatherings held frequently at the manor, displayed only as a matter of etiquette for the guests.

"I'm tired of glamor," Mariyah said, wiping her eyes as she stood. "What good are illusions? Or is this all you have to teach me?"

This was met with a dismissive flick of the hand. "Altering the perception of an adversary is far more useful than fire or lightning, and more subtle than invading their mind. Glamor is a weapon of intelligence and sophistication. One you would do well to master."

Mariyah tried to control her frustration; keep it from surfacing. But after months of lessons, she had yet to learn a single spell that could be used in self-defense or to smite an enemy. How was she supposed to fight evil with nothing but pretty lights and misdirection? "Maybe I should go to Felistal? I'm sure *he* could teach me something useful."

Lady Camdon shrugged. "As you wish. But I think you'll find life far more restrictive at the Thaumas enclave. And where I will move on to other forms of magic when I think you are ready, there you will be working with glamor for at least the next three years." She turned to the door on the far side of the room. "Let me know what you decide."

Mariyah stared after her, fuming. What was wrong with that woman? She let out a frustrated sigh, then collapsed into a chair, shoulders sagging and arms hanging between her knees. She was exhausted, both physically and mentally. And still there was more to do. Soon the guests would begin to arrive, and she would be expected to greet them looking fresh and perfectly dressed.

Maybe Lord Valmore will come tonight, she thought. Of all the nobles she had met thus far, he was easily the most entertaining to speak with. Clever and handsome, he had a quick wit and a disarming disposition. He had attended all the parties Mariyah had been to until now, and each time had not failed to gently tease out the secrets of another noble. Lady Camdon respected him as well, and from the way they interacted, the feeling was mutual. Though whether she actually *liked* the man was impossible to say.

As for most of the others, Mariyah found them to be petty, scheming, and not nearly as clever as Lady Camdon had led her to believe. A few even bordered on being dimwitted. And all of them, Lord Valmore included, had one quality in common: arrogance. In their minds, the rest of the world existed for the sole purpose of furthering their ambitions.

Well . . . there was one exception to this. But the mere thought of a compliment directed at Lady Camdon made her want to scrub clean in a hot bath. However, it was true. For all her aloofness and cold bearing, she did not use the common people to elevate her position. Quite the opposite. Mariyah learned that she was well known throughout Ubania for her generosity and kindness. Not so much in personal interactions, but in spending a great deal of gold to provide care for the downtrodden and disadvantaged, of which there were many. This drew ridicule from the other nobles. None of them were able to fathom the idea of aiding people who could never return the favor in kind.

"Most nobles are shortsighted fools," she had said, on discovering that Mariyah was aware of her altruism. "When the day comes and they find themselves in need of support from the masses, who do you think will have earned it? There have been uprisings and civil strife in the past. It's those who have gained the favor of the commoners who survive."

In this light, it appeared to be less generosity and kindness than pragmatism and caution that lay behind her building boarding houses and sending out wagonloads of food to the starving. Yet there was one thing wrong with this assumption—she rarely let the people know from where the aid had come. As it turned out, it had been her own servants who had spread the word. And Lady Camdon had been most put out that they had done this.

Mariyah glanced over to the stack of books beside her and groaned. Not even Shemi read as much as was required of her. And these were just the ones on magic. Upstairs in the library, hundreds of more volumes awaited her attention. Often she had asked herself how so many books about noble families could exist. That wasn't to say that they had not come in useful on several occasions. Her ability to memorize what she read had already gained Lady Camdon what she deemed to be valuable information. Nobles were easily goaded into a contest of wits. Fortunately for Mariyah, the majority were ill-equipped for such a contest and invariably said things they had not intended. Typically, it was little more than something mildly embarrassing. But as her primary task was to weed out those under the sway of Belkar's followers, these embarrassing tidbits could often be used as leverage to gain more valuable knowledge.

"Do not underestimate them," Lady Camdon had warned. "Feigning stupidity is a strategy often employed, and one that can be difficult to recognize until it's too late."

She picked up the top book and opened it to the first page. *The Joy and Wonder of Illusion.* The title alone was enough to make Mariyah want to rip it apart and throw it into a fire. There was no *joy* in illusion. Glamor, as Lady Camdon called it, was the first form of magic one learned. The most difficult form, transmutation, was practiced only by an experienced Thaumas and took many years of study to master. Yet when she had stumbled upon a book on the subject, she found it far more interesting and quite easy to comprehend. But the Lady would have nothing of it.

"Are you jealous?" Mariyah asked, after a particularly

difficult day when exhaustion made it impossible to govern her tongue.

"Why in Kylor's creation would I be jealous of you?"

"How long did it take you to get as far as I have?"

It was the only time since their lessons began that she had seen the woman truly flustered. And the first time she experienced aggressive magic. Lady Camdon's eyes darkened and her fingers spread. Before Mariyah could blink, a ribbon of blue light shot forth, wrapping itself around her arms and torso. The pressure was enormous, threatening to squeeze the life from her lungs and crush her bones to pulp.

"I learned this on my first day," Lady Camdon said in a low, dangerous voice.

A second later she released the spell, leaving Mariyah gasping on the floor.

"Imagine if you could have done that when the Hedran captured you."

She exited before Mariyah had a chance to reply. But the point was well made. She would not have been captured in the first place. She would be free and Shemi alive. Never again would she be a victim. And once the followers of Belkar were defeated, she would use her power to help others in bondage. At night Mariyah imagined herself raining fire and death upon the foul people who had stolen her freedom, meting out righteous vengeance on the oppressors of the innocent. Belkar was an evil without physical substance. The Archbishop, on the other hand . . . he was real. Reason told her that revenge was nothing more than wishful thinking, a fantasy to help her endure the constant pressure of the lessons compounded with her duties as the Lady's assistant. But her heart burned each time she envisioned the cages packed with helpless people, forced to suffer unimaginable abuse simply for violating church law.

Returning the book to the stack, she started for her room. Her back was aching and her head was pounding, making the long climb up the stairs even more taxing. In two days' time, Lady Camdon was due to leave for an annual gathering of Ubanian nobles. Two more days and there would be a blessed, if very brief, respite.

On entering her chamber, she saw that her attire had already been laid out on the bed. Kylanda, the young woman she'd met on her first day at the manor, was drawing her bath.

"You don't have to do that," she called to the girl. "I can take care of it myself."

"I know," she replied from inside the washroom. "But you work so hard. I thought you might need tending to."

"I'm fine, really. Thank you anyway."

Kylanda moved into the bedroom wearing her customary smile. This vanished the moment she caught sight of Mariyah. "My, you're as bent as a little old lady. How old are you? Twenty?"

"Yes. No . . . wait. I think I'm twenty-one now."

"You can't say how old you are, yet you think you don't need a bit of tending?" She clicked her tongue. "Keep it up and you'll drive yourself to the ancestors in a hurry."

She was too tired to argue. And it was obvious that Kylanda was not to be deterred.

"Now hurry up while the water's still hot," she said.

Mariyah smiled wearily. "Thank you."

Usually Kylanda would be cleaning up after the evening meal, but not today. On nights there was a party, Lady Camdon had food specially brought in from Ubania proper. While the outlying towns and villages under Ubanian control were mostly populated by tradesmen and farmers, Ubania itself boasted some of the finest fare in the north. Still, to provide sufficiently for the high-caliber events for which Lady Camdon was renowned, extra food often was brought in from every corner of the city-state, not to mention a few of its neighbors as well.

As she soaked, allowing the hot water to soothe the tension in her lower back, Mariyah went over in her mind the evening's agenda. Every social gathering, great or small, served a specific purpose. This one was to expose an enemy. The followers of Belkar had someone new among their ranks, someone influential and extremely wealthy.

At present, this was naught but a power struggle between nobles—a war without obvious casualties. And while it was hard to deny that a bloodless war was preferable to the alternative, Lady Camdon had assured her that sooner or later, the blood would flow. For now, though, it was fought exclusively in the realm of politics. Apparently, that was how the enemy had gained so much ground. They had been methodical and patient, using their foes' fear of losing position and wealth to subdue them.

Kylanda was still waiting when she finished her bath, and without prompting proceeded to help with her hair and makeup. Mariyah was still not very good at doing it herself, and this time she was grateful for the assistance.

"I see how hard you study," the girl said. "I think I would go mad reading so much."

"I've come close," she admitted.

"Lady Camdon should give you more time to yourself. You know, we have outings once a month. There's a beautiful grove near a stream on the west side of the estate that we picked out. If you could talk her into allowing it, you could come along."

This was not the first invitation Mariyah had received. Outwardly, she got along fine with the other workers in Lady Camdon's house, and the fact that she was not a believer in Kylor didn't seem to bother those who were in the slightest. Of course, Lady Camdon was wise enough to have hired people from outside Ubania, so that was likely the reason.

As Kylanda dried, brushed, and pinned her hair, Mariyah's thoughts returned to the evening and task ahead. She still didn't believe Belkar was real. As Felistal had explained, it was the name that held the power, used as it was to cloud the minds of the weak and selfish with promises of immortality and might, wrapped in dark deception. Yet there were times, particularly when she was tired, that she found herself wondering. What if it were true? A mighty sorcerer, with the power to lay low Ralmarstad? Mariyah had trouble wanting to prevent this at times. But she knew if it were true, Ralmarstad would not be the only place to suffer, and that helped her put aside those spiteful thoughts.

As it was, his followers were trying to seize power. Mariyah was unsure about many things, particularly when it came to Lady Camdon, but any group who found Ralmarstad a fertile ground to spread their cause could not be allowed to arise victorious.

Disturbingly, there were times when she thought Lady Camdon was still holding back important information. Whenever Mariyah mentioned the name Belkar, she could see the slightest of twitches in the woman's cheeks. Was it fear? The thought of her being afraid was as unimaginable as the idea of Belkar being real. Still . . . there was undeniably something.

As she finished applying Mariyah's makeup, Kylanda took a step back to regard her handiwork. "There. Finished," she said with satisfaction.

There was a rap at the door, and a young man in a neatly pressed blue-and-gold suit poked his head inside. "The guests are beginning to arrive," he informed them.

Mariyah nodded, then took a long breath. The bath had

relieved much of the soreness in her back. But it was sure to be a late night and most of it spent on her feet.

"Don't let them keep you up until dawn this time," called Kylanda.

"I won't." A definite lie. She would be required to remain in the ballroom until the last guest departed. To leave early would be noticed. *Appearances must be kept.*

The musicians were already playing by the time she arrived in the west wing foyer. Tiny lights of green and blue flitted about like fireflies. These were not insects but rather a spell of Lady Camdon's own design. In fact, the entire ballroom was filled with all manner of glamor. From a vast ceiling resembling a star-bejeweled sky to the tiny translucent-winged fairies that danced on crystal pedestals at the center of every table, each illusion was purposefully and painstakingly crafted. Even the dance floor that rippled like the surface of a pond teeming with brightly colored fish and the surrounding walls made to resemble a raging waterfall were the Lady's handiwork. When Mariyah had told her of the lights in the Sunflow River, she added them to the spell the next day. Now the fish swam among marble-sized orbs of light. Of course, everyone assumed that this had been created by the Thaumas and merely commissioned by Lady Camdon. Only a counted few knew of her magical training. Not even the manor staff was aware of it, though some suspected. This contest was still being fought in the shadows, and Lady Camdon let only a necessary few know what advantages she possessed.

Blatant opposition would only encourage more enemies to stand against her. Most of Lady Camdon's allies lived outside Ralmarstad's borders, so they could do little to help. If they did offer overt assistance, it would be taken as a sign of foreign aggression and possibly spark an armed conflict.

In that event, Ralmarstad would send an army to aid against the invaders. That could not be allowed to happen. For now, the struggle had to remain completely internal.

The guards standing on either side of the massive door were clad in shining plate armor, the sigil of the Camdon family emblazoned in black across their breasts, and holding gold-tipped spears. The armor, of course, was ceremonial, and the guards themselves far too handsome to be actual soldiers. Lady Camdon would patrol the city looking for attractive young men to fill the role—a task she certainly did not mind undertaking.

Marison was standing nearby ready to announce the guests as they passed through the foyer into the ballroom. As it turned out, he was nothing like Mariyah had imagined. Like Gertrude, he was kind and free with his humor in private, yet unflappable and proper when on duty. It was strange to see the transformation, even after all these months.

The first to arrive was Lord Chaudre Philisol, along with his wife Astrea. He was one of the lesser nobles in Ubania, and not one of the brightest. His wife, it was reported, hated that she had been forced to marry him and made no effort to hide her disgust at his overly ample girth and crude manners. Mariyah liked him, however. Once announced, Chaudre beamed at seeing her.

"A vision, as always," he said, spreading his arms wide. Mariyah curtsied to the lord, then bowed to the lady, each movement precise and meant to convey confidence.

"Why Loria chooses to have so many indentures in her household is beyond me," commented the lady, rolling her eyes. A gross exaggeration. There were nobles who had dozens.

"You're just jealous because we can't afford it," said Chaudre, his friendly bearing never fading.

"Quiet," she snapped.

One did not advertise their lack of wealth, even if it was well known.

"I must beg Lady Camdon to bring you with her on her next visit," he said.

"I would be pleased to see your home, my lord," Mariyah told him.

His wife tugged at his arm. "Come, Chaudre. I'll not be seen conversing with servants."

Mariyah struggled to contain her amusement. Speaking to household servants was looked upon as poor taste. However, she was Lady Camdon's personal assistant. This position gave her special status. She could speak to whomever she wanted and do so freely. In a sense, her role was to be the voice of her mistress, and most treated her as any other guest. Some even went out of their way to catch her attention and would often prattle on endlessly about the goings-on of their family, sneaking in a few rumors and innuendos here and there about other nobles that they hoped would reach Lady Camdon's ear.

In ones and twos, the guests continued to file in. Eventually a bell sounded, indicating that the final guest had arrived. This was Lord Landon Valmore. Dressed in an emerald-green thigh-length coat, together with a black open-necked shirt and fitted trousers, he looked every bit the youthful and vigorous noble. A green ribbon at the back of the head was neatly tied around his hair, the blond curls spilling out from this to just above his waist. His striking brown eyes and angular features, not to mention a strong build, were certainly the cause of many a young lady's swooning heart. After tossing a silver-capped walking stick over to Marison, he flashed a bright smile in Mariyah's direction.

"I see Loria has you greeting the riffraff again," he said cheerfully.

"I wait only to see you, my lord," she responded.

He gave a long sweeping bow. "Then I am shamed for making you wait, my lady."

Valmore was the only noble who called her "my lady."

He held out his arm. "If it pleases you, the bell has tolled. I would steal a dance before your mistress arrives."

Mariyah smiled, feeling a blush rise to her cheeks. "You know Lady Camdon would not approve."

"You can tell her that I insisted. Or that you were merely accommodating the desperate pleas of a guest. Unless of course, you would prefer to decline."

Mariyah took his arm. "No, my lord. I would be quite pleased to dance."

She could practically feel the eyes upon them as they entered the ballroom. It was one thing to converse with a servant; quite another to dance openly with one. But Lord Valmore seemed to care nothing for what others thought or said. And given that he was nearly as wealthy as Lady Camdon herself, no one would dare say a word; certainly not when he was within earshot.

The musicians were of good quality and playing a light melody with a moderate cadence. She was grateful it was not a slower tune that forced a close proximity. Tongues would definitely wag if people saw her wrapped tightly in the arms of Lord Valmore.

"Do you enjoy your life here?" he asked.

"Yes, my lord. Very much." He was a confident dancer, guiding her effortlessly around the floor.

He gave her a scolding look. "Must I repeat myself every time I see you? My name is Landon. Will you not honor me with familiarity?"

"It would not be proper, my lord."

"Do I seem proper to you?"

This drew a smile. "No . . . Landon. You do not."

"That's better. I was beginning to think we were not friends."

Her eyes surveyed the room as he spun her left, taking note of the guests as they tried to pretend not to be watching. She still found it odd how nobles made up their faces, men and women alike—though with the men it was centered around accentuating the eyes. Landon did this as well, but in a subtler way, where you were unsure that he had done anything at all unless you looked close enough.

She saw a few lustful stares pointed in her direction, taking note of each one. She had received a number of unwanted advances, but Lady Camdon had explained it away as being forbidden fruit. Mariyah was unattainable, which fueled their desires all the more. But it could be used as leverage if handled properly—a way to gain information, though Lady Camdon felt blackmail to be something only to be employed as a last resort. And she would never ask Mariyah to bed someone; that much she'd made sure was understood from the onset.

Lord Valmore was different, however. He often remarked on her beauty, yet never once did he suggest that they be anything other than friends.

"The man who captures your heart will be the envy of the world," he said. "A shame the closed-minded fools of society will not allow it to be me."

Mariyah smiled playfully. "A pity. But alas, I am a servant and you a lord."

"Alas," he agreed.

In another life, she thought, perhaps she would have considered it. But kind and charming as Lord Valmore was, her heart remained with Lem. She still dreamed of seeing him again, even though she knew this would never happen. Lem had no way of knowing what had become of her. As far as he was aware, she was still at home in Vylari.

368 · BRIAN D. ANDERSON

For a moment, Valmore's eyes captured hers. Yes. In another life, she *could* imagine allowing herself to feel love again. Not with this man, though. Even if one day her heart mended, he was from Ralmarstad. And that was where it ended.

"What is his name?" he asked. "The one you're thinking of now?"

The question ruffled her for a moment. "Am I so transparent?"

"No. But I can see the pain behind your eyes. Who is he?"

"His name is Lem," she confessed. It felt oddly soothing to tell him.

"Where is he now?"

"I don't know."

"I see. Perhaps one day you will see him again."

She forced a smile. "No. He is gone forever."

"You never know what the future holds. If he lives, there is always hope." The music stopped, though he did not make any attempt to step away. "Fate often provides the things we need, even when we are denied the things we want."

It was Mariyah who moved back and curtsied. Valmore bowed in return, a kindly yet boyish smile on his lips. She silently admonished herself for the attraction she was feeling. Her life was not as such to allow for affairs of the heart. Besides, even if it were possible to ignore the fact that he was from Ralmarstad, he was also a noble. Most likely his words were nothing more than false adulation designed to put her off guard.

She spotted Lady Camdon looking over at them from the edge of the dance floor, clearly displeased. Valmore saw her as well.

"Oh, dear," he said with exaggerated apprehension. "I think I'm about to be scolded. Best get it over with."

Lady Camdon was standing near a trio of young men, all of them doing their best to start up a conversation with her. In spite of their intentions, on seeing Valmore approaching, they backed away as inconspicuously as they could manage.

"My lady!" he said, kissing her hand. "You are as lovely as ever."

She responded with a tightly formed smile. "If you must insist on flirting with my assistant, please be discreet, Landon."

"My deepest apologies. But the musicians were playing my favorite song, and Mariyah was kind enough to oblige my impulse."

"So long as it is the only impulse you need obliged."

Valmore laughed. "Beauty and sharp wit. How is it you have not wed?"

"I could ask the same of you. Surely you have better prospects than my assistant."

"Sadly, no. A bachelor for life seems to be my destiny."

She turned to Mariyah. "If you will excuse us, I have a private matter I wish to discuss with Lord Valmore."

Mariyah lowered her eyes submissively. "Of course, my lady."

Valmore flashed her another smile as she left. She enjoyed that he could match Lady Camdon in wit. He was the only noble she had seen get the best of her in an exchange.

For most of the evening, Mariyah darted from one conversation to another. And as the night wore on and the wine flowed, tongues loosened and secrets began to spill out. She identified three more nobles she was sure had been compromised by Belkar's followers, plus two others whom she suspected might be.

Lord Valmore, last to arrive, was first to depart. Though he said nothing to Mariyah before leaving, he did make a point of bowing to her from across the room in full view of Lady Camdon.

After bidding Valmore farewell, the Lady stood beside Mariyah. "I hope you don't fall prey to that scoundrel of a man," she remarked.

Mariyah leaned in, as if revealing a secret. "Don't worry, we're just friends."

"What have I told you? Nobles do not have friends. There are allies and foes. And both are nothing more than tools to be used," she whispered, nodding so as to appear to be talking about something entirely different. "Do not be taken in."

Mariyah gave a small nod of reluctant agreement. "I'll remember."

After the last guest departed, Mariyah felt as if she could sleep for a year. She had informed Lady Camdon earlier of the nobles she had discovered who were compromised, so there was nothing left to do but dive into bed and pray the whirlwind in her mind would calm long enough to close her eyes.

Back in her room, she found that Kylanda had laid out her favorite nightgown. The girl must have been there quite recently because a pot of tea she'd left on the nightstand was freshly made and still steaming. Quickly changing, she poured a cup and slipped into bed. Sitting up with her back supported by several pillows, she gently blew away the head of steam before taking a small sip. Ubanian black tea, her favorite. She could feel its soothing effects sifting into her tired muscles, clearing her mind of pressing thoughts. It was the one thing she could think of that was superior to that made in Vylari.

She had just placed the empty cup on the tray when there was a light knock at the door.

Mariyah groaned, knowing who it was. "Come in," she called.

Kylanda peeked in, looking embarrassingly apologetic. "I am so sorry. I know you're tired, but someone left this with Marison for you." She was holding a small wooden box, highly polished and with a gold inlay around each corner.

"Thank you," she said. "For the tea as well."

The girl smiled, then handed her the box. "It's my pleasure."

Mariyah was relieved when she left without another word. Usually when she came to her room at night it was to plead for stories about Vylari. The others were eager to hear them too, but Kylanda was particularly enthusiastic, peppering her with questions after each tale until Mariyah was forced to ask her to leave just to get some sleep. Fortunately, tonight she could see that Mariyah was in no mood for conversation.

She regarded the box with only mild interest—another cheap bauble from a noble hoping to win her favor. It was useful, especially when the gift came from someone married. Lady Camdon could use it as leverage, should the need arise.

She caught her breath, covering her mouth upon opening the lid. This was no trinket bought in haste or pilfered from a wife's collection of costume jewelry, the like of which most noblewomen wore at social functions. This was something truly spectacular.

The diamond was as large as a dove's egg, its facets cut by a master's hand so to capture the light in such a way that it revealed the inner beauty of the stone, sending delicate rays of brilliance radiating from its center. The stone was set into a gold cradle that had been fashioned into an eagle's claw. Mariyah held it up on an impossibly thin gold chain and allowed it to slowly turn. Pinpricks of multicolored lights covered her blanket and darted across the walls.

This must have cost a fortune, she thought, unable to take her eyes off the gift. She put it on and ran over to the dresser mirror. Who could have bought this? And why? Only one name came to mind. But that was ridiculous. Lord Valmore would never be so bold. Or would he? But . . . who else could it be? Only a few nobles had the wealth to purchase such a gift, and he was definitely among them.

She considered showing it to Lady Camdon right away, then thought better of it. She might insist it be returned, and that would only provoke an argument. Right now, Mariyah was far too weary for a confrontation. She would have to tell her, but it could wait until the morning. Either way, she was keeping it. Its value in gold alone could enable her to free a dozen or more people.

After placing the necklace inside the box, she climbed back into bed. If it did turn out to be Valmore who'd sent it, what would he want in return? He was unmarried and cared little about the opinion of others. There was no note with the gift, but there never was. Marison was always the one to whom such things were initially given. He would know who had left it.

In a way, she hoped it *was* Valmore. At least then there was the possibility it was nothing more than a simple gift to a friend. And that's all he was to her: a friend.

Much as she kept telling herself this, the smile on her lips as she settled down to sleep suggested that maybe things were not quite as straightforward as she wanted to believe.

22

A FOOL'S PARADISE

The death bringer. The harbinger of justice. His hand holds
the wrath of Kylor.
Passage from *Children of the Ages*—author unknown

L em had not spoken a word in many days. There was
no one to talk to. His mind had arrived at a place of
calm acceptance; the walls of the six-foot square cell
deep in the bowels of the Temple were to be his final home.
With a pile of straw for a bed, a bucket for bodily functions, and a barred window that looked into the empty adjoining cell, it could be worse. If nothing else, the straw
kept his back away from the cold slate floor at night. It
was fitting accommodations for an assassin, he considered.
And soon he would meet an assassin's end.

The first two weeks of imprisonment had been exhausting. Two women accompanied by a giant of a man had
interrogated him for hour after hour every day. Lem held
nothing back. There was no point in doing otherwise; Farley would have told them all he knew in a vain attempt to
save his own hide. The man accompanying the women was
obviously there to mete out harsh punishment should he
not be forthcoming. They needn't have bothered. He was
caught. He would die. Why take an avoidable beating in the
process? He hoped Farley had been less cooperative. The

374 · BRIAN D. ANDERSON

thought of him beaten and weeping, begging for mercy, always drew a smile.

Eventually, however, the interrogations ended. They had what they needed, he guessed. No sense in wasting more time and energy. Lem had repeated himself dozens of times already. Short of recounting his childhood, he had absolutely nothing more he could tell them.

He often thought about the day he left home; the voice on the wind urging him to stay echoed constantly in his thoughts. If only he had listened, none of this would have happened. In spite of the prejudices, he would have found a way to survive. In time, perhaps the people of Vylari might have even learned to accept him for what he was. The stranger's warning might have been a lie or a mistake. So far he had seen no evidence of the destruction he had been warned of.

He sometimes considered what might have happened if he had been able to find the Thaumas. Could they have helped him? He should have tried harder, been relentless in his search, but freeing Mariyah had overshadowed his fear of the stranger's prophecy. He had naïvely thought he had more time.

Now it was too late, and these thoughts served only to fuel his self-loathing. His choices had doomed the two people in the world for whom he cared the most. How could he not have anticipated that they would come after him? Of course they were going to. He would have done exactly the same thing.

Stuck as he was in the semidarkness and alone, time ceased to have meaning. It could be measured only by the meals pushed through the slot in his door and whenever the waste bucket was exchanged. Even the smell didn't bother him after . . . however long it had been. Not so long, surely. He almost missed the interrogations. It was a better way to keep track of time, and the interrogators were not as cruel as he'd expected. Certainly not friendly, but they were the only company he had. People were not meant to live in seclusion.

The groan of the door's hinges had him sitting up as two guards entered, one holding a set of manacles.

It was time.

He had promised himself that he would not die weeping and begging, but he could feel his resolve sifting away. In that moment, every tiny measure of life became precious. All he could think about was how to extend it for as long as possible.

"On your feet," he was commanded.

Lem tried to stand, but his legs refused to obey. Not that this was going to delay matters. The largest of the guards quickly seized his arm and snatched him upright.

Once his hands were secured, he was shoved outside the cell and into a long narrow corridor. He was filthy. The thought of dying while covered in grime was suddenly detestable, though no one else was liable to care about his feelings on this. Who cared about the feelings of an assassin?

After being led past the other cells, he was taken into a small chamber. On the floor was a washbasin, a fresh set of pants, and a clean shirt.

"Get washed and changed," the guard ordered, removing his bindings.

Lem let out a spontaneous laugh. Was it really a last wish granted? He waited until both guards had left the room before stripping the foul-smelling rags from his body. The water was pleasingly warm, an unexpected but welcome kindness. Once clean and dressed, he sat down in the corner, taking care to first brush away the dirt from the floor with his old clothes. No need to rush.

After a few minutes, the guards returned, and his hands

were shackled once again. This time, they pulled a cloth bag over his head. It was dusty and smelled of onions, prompting a short sneezing fit. He was then led by the arm back into the corridor and, after several turns, guided up a flight of stairs.

What was the point of a bag? he wondered. Whatever he saw would quickly be forgotten. The dead remember nothing. Was it some petty cruelty? A way to stoke his anxiety? If so, it wasn't working. With each stride he took, the weakness he'd experienced only a short time ago was dissipating, and in its place came a tranquil acquiescence. He was prepared. He would not weep or beg. They would force him to his knees, place his head on a block, and in an abrupt moment of violence it would be over. The axeman's blade would end this nightmare at last.

They continued for what felt like an eternity, making turn after turn and ascending several more flights of stairs. Even through the odor of onion he could smell that the air now bore a hint of honeysuckle and roses and had cooled to a comfortable temperature. Where in blazes were they going? Finally, he heard the click of a lock and was made to sit in a chair. The feeling of the cushioned seat was surprising. His shackles and the bag were then removed.

After blinking for a few seconds to adjust his vision, Lem found himself in what looked to be a study. Directly in front of him was a large desk with a high-backed chair behind it. Shelves stuffed with books along with a few cabinets lined the walls, while the rather dim light from a solitary lantern gave the room a cozy atmosphere. It was a place to work or study in comfort. And judging by the high quality of the furnishings and artwork, a place used by someone of considerable wealth and power.

"Well, now," came a voice from behind. He recognized it at once.

Sister Dorina rounded his chair and stood beside the desk. Curiously, the guards were not present.

"You're taking quite a risk," Lem remarked. He wanted to feel anger toward this woman. But he couldn't. *He* was the one who had been the fool. She had simply behaved as he should have expected.

"A risk? Why? Are you planning to attack me?"

"Who are you really?"

"As I've already told you, I'm Sister Dorina," she replied, her smile just as warm and motherly as it had been when they met. "But if you are asking who I am aside from that . . . my official title is Light Bringer."

Lem let slip a self-deprecating chuckle. "Of course you are. Who else would you be? But why am I here? Did you want to mock me before you have me put to death?"

"Mock you? Never. I am not so cruel. And as for putting you to death, only one person in the Temple has the power to command that. No. I came simply to offer you my thanks. You have renewed an old woman's faith."

Lem cocked his head. "How did I do that exactly?"

"The High Cleric had lately begun to question my loyalty. But thanks to you, he no longer does."

Anger finally managed to surge. "So you've brought me all the way to your study just to express your gratitude? After you betrayed me? Go to the depths, woman."

Dorina frowned. "I think not. You were the one who came here with thoughts of betrayal. Was it not your intention to curry favor by exposing your employer? Your actions had nothing to do with protecting the High Cleric and everything to do with saving your own skin. In fact, I would bet my life that if you had thought it was possible, you would have gone through with the assassination."

"Coming in here alone and unprotected, it seems to me that you might have already made that bet."

"I am neither alone, nor unprotected," she told him, unmoved by the implied threat. "Feel free to test my assertion if you must."

Lem's muscles tensed. It would be quick. In the blink of an eye he could be out of his chair and have his hands around her neck. He sniffed, then allowed himself to relax. No. His last act in this world before dying would not be another murder.

Her smile broadened. "A wise choice, young man. More so than you realize."

As she started moving toward the desk chair, a soft aura of blue light surrounded her. Her form began to ripple, as if he were looking at her image through the reflection of a pond. Lem's eyes grew wide. She was changing. But into what? By the time she was seated, the old woman was gone, replaced by a man of about fifty with a square jaw, bald head, and deeply set hazel eyes. He was wearing a yellow-and-purple satin robe with the eye of Kylor stitched in silver on its chest. His hands were adorned with gold and gems, and a gold hoop hung from each ear.

He smiled at Lem's astonishment. "You didn't think I would send Dorina in here alone with the infamous Shade, did you? I had to be certain that you were not prone to violent outbursts."

Lem's voice dropped to a half-whisper. "Who are you?" he asked.

"I think you know that already," he replied, leaning back in his chair.

"The High Cleric."

"Of course. Guillard Rothmore at your service. Or more accurately, you are at mine."

Magic. No wonder he wasn't afraid. The High Cleric was a sorcerer. "I . . . I don't understand," Lem stammered. "Why am I here?"

He folded his hands and pressed them beneath his chin.
"That, my boy, is a question I have been pondering for
some time. When Dorina came to tell me what had happened, my initial reaction was to drag you and that shady
dog of an employer of yours straight to the executioner.
Honestly, did you really think your plan would work? That
you could bargain with me?"

"I . . . I was trying to—"

"You were trying to avoid justice. The kings and queens
of Lamoria may turn a blind eye to your kind, but the
church does not. Were the circumstances different, you'd
be dead already."

"I don't understand. What circumstances?"

"For such an accomplished killer, you certainly are
impatient." He waved a dismissive hand. "But I suppose
you're right. We should get down to it." He leaned in to get
a closer look. "I thought I would see it in you. But now that
you're here . . ." He squinted, then shook his head.

"See what?"

"It is said that those from Vylari possess an inner light."

"So you know?"

"Of course. I read the report on your interrogation. And
your former employer confirmed it. You were wise to hold
nothing back. It's remarkable, actually. A great pity you
chose the path you did. Your talents could have taken you
quite far." He paused for a weighty moment. "Though
even now, perhaps it's not too late."

A shiver ran through Lem. "What are you saying? That
I'm to be spared?"

"That all depends on you."

Lem knew he should feel elation, or at the very least relief. The trouble was, he'd already come to grips with the
hopelessness of his situation. Though he heard the man's
words, he could not yet bring himself to accept them.

"Do you believe in destiny?" the High Cleric asked. "That the creator of all things has a plan for us?"

"No. I don't believe in Kylor, if that's what you're asking. If you must know, I believe that our ancestors watch over us. But they do not interfere. Nor do they alter our course."

"Yes. That keeps it nice and simple for you. Without the need for clerics or worship. Or faith, for that matter. Tell me, do you ever ask your ancestors for guidance?"

"Occasionally. Though I can't say if they hear me."

The High Cleric thought on this for a moment. "I see. Are you not the least bit curious to understand our faith?"

"I've read about it. But more out of necessity than curiosity. I needed to be able to blend in."

"Yes, your homeland *was* the biggest surprise of all. Vylari, of all places. I confess I didn't believe it. Not even when your employer confirmed it. It took your uncle to convince me."

"What did you do to him?" Lem demanded.

The High Cleric held up his palms. "There is no need to worry; he's perfectly fine. There is no law against being from—and I still can't quite believe I'm saying this—Vylari. So far as we are concerned, he's done nothing wrong. And if you're worried about the same thing your uncle was, I have not the slightest interest in finding your homeland. So rest your fears."

"Where is he?"

"For now, he's here in the Temple. As for Farley, in case you're wondering, I turned him over to the king's executioner. So what's left of him is probably ash."

A smile formed before Lem realized it was there. "And you intend to let my uncle go?"

"As I said, he faces no charges. Sister Dorina offered him accommodations while your fate is being determined.

She really is a kind woman, you know. She even pled for leniency on your behalf."

"So what is it you want from me?"

"Faith."

Lem creased his brow. "You want me to worship your god?"

"Kylor is everyone's god. So yes."

Lem huffed a laugh. "You can't force a person to believe."

"A bold statement from a man a hair's breadth away from execution."

"I'm only saying that you can't make me believe. If it saves my life, I'm willing to lie and tell you I have faith. But it would only be words."

The High Cleric scrutinized him for a time. "You are indeed different. Most people faced with death would not be so honest. They would say anything they thought I wanted to hear."

"If I did that, I have the feeling you'd see through me."

"Indeed I would. And you're right—you cannot force someone to have faith. They either have it or they don't." He dipped his head, eyes darting around as if checking to see that no one was about. "Do you want to know a secret?"

A touch confused by this odd behavior, Lem nodded.

"I had all but lost my faith. Until very recently, in fact."

"What changed?"

"You, as it happens. When you came here on what amounted to a fool's quest, you could have run into any number of people. Likely none of them would have taken you seriously. You certainly wouldn't be sitting here now. But you didn't run into just anyone. Three thousand men and women live within the Temple, and thousands more visit here each day on business. That's not even counting

382 · BRIAN D. ANDERSON

those who come on pilgrimage. So what are the chances that you would end up encountering the one person who would be able to help you? The one person who could see me without anyone stopping them? In fact, the second most powerful person in the Temple. What are the chances?"

Leaving this question hanging, he stood up and rounded the desk, sitting on its corner directly in front of Lem. "There is a new enemy arising. One who is bent on the destruction of the Temple . . . and myself. One whom I know how to fight, yet do not possess a weapon with which to do so." He laughed loudly, sweeping a hand toward Lem. "Just when I think I cannot prevent what's coming, when all my prayers have been ignored, *you* arrive. The Shade. The perfect weapon for me to throw down my enemies. And if there was any doubt left, I hear that you are from Vylari—a land believed to be nothing more than a myth. I would be a great fool not to see this as anything other than divine intervention. You were sent here. A miracle. I can see no other explanation."

Lem was unsure what to say. He was no miracle. And he certainly did not believe he'd been sent by a god to help this man. But it was obvious that the High Cleric believed his own words, and it would be foolish to contradict them out of hand. He spoke carefully. "Even if what you say is true and I was sent here, I don't see how I can help you."

"Of course you don't. But you're about to." He returned to his seat behind the desk and opened a drawer, producing a sheet of parchment along with a small gold box. Both were placed on the desk and pushed toward Lem. "This is the choice I give you."

Lem read the parchment. Much of the language was confusing and cryptic, but he was able to divine it to be a contract of sorts—one that required him to become something called the Blade of Kylor. "What does this mean, exactly?" he asked.

"It means that you will serve me," the High Cleric explained. "Until such time as I release you or you are killed."

"What would I be doing?"

"The same thing that you've been doing all along. Only this time you would kill for the good of this world rather than serve the darkest side of its nature."

"So I'm to be your personal assassin?"

"Putting it crudely, yes. But it is so much more than that. The Blade of Kylor is a sacred charge, highly regarded among the faithful. A position for which you are uniquely qualified."

Lem stared down at the parchment. Within its intricate lettering and flowery words was his salvation. And yet once again, he was trapped. Though he had no desire to be this man's killer, to refuse meant to accept death. Yes, he had been prepared to die. He still was. But hope has a clever way of worming into one's heart. The hunger it creates for another day of life is powerful.

Too powerful to resist.

"If I accept, there's one thing I would need," he stated.

"The girl, yes? Farley told us about her as well. Unfortunately, we have nothing to do with that. Indenture is a practice sanctioned by the Archbishop and only in Ralmarstad." The word *Archbishop* came out like a curse.

Lem was aware that the two churches had nothing to do with one another. Still . . . "But you *could* find her? You have ways of finding out, don't you?"

After a long pause, he nodded. "Yes. We have spies among them. But it would take time. Months, perhaps years."

"If you promise to find her, I will serve you for as long as you want."

"So you would serve me not to save your own life, but to save the woman you love?" He lowered his head and chuckled softly. "Yes. Uniquely qualified." After a moment he cleared his throat and placed a quill and ink beside the parchment. "I will make you a bargain. Become the Blade of Kylor, prove your loyalty to me, and in return I will do all I can to find her, regardless of the cost."

"How will I prove my loyalty?"

"You can start with your signature."

He locked eyes with the High Cleric. He didn't trust him any more than he had Farley. Of course, thus far he'd been unable to trust anyone in this world. Why should he think the High Cleric's word would prove to be any better than the rest? But did that really matter? By signing, he would save his own life, and gain the one thing he needed most of all . . . time. Even if the man *was* lying, it would still give him time to find Mariyah himself. Without dwelling on the issue a second longer, he picked up the quill and scrawled his name at the bottom. The High Cleric smiled, then did the same.

"Inside the box is a pendant bearing the sigil of your title," he said. "Keep it with you at all times. It will ensure that no temple, church, or monastery will deny you."

After removing the pendant, Lem examined it closely. It bore the eye of Kylor on one side and a curved dagger on the reverse.

"There hasn't been a Blade for several generations," the High Cleric told him. "So you may receive a chilly reception in some places. But no one would dare turn you away."

"So what happens now?"

"Now you are free to go," he replied, gesturing to the door. "Your uncle will be waiting for you, along with your belongings."

"Where should I go?"

"Wherever you please. Don't worry. I'll know how to find you. When you are needed, I'll send word."

Lem stood and placed the pendant around his neck, shoving it beneath his shirt. He stared at the High Cleric for a moment, then, with a curious feeling of serenity and relief, he turned to the door.

"By the way, I've heard you play," the Cleric called just as Lem's hand touched the knob. "You were most impressive, so perhaps you should consider heading north. I hear there is a great deal of coin to be made for a musician of genuine talent. Not to mention that the Bard's College is in Callahn. Nothing forbids the Blade of Kylor from being a bard."

Outside, the guards were still waiting. This time there would be no shackles or bags. Instead, after bowing low, they silently led him through the labyrinth of corridors and chambers back to the main gallery. The light pouring in from outside told Lem that it was now midmorning. The air was warm and fragrant, and the bustle of people going about their business was already loud enough to reverberate from the marble walls.

As promised, Shemi was waiting outside at the bottom of the steps. The moment he saw Lem approach, he ran to greet him, embracing him tightly.

"I thought they had killed you," he said, weeping with joy.

Lem returned the embrace. "Not yet. But the day isn't over. Who knows what could happen?"

23

THE TRUTH REVEALED

Beauty can be as deceptive as the cleverest lie. Do not be fooled by a bright smile and friendly eyes. It is the deeds of a person that will give away their heart.

Book of Kylor, Chapter Six, Verse Three

Wake up, my child.
Mariyah rolled over onto her side and pulled the blanket tight. Not yet. Just a few more minutes.

Wake up.

It couldn't be time. Her muscles still ached, and she could feel her body insisting that she remain in bed. But the voice would not be denied.

Wake up.

She peeled open one eye. Utter darkness. The lights were out, which meant it was not yet dawn.

"Whoever it is, go away," she groaned.

I cannot go away. Not until we have had a chance to speak.

"It's not morning yet. Let me sleep."

You have slept all your life. It is time for you to wake.

"This isn't funny," she snapped. "I have a long day ahead. Now, for the last time, *let me sleep.*"

The end is coming, my child. I am coming. I need you to hear me. Open your eyes. See me.

This was too much. Flinging her pillow across the room, she sat up, fuming. "I'll bloody throttle you."

The lights should have brightened the moment she sat up. But they remained dark. A tingle of fear rose in her chest. "Who's there?"

Don't you know me? Have you not seen me deep in the corners of your heart? Surely you have felt my call.

"This is a dream," she said, doubting her own words even as she spoke them. The voice . . . it was inside her head.

Step outside and you will see that I am quite real. I await you beyond your door. There is no cause to fear. I would never harm you.

Mariyah felt herself drawn, as if some invisible force were urging her to rise. Without knowing how she got there, she found herself standing beside the bed. There was no recollection of pulling back the blanket or feeling the shock of the cold floor on her bare feet. Yet there she was.

"You will not control me," she said through clenched teeth.

I have no desire to. I wish only to speak with you: to show you the folly of the path you have chosen and beg you to see through the lies you have been told.

"Leave me alone."

I cannot. For it is you who have summoned me. I am your servant. I will never abandon you as others have done. As Lem did. I will stay by your side until the stars cease to shine. And beyond. Through time everlasting.

The compulsion to open the door and discover the source of the voice was overwhelming. She crossed the room and gripped the knob. "You say that you are my servant?"

Yes.

"So if I command you to leave?"

I will obey. I ask only that you first listen to my plea. Hear my petition before passing judgment.

She stepped into the hall. It was empty. "Where are you?"

Speak my name and I will be revealed.

"Belkar." The name slipped out without thinking, her voice barely above a whisper.

At once, the door to Lady Camdon's chamber opened and a tall figure emerged from the shadows. Mariyah took a quick step back. He was a man, yet like no man she had seen before. A full head taller than most and twice as broad in the shoulder, he was wearing black pants and a simple white vest that revealed a well-muscled frame. His feet were bare, and aside from a thin leather circlet holding back his silver waist-length hair, he wore no jewelry or any other form of decoration. As he stepped closer, she could see that his flesh was slate gray and smooth, much like polished granite. With long, angular, and perfectly symmetrical features, he was undeniably beautiful. His broad smile was warm and welcoming, yet gave off a sense of humility, as if he felt honored to be in her presence.

"You see? Am I as terrifying as you have been told?"

Mariyah was too stunned to speak, and took several seconds to compose herself. "No. You are nothing like I expected."

"And your beauty far surpasses my loftiest expectations." He gestured down the hall. "Will you walk with me?"

"Where are we going?"

"For a stroll, nothing more. Though if these surroundings are unpleasant for you, I can take you wherever you wish to go."

Home flashed through her mind.

"You would like to see Vylari again? I can take you there. Would you like that?"

"Only if it's real," she said, ignoring the fact that he had just read her thoughts. "I'm sick of glamor."

"What is real? If you believe it to be so, is it not just as true?"

"No," she stated flatly. "It isn't." This was a dream, she decided. It had to be.

"Not precisely," he replied. "A dream is contained within one's mind. You could not speak to me in a dream. If you want to know if your body is still lying safely in your bed, then the answer is yes. But I assure you, this is very real. As am I."

"How is this possible?"

"All things are possible if only you allow yourself to believe. You will learn this in time."

Mariyah looked up. They were in the south garden walking down a stone path between a row of tulips. "Please don't do that," she said, unsettled by the sudden change in location.

Belkar laughed. "It was not I. You possess more power than you yet understand."

"Is that why you're here?"

"In part," he admitted. "I cannot deny that your strength draws me to you. With you as an ally, my return would be much hastened. But I desire more. I will shatter the prison that holds me. Nothing can prevent that now. Those who would poison your mind against me know this all too well."

"Then what is it you want?"

"Long have I searched for one who could stand beside me as my equal—someone with the power and the courage to see the world as I do. A mate to give me the balance I have lacked. For countless lifetimes I have waited and watched as mortals struggled uselessly against the demons of their nature. You, Mariyah, have the power to make them understand. To open their eyes to the futility of their petty ambitions."

"Not everyone is like that," she protested. "There are good people in the world."

Belkar sniffed. "Do not be deceived. Human hearts never change."

"That's not true. People can change. I've seen it with my own eyes." But even as she spoke, she thought of the cruelty and senseless pain visited upon her—and others—since leaving Vylari. But there were also people in the world like Gertrude, like Trysilia, even Marison. People with kind hearts and gentle spirits. They could not be held to account for the wickedness of others.

He let out a long, sad breath. "If only you had seen through the ages as I have, you would know how mistaken you are. But mortal memory fades, altered by the victor and forgotten by the subjugated. Those in power in this age have fought and killed over nothing more important than to whom they offer their prayers. No, sweet lady, mortals do not change. They throw off one yoke only to put on another. Nothing differs aside from the hand holding the whip."

Mariyah found his words oddly compelling. Still, she had doubts. "I refuse to accept that peace is impossible. Surely it just takes time."

"Were it only so," he said softly, sounding to Mariyah as if thinking about an unhappy memory. "Old ways return, no matter how hard they try. They cannot help themselves. It is written into their very essence. Only through me will peace be eternal. This has been my sole ambition: to finally bring harmony to the world and ensure that never again will one be subjected to the cruelty of another."

"How will you do this?"

"Long ago I discovered the secret to eternal life. I thought it gave me the right to rule . . . to conquer. And in my arrogance, I set forth to bend the people of Lamoria to my will. But I was foolish and did not yet understand the truth of what I had become. I had yet to see the potential of the power I wielded. In the end, it was my undoing. I have since become wise. I see where my mind was flawed. Now, I am coming to right the wrongs of the past."

"And you want me to help you?" His words were reaching deep into her spirit, pleading with her to trust him. But she wasn't able to. There was a barely discernible look in his eyes that troubled her. He was hiding something.

"I did not come here to trick you," he insisted.

"I . . . I want to believe you."

He turned and placed his hands on her shoulders. "Then do. I cannot face the ocean of time alone. That is another lesson I have learned. The moment I felt your spirit, I knew I had found my mate. My queen. Join me. Help me to bring peace to this troubled world."

His touch was warm and soothing. And his voice . . . like the song of the wind whispering gently through fall leaves. "If there can be peace, why would you be alone?"

"It is the price I have chosen to pay for the good of all. Only you have the strength to span the ages with me."

For a brief moment, she felt as if her will was about to break. Then she saw it: the faintest of lights hidden deep within his dark eyes. This was what he did not want her to see.

"What are you doing?" he demanded, his tone hardening. He shoved her roughly away. "Stop this at once."

But Mariyah's mind was set. Just as earlier, when she had been compelled to meet with him, she was now equally driven to know what he was concealing. There was

392 · BRIAN D. ANDERSON

a rush of motion, as if falling from a great height. The garden disappeared and the world around her was now a blur of color. Then, in the far distance, a single point of light shone. No; not light. The veil of deceit fell away, and it was transformed. It was darkness. *Belkar's* darkness. Like a dying star, its absence of light was in an ominous way dazzling to behold—a deep pit of oblivion fixed in the night sky. Looking closer, she could see tiny filaments of mist spewing forth, creeping throughout the world, intent on invading the spirits of all it touched. Turning them to his cause. Infecting them with his power.

She wanted to pull away but was drawn irresistibly closer until finally passing through the darkness and seeing what lay beyond. Before her now stretched an endless land of ash and fire. Not a single tree grew or bird sang. It was lifeless, as if death itself had come to claim it as its own. Flames erupted from thousands of jagged fissures, and a cloud of thick, acrid smoke hung in the air just a few feet above the rocky ground. Mariyah knew instinctively that no mortal foot had ever trod in this place.

But it was not the desolation of the land that was causing her tears to now spring forth. It was what lay within. She wanted to cry out, but the knowledge of what she beheld had robbed her of speech. This was Belkar's prison: the place where the ancient Thaumas had sealed him away countless lifetimes ago. And inside this prison, she could see what he intended to unleash upon the world: thousands upon thousands of men and women, every one of them clad in black armor, with spears planted in the ground at their sides and swords hanging from their belts. Motionless as statues, they stared unblinkingly with black, soulless eyes into the void, awaiting their master's command.

Belkar was standing beside her. Horrified, she spun to face him. "You did this to them. And this is what you intend to inflict on everyone else." Rage filled her. "This is the kind of peace you bring?"

"You see without understanding," he replied. "It is the only way. They are a part of me now. They know nothing of hatred or jealousy. They are at peace. And so long as I live, they will endure. They are bound to me, and I to them. Can you not see the beauty in this?"

"What I see isn't beauty; it's a nightmare. And you are a monster."

He dropped to one knee and took her hands. "I beg you to listen. You need not become like this. I cannot bear the emptiness of time alone. Join me, and I swear you will remain as you are. I would never allow your spirit to dim."

She jerked free. He was no longer beautiful, and his warm, tender voice now sounded as if every word were a vile curse. "You think I would sacrifice the entire world to save my own life? No. You may have touched my spirit, but you do not know me. If you did, you would flee this instant. Now that I have seen what you really are, I swear that I will never stop opposing you."

Her fury built with each second until it threatened to overcome her reason. She charged blindly forward, ready to rip him apart, but he vanished in a blink, and she found herself once again in her room, standing beside the open door.

Fight me if you must. Kill my servants, oppose me at every turn. It will do you no good. I am coming. You cannot prevent it. I will bring peace to Lamoria. And in the end . . . you **will** *be mine.*

Mariyah's eyes popped open. She was now back in her bed, her heart pounding and her nightgown soaked in sweat. Then, just as she was sitting up, the box on the nightstand containing the pendant burst into flames. Quickly, she doused the fire with what was left in the teapot. As the water bubbled away, thin lines of red smoke snaked out, filling the room with a sickly sweet odor. With a hand covering her nose, she slid from the bed, the light brightening the moment her feet struck the tiles. This was a magic with which she was unfamiliar. And whoever had given this gift to her had to be a follower of . . .

A terrible thought invaded her mind. He was real. Belkar was more than a mere name by which to rally support. He *was* real. There was no doubt. And he was coming.

She tried to calm her breathing. Lady Camdon had to be told. While reaching for the door, she hesitated. Just outside she could hear the soft scraping of shoes. Her heart raced once again. No one should be in this part of the manor at such a late hour. It was a rule that none of the servants would ever dare break. She looked over at the smoldering remains of the box. This could not be a coincidence. Whoever was outside should not be there.

Her eyes darted around the room for something to use as a weapon. Finding nothing, she picked up the now-empty teapot and pressed her ear to the door. The clack of a doorknob was barely audible. Someone was sneaking into Lady Camdon's chambers; someone who knew how to pass through her wards. Holding her breath, Mariyah eased the door open just enough to peer into the hallway. A silhouetted figure was entering Lady Camdon's chambers with slow, cautious steps. The shimmer of a blade in their hand caught the light from the corridor.

Fear and panic threatened to rob her of courage. She had never faced anything like this. Yet if she didn't act, Lady Camdon would die. And after her encounter with Belkar, she knew that could not be allowed to happen. Squeezing her eyes shut, she took a series of short breaths. She could cry out a warning, but that might only get herself killed. There were no wards guarding her own door, and the lock might not hold a determined attacker long enough for help to arrive.

She pictured the layout of the Lady's chambers. The first room beyond the entrance was a spacious parlor. Lady Camdon would be in her bedroom, which was through a door on the left. Her muscles twitched and jerked with nervous anticipation. She only needed to buy enough time for Lady Camdon to wake. Surely she could do that much.

Gripping the handle of the teapot in her right hand, she burst into the hallway, shouting out a warning the instant she crossed the threshold. The alerted intruder spun around just as Mariyah brought her arm down hard, the pot aimed at their head. Her makeshift weapon shattered into countless pieces, though where it had struck she could not tell. The next thing she knew their bodies collided, sending them both tumbling to the floor. They grappled for a moment, then pain ripped through her left shoulder as the dagger sank deep into her flesh. Mariyah attempted to twist away, but the pain had caused her muscles to momentarily seize. In an instant, the blade was pulled free and she found herself rolled onto her back, her enemy kneeling on top of her. The flurry of movement had prompted the light overhead to brighten, though a black scarf covering the intruder's face masked their identity.

There was a split second of terror as Mariyah realized her helplessness. Deadly steel hovered, poised for a killer blow. Unable to resist, she closed her eyes and waited for death. But it didn't come. Rather than feeling the bite of cold steel, there was the glorious relief of her foe's weight being lifted from her chest. She opened her eyes again just in time to see the masked figure's body crashing hard into the far wall. Lady Camdon was standing in the doorway of her bedchamber, her hands pitched forward with a furious expression. A flash of green light flew from her left palm, smashing into the assassin's chest.

Clutching at the wound, Mariyah struggled to her feet. Blood oozed out between her fingers, each droplet dissipating with a hiss as it landed on the floor. Lady Camdon, ignoring the assassin for the moment, raced over to examine the injury.

"You're lucky it wasn't your heart," she said. "What in the world possessed you to do such a thing?"

"Whoever that is had passed through your wards," Mariyah replied through a clamped jaw. "What else could I do?" She was about to point out that she had saved her life when a fresh wave of pain had her sucking her teeth and stumbling back.

Lady Camdon helped her into a nearby chair. "Next time, Mariyah, a warning will do just fine."

Next time I'll just let them kill you, she thought.

From a nearby cabinet, Lady Camdon retrieved a small metal box. "This is not going to be pleasant," she warned, scooping out a thick blue paste with the tip of her finger and applying it directly to the damaged flesh.

The pain intensified to such an extent that Mariyah was unable to contain an agonized scream. Mercifully, it was fleeting. Within a matter of seconds, the pain was no more than a dull throb, and the bleeding had stopped completely.

"You need proper treatment," Camdon told her. "But this will do for now."

Though the pain had lessened, Mariyah found that her arm was now completely paralyzed. "What did you do?" she asked.

"I saved your life. A wound like that could have seen you bleed to death. Don't worry, you'll be able to use your arm again soon enough." She placed the salve on a table beside

Mariyah, then stepped over to where the still-unconscious assassin lay. Kneeling down, she ripped away the scarf.

Mariyah gazed in stunned disbelief. "Kylanda!"

Lady Camdon appeared unmoved by the revelation. She checked the girl's pulse. "Whoever sent her made certain that she would not be able to talk." She rose, tossing the scarf onto Kylanda's lap.

"She's dead?" asked Mariyah.

"Nearly. The spell I used should have only disabled her. Someone must have used a binding spell to make sure she went through with the attack. Clever."

"Can you save her?"

"No. She'll be dead in minutes." This time her face bore clear disdain. "She'd be in quite a lot of pain were she conscious. A pity I can't wake her." She returned to Mariyah's side. "How did you know she was coming?"

Mariyah recounted her experience with Belkar. "I awoke just as she was sneaking into your room."

"It was fortunate for me that you did." She looked again at Mariyah's wound. "Come. I'll send for a healer in the morning. I promise there won't even be a scar."

Mariyah remained seated, confused as to Lady Camdon's lack of reaction to what she had been told. "Then he is real?"

"I'm afraid so."

"You said he was a myth. Just a name people used to intimidate others. Why not tell me the truth?"

"Honestly, I didn't think you would believe me. Neither did Felistal. And before you look at me with those angry eyes of yours, ask yourself this question: If I had told you that an immortal sorcerer of legend was influencing the minds of the nobles to prepare for his return, what would you have done? I couldn't risk you leaving."

Mariyah wanted to argue, but the woman was right. She

wouldn't have believed her. Even after having seen Belkar for herself, it was difficult to grasp. "Why is it so important that I stay?"

"For the very same reason Belkar wants you. Even though I still have my doubts as to your resolve, your natural talent is undeniable. In time, you could become very powerful indeed. Unfortunately, our foes are now aware of this as well." She glanced over to Kylanda. "And it seems they are also aware of me. This complicates matters."

"Why?"

"Those of us opposing Belkar have tried to remain hidden. We need to learn more about what we're up against. So long as our alliances are secret, we can more easily acquire the information we need." She held out her hand. "Why do you think I endure those wretched parties?"

Mariyah allowed herself to be pulled up and led back to her room. After cleaning the wound and applying a second coating of salve, Lady Camdon helped her put on a fresh nightgown. It felt strange being attended this way, but as her arm was still useless it was a necessary measure.

Once this was done, Lady Camdon examined the ashes on the nightstand. The gem was gone. With a barely audible grunt of annoyance, she used the blood-soaked cloth to brush away the ashes. Sparks crackled and snapped as they were consumed by the floor's magic.

"You should have informed me at once when it was brought to you," she scolded as Mariyah climbed into bed.

"What was it?"

"Some sort of beacon, or perhaps a charm used for communication over vast distances. I've heard of them, though I've never seen one before. They are quite rare. And this one was apparently powerful enough to penetrate the barrier."

"Belkar's prison . . . it's in the mountains." Mariyah was not sure how she knew this.

Lady Camdon nodded. "Yes. Beyond the Teeth of the Gods. Belkar is struggling to break free, and for now he can only reach out with his spirit. But with each day that passes, the magic is weakening."

Mariyah could still see the vacant soulless eyes of Belkar's vast army. They were immortal, their existence bound to their master. How did one defeat that which cannot die?

"Can we do anything to stop him?" she asked.

"Of course. We can fight." Lady Camdon turned to the door, pausing just outside. "Thank you. What you did tonight was very brave. I won't forget it."

The rest of the night she could hear the servants coming and going. Several times Lady Camdon insisted that Mariyah be left alone, assuring the others that she was unharmed and needed her sleep after the ordeal. Gertrude could be heard actually arguing with the mistress to be allowed to check on her. Only after repeated assurances did she agree to wait until morning. Kylanda's betrayal had upset everyone.

It was well past dawn before she finally closed her eyes. When she did, Belkar's face haunted her dreams. Of all the lies he had told, one thing was true: He was coming. And whatever she had to do, she would be ready. The people of Vylari would not be turned to mindless fiends. He had been driven back once. The Thaumas of long ago had found a way to defeat him.

She would find a way to do so again.

24

THE PAIN OF REUNION

The husband wept, and begged of Kylor: Can you not save
her? Kylor knelt and touched the body of the fallen woman.
But she did not rise. Kylor stood and looked to the grieving
man and said: She has given her last measure so that you
might live. Her sacrifice is eternal. Do not weep for your
loss. Rejoice for the love she has deemed worthy of her own
life.

Book of Kylor, **Chapter One, Verse Seventy-Six**

L em adjusted his elegant wide-brimmed hat and
checked to see that his veil was secure before approaching the door to the lavish manor. This would
be a quiet kill, the victim dead long before he knew what
had happened. He preferred this to the messy assassina-
tions the High Cleric occasionally ordered whenever suffering and blood was required as penance. Those didn't
happen often, for which he was grateful.

The Head of Household greeted him at the rear entrance just off from the kitchen with a rigid expression.
"You're late. The guests will be arriving within the hour."

"Your mistress contacted me only a week ago," Lem replied. "It was a long journey."

His reputation as a musician had grown. He was now
highly sought after and paid almost as much as a bard for

his services. Had he not been the Blade of Kylor, he would have considered the life he'd carved out for himself to be quite rewarding. In the six months since leaving the holy city, he had saved nearly one thousand gold, more than enough to keep Shemi well stocked with books and their bellies full. Which was all they really needed, although there were times when he thought his uncle would have liked to settle down. In fact, Lem had offered to buy him a small home in Lytonia or wherever else he might want to live. But the old man refused for them to be separated.

He spotted a servant standing over a steaming pot as they passed the open kitchen door, almost certainly a convict from Ralmarstad. He had been four times to the Ralmarstad-controlled city-states, and it always made him uneasy. Gothmora was by far the worst, with the indentures there treated no better than animals. Here in Ubania, it was not quite as bad. Most worked for rich nobles, their duties limited to household chores. Here they were a status symbol more than anything. At least the extreme high tax placed on indenture ensured that their treatment was typically humane.

"Are you prepared?" the man asked, guiding Lem down a long corridor.

"Of course," he replied. "Is there a particular style of music preferred?"

"I understand that you are quite versatile. Feel free to use your discretion."

This was to be a small event—just him alone playing for about thirty people. Normally he performed at far larger functions, sometimes together with other musicians, in front of hundreds of guests within massive ballrooms. On these occasions, those he played with tended to look at him with animosity. This was unavoidable. Inradel Mercer, the name he had chosen as his alias, was well known for being a man who did not socialize with others. Mostly, though, they resented him for the same reason that Clovis had when they first met. His superior talent was obvious, and in Lamoria, musicians were often jealous and spiteful creatures.

He had run across his old troupe a few months after becoming the Blade. Though he chose not to approach them, from what he could see, Clovis had taken over the management. In Lem's opinion, the plays were even better now. Clovis had hired a lutist and a singer with a powerful, belting voice to entertain during the intermissions, and the crowd seemed to enjoy them immensely. Lem was glad they were continuing to do well, though admittedly he felt a small touch of jealousy. He had always thought his talent could not be replaced. A petty thing . . . but not even he was above baser feelings.

The manor was impressive by any standards, although this was to be expected, considering the affluence of its owner. Ubania as a whole was wealthy, and unlike Gothmora, did not solely depend on Ralmarstad for support. This was mainly due to proper management of resources. There was little difference between Gothmora's permanent governor and a king or queen, whereas Ubania's High Chancellor was not a lifetime position. That wasn't to say there was no corruption, a thing Lem had found to be universal regardless of where he went. It was just that in the kingdoms where power was shared and the monarch given limits, there was far less.

The parlor in which he was to play was large enough to accommodate many times the scheduled number of guests. Crystal chandeliers, ornate furniture, fine works of art, and masterfully woven rugs made certain that the owner's status was never in question.

A woman in a sleek red gown, her neck and fingers dripping with jewels, entered just as Lem was being shown the corner in which he was to play.

"Must you cover your face?" she demanded.

"Lady Camdon, I presume?" Lem responded, bowing.

"Indeed," she confirmed. "Now do please remove that ridiculous scarf."

"I'm afraid that is out of the question, my lady."

"You look like you're here to rob me, not to play music."

"I assure you I am not."

"I should have called for a bard."

Lem's smile went unseen. "As my lady is probably aware, the bards refuse to play in Ubania. However, if my veil bothers you, I can leave."

Lady Camdon gave a scornful look, though it quickly melted to impassivity. "Let us hope you are as good as they say."

"I will do my best, my lady."

Without another word, she spun gracefully around and strode off toward an archway at the far end of the room that led out onto a courtyard.

"Is she always so pleasant?" remarked Lem.

"Please refrain from speaking about Lady Camdon with disrespect," the man told him sternly.

"My apologies."

The Head of Household gave a curt nod. "You should begin playing." He started to leave, then paused after taking only a single step. "And yes. She is always precisely that pleasant."

Lem stifled a laugh. He had heard that Lady Camdon was a difficult woman. As a consolation, the pay was exceedingly good. Shemi, however, refused to step foot in a place where the Archbishop had influence. He was presently staying with a family on the Lytonian side of the Trudonian border. Lem's oath never to return to Ralmarstad had soon been broken. How else was he to find Mariyah?

While settling into the chair provided and placing his balisari on his lap, Lem's mind turned to the message he was awaiting. He needed to get back to Ralmarstad to continue his search for Mariyah. Frustratingly, the assignments he was given invariably drove him farther away. He had given up waiting for the High Cleric to discover who had taken her, though the more Lem learned, the more he came to believe what he had said about it not being a matter of a simple inquiry. Yes, the High Cleric was powerful. But his influence in Ralmarstad was almost nonexistent.

Lem plucked out a soft tune with a moderate tempo as an opener. It was a favorite among the people in the north, though seeing as Lady Camdon was unwilling to pay the extra five gold for vocals, he would not be singing the lyrics. Perhaps that was why she was being so inhospitable, he mused. But if you wanted the voice of Inradel Mercer to grace your event, you had to pay. One lesson Farley had taught him: Never do anything for free. If you do, people will take advantage of you. He had found this to be the case with the nobility in particular.

The first of the guests began filing in and wandering around the parlor, most of them pretending to appreciate the art and décor as if they were experts on the subject. The truth was, most nobles were far from knowledgeable on matters that did not involve politics or commerce. They might pretend to be cultured, but their education rarely went beyond the rudiments of scholarship. It was the lower classes, true scholars, and tradespeople who were generally the most educated.

It was another hour before all the guests had arrived and Lady Camdon reemerged from the courtyard. Though she didn't approach Lem at first, she did take the trouble to cast a sour look in his direction. Several men and women were gathered nearby, a few remarking quite loudly on the quality of his playing. When Lady Camdon did eventually deign to come near, he grinned at the fact that three guests begged to know where she had found such a marvelous musician.

"I have my sources," she told them. "Though I'm hoping to bring an actual bard for our next gathering."

This was an absurd statement, likely meant as a dig at Lem.

"I don't know about that," remarked a woman. "I heard a bard play a few years ago, and I must admit he wasn't as good as I thought he'd be. And this one . . . so mysterious, the way he hides his face."

"I've heard of Inradel Mercer," an older man, presumably the woman's husband, chipped in. "I was told he covers his face so that he can walk about in public without being bothered with requests to play." He turned to Lem. "Is that true?"

Lem nodded. It was true, at least in part. As the Blade of Kylor, he had found it useful to separate his Inradel identity from his true self. This was far from the first time he had infiltrated a noble house in this way. Much better to be able to blend into a crowd should things go awry and the local authorities become involved.

The man's attention switched back to Lady Camdon. "Where is that lovely assistant of yours? I hope she isn't ill."

"She should be along shortly," Camdon replied. "She is seeing to the preparations for my trip to Mardyna Lake tomorrow."

Assistant? You mean servant, thought Lem.

The woman rolled her eyes. "My husband is quite

smitten. If he were twenty years younger, I do think he might leave me and spirit her away."

"I would never consider leaving you, my love," he protested with a soft chuckle. "And I am not smitten. She is simply a charming young woman. I enjoy her wit."

"Yes," Lady Camdon agreed. "She is quite talented."

"You wouldn't consider transferring her indenture writ, would you?" he asked. "I would pay you handsomely."

His wife gave him a scolding frown. "We have plenty of servants already." She smiled at Lady Camdon. "Please forgive my husband. He simply cannot govern his tongue at times."

"No need to apologize. I would never let her go. I've too much time invested in her training. To find another would be a labor I would not want to undertake."

Lem felt his anger boil. Speaking about people as if they were nothing more than a horse or a sheep to be traded on a whim . . . He took a breath and tuned out the conversation. He was there to do a job. And somewhere among the guests was his objective.

It took another few minutes before spotting him: Lord Ranson Lupardi, a tall, rather thin man with lank brown hair and a sickly pallor. Unlike when working for Farley, Lem was seldom aware of why his victims were to die. This time, however, his research revealed that his target had been part of a failed plot to kill a monk who had come to Ubania to visit relatives. Precisely why Lupardi had wanted him dead remained a mystery, one that Lem did not care to solve.

The target was skulking about, clearly avoiding conversation and drinking copious amounts of wine. He looked nervous, even allowing for his naturally uneasy bearing. Likely he was expecting the High Cleric's office to retaliate, though he would never expect it to happen here, which was why Lem had chosen the party to strike. And why he had made sure his availability was made known to Lady Camdon. The tiny dart in his pocket had been tailored especially for the task. The poison would act slowly, and the anesthetic blended in would ensure his victim did not feel a thing. He just needed to be close, no farther than a few feet away. Seeing as he was expected to mingle with the guests during his breaks, that should not be a problem. Just so long as Lupardi did not leave early. From what he knew of the Lady, to leave before midnight would be considered a grave insult. And one did not insult Lady Camdon.

By morning, his target would be dead, and Lem halfway back to Lytonia to meet Shemi.

"Ah, Mariyah," called the man standing beside Lady Camdon. "We were just talking about you."

Never before had Lem even come close to playing a sour note during a public performance. So off-key was the one he now produced that it prompted an appalled look from several of the guests, Lady Camdon in particular.

"Apparently your reputation is exaggerated," she remarked, ice in both her expression and tone.

Lem had stopped playing completely and barely heard her rebuke. There she was: Mariyah. After more than a year of searching, barely clinging to the hope of ever seeing his love again, she was now standing not a dozen feet away.

She was wearing a blue-and-white gown, split up her left leg just above the knee. The sleek material shimmered in the soft light, casting a faint aura around her entire body. Her hair was adorned with delicate white flowers attached to silver threads and pulled back away from her shoulders with diamond-encrusted combs. It was as if she had been transformed into someone new. And yet the woman he loved remained unchanged. It showed in her smile, the confident grace with which she crossed the room, the way her head tilted ever so slightly when greeting those she passed. It was Mariyah, and yet she had become something more. She was utterly radiant.

It took all his self-control not to leap from his chair and wrap his arms around her, right there in front of everyone.

"Do continue, or I will have to ask you to leave my home."

Lem had not noticed Lady Camdon move closer.

"Forgive me, my lady. I was struck for a moment by your assistant's beauty. It will not happen again."

"See that it doesn't," she said in a harsh whisper. "And I expect you to sing before the night is done to make up for your incompetence."

"Of course, my lady."

He continued playing, though his eyes never once left Mariyah as she moved confidently about the parlor, engaging in one conversation after another.

A few times, Mariyah looked over to him, and for a moment he thought he saw a flash of recognition. But it was fleeting. His mind raced as to what he should do. She would be wearing an anklet, so simply stealing her away was not possible. And from the conversation he had overheard, any offer of purchase would be declined, even if he had the gold, which he didn't.

He nearly played another sour note when he saw Mariyah leave a small group of noble lords and walk directly toward him. She had a curious expression, one eyebrow slightly lifted, her lips turned to a half-smile.

"You play beautifully," she said.

"Thank you, my lady." Hearing her speak was almost enough to cause his hands to fumble over the strings. Unseen tears fell as he did his best to keep from choking on his own words. Though he thought she might recognize his voice, she did not appear to.

"That's a balisari, yes?"

Lem nodded.

Her eyes filled with sorrow as she gazed upon the instrument. "I knew someone who played one quite similar. Only his was a bit more worn."

Lem had recently refinished the instrument, and was now cursing himself for having done so. "Did he play well?" he asked.

"He was brilliant. Though not as good as you."

"You are too kind, my lady. Perhaps you would like me to play something special for you?"

How did she not recognize his voice? Or did she, and was able to hide it?

"There is one song . . . though I doubt you would know it. It's a song from my homeland."

"I know songs from many lands, my lady. I might know it."

"It's called 'The Flower of Winter.'"

Lem remembered it well. He used to play it for her often, and since leaving Vylari would still play it on nights when he could not sleep, imagining that she was lying on the grass beside him humming softly to the music.

"A silly request," she said, her cheerful and clearly practiced demeanor returning. "If you will excuse me, I must return to my duties."

Lem finished the song he was playing, unable to tear his eyes away, his thoughts a tangled jumble of self-recrimination.

What a damn fool he was! She was right there in front of him. Why hadn't he said something? He had to let her know he was here.

But how? He could not risk her mistress becoming aware of him. He needed to keep his wits if there was to be any hope of freeing her. The problem was, how to remove the anklet that peeked out each time Mariyah took a step? A plan began to form as he strummed out the opening notes of "The Flower of Winter."

The reaction was instantaneous. Mariyah spun around, a hand covering her mouth. The glass of wine she held slipped to the floor, shattering into innumerable pieces. Tears welled in her eyes.

From a few feet away, Lady Camdon turned to see what had happened, looking alarmed by Mariyah's reaction. Before Lem had reached the end of the first verse, Mariyah bolted from the parlor, tears streaming down her cheeks. After shooting Lem an accusing look, Lady Camdon followed after her at an urgent pace.

Several minutes passed before the woman returned. She strode directly over to Lem, her expression hard and eyes burning with anger.

"You will leave my home this instant," she said, taking care to keep her voice low.

"Have I displeased you, my lady?"

"I don't know what you did," she said. "Regardless, you have somehow managed to distress my assistant most terribly. I insist you leave without delay. Your pay will be waiting at the door."

"As you are dissatisfied, I will accept no payment."

"Then we have no further business." She turned, a smile appearing as if nothing at all were wrong.

The target was standing near the rear exit. Lem had almost forgotten about him. He stood, slinging his balisari across his back and reaching into his belt, where the dart was waiting to do its deadly work.

Disappointed voices complaining that they wanted him

to keep playing followed him out. Lem simply bowed, telling them that he was feeling unwell and had requested the Lady give him leave to depart.

As he passed Lord Ranson Lupardi, a quick flick of his finger completed his assignment. It would be a few hours before the poison took hold, long enough so that no one would ever discover who had done it or how.

A servant then led him to the back entrance at which he had arrived. Along the way, he hoped to catch sight of Mariyah. But she was nowhere to be seen.

"Can you convey a message to Lady Camdon's assistant?" he asked the servant.

"It depends on the message," she replied.

"Tell her I'm sorry if my music upset her."

The woman nodded, then closed the door. The path leading to the edge of the east garden was well guarded. In fact, he had noticed guards positioned throughout the grounds. It was an unusual degree of security, even for a noble as wealthy as Lady Camdon. There were certainly wards in place to keep people out at night. Normally, this would be enough to deter him from what he intended. Now, however, nothing would stop him. He had found Mariyah. One way or another, he was determined to let her know that he had not forgotten her.

The tingle of shadow walk itched in his belly as he ducked behind a low hedge. Wards were designed to keep people out. But he had no intention of leaving.

25

THE SORROW OF A DREAM COME TRUE

To bathe in the joy of life, you must first learn to accept that
one day it will end.

Mannan Proverb

It couldn't have been him, she thought, unable to contain her tears. Despite telling herself this repeatedly, merciless doubt still tore at Mariyah's heart like savage talons. How else could he have known that song? She had mentioned it purely as a jest: one only she would understand. She cursed herself for running out the way she had. She should have insisted that the man show her his face. At least then she would know that it wasn't Lem. But the balisari . . . and the way he played it . . .

"Are you all right?"

Lady Camdon was standing in the doorway.

Mariyah wiped her eyes. "Yes. I'm fine. Give me a moment and I'll return to the party."

"I've sent the guests home," she said. "Along with that dreadful musician."

"No!" The desperate word flew out before she could contain it. "What I mean is, why did you do that?"

Camdon let out an exasperated sigh. "I was in no mood for the idle banter of fools. And your sudden and quite conspicuous departure set tongues wagging. The thought of explaining what had happened was giving me a head-ache."

"I'm sorry," she said. "It really was nothing. The man playing the balisari reminded me of someone, that's all." Saying it out loud was making her feel ridiculous. Of course it wasn't Lem. How could it be? And the song he played, "The Flower of Winter," could easily be known outside of Vylari. For all she knew, Lem's mother had learned it during her time in Lamoria. She was jumping to conclusions.

"That *someone* wouldn't be the young man you followed from Vylari, would it?" Camdon asked.

Mariyah nodded. "Yes. But I was wrong. It wasn't him."

"So you don't want me to find him and bring him back?"

The temptation to accept the offer was almost too much. But the dark vision she'd seen with Belkar flashed in her mind. The emotionless soldiers. The fire, the ash. "No," she forced out finally. "I can't keep dwelling in the past."

"In that case, I think it is time we moved on to more useful endeavors. Tomorrow I will begin teaching you transmutation."

Mariyah's eyes lit up. "Are you serious?"

"When am I not?"

Of late, Mariyah had become even more frustrated with the lessons. She found glamor tedious, and in her opinion had already mastered as much as she would need. She desperately wanted to learn things that could help her to protect Vylari from the evil she knew was coming. Belkar would not be defeated by glamor.

Lady Camdon moved to the edge of the bed. "Let's say for a moment that you did find this love of yours. What would you do then? After all, you braved the unknown to find him. Would you not want to go away with him?"

Mariyah tucked her knees to her chin. "I'm not sure. Yes, I still love him. I think I always will. But now that

I know what's coming and what I must do to fight it . . . I . . . I just don't know."

Camdon regarded her for a long moment. "Even if it wasn't your young man, there's always the chance you will see him again. So I suggest you decide where your duty lies. I need to know that I can count on you. I can't have you falling apart. Not with so much at stake."

The coldness of her remarks sparked a surge of anger. "Yes. I'm sure love isn't something that you would know a thing about," she retorted. "I . . . I'm sorry. I shouldn't have said that. I'd just like to be alone, if you don't mind."

"I understand. More than you realize." Lady Camdon turned to the door and then paused. "We *are* alone, Mariyah. It's a bitter thing to learn. But better that you come to terms with it now."

"Were you ever in love?" The question was spoken before Mariyah could think about why she had asked.

Lady Camdon lowered her eyes, looking almost remorseful. "Yes, I have loved," she said. "And I've been loved in return. I know you may not believe this, but I do understand how you feel." She looked up, the hint of emotion gone as quickly as it appeared. "But you know as well as I do what is coming. Love will not stop Belkar. Evil is not defeated by good, Mariyah. Evil is defeated by the strength and conviction of those who refuse to break. You have chosen to fight. As have I. Love is not a luxury people like us can afford."

Having made her point, she swept from the room, closing the door firmly behind her.

A chill ran through Mariyah. *People like us.* Was that how Lady Camdon saw her? A younger version of herself? The thought was unsettling. The possibility that one day she might become as cold and callous as the Iron Lady . . . never. Yet the truth in her words could not be denied. It would take strength and conviction to defeat evil. But did that have to mean to the exclusion of all things good? What was the point in protecting the world without knowing kindness and love?

While settling into bed, Mariyah was not sure she was capable of turning away from her own feelings. It truly would mean becoming like Lady Camdon. Still, it had been surprising to hear that she had once been in love. Gertrude had said on several occasions that the Lady was not always so distant. Though she was not forthcoming about the details regarding the Lady's past, claiming it to be private and not a proper topic for casual discussion.

While drifting to sleep, "The Flower of Winter" played in her mind. Curiously, for the first time, Lem was not the one she imagined playing it.

———

Mariyah awoke with a start. For a moment she thought to call out. Then a draught blew over from the open door, drawing a relieved smile. Lady Camdon must not have closed it properly. She slipped from the bed and pushed it shut.

Kylanda's attack had prompted Lady Camdon to believe more security was warranted, and guards were now patrolling throughout the manor. Her wards would still keep out most adversaries, but as they had learned, once inside, there was very little to prevent someone from moving about freely. Mariyah didn't like this new arrangement; it made her uneasy when she heard their boots stomping along outside her room at night. Nevertheless, Lady Camdon had insisted it was a necessary precaution.

She double-checked to be sure the door was securely closed, then turned to the bed.

"Mariyah."

416 · BRIAN D. ANDERSON

"Lem," she gasped.

She backed into the door, hands clutched to her chest. Though she had uttered his name, she still could not believe what she was seeing. There he stood beside her bed, his balisari slung across his back and the wide-brimmed hat she had seen earlier now in his hands. He was smiling nervously, tears welling in his eyes. He looked exactly the way she remembered, yet at the same time somehow changed . . . Older? . . . No, that wasn't it. But something was different about him.

"Yes, it's me," he assured her.

Mariyah felt her knees weaken. Lem tossed the hat away and was at her side in an instant. His hands against the exposed flesh of her arm sent currents racing throughout her body. She had never thought to feel his touch again. Gently, he helped her over to the bed and then took a seat beside her.

"It *was* you, wasn't it? This evening . . . in the parlor."

He placed his hand on her cheek. "Yes. You have no idea how hard it was not to say something."

"How did you find me?"

Before he could respond, a colossal rush of emotion overcame her. Without thinking, she threw her arms around his neck and kissed him with utter abandon. He tensed for the briefest of moments, then returned the kiss with a passion to rival her own. Time lost all meaning. The world around her simply dissolved. The only thing that existed was the unbridled joy of reclaiming the love she had carried with her throughout the worst nightmare imaginable. And amazingly, it was undamaged. No . . . better than that. Their love was stronger than before. Made so by the power of undying hope.

When their lips finally parted, she buried her face in his shoulder, the salt of their combined tears lingering on her tongue, clinging to him as if fearful that should she let go, he might evaporate.

"I thought I would never see you again."

His voice was a gentle whisper. "I will always find you. Nothing can keep us apart forever."

After a time, she released her hold and gazed into his eyes. Those beautiful gray eyes. "How did you know I was here?" she asked.

"I didn't. All I knew was that you had been imprisoned and forced to serve some noble."

"No, I mean, how did you know I left Vylari?"

"Shemi told me."

Her eyes shot wide and joy instantly swelled her heart to near bursting. "He's alive?"

Lem smiled. "He is. And he'll be happy beyond belief to know you're all right."

"But how? I thought for sure they would send him to the mines, or worse."

"It's a long story. One I can't wait to tell you. But first, we need to get you out of here."

"Lem . . . I . . ."

"I haven't yet found a way to release you from your anklet. But there must be a way."

"Lem."

"Once you're free, I can get you out of Ubania easily enough."

"Lem. Listen." She could tell he wasn't hearing her. His joy and excitement were too great.

"I have enough gold saved to buy us a house," he continued. "Or even a farm if you want."

She gripped his arms. "Lem. I need you to listen to me."

Cupping her face in his hands, he kissed her tenderly. "Forgive me. I'm just so overwhelmed. I will listen for as long as you want."

"Can you make it to the east gate without being seen?"

"Of course. Why?"

"Wait for me there."

Lem furrowed his brow. "What's wrong?"

She took his hand and pressed it to her cheek, then kissed his palm. "Nothing. I'll be there shortly. Just make sure no one sees you." When he hesitated, she said, "Please. I promise I'll be just behind you."

Lem stood and kissed her once more. "Are you sure? The anklet . . ."

"Don't worry about that. Hurry now."

She could see the excitement in his eyes. It was clear he had longed to be with her as much as she had longed to be with him. And now . . . they would be together. He smiled at her over his shoulder as he opened the door. "I've been dreaming of this moment," he whispered.

She returned his smile. When the door closed, she said, "So have I."

She assumed Lem had not left the grounds; otherwise the wards would have been triggered. Lady Camdon was particularly adept at creating them, so unless Lem had brought a powerful Thaumas along, it was the only way he could have gained entry. He had likely used shadow walk to evade the guards on his way to her room, which meant he'd be able to make it back to the gate unseen just as easily.

Mariyah crossed over to the wardrobe and changed into a pair of silk pants and blouse, together with a pair of suede shoes she often wore when walking the garden. While passing the dresser mirror, she paused. Her tears had ceased.

Only moments after leaving the room, she spotted one of the guards rounding a corner in the hallway. As he drew closer she recognized him as Bram, among the first to be hired after Kylanda's assassination attempt. He had taken a liking to Mariyah from the first moment he arrived, saying that she reminded him of his younger sister, and always made a special point of patrolling the corridors near her chambers. Mariyah thought it sweet that he was so protective of her.

"Are you all right?" he asked, upon seeing her approach.

Mariyah pressed a finger to her lips. "Please. I don't want to wake Lady Camdon."

The guard lowered his voice. "Are you well? I heard you left the party early."

"Too much wine," she said. "But I'm fine now." A feeble lie, but Bram was not the brightest of men.

"What are you doing up at this hour?" he asked.

She gave him a quick smile. "I just need some air. You know how it is when you fall asleep too early. I thought a walk around the garden might help."

He nodded understandingly. "The same happened to me at my nephew's birthday. Fell asleep before the sun set. Took me days to get back right again."

Mariyah knew that if she didn't stop him, he would chatter on endlessly. "Exactly. Thank you for the concern, Bram." She started to move on.

"I can walk with you, if you like."

"That is very kind," she told him. "But I think I need to be alone right now. Another time, perhaps."

"Of course, my lady." He gave her a polite, graceless bow. "But if you need some company, I'm always around."

"Thank you, Bram. I will remember that."

She waited until he continued down the corridor before starting toward the east wing. Along the way she passed a few more guards, but once they saw who she was, none attempted to stop her.

She tried to picture Lem ducking through the halls

420 · BRIAN D. ANDERSON

and chambers, nimbly staying hidden by using a skill well learned while hunting in the forests of Vylari. She wondered what he had been doing all this time. Clearly he had found his niche as a musician and built up quite a reputation. She had heard the name Inradel Mercer being spoken on a few occasions. But there were still other unanswered questions she was eager to hear explained. For a start, how had he managed to find Shemi? And why was he going by a name other than his own?

Arriving at the servant's entrance she stopped, shut her eyes for a few seconds, and focused on the beating of her heart. Just one more step, she told herself. That was all she needed to take.

With her resolve firmed, she exited the manor.

The night air carried with it a powerful scent of lavender and jasmine. Though the garden was bursting with all manner of sweet-smelling flowers, these two were Lady Camdon's favorites, and she had cast a charm so that it was their fragrances that dominated each of the three gardens surrounding the estate. Mariyah paused beside a wooden bench beneath a large willow in the garden's center. On warm days, she would leave the library and bring her books here to study. This had raised a few eyebrows in the beginning. The freedom she was allowed was unusual, even by Lady Camdon's standards. She huffed a contemptuous laugh. For all the glamor she had learned, freedom was still the greatest illusion.

The gate was watched by a single guard. Mariyah could not recall his name. Bartimus? He was newly hired, and patrolled outside for the most part. Both the narrow path she was currently on and the service road farther ahead spanning from the main entrance to the cliff overlooking the sea were well lit. The wrought iron gate, typically used for kitchen and various other household deliveries, was shut. The ward would need to be disabled before it would be safe to leave.

The moment the guard saw her approaching, his hand shot to the hilt of his sword. "No one is permitted beyond the gate at night," he told her, his deep, gruff voice a perfect match for his menacing bearing. Though not as large a man as Bram, he was older and bore several facial scars that served to enhance his fearsome appearance.

Lem would be nearby, watching. She hoped he would not do anything rash. Quickly she held up her hands and put on her friendliest smile. "Bartimus, isn't it?"

"Harmin," he corrected. "And you're not supposed to be here. I have orders . . ."

"Calm down," she said. "Lady Camdon sent me."

He eyed her suspiciously, hand still resting on his weapon. "And why would she send *you*?"

"How should I know? All she told me was that she wanted to see you in the west wing dining hall."

It was clear he was not believing her story. She took a short step forward into the shadow of the eight-foot-tall fir trees lining either side of the path. "Look, if you don't believe me . . ."

She turned away just enough to hide the movement of her hands.

"Is that lout coming or not? I don't have all night." It was Lady Camdon's voice. And it sounded as if it were coming from the direction of the servants' entrance.

"You see? I told you."

It was all the convincing Harmin needed. "I . . . yes. West wing dining hall. On my way, my lady." He set off at a quick jog.

Mariyah suppressed a laugh as the guard nearly tripped over his own feet hurrying down the next path. It would take him at least ten minutes to get there. Then a few more to realize that no one was coming. Plenty of time . . . she hoped.

"How did you do that?"

Lem appeared from between two firs, seemingly out of thin air.

"Glamor," she replied. On seeing his confusion, she added, "It's hard to explain."

He started toward her but stopped in his tracks, his eyes fixed on her exposed ankle. "How did you get it off?" He wrapped his arms around her. "It doesn't matter. Not right now. You can tell me once we're well away from here."

Mariyah met his gaze silently. The warmth of his body—the love she felt in his touch—it was maddening. She crushed her lips to his. She had not known what she was going to do. Not until this very moment.

It was Lem who pulled away. "We should hurry," he said.

"I need to take down the wards first." The absence of his touch, even in the brief time it took to step to the gate, was painful. She spread her arms. *"Mepas ku deharuun."*

The ground just beyond the gate glowed with a faint blue light for a few seconds, then went dark, and the gate slowly swung open. Lady Camdon would know that the ward had been disabled immediately and would send guards to investigate.

Mariyah took Lem's hands. "I want you to know— through it all, I never stopped loving you. And I never will. Not for a single minute."

"I'm so sorry for what happened," he said. "I know it's my fault. But we're together now. That's all that matters."

"No. I can't go with you."

If she had said that she despised the ground he walked upon, he could not have looked more shocked. He stared at her uncomprehendingly. "What? Of course you can.

Don't be afraid. I can get you out of Ubania." He pulled her toward the gate, but she jerked her hands free.

"Listen to me, Lem. I'm not leaving. I have to stay here." His agonized expression and confused, pleading tone threatened to rip her soul apart.

"I don't understand. What's stopping you?"

"I wish I could explain . . . just know that it is my decision. No one is forcing me to do this."

"I will *not* leave you here," he shouted.

"You must. Just like you left Vylari to protect me, it's my turn to protect you. I cannot let you be a part of what's going to happen."

"What are you talking about?"

She took a step back. "The stranger. He didn't come to Vylari looking for you. He came there for me. So please—if you love me, just go. Watch over Shemi. He needs you."

"The stranger? What are you talking about? I can't . . . I *won't* leave you behind. Not again. Whatever is happening, we'll face it together."

She placed her hand on his cheek. He would, and she knew it. Lem would stand by her side while the world burned to cinders. He would lay down his own life without so much as a second's pause. And she could not bear the weight upon her heart if he did. There was only one thing left to do.

"I'm sorry," she whispered, then moved away.

"No!" he cried out. "I won't leave you."

He reached out to grab her arm, but she twisted free. Already the sound of the guards could be heard exiting the house. Mariyah realized she wasn't going to convince Lem, still in shock and denial, to leave the grounds before they were discovered.

In that moment, she did something she would have thought impossible. Running at him full tilt, she buried her shoulder into Lem's chest, and with all of her strength, shoved his body through the open gate. Completely unprepared, Lem took the full force of the blow and let out a gurgling groan. The momentum was enough to send him crashing through and sprawling onto the road. Mariyah quickly shut the gate and raised the ward once again.

Even through the pain, Lem did not give up. He continued to look at her pleadingly from the other side. "I won't leave you."

"Run." She could not bring herself to look into his eyes. "Please. Just run."

Three guards were rounding the hedge, swords drawn. Lem struggled to his feet and staggered away, vanishing behind the trees on the far side of the road. Mariyah turned toward the manor.

"What happened?" It was Bram.

"Nothing. A deer wandered too near the gate, so I disabled the ward. It's fine now. I chased it away."

"I thought I heard—"

"There was a strange sound in the bushes. It startled me." The smile she forced onto her lips was excruciating. The deep emptiness in the pit of her stomach threatened to rob her legs of strength.

Bram looked at her for a long moment, then motioned for the other guards to go back inside, ordering them to report the incident to Lady Camdon. "Come," he said, offering her his arm. "I'll take you back to your room."

Mariyah knew that without help, she was about to collapse. She took Bram's arm, allowing him to lead her back inside. The pain on Lem's face would not leave her. And yet . . . the tears were gone. In their place was a dark, empty shell where her heart had been.

Bram, to his credit, could see her distress and was silent

THE BARD'S BLADE · 425

the entire way. Upon reaching her door, Lady Camdon entered the hall in her nightgown, hands planted on her hips and looking none too pleased.

"A deer?" she remarked, clearly not believing the story the guards had passed on.

Mariyah did not so much as look up. "Yes. A deer."

She entered her room and, barely able to lift her feet, crossed over to the bed. Yet rather than lie down, she leaned her hands on the mattress and lowered her head.

I will not leave you.

Again and again Lem's words persecuted her thoughts. They encapsulated the sheer depth of his misery and torment—as well as her own. She imagined actually hearing his heart fracturing into pieces.

Yet it had to be done. Evil was not defeated by good. No. It was defeated by people like Lady Camdon. Cold, heartless, ruthless people. Those without a trace of pity or love.

Pushing upright, she stood in front of the mirror.

Her hair was in wild tangles and her cheeks red from the cold night air. "Yes, and people like you too," she whispered.

The sight of her own reflection caused a blinding anger to rise. With a primal scream, she picked up a perfume bottle from the dresser and hurled it straight at the glass, shattering it to pieces. She let out another scream. This was not enough. She wanted to tear the whole world apart. Her fury continued to rise. What else could she destroy? Grabbing the dresser, she pulled with all her strength, sending it crashing to the floor.

The door flew open and Lady Camdon rushed in. "What's wrong with you?" she demanded.

Mariyah ignored her completely. Stalking over to the

wardrobe, she threw it open. Every dress, shirt, and jacket hanging within taunted her; all the things required to present herself as something she was not and never could be. In a renewed burst of rage, she tore at every last item of clothing, flinging their tattered remains about the room in feral abandon. How long this went on, she didn't know. By the time she finally stumbled back, nearly everything she owned had been left in ruins.

Lady Camdon had stood in the doorway throughout, calmly watching and saying nothing.

Mariyah spun to face her. "I hate you! I hate this place. I hate . . ." She dropped to her knees. "I hate myself."

"So you sent him away?" The woman's voice was almost tender.

"Get out!" More than anything she wanted to weep. But her tears still would not flow.

Lady Camdon closed the door and knelt beside her. "Tell me what happened."

"What do you care? He's gone forever, and I'm still here. That's all you want from me, isn't it? To be strong and unfeeling like you. Well, congratulations, I did it. I destroyed the one thing in my life I have ever loved. Now I'm just like you wanted me to be. Are you satisfied . . . my lady? I'm broken. Just like you."

"You may stop calling me my lady," Lady Camdon told her. "Loria will do fine." She cast her eyes at the floor in silent reflection for nearly a minute before speaking again. "Do you remember earlier today when I told you I had loved once?"

Mariyah looked up. Loria was looking back with an expression she had never seen on her before. Tenderness. Compassion. And it was genuine. Despite her pain, it was startling to see.

"I was nineteen and had just come into my inheritance.

He was a young merchant I met while on holiday." A far-away smile appeared. "He was so handsome. Deep olive skin, wavy black hair, and a smile that could make you blush from a mile away. I fell in love the first moment I saw him. You might find it hard to believe, but he fell in love with me too. Of course, I wasn't the Iron Lady back then. I was just Loria."

Seeing her this way, hearing the sincerity in her words, made Mariyah forget her own heartache. At least for a moment.

"I was so naïve. I actually thought we could be together."

"Why couldn't you?"

Loria sighed. "Because the world is cruel. It cares nothing about how someone feels. I was a noble and he a commoner. And that was the end of it."

"So you just gave up?"

She gave Mariyah a sideways look. "In the time you've been here, have I ever given you the impression that I concede easily? No. I was like you are now, defiant and strong willed. I was not about to let people tell me whom to love. Unfortunately, my brother had other ideas."

"You have a brother?"

"I did. He was a year younger and none too pleased that I had inherited the family's wealth. Fortunately, my mother outlived my father and saw to it that I was given control of our holdings. She knew Alimar would squander it all. He wasn't a very bright boy, and even from a young age had developed some . . . let's call them *expensive* habits."

She paused briefly to give a sad shake of her head. "Needless to say, the possibility of my marrying into another noble family was foremost on his mind. When he learned of my relationship with Carlo, he was furious. It didn't matter a wit that he bedded every wench stupid enough to believe his lies or greedy enough to spend his gold. I was the only daughter—the one expected to increase our family's standing through marriage. That was my duty."

"How did Carlo feel about it?"

"He was as naïve as I was. He believed our love was powerful enough to change the ways of the world." She lowered her head. "Sweet boy. He couldn't see the storm coming. Neither could I. Not until it was too late."

"What happened?"

"My brother had him killed."

"He did what?"

Loria's jaw tightened as more tears fell. "When he discovered that we planned to wed in secret, he hired an assassin to murder him."

"Sweet spirits of the ancestors. I . . . I'm so sorry."

She smiled over at Mariyah while wiping her eyes. "It was a long time ago. I'm no longer the young girl I was. But I must admit there are times when I wonder what my life would have become had we wed." She laughed softly. "Most likely we'd have been driven from Ubania, one way or another."

"And your brother? Where is he?"

"Dead. Killed by the hand of the same assassin he hired. And yes, I was the one responsible."

"You had your own brother killed?" Though Mariyah knew it should not be, the confession was still surprising to hear.

"Yes. I hated him for what he did to Carlo. But that was *not* why I did it. Well . . . not entirely."

"So why did you?"

"In a single word: security. I was not about to be married off simply to increase my family's wealth and position. So long as my brother lived, even though I controlled the family's holdings, he still possessed the power to force me into marriage. Not as a matter of law. But he could have found a way to have me stripped of my title and position should I refuse."

"I don't understand. How could he have done that?"

"Simple. Petition the Archbishop and claim me to be incompetent. If he succeeded, he would gain control over all matters of finance. I would remain as head of the family, but in name only. Refusing a socially advantageous marriage would be used as evidence against me. My affair with Carlo would have been seen as impulsive, easily dismissed. But failing to increase our holdings through a union . . . that would be thought of as irresponsible beyond measure."

Mariyah's expression was one of pure disgust. "What kind of world *is* this?"

Loria cocked an eyebrow. "You thought the common folk are the only ones who suffer under Ralmarstad law and bigotry? My dear, outside these borders, people are free to live as they choose. But here we are not so fortunate."

"Then why do you stay?"

"Where should I go? This is my home. If people like me abandon it, what do you think would become of those left behind? Those unable to fight for themselves? It has taken most of my life to elevate myself to the point where I have any hope of changing things. As I told you before, evil is defeated through strength and conviction. I refuse to run."

"I . . . I understand. At least, I think I do."

"I want you to know that I am truly sorry you were forced to choose between what is right for you and what is right for the world. But if I did not think you had the strength, I would tell you to leave this instant and chase after him: to go live your life and let others do the fighting. Sadly, as painful as it might be to hear, you *are* like me. Maybe not in every way. But we bear the same curse: strength. We fight so others have the chance to live . . . and love."

Mariyah noticed that the pain she'd felt only a few minutes ago, though not completely gone, had dulled considerably. "Thank you, my lady."

"I thought I told you—it's Loria when we are alone."

"Loria, then." She met her eyes. "I have to ask: Why tell me all this?"

Loria rose to her feet and offered a hand. "Because I learned something tonight that I've wondered about since the day you arrived."

Mariyah allowed herself to be helped up. "What's that?"

"That you will not give in. Not even to yourself. We have a long and dangerous road ahead of us. I've prayed to Kylor to send me someone like you, someone who can see this through to the end. There are few people in this world to whom I give my trust. You are now among them."

Mariyah felt a wave of affection that she would have previously thought impossible. Were they now friends? Perhaps not yet. All the same, something had irreversibly changed between them.

"Come," said Loria. "You will sleep in my room tonight." A good-humored smile rose. "Yours is quite a mess at the moment." As they started to the door, she added, "You never know what the future holds. Perhaps one day, when this is over, you can still be with your love."

Yes, thought Mariyah. There *was* still hope. She would allow it to salve her wounds. Lem was alive, and so was she. So long as this remained a truth, hope would be her banner and her battle cry. With hope, she *would* destroy Belkar.

And then she would find the peace and love she yearned for . . . and deserved.

ACKNOWLEDGMENTS

My loving wife and son, Eleni and Jonathan Anderson. Hunter, Sarah, Elle, Donna, and Gerald Anderson. George Panagos. The Di Battista family. The Ramos family. My agent, Laurie McLean, and her team at Fuse Literary (it took some time, but here we are). My editor at Tor, Lindsey Hall, for believing in my work and taking the leap. Devi Pillai, for the wisdom to hand Lindsey the manuscript in the first place. Felix Ortiz, for his amazing talent and creating the perfect cover. My indie editors, George Stratford and Dorothy Zemach. Helen Paton and her family, especially Kristie. Michael and Robin Sullivan—thanks for the advice and for letting me shoot bows in your front yard. James Inman and his parents, Mindy and Tom. And to everyone who reads fantasy and keeps the genre alive and strong through your patronage and love for the fantastical. Without you, the world would lose its magic.

ABOUT THE AUTHOR

BRIAN D. ANDERSON is the bestselling fantasy author
of the Godling Chronicles, Dragonvein, and Akiri (with
coauthor Steven Savile) series. Currently, he lives in the
sleepy southern town of Fairhope, Alabama, with his wife
and son, who inspire him daily.
You can learn more at:

BrianDAndersonbooks.com
briandandersonbooks.blogspot.com
www.facebook.com/#!/AuthorBrianDAnderson